COULEE

THE GROWING YEARS A NOVEL

*When we were young everthing
was an adventure."
J.C. Cantle
Jaurè AA 2012*

J.C. CANTLE

authorHOUSE®

AuthorHouse™
1663 Liberty Drive
Bloomington, IN 47403
www.authorhouse.com
Phone: 1-800-839-8640

This book is a work of fiction. Places, events, and situations in this story are purely fictional. Any resemblance to actual persons, living or dead is coincidental.

First published by AuthorHouse   11/12/2011

ISBN: 978-1-4670-4217-8 (sc)
ISBN: 978-1-4670-4216-1 (hc)
ISBN: 978-1-4670-4215-4 (ebk)

Library of Congress Control Number: 2011917321

Printed in the United States of America

Any people depicted in stock imagery provided by Thinkstock are models, and such images are being used for illustrative purposes only.
Certain stock imagery © Thinkstock.

This book is printed on acid-free paper.

To our faithful Australian Sheppard / border-collie dogs
for their years of devotion;
Mesa, Chamisa and Willie Jane

CONTENTS

ACKNOWLEDGEMENT PAGE

I wish to acknowledge all my good friends, family and of course the horses, dogs and cats who contributed and thus made it possible for me to enrich this novel. I wish to recognize Art for his aid in the authenticity of that time period, Larry for his western terminology, Grace and Nicki's aid in proofing and editing and to my wife Beth for her constant support.

"When I was younger, I could remember anything, whether it had happened or not."

Mark Twain

COULEE
THE GROWING YEARS

BLAST
CHAPTER ONE

I awoke early, 4:00 a.m. Turned on the bedside light and swung out of the rack. I'd had enough sleep. Besides I was to be at the yards and feedlot by 5:30. There would be a convoy of trucks loaded with steers and heifers coming in for feeding before being sold to Pierce Packing Company and Midland Packing Company in Billings or shipped out by rail in cattle boxcars to out of state meat packing buyers. The first shipment of stock would arrive at six and periodically coming back in with more beeves the rest of the day until all the Milliron slash B Ranch cows Archie Braddock was selling early were penned. In these pen lots the beeves would be fed and fattened up. Once the cattle had gained some fat they would be weighed and then sold, slaughtered and eventually end up on someone's dinner plate.

Today was also the day old man Blastingame was going to court for driving without a driver's license. He hadn't renewed it since it had expired sometime after he had been discharged from the Army in 1945.

One night while Ben was on his way home a sheriff's deputy stopped him, because the old Dodge one-ton had a taillight out, he asked Ben for his driver's' license and registration and he only had the registration.

"I don't need no damn driver's license to operate this truck. I'm not drivin', I'm operating a vehicle! And furthermore I'm not signin' anything!" advised Ben. He was going to fight the law on these grounds.

That's when the deputy arrested him for not signing his traffic citation, and hauled him off to jail with some resistance. Ben sat in the hoosegow as he called it until his wife came to bail him out.

The Dodge truck was left parked off the road and hub deep in weeds. I had to hitch a ride and get the truck along with a new bulb for the taillight and drive it (*I mean operate it*) back to the yards.

I put on clean socks, underpants and grabbed the blue jeans that I'd thrown on the ladder back chair and pulled them on. The plaid shirt I yanked off the back of the chair where I'd hung it that evening. It was one I had worn for the last three days. As I was about to put it on I discovered it had a sizable smear of dried cow shit on it. I couldn't recall how it had happened but it wasn't that uncommon to have my clothes branded with manure, slobber or my blood. In the bathroom I tossed it into the clothes hamper and found a clean faded denim shirt in the closet, slipped it on and before snapping the pearlescent snaps, noticed the sleeves at the elbows were about to blow out. They were worn to the point of being threadbare. I'd have to ask Ma to patch them both and flip the frayed collar over for me. My boots sat where I had taken them off. One laid on its side, the other upright, the heel still caught and held in the bootjack. Normally I'd leave my boots by the back door if they were caked in corral mud. Carrying them by their tops I made my way down the dark hall in stocking feet.

At the stairs I made sure I didn't step on the fifth step down, because it would let out a squeak that was louder than a cat in heat. I didn't want to wake Ma, the old man or Kipp, not that waking Kipp was an easy thing to do. Ma always had the coffee in the percolator ready to go the night before and I set a match to the gas burner under it. Then turned the flame down low and tossed the spent match into the sink.

Snatching the near empty pack of Lucky Strikes from the kitchen counter next to the radio and a couple of wood matches by the stove, I left the house by the back mudroom porch, clutching my boots under my arms. I stepped outside in stocking feet, making sure the screen door didn't slam as I shut it behind me. Now I would smoke while waiting for the coffee to perk.

Shaking out a Lucky from the pack and grabbing it with my lips, I then snapped the match head with my thumbnail; a strong smell of sulfur wafted into my nostrils as I lit the cigarette and inhaled, then allowed the smoke out from my lungs and into the cool morning air. Smoking in those days was as accepted as breathing air itself. People smoked on television, on the silver screen of the movies, at home, in their cars, at work and in any and all public places. The arrival of filtered cigarettes was slow in coming, but almost without fail one bought the brand or two that had come into being.

Sitting on the steps with the Lucky hanging from my mouth, I pulled my boots on, then stood to set the left foot into the mold of the boot better. The inside leather liner had come unstitched and at times I'd have to stomp my foot to have it set back in place so that it wouldn't wear a hole in the heel of the sock. Whenever I bought new boots they would have to fit tight. The first morning, after I fought to get them on, I'd go out to the horse trough and stand in it until the leather was saturated by water. I would wear them water soaked all day until both socks and boots had completely dried on my feet, conforming to their shape. Sometimes it meant wearing them while I slept on top of the bed while wrapped in a blanket. The following day before bed I'd detach the boots from my feet with hard tugs on the bootjack and then pull my socks off and my feet were wrinkled and somewhat swollen. From then on my boots fit perfectly as if custom built and molded over wooden lathes to the size and shape of my feet.

With the boots well seated on my feet I sat back down on the steps to finish my cigarette while I gawked up into the sky and watched the stars wink at me. The Big Dipper had by now moved off and the hint of the oncoming dawn approached in the eastern sky and began to neon towards a new day. The far distant pin point stars blinked out and only the brightest stars still radiated and stood out like billboard lights in the inky-gray morning. I smoked and gave thought to the heavens and the billions of stars, mulling and speculated that somewhere out there had to be another world like this one with life on it. We couldn't conceivably be the only ones in this galaxy or universe that had water, air and a climate for living things.

Most of Billings was still asleep. There was coolness in the light breeze that Dad would call, "A cat's paw," because of its softness. The smell of damp grass made me glad to be alive. As my eyes had now adjusted to the night and as day light began to show itself, I could see the two horses in the corral watching me, Jeep and Sioux. Jeep let out a nicker and Sioux stomped the ground impatiently, wanting me to feed them now since I was up already. *You can wait until I've had a smoke and a cup of coffee before I feed you two wing nuts. God, I've got to get out and ride Jeep. This weekend maybe I can get Kipp to go along and we'll haul them down to Pryor Creek and ride up into the hills on the Crow Res. together, camp out for the night*, I was thinking. Then there was that sudden enormous explosion from the Rim, rocking all of Billings and me just about off the back steps.

The horses raced about the corral in a panic and lights came on in all the houses around town and dogs started to bark and howl. Upstairs the old man switched on the bed lamp, then a second later the overhead light lit up the back yard, part of the barn and corral.

Well the town's awake now. What the hell was that explosion? The Japs attacking Montana? Thought they'd given up fighting with us years ago.

I went back into the house and the old man was just coming into the kitchen barefoot and was only wearing his tank-top t-shirt and black gabardine dress work pants and suspenders. As he zipped up his fly he swore, "What in Hell's going on? What was that explosion?"

"I don't know, but it shook the shit outta me and all of Billings. Got Jeep, Sioux and all the damn dogs spooked. I haven't a clue what it's all about. Sounded like it came from west of the Rim."

Ma came down stairs wearing her old long lilac chenille robe and felt slippers, "Where's Kipp?"

"Still in bed, an A-bomb couldn't wake him outta the cradle," I suggested.

"Kid's deaf when he's asleep. Always has been, ever since he was a pup," Pa put in.

"Well I'm sure all of Billing's up and about by now. D'jou call the law to find out what blew up?" Ma asked.

"No, ain't had a chance, an' chances are they're bein' swamped by calls already. I'll turn the radio on and maybe they'll have it on a bulletin or news after the livestock and grain report," Dad ventured.

"Maybe the oil refinery in Laurel had an accident or one of the grain silos blew up, they'll do that once in a blue moon," Ma put in.

The comment made me smile, since silo explosions most normally happen in the heat of the day.

"Well, all the silos in Billings would have to blow at the same time to make an explosion like that, an' it's against all the odds I'd say, but it might be the refinery. Well, I might as well get dressed, sure not going to get back to sleep now. It'll be daylight soon anyways."

The coffee had by now perked to its ebony tincture and Ma had turned the heat down until only a very small flame trembled under the pot.

"You two want breakfast now?" she asked.

"Might's well. How come you're up and dressed this early, Dakk?" Dad asked as he glanced back from going upstairs.

"Got an early load of yearlings, old-man Braddock's having brought in and Ben's going to court today. I have to be there by six and take care of things."

"When's that cheap S.O.B goin' to raise your wages? Ben couldn't keep help more than a month. He's so crouch-a-dee. I've known Blast forever and he's always been tighter than a wood tick in a dog's tail," Dad accused unforgiving.

"That he is. I won't deny it. I'd love to get another job, but it's not a heyday out there. Trying to get cow riding jobs don't spring up every minute now days." I replied.

"Doesn't," Ma corrected.

"The mills will be hirin' soon, they pay a bit more than ol' Ben Blastingame. Blastingame, maybe he blew up and that's the racket we heard. He's always been full of hot air. Sounded like a munitions dump of TNT blowing up," Dad mused with a twinkle in his eye.

"Dad, don't be ridiculous. That's balderdash," Ma guffawed. "Go get dressed. I'll have breakfast ready in a minute."

Ma always loved the words balderdash, debacle and discombobulate whenever it was appropriate for her to use them.

While Ma was fixing breakfast I thought I'd go out and feed the horses. I was part way to the barn when I remembered leaving my wallet on the dresser. I didn't want to forget it and my driver's license, besides I knew Ma had the curiosity of a cat and she couldn't resist looking into the billfold if she saw it lying there. If she did, she'd find the foil packaged Trojan rubber I kept in there, for safety sake, in case I got lucky, which wasn't too often. The damn condom left a permanent round impression in the leather like a can of Copenhagen against your hind pocket or shirt if you dipped snuff as some of the guys did. I never took to dipping. I had tried it once when I was twelve. Got green behind the gills and heaved bile until I had nothing more to toss but my guts and they refused to come up. That was the sickest I can remember ever being in my life. Dippin' snuff was getting popular with a lot of the young cowboys while the old timers still chawed on Brown Mule plug or leafy Redman chewing tobacco.

As I left my bedroom, I heard the Old man set his weight on that squeaky step as he made his way downstairs. In the hall I decided to take a look see at sleeping-beauty and see if Kipp was awake, even though I knew the chance was very unlikely. Opening the door to its fullest the hall light made an oblique rectangle into the room and bed. No Kipp. The bed was un-made. I looked in the hall bathroom he and I shared, but he was not in there either.

What's that little shit up to this time? If Pa finds out he's skipped out of the house in the still of the night, he'll skin him alive, ran through my mind, *He must be with Cody and Cooper. Those three sure can get into more crap than a whole pack of pigs. Hell, and as happy as pigs in shit while pulling some dumb stunt.*

Downstairs, Dad was at the table with his first cup of black coffee and leafing through a Popular Mechanics magazine. He always loved reading about someone's new brainstorm of how to build a better mousetrap or improve on the windmill.

I didn't dare say anything about Kipp not being in his bed.

"I'm going to feed the horses. It'll only take a minute," I told Ma as I poured myself a cup of coffee and tried to take a sip. It was too hot and I set the steaming cup on the table to cool.

"Well, take an extra minute and check for eggs. I'm short a couple for when Kipp gets up. Those chickens sometimes hide their eggs behind the door instead of using the nesting boxes," she said.

I grabbed my beat up old 5x beaver Resistol from one of the elk horn tines hat rack and set it on the back of my head loose. Sweat, dirt, oil, horse and cow shit stained the tattered black cowboy hat that had seen better days but the sweat formed felt fit my head comfortably. The hat looked more brown than black.

The horses were right there waiting their morning's bait and with the usual hungry anticipation now that the explosive calamity was over. We had had Sioux since he was seven and he came with that name, so we kept it. On the other hand, Dad re-named Jeep from the name he came with, which was Miles. Because he was ten years old at the time and was capable of going anyplace and everywhere, is as strong as a mule, as agile as a mountain goat and as faithful as an old dog, Dad called him Jeep.

The name Jeep came from the Popeye comics and the character Eugene Jeep. Eugene Jeep was a small dog-size animal that walked on his hind legs, was able to cross into the fourth dimension, and could fly. It was thought that was where the name of the Army Jeep came from because it was extremely capable and reliable.

Venus, the Morning Star, was in its full brilliance to the east. I switched the lights on in the barn. Pa only had two 20-watt bulbs to light up the barn and one was just outside the door. In the pale amber light, I was almost better off with a flashlight, but as Dad would put it, something is better than nothing. So I went about getting feed for the horses and let my eyes adjust to the poor lighting.

Black Jack looked at me, blinking his yellow eyes. He'd just finished eating a mouse. The critter's head, tail and guts lay scattered on the dirt floor in front of him. Black Jack had adopted us a year ago. A stray that stopped by then stayed. The cat was a killing machine towards any rodent, rabbit and occasional robin or sparrow. He hunted in the barn or around the surrounding territory. Blackjack was smooth and as shiny as obsidian, long slender, streamlined and with a tail that looked longer than that of an average cat. He made one handsome feline. He was a panther for sure.

The barn housed two cats. The other one was a tail sucking little calico, sweet as they come. She must have been taken away from her mama too soon. She had the habit of sucking the tip of her tail until it was soaked, sticky and as pointed as a newly sharpened pencil. Dad named her Barley.

Normally Pa did the honors of naming the cats and all had had the names of grains. He was in the grain business, so to speak. We had had a male Manx red tiger cat he named Buckwheat. There was another black and white feral cat he called Oats that was around for only a few months, and then disappeared. After which a real beauty appeared on a hot August day. She was a Persian-Siamese mix, with a tail that spiraled in a screw like fashion over her back. He called her Rye, but we all called her Corky as in corkscrew. Dad worked for Cream of the West Cereal Company since after high school. He was drafted into the Army on August 17, 1942. Then he went back to working for Cream of the West after being discharged in 1945. When Black Jack came along Pa had run out of grains that would be appropriate for cat names. Rice was no one's favorite so I named him Black Jack after the card game.

Ma didn't mind having animals around but she refused to allow them in the house at any time. All animals stayed outside, even if it was twenty below zero they had the barn to live in. That was her law. Kipp was the first to break the law and wished he hadn't. Kipp at the time was fourteen, he's two years younger than me; he had brought home a five and a half foot long diamond back rattler. He and his two buddies, Cody and Cooper, the KCC we called the trio, would hunt snakes in the spring then sell them for a few bucks to Mr. Fouche who had the Wonderland Amusement Park and a small snake museum along with a glass display case with a collection of supposedly George Armstrong Custer memorabilia. The park and museum was located to the east of Billings at the edge of town.

The museum had all sorts of snakes, most of which he kept in varying sized rectangular glass fish aquariums with wire screen lids on them. Each aquarium had a sign identifying the particular snake, lizard, toad, spider and scorpions with their common and Latin scientific name. The museum also displayed live poisonous tarantulas and deadly black widow spiders. The Fouche Museum had a good collection of snakes besides the poisonous ones. He had coach whips, a pink blind snake, lyre, leaf nose and hognose snakes. A colorful lot of yellow, red and black-banded snakes like the Mexican king snake, and lethal coral snake. At the coral snake display he had another sign under the snake's name that read, "**Red next to yellow kills a fellow. Red next to black is a friend of Jack**." At the end of the tourist season, Fouche would take all the rattlers Kipp and the others had caught that he'd kept in what he called, "The Snake Pit," a round 800 gallon metal stock tank and release them back into the wild, back on the Rim and let them head into the crags, back to snake heaven and another winter of hibernation. By fall most of the rattlers had lost weight since Fouche never fed them enough for them to grow and I'm sure many died or would die of starvation soon after their release back into their home ground that late in the year.

The big diamondback Kipp had caught was in a potato gunnysack with the top knotted closed. He had come into the house and set the bag next to the back door while Ma was out hanging up the wash. Kipp had gone to the fridge and as usual just took the cap off of the quart milk bottle and drank down a few gulps from it, being too lazy to bother with a glass, after which he headed upstairs, to tell me about his catch. Ma was just coming back into the house as Kipp burst into my room. I was lying on my bed reading the "Sagebrush Savvy" quiz, subscribers had written to, in the magazine called, 'Texas Rangers' Meanwhile Ma, seeing the burlap bag and thinking it was a sack with potatoes in it, opened it up to see. No potatoes there. The sack only held one hell of a good size venomous viper.

She screamed and dropped the bag. The rattler slithered out onto the linoleum. It headed under the stove. Ma had grabbed the skillet and paring knife as she climbed onto one of the kitchen chairs and shrieked. I jumped from the bed and followed Kipp downstairs two and three steps at the time to see what was amiss with Ma. She was standing on a chair holding a paring knife in one hand and her 9-inch iron skillet in the other. She screamed, "Get it out of here! Kill it! Kill it!"

Kipp saw the sack, opened and lying on the floor. He dropped to his knees and carefully peeked under the stove. When I heard the familiar, "Tisss, tisss," I knew there was a viper in the kitchen. I grabbed the broom and looked under the stove with Kipp and sure enough it was a rattler, a big one that was coiled tighter than a spring, the tail shaking up a storm, letting us know he was pissed off, and big time.

Ma kept yelling hysterically while shaking the frying pan in the air and repeated, "Get that thing out of here! Get it out of here! Kill it! Kill it!"

I poked at it and it struck out at the broom, spraying venom from its fangs each time it hit. Finally I turned the broom around and using the handle I poked at it some more until it had enough of that, uncoiled and slithered out from under the stove as Kipp got out of the snake's way. Ma was still screaming. I managed to set the tip of the handle behind its head, which looked as big as a saucer with black beady eyes that penetrated its anger at us.

"Hold 'em, hold 'em good!" Kipp said anxiously.

The snake twisted and curled over and around itself trying to get loose, its black forked tongue jetting out testing the air. He was madder than a Holstein with her tit caught in a wringer.

"I got 'em!" I told Kipp.

Kipp snatched the snake just behind the broom handle where I held the snake down. When I saw he had a good grip of the big beauty, I took the pressure off of the snake. Kipp had the rattler by the neck and tail; I could see its big swollen glands still full of poison behind the eyes.

As I held the sack open he placed the tail into the bag, and then lowered it down and after releasing the head, the rattler dropped down into the burlap sack.

"Get that thing outta here! Now!" Ma demanded as she stood on her chair, looking scared shitless and shaking.

I closed the bag and tied a knot at the opening.

"Get it out of my house now!" she shrieked at us.

Kipp took the potato sack and snake, made a beeline out of the kitchen door like an antelope being shot at. Ma, being so mad, threw the skillet at him as Kipp let the screen door slam behind him. The skillet missed the screen and hit the wall next to the door jamb, knocking a hole in the plaster and chips of gypsum flew out like a covey of quail.

Ma got off the chair, tossed the knife on the counter and marched upstairs. I heard the bedroom door slam shut. She was more peeved than the diamond back.

"Ma sure had a cow," Kipp said, wincing as he came back in the house for his shirt and sneakers.

Kipp had found the rattler under the hood of a rusted out old junker automobile, that someone had years ago dumped into a coulee as a form of erosion control. The snake had been coiled on top of a pack rat's nest built up against and over the engine; waiting for the rat to appear and make the rodent his dinner.

Fouche paid Kipp $5.50 for the big diamondback rattler, a buck a foot.

We didn't see Ma for two days, she stayed locked up in the bedroom. The old man had to sleep on the sofa downstairs. We had to make our own meals. Pa only claimed to be able to cook hot cereal and make coffee, so he made breakfast and I'd burn meat for supper. Kipp, that little shit, ate at Cody's house for a week. When Ma decided she had been infuriated and craven long enough she came out of the bedroom. Everyone knew she was still on the warpath; she went about not talking to any of us including Dad for the rest of the week. Then one evening while doing the dishes and listening to "Our Miss Brooks" on the radio, she started to laugh at something Miss Brooks said and she was back to her old pleasant self again.

Our three Rhode Island Reds and Two White Rocks are all the chickens Ma kept these days. She had twenty or twenty-five at one time but that was more eggs than we needed so every now and again she would cull one. When we had too many eggs Ma would sell a dozen or two or just give them away to the neighbors. The poultry resided in a small pen with a white board hen house that had an east-facing window. She had Dad build the hen house next to her garden for easy access to chicken manure for her special plants, tomatoes for one. Ma didn't care all that much for flowers except for Dahlias of which she had and pampered eight species. She had inherited the love for them from her mother who was a member of the Dahlia Society organized in 1915. There were Dahlias all around the house and yard. Every fall she'd dig the Dahlias rhizomes out of the ground and keep them in the basement, laid and covered in a bed of vermiculite, until spring and then she would replant them around the house. In the vegetable garden she grew what was needed to feed us, corn, beans, squash, potatoes, tomatoes, cabbage and a variety of lettuce to name a few. The irrigation ditch running along the edge of the one acre we live on from which everything is watered did very well until the first frost that appeared sometimes as early as September. Living in town, south-east of the Rim with neighbors only an acre or two away gave the neighborhood ample elbow room from one another. Just about everybody having a horse or two or having had horses kept the feeling of country living in a city environment.

I opened the hens' coop and plucked the green plastic Army flashlight that was clipped on a nail next to the inside of the coop door. Immediately the hens started up their worried, nervous chatter as I entered. Fanning the light, the hen house lit up. I could see the hens sitting in their nesting boxes. Everything was covered with thick pollen of chicken shit dust that covered and clung to every surface, including the cobwebs that hung everywhere. I went from nest to nest and reached under each hen, they all in turn pecked at my hand and wrist with their rounded beaks. I retrieved four eggs from the nest boxes and one more that lay in a twig, feather and straw makeshift nest behind the door as Ma suggested there would be. I shut the flashlight off, re-clipped it on the nail that held it and stepped out of the coop, closing the door behind me. By now daybreak was apparent, as the sky was light blue to the east. Carrying the brown eggs in my Resistol hat cradled to my chest I heard a clamor. I didn't think much of it since it was that time of morning the milkman made his delivery of two quarts of milk and pint of whole cream. He never had to leave us eggs. We grew our own. But it wasn't the milkman making his delivery.

I heard, "Psst, psst Dakk," from above the side of the back porch and looking up could see the figure of Kipp half on and half off of the roof.

"What the Hell are you doing up there, you dumb shit?" I whispered.

"Tryin' to get back to bed," he stated, "I'm stuck. My cuffs caught on a branch. Help me out before Pa finds out I've been out of the house all night."

A stubborn limb tangled in the large cuff of his dungarees caught his left leg. Dungarees or jeans all came in long sizes and you would roll up and make cuffs about six inches high or so to fit your leg length. He was shaking his foot, in the black high top Keds he had on, trying to get himself loose. I set the hat, with the eggs nestled next to one another in the crown, down on the ground and climbed up the tree. With my pocketknife I hacked at the half-inch branch that held his cuff until it snapped off of the main limb.

"There you go," I grumbled as he pulled his foot away and clambered on through the window of his room.

"Where you been? Everybody's up. They all think you're still asleep. Ma's makin' breakfast," I whispered and forewarned at the same time as he started to close the window.

"Tell you later. Thanks. What time is it?"

"Close to 5:30, I'd guess."

"I'll be down in a while. Don't squeal on me."

"I wouldn't, you know that. But if the Ol'-man finds out, your ass is grass and he's the lawn mower."

Dad could be a hard ass when he had to be, but most of the time he was easy going. He did have the propensity of getting real angry when people pushed him into a corner and especially if they were wrong and he was right, then the shit would fly.

When dad was fresh out of high school he cowboyed a little but it didn't take long for him to figure out there was no money to be made in that dying trade and so went to work at Cream of the West Cereal Mill as an accountant. He had a great aptitude for mathematics and organizing, cutting cost and making a profit. I wish I had a dime for every time I heard him say, quoting Benjamin Franklin, "A penny saved is a penny earned." It's not that Pa is cheap, just careful about not wasting money. That's why we didn't get a television until 1952, unlike most of our neighbors' homes in Billings who sported TV antennas poking over the roofs for what seemed like years. He had bought a Traveler Television. Dad had said, "Let them work the bugs out of television. They're in business to make money. They'll bring the price down in order to sell more. With anything new, it's always been that way. Only when there's a shortage does supply and demand play into the picture, then there is escalating cost and a black market flourishes."

Dad also repeated, "Make your money grow. Money is like seeds; if you just keep them in a coffee can on a dry dark shelf they'll never sprout and grow. Money should be invested wisely so it will produce more money. Banks are just coffee cans."

Two years after working at the mill, Pa and Ma married in 1936 and that's the first time Ma had been out of the state of Montana in her life. They honeymooned in Yellowstone National Park, Wyoming, staying at the Old Faithful Inn for a couple of days and toured the park and its wonders of natural beauty, its geysers like Old Faithful erupting every 35 to 95 minutes, shooting a steam plume 100 to 185 feet high for two to five minutes, hot pools of brilliant colored crystal clear hot water and others of bubbling boiling mud, colorful icicle layered wedding cake terraces of Mammoth Hot Springs and the many fumaroles discharging steam from hundreds of earth's vents and the beautiful Lower Falls on the Yellowstone River.

They remembered counting 98 black bears while doing the 142-mile park's loop. After leaving Yellowstone they drove south past Jackson Lake, Mount Moran, and did the loop past Jenny Lake at the base of the three Cathedral group of snow laden peaks known as the Tetons in the Grand Teton National Park. In the town of Jackson at the south end of Jackson Hole they spent a night at the Wort Hotel. They came back to Montana by traveling back through Yellowstone again and via Cody, Wyoming, staying at the Irma Hotel that William Cody had built and named after his daughter Irma Cody. The following day they visited the Buffalo Bill Cody Museum located in a log cabin filled with memorabilia of William F. Cody's Wild West Shows and his western escapades. They drove up highway 120 through Clark to Red Lodge, then back to Billings and a small white wood clad house.

I was born nine months later on a cold February 14, 1937, Valentine's Day. Kipp was born in January 13, 1939, a Friday. He took the number 13 as his lucky number and by the many scrapes he escaped, it must be. The family moved into this house that belonged to Gram and Gramps after they died in a winter whiteout car crash after hitting some black ice. The vehicle had slid off the road and down into a deep snow drifted coulee, rolling over and over until it came to rest at the bottom. Both Gramps and Gram had been ejected from the vehicle and killed. A week later the car was found south of Acton after a warm spell only 15 miles from Billings. That was in 1947, two years after dad had been discharged from the Army. Mother had lived with Gram and Gramps while raising us babies during the time Dad was in the military.

Kipp came downstairs, making sure he stepped on the stair that squeaked.

"Oh! Here's Kipp now," Ma ventured when she heard the squeak.

Kipp was a bit of an actor, if not a real ham, genuinely theatrical at times. He entered the kitchen half dressed, yawning, looking sleepy eyed and asking why everyone was up so early.

"I smelled breakfast cookin'," Kipp lied.

"Didn't you hear and feel the explosion?" Ma asked, knowing full well Kipp wouldn't if he was asleep.

Kipp answered with the question, "What explosion?"

"There was a terrible blast. Up on the Rim, they said on the morning news. But no one knows what or where. I'm sure they'll know more by tonight's news after they investigate."

"Well, whatever caused it, I hope no one was hurt or killed," Dad put in.

That's when I noticed Kipp had a slight worried look on his face, which he covered up by hiding behind the glass of milk that he was sipping.

Ma had just placed the plates of eggs, sausage and home fries in front of us, and then cursed herself because the toast in the old toaster was burning on one side.

"I'll take the burnt toast," I told her, "Charcoal's good for you." And I asked Dad to pass the oleo.

"I hate this oleomargarine. Had enough of it in the Army. The stuff is made of plastic. I'll get some butter from Missis Wilson. She makes her own from her dairy cows." Dad put in as he spread blackberry jam on his toast.

Kipp had his head down and I almost asked him what was the matter with him but changed my mind.

"Kipp, you look awful tired, are you okay?"

"Yeah, Ma. I'm fine. I'll get the grass cut this mornin'. Cooper, Cody and me are goin' fishin' this afternoon."

"Cooper, Cody and I," mother corrected, "You know, like me, my shadow and I."

I wolfed my breakfast down and said, "I've got to get to the yards. See you all tonight. Kipp, you want to go riding this weekend down to Pryor? We could camp out. Jeep and Sioux need to get out. You and I haven't done anything together this summer and you'll be back in school soon."

"Sure. Cody has to be at his new little sister's christening and Cooper's goin' up to Helena with his folks. So I might as well go with you."

                              *   *   *

Driving towards the refinery east of town I watched its lights shining up and down columns of enormous cylindrical tubes, tanks and catwalks. A tall narrow stack spewed yellow and blue flames that licked out at the sky like a fire-breathing beast. Steam plumes escaped from various orifices and disappeared into the air that was choked with the acrid smell of petroleum.

I pulled into the stockyards and feedlot near the hay barn and parked my International pick-up next to Cliff's car at the side of the diner, I could see from the back window of the diner that Cliff and his wife were already at work, the kitchen lights on. Cliff owned the small two story red brick building with dressed stone corners and the doors as well as the window trim was newly painted white. Upstairs, Ben Blastingame leased his 10' by 16' office space equipped with desk, three chairs, telephone, a radio and a bank of file cabinets, four drawers tall. On the wall hung dusty and slightly sun-faded photos of some of the top horses and bulls bucking cowboys off of them. These photographs were from when Ben owned rodeo stock, before old age took over and Blastingame bought the stockyards. His desk always looked stacked with the same pile of papers and an ashtray heaped with old cigarette butts. Hanging on the wall behind his desk was a glass and framed sun-faded print called "Sagebrush Sport." It was a lithograph copy of a painting by Charles M. Russell. It showed a couple of cowhands roping a coyote. On the same wall was a calendar from the feed store with torn off months which also had a color print of one of C. M. Russell's paintings depicting a bucking horse wrecking the cook fire and vittles of a cow camp chuck wagon titled, "A Bronc To Breakfast." In the right desk drawer he kept a loaded Smith and Wesson .38 double action revolver and in one of the bottom drawers of a filing cabinet he kept four glasses and a fifth of Jack Daniel's. Also upstairs on the second floor and next door was a slightly larger office space rented to a guitar maker and repairer, who wrote western songs and occasionally gave lessons to would-be guitar and fiddle players.

The whole downstairs was Cliff's and the red and black sign on the side and front of the building read, "The Hoof and Horn Diner." Cliff, the diner's cook and his wife Donna, 15 years younger than him, the waitress and sometimes dish washer, were the only employees. Cliff had it pretty good in the diner; he would open most mornings at 5:30 and close after lunch around 2:00. Cliff was renowned for his famous chicken potpies that he made as a special every Wednesday of which he refused to give out his secret recipe. Thursday's special was what was called on the menu Patty's Meatloaf in which there was a bit of a bite of New Mexico, Hatch green chili that his brother would send him every year from Alamogordo. Cliff would in exchange send his brother some of his pickled beets. Most of Cliff's customers were cowhands, truck drivers, occasional rail-road hands shipping out stock or delivering feed, as well as all the good old ranchers, grain, or sugar beet farmers coming in to buy a nickel cup of coffee, a 25 cent pack of cigarettes and catch up on the local news.

I started feeding and watering the stockyard working horses and the few old bony horses we had in a pen, awaiting their fate of being sent out to a slaughter house and becoming canned dog food.

The poor old nags had been bought for slaughter for a few cents a pound, making them worth only 30 to 50 bucks to the owner after their many years of service. I could never sell Jeep or Sioux in their old age; I hoped to see them end their days with me close by. I've always known "stock is just stock and not pets," but when you've been that close to an animal that's worked for you and you fed and did veterinary work on them when they needed it for so long, they became old and loving friend not just stock. I guess I've just got a soft spot for loyalty to the animals.

One of the horses waiting shipping stood 16 and a half hands tall. He was a black, bald face quarter horse gelding with clouded mooneyes, a virus infection that causes blindness in horses. The old boy was almost 30 years old and sported six brands, three on the left hip and two on the right hip and a quarter circle lazy J on his left shoulder. He'd been around.

A few days after this old horse arrived, a cowboy looking like he was in his seventies happened by and before getting back into his truck after eating at Cliff's, came over to look at the old horse that I was feeding at the time. He looked the horse over, pulled a pack of Pall Malls from his shirt pocket and asked, "Want a smoke?"

"No thanks," I declined, smiling.

He pulled a cigarette from the pack and lit it with a wood match after he snapped the head with his thumb nail.

"Hell, I know this here horse, if my memory serves me right," he told me.

"That old horse called Phantom an' way back when I worked for the Bar Z 4 outfit up north; I recalled that ol' Phantom then was a good lookin' gelding of about 15 or 16 years old. He was a diehard bachelor by then. He would find a way to always try to hide from the wranglers and not hang close to the bell mare after he was put out for the night with the rest of the remuda. And that's why they called him Phantom." He admitted.

"Pore old horse looks like his teeth is worn down ta nubbins and he's just 'bout starved to death. Surprised he ain't gone tits up in some ditch before now," he grumbled as he waved goodbye to me and opened his truck door, stepped up onto the running board and eased himself onto the seat with the help of the steering wheel. He started the engine and drove off in his rusting 1931 Chevy truck, that coughed once as he shifted into second, leaving behind a cloud of dust and blue smoke.

I would sneak Phantom mush I'd make with a combination of grain, oats, beet pulp and warm water and let set for a bit until everything was soft then feed it to him. Had to do it when Ben was having his coffee in the Cliff's or off somewhere away from the stockyards.

I heard the trucks coming up Montana Ave. as I walked around to the front to the diner. Donna was turning the "Closed" sign around to "Open" in the window. The truck drivers down shifted using their jake brakes to slow the rig and instantly the sound of the mufflers piped up a chorus of bellowed put-put-putting that echoed off of the surrounding buildings as the engines idled down. Ahead of the convoy of four trucks was old man Archie Braddock, owner of the 16,000 acre Milliron slash B Ranch, driving his $6,000 lily white Cadillac, Coupe de Ville straight for the diner. A surge of gray dust lofted and palled over the vicinity from the unpaved yard road behind the car and trucks. The sound of bellowing stock being jarred over the pothole drive and the resounding truck muffler broke the otherwise stillness of the morning as the pigeons flew from the power lines in groups and circled, only to land again in beads on the same telephone and power lines to wait for the opportunity to find food dropped on the ground by man or beast.

I came up to see Mister Braddock as he was opening the car door. Archie Braddock seemed to have a sixth sense about when the price of beef was about to escalate and this is why he had his herd rounded up a month or so before this Fall and was now selling off what steers and heifers he needed to at a very good market price.

"Okay!" he told his old red, stubbed-tailed Heeler that rode shotgun on the seat next to him and she jumped out of the Caddy, ran next to the side of the building and peed squatting while at the same time lifting a hind leg off the ground like a male dog. She then ran around, with her stub of a tail wagging, sniffing Cliff's car tires and those on my pickup truck.

"Stick around, Sylvia," he told the dog, "Mornin', son. Is Blast in his office?" Braddock asked.

"Morning, Mister Braddock. No sir, he's got to be in court first thing this morning. So I guess he's home preparing his defense. He said he'd be here as soon as he got out of court."

"Hope he wins. Law around here has gotten outta hand. Can't piss on a Jackrabbit without the son-of-a-bitch havin' you arrested and takin' you to court an' suing' you for a life-time of carrots."

"Yes sir, I reckon."

"Well, I'll be in the diner havin' coffee and checkin' out Donna while you get the beeves settled an' counted."

By 6:30 A.M., the first of the day's five loads of what would be eight hundred head of big healthy steers and heifers were unloaded and counted and settling in one of the pens. I'd count in units of ten and keep track of the units by lifting a finger and when all ten fingers had been used up I'd say one hundred, then two hundred after the next ten fingers had raised and so on, until the tally was finished. Dad had taught me how to tally this way when I was just knee high to a grasshopper. I went upstairs to the office and made Braddock an invoice for the stock received and went down to the diner to hand it to him.

"Hey, Donna," Archie was saying, while gazing at her well—rounded butt in tight jeans accented by the wide pink bow of her waitress apron tied around her waist. He watched as she reached up at the shelf over a narrow back counter to the serving shelf for a plate of food, "have you ever heard the sayin', 'She was a horseman's daughter an' all of the horsemen knew her?" He smiled and winked at one of his cowboys sitting at the counter next to him sipping coffee.

"Are you a horseman's daughter? 'cause I'm a horseman an' I'd sure like to know you better." Cliff was glaring from behind the kitchen stove frying up bacon that sizzled in its own grease and the eggs sat on the grill next to a short stack one of the drivers had ordered for breakfast.

"Mr. Braddock, you know enough about me for my likin' and any small curiosity I might have about you, I can ask your wife."

"Well you'll never know unless you've been ridden hard and put away wet," Archie joked as the cowboys and drivers snickered and hid their chuckles with bent heads, their faces hiding behind coffee mugs.

"I'm sure your wife Emma knows all about that and she can tell me about it one of these days," Donna retorted. Cliff was now smirking. Braddock said nothing more.

The diner was already filling with cigarette smoke, driving the flies crazy. Around stockyards and feedlots there is always an abundance of flies everywhere. Cliff had four strips of sticky flypaper corkscrewing down from the ceiling, dotted with dead or dying flies. A few flies crawled about the glass pie case looking for a breach in which to enter but without success. By the door hung a bulletin board that held handwritten odd-size bits of paper advertising everything from someone selling a horse, giving away puppies to selling a sewing machine and it included a poster of the last spring's high school rodeo schedule that was pinned at one corner. It was a scramble of whatnot notes and ads tacked helter-skelter to the cork board for the customers to gander at.

The Wurlitzer jukebox came on after one of the cowboys pressed C-4 and began the riff of a Hank William's song over the idle conversations in the diner. On the wall next to the cash register hung a rack of cigarettes and another displaying a selection of candy bars; a can bank for the March of Dimes sat on the counter. The place was pretty plain from a decorating standpoint, a calendar, the same as Ben had in his office, a color Anheuser-Busch Brewery replica of the famous 1895 lithograph, "Last Fight", depicting George Armstrong Custer on a knoll at the Little Big Horn fighting off Sioux and Cheyenne warriors, a framed black and white ink line drawing of a cowboy on a bucking horse signed "Will James" and dated 1942, the glass protecting the art work filmed by smoke. Hanging on the sidewall over a two-top table near the ceiling was a stuffed head of a Texas Longhorn, its horns now yellowed with age, with black tips reaching over five feet wide from point to point.

"Mr. Braddock," I put in and handed him the invoice as soon as Donna had finished down-sizing the old man, "A hundred and twenty six is the count I got for your first load, sir."

"Walt!" Archie said loudly, sticking his head out over the counter and looking past the row of men and their beat-up, sweat stained straw and felt cowboy hats at one of his contract cowboy-truck drivers, "You're off by one heifer on this count. You let one too many get by you."

Archie Braddock was what women thought of as a handsome man. A slim, six foot plus cowboy, in his late 60's, tanned face, clean shaved, white wavy hair, gray-green eyes and a face with chiseled features, a real ladies man with an infectious grin.

"Have a seat," he told me, motioning to the empty stool to his right, as he pushed his Stetson, a finely woven straw hat, with thumb and forefinger back on his head. "I'll buy your coffee, son."

"Thank you sir," I said as I sat down next to him and pulled out my pack of Luckies and fished the last one out, and then fumbled trying to find a book of matches in my pocket.

He turned and slid his Zippo lighter towards me and said, "Have a light." The Zippo had an insignia of the 101st Airborne, the 'Screaming Eagle.'

"You were a paratrooper?" I asked while examining the lighter.

"No, it belonged to a good friend of mine's son. His father gave it to me a few years after Russell was killed. He had been shot after he jumped into Holland and was fighting in Bastogne. He kept Russell's Purple Heart, dog tags and the winged qualification paratrooper patch. He also had his son's 501st Airborne command patch which he had worn before the command became the 101st Airborne."

"He gave me the Zippo," he went on, "knowing that I really liked his boy, and should have his lighter as a memento of Russell. He has never smoked but knew I did. Got to put lighter fluid in it from time to time, but it has never let me down. Lights most times with the first try."

I nodded as if I fully understood and after a short silent time thinking about what Archie had said, he opened into a new subject.

"You know, son," Archie began, "I'm losing a hand at the ranch, he's quitting. Thinks he'll try his luck in Hollywood tryin' to become a movie cowboy like Will James was. Anyways, my question to you is can you rope and work stock? If so I'd hire you from Blastingame's employment if you're willing to quit riding for his brand."

"Yes sir, I can ride and rope and work stock and can break colts," I answered him, "Besides, I think Ben was thinking of having his grandson come to work for him full-time." *And he and I don't get on too good anyways, He reminds me of thunder: lightning does the work, thunder takes the credit,* entered my mind, "So I'll probably be laid off as soon as things slow down first of the winter. I was going to move on and hopefully find a riding job at some point."

"Good. Job pays a hundred and fifty bucks a month, room and board; you can throw your horse in with the ranch remuda. I use to pay twenty-five bucks per colt-breaking in the spring. But I'm out of the colt business these days and so you're out of luck there. You'll spend the summer months in the Jackrabbit line shack near the Arrowhead Coulee. Hope you can cook your own vittles."

"Yes sir, I can cook for myself. When do you expect me to start?"

"Brent's leaving the outfit end of October. Things are quiet around the ranch then, so I'd say you can start right after Armistice Day, I mean Veterans Day," he corrected himself and went on, "Live in the bunk-house with the rest of the boys and take your meals in the main house," he suggested with a forlorn look on his face while staring into his half empty cup of coffee just as Donna came to refill his cup. I had a feeling he was just then thinking of Russell or his own son as he put the Zippo back into his pocket.

Armistice Day had been just changed to Veterans Day by President Eisenhower in 1954.

Archie Braddock's son had been drafted at the beginning of the Second World War and was one of the first fatalities on D-Day at Omaha Beach in Normandy. They say he caught a bullet and drowned when he fell into the water, as he was about to wade towards shore after leaving the L.S.T. he had been on.

"You want coffee, Dakk?" Donna asked me as she poured more coffee into Archie's cup.

"Sure, and a pack of Luckies too, please," I told the waitress.

"I've got his coffee," Archie told Donna. Then looking at me said, "Well, I guess we've got a deal son." and he put out his hand to seal the offer.

"Thank you, sir. I'm much obliged," I said shaking his hand that had a strong grip.

*   *   *

HOOF & HORN
CHAPTER TWO

It had been a long day without any help. Roy, Blastingame's grandson, never showed up. Ben showed up by mid afternoon, drunk and pissed off at the judge and the justice system. He'd put up a logical defense remonstrating that he wasn't driving because there was no stock in front of him. No horses, oxen, mules, donkeys, sheep, goats, cows or any other kind of domesticated animal. He was operating a truck and "therefore," didn't need a driver's license, "there for," didn't have one. What he needed was an operator's license, but the state didn't issue such a thing and "there for," he wasn't guilty as charged. The magistrate judge told him even though he had a good argument, he was splitting hairs and "there for," found him guilty, fining him fifty dollars or two weeks in jail. Blast almost took the jail sentence, but had a sudden last minute change of heart. He begrudgingly coughed up two twenties and a ten and paid the fine off with a clenched mouth and a fit to be tied look on his face.

The clerk thanked him as she gave him a receipt and he mumbled, "Blood suckin' bureaucrats."

Now he had to take the damn written and driving test so he could have a new Montana "Driver's License" issued to him.

After court, he went to the Cattleman's Club at the Northern Hotel, Stockman's Bar. There he and his buddies hammered down a few too many drinks. All of the pals sided up with him and said he put up a good fight, but the cards were stacked against him and the judge was no more than a wolf disguised as a coyote.

After he was chauffeured by one of his friends to the stockyards, Ben went straight up to his office, pulled the shades down, and slumped in his chair. He leaned back, put his feet on the desk and pulled his hat down over his face. Within seconds he was sawing logs and for the rest of the afternoon slept. Around 6:30 I walked into the office and set the day's paper work on his desk. Blast woke with a start.

"What time is it?" he asked after jacking himself to a proper sitting position.

"Six-thirty," I said in a non-committal tone. It had been a long hectic day.

"Put your horse up yet? How's the Braddock beeves he brought in today?"

"You bet. He's in his pen and has been fed as usual. And the Milliron slash B stock all look okay. Have a steer with only one eye but it's an old wound. They must have sewed it up after it happened sometime ago."

"Well, I don't suppose it will affect him none once he becomes steaks," he gazed at the tally sheets I'd put on his desk. "Do me a favor, son. Give me a lift home. Damn, the ol' lady's goin' to be peeved off at me again. By the way, did the Rafter Box Dot foreman call today?"

"No he didn't, at least not while I was in the office. Yeah, I'll give you a ride home, it's on my way." I said.

His eyes looked swollen and watery. He spit in the full wastebasket. Went to the filing cabinet, opened the bottom drawer and took a pull on the bottle of Jack Daniel's, washed out his mouth and swallowed. "I'll be just a minute," he said and went into the small rest room pulling the door shut behind him.

I lit a Lucky and waited for him while filling out my time card.

As the toilet flushed he came out buttoning his fly. "Dakk, son, when you get to be my age, no matter how much you shake, dance and prance, the last drop goes down your pants."

All I could think of saying was, "Yes sir," with a grin.

"Take my sorry ass home to face the music, son. I'll have Roy bring me here in the mornin'. So don't worry about comin' by to get me. I've got some of the waddies comin' in to help out for a while. Also have a semi of hay comin' in tomorrow," he assured me, "Hays from the Rafter Box Dot Ranch."

Waddies are what we called day help, mostly working cowhands that work for whoever needs help for a short time.

"Gonna need all the help I can get. Hope they're working this weekend because I haven't had a day off in weeks and I plan to spend time with Kipp riding the backcountry and camping." I said.

Now watch Murphy's Law come into effect, I thought to myself as we reached my truck.

"Yeah, they and Roy will work. Not a problem," Blast said as he hoisted himself into the truck cab and slammed the door closed. I climbed in behind the wheel and we drove off.

"Did you hear that explosion this morning?" I asked, changing the subject.

"It don't figure, rattled the windows and damn near shook me outta' bed. Nobody knows what's it all about. But the paper will have the skinny on it. Sure they know what it was all about by now."

I left Ben to make his way from the street to his house and as I drove off he gave me a halfhearted wave of his hand without looking back.

A little after seven o'clock, I pulled into the parking lot at the Pronghorn Cafe and went in for a cup of coffee and a piece of pie. I was starved and though I knew Ma would have dinner in the oven warming, I wanted to see if Sue Palmer was waiting tables. She was. I sat at a double-top facing the door. Fumbling with the menu, the day's special held by a well-used paper clip slipped off and fell on the table, then my lap, and finally the floor before I could grab it. I was bent down trying to get a hold of it, when I saw the waitress standing next to me.

"Hi! Can I get you something to drink?"

"Yeah, Sue, please, a cup of joe and a piece of apple pie," I said as I straightened up, holding the day's special in my hand.

"Heated and with a piece of cheese on top?"

"Sure, thanks."

She poured me a mug of coffee from a steaming full pot, while she smiled warmly.

"Be back in a couple, I'll ask Cookie to heat it under the salamander," she smiled again.

Sue Palmer was my heartthrob, though I never admitted it to her. I was in love with her, or maybe it was just lust. I wasn't sure. She must have known I had a thing for her. At least I hoped she did. But then again, maybe she didn't realize it. She was maybe a year younger than me, a touch on the heavy side, big-boned I guess you'd say, not beautiful but pretty in her own right, a good figure. She had blonde hair, on the dishwater side that she wore in a single long braid most of the time. Her eyes were a deep blue and she always had a warm smile that could melt a river of ice on a Montana January day.

I got up from the table, left my pack of cigarettes and matches by my coffee cup and went to wash up. As I was about to enter the can, the door opened and Lee Pekhead came out. Seeing me, his zit pocked face became all smiles, exposing a mouth full of stained teeth with gums covered black from always dipping Copenhagen.

"Hey! If it ain't Dakk, the shitstomping cowboy."

"How you doin,' Peckerhead? Been stealing any cars again lately, or peeping into windows?"

"Fuck you!" he sneered.

"I'll take that as a no. Hope the windows open in here to let out your stink." I said curtly as I looked back at Sue and winked.

"One of these days I'm goin' to open up your head, asshole, and dump your body into a coulee," he mumbled.

"I can wait. I'm not leaving town just yet," and pushed my way into the rest room. My bloodstream now stirred with rancor. I could feel the adrenalin pumping in me. Over the urinal, I noticed someone had written a poem in pencil. It read, "Here I sit broken hearted, ran three blocks and only farted." I pulled a pencil stub from my pocket and signed the poem, Lee.

When I came back and sat down, Sue was just bringing my pie to the table. The cafe was empty except for three guys and a gal sitting by the window. Lee had left.

"Here you go. Anything else I can get you?"

"Thanks, no."

And as she started to walk away, I said, "Yeah, Sue, you got a minute."

She turned back to me, "Sure."

"You work in here every day?" I asked stupidly.

"All but Sundays and Mondays. Why?"

"Maybe we could take in a movie or something. Sometime, if you're not seeing anyone."

"Dakk, are you askin' me out on a date?"

"Yeah, I guess I am," I said sheepishly.

"Something must be in the air. Lee just asked me out earlier also."

"Oh," I muttered.

"I wouldn't be seen with him in church in a month of Sundays."

I let out a choking laugh.

"Sure, a movie would be fun," she remarked, "I was hoping to see the new Alfred Hitchcock, *To Catch a Thief* with Cary Grant and Grace Kelly one of these days. I hear it's great according to Rose, my neighbor. It's playing at the Fox Theater. The Billings Gazette had a good review of the film."

"Yeah, I like Hitchcock's films. Did you see *Rear Window* last year?"

"Yeah, he sure makes good mystery movies."

"Well, how about this Monday night? Meet you here around this time, seven-thirty?" I asked with anxiety.

"Okay," she smiled.

I wolfed down the pie, blowing on every forkful to cool the hot cheese.

Sue came back with the Billings "Gazette" and pot of coffee. She refilled my cup. "Some ranch hand left this paper. You can read the movie review if you want."

"Sure, thanks, I will. And I'd like to see if they've found out what that explosion was this morning."

"Wasn't that something? Scared the bee-gees out of me. So sudden and at that hour. I couldn't get back to sleep."

"The whole ground shook under me. I was up and having a smoke on the back porch when it happened."

"It says on the front page they think it was a sonic boom from an Air Force jet. But I heard on the radio that Montana State University claim it was a seismic tremor."

*   *   *

I pulled my boots off with the "Naughty Nellie" bootjack which always sat on the back porch that Ma hated because she saw the bootjack as a form of suggestive pornography since it was that of a woman laid on her back with her legs spread out to catch your boot heel on while standing on the rest of her with your other foot.

I walked into the kitchen as the smell of a pot-roast entered my nostrils and saw that Ma was sitting at the table thumbing through and reading recipes in the American Women's Cook Book.

"You're home late, son. I'll bet you're starved. Wash up and sit down. I'll get you some pot-roast, potatoes and carrots."

"Yeah, long day."

"You want milk?"

"Sure," I hung up the hand towel next to the sink.

"Dad wants to talk to you before you turn in."

"What about?"

"Oh, he'll tell you."

"Where's Kipp?"

"He fed the animals after dinner and went to bed early. It's not like him. Hope he's not coming down with something."

He's coming down with lack of sleep. He'll make that up in the next twenty hours, went through my mind, *What's he and the CC's been up too?*

I could hear the TV's sound getting louder when the program broke for commercials. Dad entered the kitchen with his empty water glass.

"How your day go? Besides long."

"Not bad, actually real good. Archie Braddock who owns the Milliron slash B asked me if I wanted a job on the ranch. Said he was losing a hand and wanted to know if I'd be interested in working for him. Room and board, a hundred-fifty dollars a month and I can put Sioux and Jeep in with his remuda. He doesn't have colts to break anymore so Ma doesn't have to worry about my getting my neck broke."

"And are you quittin' Blast and takin' the job?"

"I told Braddock I would. Job starts after Veterans Day. He'll have me winter at the ranch then in one of the line shacks after spring roundup."

"That will make for a long winter for you, Dakk. Are you sure you won't get cabin fever?" Ma put in.

"Cabin fever will have to come and go, that's all part of the job. Besides he said my main job this winter will be feeding his bulls in the bull pasture. He's got 28 that I'll be feeding twice a day, snow, rain or shine."

"Humm," Dad sighed.

The TV muted some as the evening program resumed.

"Besides it may give me a chance to do some writing while holed up at the line shack. I've got a couple of ideas for short stories. Maybe I can sell to magazines like "Outdoor Life" or "Western Horseman." Anyways, being alone for awhile might clear my mind up about what I want to do with my life and future."

"Well, this is along the lines of what I wanted to talk to you about, Dakk."

"Yeah, what do you mean?"

"We've been puttin' a bit of money away in a savin's account at the bank for some years now hopin' you'd be the first of the Lovetts to make it into college. Ma has also been addin' the money you've paid for room and board every week since you've graduated from high school to the college fund. I also bought stock in your name, some time ago at 15 cents a share and now it's up to almost a buck a share. You can use it as a reserve and sell it or part of it to further your education if you wish. That's what I planned it for anyways. It isn't much but everything adds up. Anyways, if you want to go to college it isn't out of the question. We can help some financially."

"I appreciate that. And maybe next year after I've thought things out this winter I'll see about college and making my major in English Literature, you know, writing. I don't really know which way to go. But I've got to get this cowboy feelin' either deeper into me or out for good."

"I did it, as you know. So maybe you need to also. I liked cowboyin' but there was no future in it unless you own the ranch you cowboyed at. It was a dead end in those days as it is now, even with the growin' demand for beef. Ranchin's iffy. But as they say, life is a gamble and you can only play the cards you're dealt and hope you get a winnin' hand now and again before you end up with 'ace's an' eights'."

"Yeah," I said as I stood up and took my plate and glass to the sink to wash.

"I'll get those," Ma said gingerly, "Dakk, you've always had good stories to write, like the one you did a year ago in your senior English class about the elk hunt and the one on wheat fields. That was almost poetic. I think you could become a very good writer. You have a way of painting a picture with words. John Steinbeck had to start at some point. I think you can. If you set your mind to it. Why if Steinbeck had ever been on an elk hunt, I think he would have written about it as you did."

Dad had settled himself at the table and had taken his pencil and pad out of his pocket. I dried the dishes and put them away as Ma was wiping down the sink and table.

"Just doin' a few figures here and even now with the minimum wage set all the way up to a dollar an hour and you workin' on the ranch seven days a week, ten hours a day, give or take. That's two—hundred-eighty hours. Therefore you should be your makin' two hundred and eighty dollars a month, before taxes and social security. And you say Braddock's payin' you a hundred-fifty a month even with room and board, feedin' the horse and all, you're coming up short some. I know ranch work pays under different guide lines than workin' at the refinery or any other normal trade, but you should think about it in terms of wages."

"Yeah, and maybe if I decide to go to college by next spring, I may quit the ranch after calving and work turn-around at one of the refineries in Billings or Laurel and save up for school in the fall. That's if I find working for the Milliron not to my liking for one reason or another," I told him.

"Yes, well you could maybe save up close to three hundred dollars in a couple of months if you didn't spend a penny while working turn-around," Dad rationalized.

"Kipp talked that he planned and hoped to get a job at the refinery during turn-around next summer. He wants to save up to buy a used car now that Cooper has that old Pontiac with the beat up running boards and smashed-in grill his grandfather sold him. Kipp says he's paying his grandfather off with money he makes doing occasional odd jobs," Ma put in.

Yawning, I said, "I've got to hit the hay. I'm beat."

"You think about what we discussed. I sure would be proud to see a Lovett graduate from college," Dad urged.

* * *

The following morning, I was at the stock yards before anyone else except for Cliff and Donna who I could see busy setting up for breakfast. Cliff had ordered a new color neon sign for the window and it was now turned on for the first time. HOOF & HORN DINER it read with a logo of a longhorn cow's head above the name, it lit up in tubes of red, white and blue. The blue neon had a slight dither. The waft of bacon hit my nostrils as I got out of the truck. Donna, I could see, was working in the kitchen and as she turned towards the window she waved to me and I waved back. I tossed my cigarette butt to the ground among fifty others and stepped on it. At the pens, there was a very strong smell of cow manure and urine, the yard lights still beamed in the early morning radiance of another sunny day. White and blue-slate colored pigeons cooed and flew from the hay barn's beams and rafters, circled the pens, then returned, landed, cooed some more while looking for spilt oats and grain. The beeves milled and bellowed with moos of hunger.

It had rained that night, a short thunderstorm that dumped a half-inch of rain down on Billings in an hour. With the damp earth you could now smell the distant hog pens, which to me was never pleasant. It was not at all earthy as the scent of horse or cow manure, which I always found rich and pleasant to my olfactory senses.

Billings at one time had the largest stockyards in the nation, even bigger than Kansas City stockyards. The Pierce Packing Company, a tall two story red brick and concrete building dominated two and one half city blocks alone. Feed lots with the acres of wood and iron pens covered acres on the east end of First Ave. of North 13th Street and a large part of the south side of Montana Avenue up towards North 9th Street and the pig and chicken farms. The tunnel under North 13th Street was used to drive the cattle under and into dip vats filled with pesticides to rid the animals of ticks, lice and other external parasites and then down along a chute to the slaughterhouse they would go. In the Pierce feed lot the cows were fed for some time before butchering to add weight and also so that the meat had ample marble and therefore taste. Corn as well as sugar beet mush and just about everything but the kitchen sink was fed these animals before they were all decimated.

I fed my workhorse Amigo and the other workhorses first from hay-alfalfa mix bales stacked near the feed bins at the paddock pens. I'd saddle Amigo later after he'd eaten. At the hay barn, I started the John Deere tractor; she fired up on the first try with only one or two short sputters. Then I pulled the flat bed hitched to the Deere close to the stacked hay. Leaving the tractor running, I went to the tack shed and put on my beat up hay chaps, with the belt strap held together with a piece of baling wire sewn through the leather, grabbed a set of hay hooks and work gloves off the shelf and headed back to the wagon. Dwayne, one of the waddlies, had shown up and was already tossing bales onto the flat bed.

"Mornin' Dwayne."

"Howdy. Looks like it's gonna be another hot one."

"Yeah, sure does."

I stacked while Dwayne pitched the bales to me. Every bale hit the trailer's wooden deck with a thud that shook it with each landing. The air now smelled of hay and it hung there heavily. Already I was covered with bits and pieces of hay and the clouds of chaff rose into the slanted morning sunlight.

George showed up and climbed on the wagon and pulled on his gloves. George, in his thirties, a decorated Army veteran of the Second World War, having served in North Africa and Italy, now worked odd jobs, was married with a five-year-old daughter.

"Georgey!" Dwayne called.

"Mornin', Dwayne, Dakk."

"What's up, George?" I asked.

"Not much. Same ol' shit, different day, I guess. Was sick with somethin' for couple days, but I'm okay now. Well it's like my ol' man use to say, 'You was sick, but now you're well again, there's work to do.' So here I am."

"We get the stock fed and watered and I'll buy the coffee," I insisted.

"Good, 'cause I've just 'nough for a pack of Chesterfields and lunch," George sighed. "Ol' lady only let me have a buck and a half. She don't trust me with more. Thinks if I have five-six bucks or more, I'll blow it all in a bar, suckin' down beer or lose it at poker."

"Sounds like she really knows you by now after bein' married to you, for how long, five-six years?" Dwayne said.

"Six, I reckon."

Finished loading the thirty bales, I drove while and George cut the baling wire with dikes, folded and wrapped the two strands into a bow with a twist and tossed it into a wood trash box in the corner of the head-ache rack on the wagon. Dwayne with George's help pitched hay flakes into the lengthy feed line of mangers along the welded iron pipe fence line. We heard Roy pull his truck into the lot. *Day late and a dollar short*, ran through my mind. I saw Roy followed Blast up to his office.

After feeding and watering, we three whacked the hay chaff off ourselves. George used his sweat-stained beat up straw hat to smack the chaff from his clothes. We took turns washing up at one of the hose bibs. The water felt cool and refreshing when I washed my neck with a wet neckerchief. I wrung it out and hung it on a nail along with my hay chaps outside the tack shed before we headed for a ten-minute coffee break and smoke. My gloves I pushed into my back pocket.

"Three coffees please, Donna," I ordered "And I'll take up the tab."

"I could use a glass of water alongside the coffee," George said, "An' a pack of Chesterfields too! If you please."

"You men look like you already have put in a full day," Donna commented as she filled the three mugs with steaming black coffee.

"Almost feels like it," Dwayne laughed.

Donna set three glasses down in front of us with ice cubes floating in the water. She took George's fifty-cent piece and brought him back a pack of cigarettes and change.

Coffee was a bit too hot so I fished out an ice cube from the water and let it float and melt in the mug. Then I drank the glass of water in one long gulp.

"What time is the truck load of hay comin'?" Dwayne wanted to know staring straight, as if he was asking the glass pie and doughnut case that sat on the back counter across from him to befall to him.

"This a.m. I was told. No particular time, I kind of thought the load would already be here when I arrived," I answered and sipped my coffee.

"Hey! Donna, how about one of those doughnuts, a plain one. Here's a nickel or are they a dime?"

"For you Dwayne, five cents."

George had just put out what was left of the cigarette butt in the glass ashtray and held up his mug to Donna for a refill. She came by with the pot and filled our mugs again. Dwayne stuck a dime into the jukebox and pushed G-8 and a second or two later the machine played "The Yellow Rose of Texas" and Donna started to sing along.

"She should be a Western singer," I whispered to Dwayne.

"Yeah, she's even got the looks to go along with the fantastic voice."

As the song ended and I was thinking of dropping a dime into the juke so we could hear Donna sing along to, "Cherry Pink and Apple Blossom White" when we heard the Reo semi engine idle down. Its dual exhaust pipes trembling as the truck and trailer coasted past the café and onto the dirt drive to the metal barn, splashing brown water out of the puddle potholes.

"Look's like our break's over." I washed down the rest of my coffee, stood up reached into my jeans and pulled out some odd change, tossed two bits and a dime and nickel on the counter, "Thanks for the song, Donna. See you at lunch."

The hay farm semi driver was backing into position next to the barn. The signs on the truck doors read, Rafter Box Dot Hay Sales, Harlowton, Montana. We got set up, and waited for the driver to untie the load. That's when I noticed Roy was out on my working horse riding around the Milliron slash B beeves checking the stock. I made a nod towards the pens with my head and both George and Dwayne looked over to that direction.

"Thought he rode that appi? What's he doin' on your work bay horse?" Dwayne asked.

"It's the horse I normally use. Hope he hasn't takin' to using my *Heiser* saddle also, the pencil neck. His appi, Dipper, should be called Dip-stick, damn horse's brain is short two bales of makin' a ton when it comes to smarts."

"Heads up!" shouted the driver as he threw one of the lines over the top of the load. We moved out of the way from the flying rope.

"Roy was out ridin' Dip-stick last week, had on a new plaid shirt tryin' to look good, when ol' Dipper saw a crumpled sheet of newspaper flying across the ground in the wind. Roy had his nose in the air as Dip-stick boogered up, blew a gasket and dumped Roy head over tea kettle into the air and he landed in a pile of fresh green horse shit."

Dwayne and George started laughing hard.

"Oh, he split his new cowboy shirt right up the back slicker than you could with a pair of scissors."

"He's a piece of work, one sorry cowboy. He'll never make a hand, too lazy." George shook his head back and forth with a disgusted look on his face.

"I don't suppose he'll make his way over here and help stack this hay," Dwayne ventured.

By one-fifteen all the hay was unloaded, stacked in the barn and the semi with empty trailer pulled away, leaving behind a cloud of green hay floating off the deck and swirling in the still air. The Reo belched black smoke from its pipes as the driver shifted up in gears. Again we washed ourselves off, it seemed that every pore on our arms and neck had opened, then filled with chaff, making the sweat sting as it ran from our bodies. The backs of our shirts had darkened with sweat and clung to our backs. It was overdue time for lunch and we headed for Cliff's Diner, more coffee and food. Roy had already taken his meal at noon. I saw my working horse tied at the hitching post at the back of the Hoof and Horn at twelve sharp. Roy never came by to even say hi, not that we expected him to.

After we had eaten, we went back to mop up, so to speak and re-stack one of the stacks that was listing precariously. Roy rode over and said to us, "When you boys get finished around here, Ben wants the manure mountain moved to the old spot. He's got it sold to . . . ."

"Who the fuck you callin' BOY? I for one ain't your nigger, sonny!" yelled George, all red in the face, and he spit his wad of Redman onto the dirt that hit like a bullet.

"I-I-I didn't mean nothin' by it. I-I called you boys as in cowboys," Roy stuttered.

"If'n that was what you meant by that remark, why in hell didn't you say cowboys, you sorry little shit?"

"I-I-I'm only tellin' you—."

"You ain't tellin' me shit, you little fart. For Christ-sake I was fuckin' a long while before you were just learnin' to suck your mother's tit!"

I was about to intervene before things escalated into George dragging Roy off of Amigo, when Roy turned the horse around, tapped him with his heels and rode off at a trot towards the paddocks.

"What got into you?" Dwayne asked dubiously with a chagrined look on his face.

"High and mighty little turd thinks he's king of the fuckin' hill, just 'cause Blast is his gramps. Well he ain't no king-shit to me, that *pendejo*. And I don't give a rat's ass if I ever work for Ben again," George steamed.

"What's a ben-day-hoe?" I asked, surprised by hearing the term.

"It's pen-day-hoe and it means asshole, stupid, dumb-shit in Mexican," George remarked, "An' it fits him!"

By the end of the day I put my saddle, blanket, headstall, bridle, reins and rope in the cab of my truck. George took off without filling out his time card. I had half a mind to give Ben my notice, but thought better of it. Not until things got closer to the end of October. I'd just have to put up with Roy for a while longer.

"Think George will work tomorrow?" I asked Dwayne.

"Yeah, he needs the money, same's me. I've got a month to go before I go into the U.S. Marines. I enlisted, took the oath last week."

I didn't know what to say except, "I wish you luck. Marines are tough bunch, all bulldog. At least we're not at war. The Korean Conflict is over and Ike is president so I don't think we'll be at war for a while, I hope."

"Well at least it's one way to get out of Billings an' see what else is out there in this big world."

"Yeah, I guess. Has ahh—, Blast talked to you about working this weekend? I was hoping for a couple days off and go camping with my brother Kipp."

"Ben told me on the phone that I was to work an' help you an' Roy out, an' take care of the feedin' Saturday an' Sunday. So I guess you've got the weekend off. No worry, cowboy," and he winked as he got into his truck and said, "At a lope," and drove off nice and easy without stirring up dust.

*   *   *

ROADSTER
CHAPTER THREE

Friday came and went. I made sure the first thing I did was to put my saddle on Amigo before I fed him and Roy got there. George did show up to work and Roy stayed as far away from him as he could. George had given Ben a call Thursday evening, still pissed at having been called a boy. He told Blast that if he wanted him to come in on Friday with his welder and cutting torch to make up some new fencing out of the old pipe casing Ben had bought, he would have to pay more than the one dollar minimum wage. He wanted three bucks an hour and two dollars an hour for Dwayne as his helper. Or Ben could have another welder come out to do the job for five bucks an hour plus three for his helper. Ben pondered this for a minute then agreed as long as George didn't charge him for the welding rods or any other extras.

At noon Roy ate in the diner but sat at the other end of the counter talking to a young high school cowboy from the Double Diamond Ranch who was a pretty good bull, bareback and saddle bronc rider. In time he might give Casey Tibbs of South Dakota the all-around cowboy for the second time, some competition, as age would give the younger cowboy an advantage and age would in time wear down Tibbs.

After work I stopped and had coffee at the Pronghorn Café to see if Sue was still going to the movies with me on Monday night. When she said of course, my heart pounded and the aches and pains in my body from the day's work seemed to have instantly disappeared.

Kipp and I had hitched the homemade iron and oak wood horse trailer Dad had bought some years back to my truck. We made sure the air pressure was up in all the tires. I got under the truck and found the loose trailer wires I'd taped up under the bumper. They were caked hard with mud and I cleaned the connections off. Then I twisted them to the trailer wires, re-taping them together so we had the one red tail-brake light working on the trailer. Then we went over the tack and gear we'd need for the trip.

"Cooper has an uncle who has a ranch, the Rolling U, around Pryor someplace. Coop said his uncle has found stuff from time to time around Canyon Creek and the coulees. The creek runs through the ranch where Chief Joseph killed a lot of cavalry soldiers and there's a mass unmarked grave some place on the ranch. No one's found it yet. Coop said that when the soldiers found their dead, the bodies had been ripped apart by coyotes and bears so they had to gather the bones and put them in one big hole. Maybe we ought to call them and see if he'll let us camp there and ride around the place and find stuff. I can get his phone number from Coop," Kipp informed me in an anxious voice.

"It sounds like a plan to me. Sure beats anything I had in mind. Let's give them a call. You know that when someone does find that grave you can bet that there's nothing more than bones in it," I told Kipp.

"Why?" Kipp wondered.

"Because Joseph and his band would have taken everything from the dead soldiers, stripped them clean," I told him.

"Yeah, you're right. I should of figured that."

Kipp was one that was always kind of nuts about Indians and Indian culture and artifacts. He had granddad's collection of arrowheads glued on red felt and framed hanging on the wall in his room along with a bowl carved out of steatite. The KCC's spent many summer hours looking for snakes, fishing the banks of the Yellowstone River and always looking for arrowheads on the rims, coulees and waters cut banks. He had a cigar box full of arrowheads, scrapers, beads, old bullets and even part of a human skull, the frontal bone with a bullet hole in it. He had all the gum cards with the famous Indian chiefs pictured on them instead of collecting the more popular baseball player bubble gum cards. When he read anything it generally had to do with Indians or hot rod cars.

At five-thirty, I woke Kipp up and he was, 'up and at 'em' the second I shook him. It normally took a crowbar to get his butt out of bed. My guess is he rose without a fight because we were given the okay to camp and hunt around on the Rolling U Ranch and had been clued in on where to go search for arrowheads over the telephone. The owner also invited us to see what they had found while looking for his cattle or mending fence in the many years that he, his father and grandfather had picked up around that part of the country.

Kipp and I loaded the horses into the green trailer hitched to my 1939 International. We had already stowed both saddles with the head stalls and our saddle bags stuffed with chuck and cooking utensils as well as basic first aid kit for man and beast. Our bedrolls were each a couple of old wool blankets rolled up in canvas manties tied to the back of the saddle cantles along with our yellow slickers and everything sat in the truck bed. The horses were tied to the front of the trailer with their cotton lead ropes snapped to the leather halters and the leads hitched with quick release knots up to the trailer tie-ups. We were ready to get on the road.

"You don't plan to ride in your Keds, do you? Where's your boots?" I asked.

"Dakk, those old boots don't fit any more. My feet grew a size or two since I was twelve. So my Keds will have to do."

"If Sioux spooks and your foot slips through the stirrup and you get dumped, she'll drag you into coyote bait."

"Well that's the chance I'm goin' to have to take at this time. Besides Sioux wouldn't spook even if a black bear stood up and slipped a paw in the stirrup and climbed aboard, and you know that."

"Maybe, and you could put a new born baby in the saddle and she'd take it to the high and low, feed it and change its diapers, bring the kid back without a scratch. But accidents happen. That's why they're called accidents," I reminded him. "Go up to my room, I've got an old pair of Acme boots in the back of the closet somewhere. If they're too big, stick some TP in the toes and they'll do."

"Oh, all right but I'd rather wear my sneakers," Kipp complained, "they're easier to walk around rocks and stuff than cowboy boots."

"Bring them along. You can put them on when we find a spot we'd like to hunt around at. We'll let the horses graze while we're checking the ground."

We finally got underway heading southeast, then southwest through the Crow Indian Reservation. At the town of Pryor, home of Chief

Plenty Coups, I turned west and drove the dirt and washboard road towards Edger. At 35, both truck and trailer rattled like the tail of a pissed off diamond-back rattler. The brown dust pluming a clouded a wake behind us for a quarter of a mile before it settled to the ground again.

About five miles down the road the trailer started to wobble and I braked to a slow stop. We had a flat tire on the driver's side of the trailer.

"Shit! Hope the spare will hold up. It's getting down in tread."

"I'll get the horses out while you set up the jack," Kipp offered.

I stuck a piece of board I kept in the truck under the jack and raised the axle to get the weight of the rim off the tire, loosened the lug nuts and jacked the trailer up to get the flat tire off. Kipp had tied the horses to the other side of the trailer and was rolling the spare to me.

"Truck's comin'."

"Yeah, I hear it."

The truck slowed as it came along side then stopped.

"Need a hand?" the Indian driver asked.

"Don't reckon, just a flat. Dakk's got 'er whipped, thanks."

I stood up, "If you don't mind my asking, how far is it to the Rolling U Ranch from here?" I asked as I looked into the truck cab at the man.

"Oh, just down the road a piece. Maybe two miles. Can't miss it. Got a sign with a Rolling U brand burnt into it and an arrow pointin' to the right down a rutty road."

"Thanks."

"No problem. Hey, got a cigarette?"

"You bet," I tapped one out of the pack and handed it to him, then took one out myself and lit it, then handed him my matches.

After lighting his, he gave me the matchbook back, nodded, then shifted out of neutral into first and pulled off slowly.

"Nice porcupine quill hat band he had on his straw," Kipp commented, "I'd sure like to have a Golden Eagle feather like he had tied to his hat."

"Yeah, I noticed. We should make next year's Crow Pow-wow and see if anyone has some hat bands for sale."

"I'd like to buy a pair of beaded moccasins there. Yeah, let's plan to go."

"The mocs will probably cost you fifteen to twenty bucks these days. Better save up. You need cowboy boots more than moccasins. How those Ache-me's (*Acme's*) of mine feel on your feet?"

"They're fine. Not all that much bigger really."

"Well you keep them. I like my Justin's better."

"What you have to give for them?"

"Thirty-six fifty."

"Shit, that's a weeks worth of work.'

"Yeah, but they're worth it," I said as I torqued the lug nuts down once I had the spare on the trailer.

"Load the kids while I put the jack and flat tire away."

Kipp walked Sioux in, then Jeep; and I helped him lift the ramp-gate up and shut. And we were off again.

"It'll be after eleven maybe by the time we get to the ranch house," I pondered out loud.

*   *   *

When we reached the Rolling U Ranch sign, it had a bullet hole mid-center of the U, and a Meadowlark was perched on the branded weathered board. The lark flew off as we neared, with short wing beats and alternating brief glides to a fence post and there sat, then warbled an alarm. Old railroad ties made up sturdy corner posts for the four strand barbed wire fencing linked by cedar posts and narrow split cedar staves. The truck and trailer rattled over the cattle guard, my "*Crocket*" spurs that I kept buckled and dropped down over the long floor gearshift, jumped and clinked against one another. The rowels chimed and jingled. The road headed north now, and nothing much beyond a dirt track of worn ruts. A line of telephone poles followed the track. Black birds of some kind flocked in small groups on the electric and phone wires. Ahead, on one of the poles a Red-tail Hawk stood sentinel and watched as we approached, at the last second before we passed he spread his wings and glided away on large broad wings. On each side of the valley lay stone ledge cliffs about two and a half miles apart. I took my time driving the track bordered by green sage and grassy meadows. Cows lay or grazed, scattered about the landscape.

Hereford cattle, all a reddish-brown, white faces and bodies blotched with white.

"Good looking beef stock," I put to Kipp.

"A cow is a cow to me, I'm not into this cow and cowboy stuff like you are."

I guess he never was and wouldn't be. He loves cars especially "Hot Rods" and Indian stuff. Horses he could take or leave. To Kipp as it seemed it was to dad, horses were like an extension ladder, if you really needed one you got one. Horses were not in his blood like taking apart an engine and putting it back together without ending up with a coffee can of spare nuts and bolts. If anything was wrong with my International he'd figure out what it was and fix it. The auto parts store knew him well, even sent business his way from time to time.

We crossed the low-flowing clear Canyon Creek at stony shoals a couple of times where it meandered back and forth before the road to the Rolling U Ranch headquarters ended. The creek ran through willows, Russian olive groves, tall cottonwood trees and lush pasture, heading north before ebbing into the Yellowstone River where it merged. And eventually the waters would unite with the Missouri River and on to Saint Louis and the confluence of the Mississippi River and would then flow south to the Gulf of Mexico, ending its two thousand mile journey.

With each ford, water sloshed and gravel churned beneath us. Sioux nickered each time. *Must be thirsty,* I thought, *They'll have to wait until we're at the ranch headquarters.* The sun was now above us, and the sky in its immensity made me think it was as blue as Sue Palmer's eyes.

"Hey, look over there, a couple of bucks," Kipp half whispered.

"Yeah, I see them. Nice rack on that one mulie."

The bucks stared at us with fossil coal eyes, then turned and bounded into the willows that blotted him from our sight.

"Camp meat. You got Dad's Luger with you?"

"Hell that's more camp meat than we need and besides it's not hunting season. Plus, chances of nailing him with the nine millimeter is real iffy."

"Just kiddin'. They're long gone now. Besides where's your head at? That you can't take a joke. Sure as shit not in the clouds, there ain't one in sight."

"Just day dreaming."

"About what? D'ju bring Dad's Luger?"

"Yeah, it's in the glove box. Leave it there."

The Luger was one of the few items Dad had brought home from the war along with Nazi pins with swastikas, Maltese iron crosses, SS (*Schutz Staffel*) skull and cross-bone lapel insignias, campaign ribbons and the photos of *Auschwitz* he'd taken after the Germans had surrendered. Pa had managed to smuggle the gun and holster back to the states. How, he never divulged. He bought it off of another GI in North Africa that had lost all of his African Francs playing poker and needed a little spare dough to make it until Uncle Sam paid him again in a month. The Luger, the Infantry Soldier claimed, had been taken off of a dead German officer.

Dad's ship, the SS West Point, a liner made Troop carrier, previously called SS America, docked in Casablanca, Morocco, after his Atlantic crossing in 1943. The Americans and British had defeated Hitler's Field Marshal Rommel, "The Desert Fox," head of the armored panzer division at that time in North Africa. Dad was in the 680th Ordnance Company that supplied ammunition for the big guns. After Africa, Dad and the other soldiers proceeded from Tunisia to Italy. Then he was sent to Southern France in 1944 near the town of Frejus on the Mediterranean Sea for the secondary invasion of France. They landed by L.S.T. (Landing Ship Tank). The night before the landing he slept on a coil of rope at the bow of the ship, so when the fireworks from the destroyer's big guns began firing on the coast, he woke and watched it happening in a blazing barrage as if fired from Hell.

Dad was a Pfc as a munitions handler. He had attained no rank higher than Private First Class by the time he received his discharge in November 1945. The European-African-Middle Eastern Service Medal with arrowhead was the only decoration he received. Dad had no interest in being Army any longer than what his draft obligation warranted. He had a family to take care of back home.

In September of 1945, Dad was in a train wreck, outside of Romans, France, over the Isere River. The bridge had been bombed and only a one lane track had been rebuilt over the partly repaired trestle, there was a signal mix-up and two passenger trains had a head on collision. Seventy-eight people were killed, Dad escaped with only a bruised knee. Right after the crash people piled out of the burning cars, disoriented, many fell to their death off the trestle forty feet into the fast flowing river. Dad had helped a three-year-old girl out of the burning car they were in and across the trestle to the safety of the bank from which they had come.

All of Dad's luck during the Second World War, including accidentally walking through a mine field that hadn't been cleared, came from what he believed was his talisman, a 1934 aluminum coin stamped "Union Pacific Lucky Piece" and showing a Streamliner locomotive on it, which he still carries in his wallet.

Among the souvenirs Dad brought home were hundreds of black and white photos and muted color post cards of Algeria, Italy, Germany, and France. As kids we loved looking through them. They were kept in a shoebox along with his dog tags, sharp-shooter's medal and other military paraphernalia of his. The most interesting cards were from Algeria: the white government palace, Moorish architecture, Arabs on camels with date palm trees behind them, Arabs in the *Kasbah,* and a card showing an Arab falconer with one hawk on his gauntlet and another perched on top of his turban-covered head. The photos he had taken of the gas chambers and crematory ovens at Auschwitz were grotesque and made one think of the millions killed and disposed of this way. Dad and some of his Army buddies had visited the place on a cold gray day and he recalled that as soon as they entered the concentration camp they all became silent, sad, and remorseful. One of the soldiers with Dad was called Sal Goldbloom and the soldier cried uncontrollably for some time.

"I got to fix this radio in here one of these days," Kipp said out of the clear blue, "How you get along without music? Like, 'Sixteen Tons and what do you get? Another day older and deeper in debt!' Should I go on?"

"No! You're voice sounds like a cat in heat."

"Thanks, you don't sound like no Frank Sinatra by the last time I heard you crowin' in the shower."

"It's got to be better than your screechy cooing."

"No! It ain't!" he exclaimed, "Hey! Did I tell you what happened last week?"

"No, what?"

"Well, a month and a half ago, middle of July I think it was. Yeah, I remember it was after the Fourth. Me and the boys were hanging out back of Cody's house shootin' the breeze smoking Pall Malls Cody ripped off from his Ma. She had left the pack of cigs sittin' on the kitchen table. We were smokin' and watchin' Cody's Dad's rabbit's in their individual hutches. When I decide we should see what would happen if we, I mean "I" put the buck in with one of the does. Cody's going, "No! No! Dad will be pissed if she gets knocked up." And goes on about how his Dad keeps close tabs on these Silver Marten rabbit's breedin' habits. He raises them for competition you know. Well I say, Hell, nothin's gonna happen. If he goes to nail her I'll just jerk him out before you can say Jackie Robinson."

I take my eyes off the track and look at him sideways, "Yeah, so?"

"I put the buck in with the doe. Well every time he worms his way around behind her, she up and lets him have it with both hind feet and hits him square in the breadbasket and he goes head over teakettle from the kick. Then gets himself up and thumps his back feet like he's real pissed off. Hell, we're laughin' so hard our sides ache. Even Cody's about to pee in his pants laughin'. That old buck tried to mount her a good ten times and each time got kicked in the nuts for tryin' and each time thumps his hind feet to let her know he wants it and goin' to die getting' kicked in the guts tryin'. Funniest thing we ever saw."

I myself was now laughing at the visual picture Kipp was talking about.

"Shit, we're laughin', tears pouring out of our eyes. I had to wipe them off with my sleeve. I finally got hold of the buck and stuck him back into his hutch before he knocks the doe up. Didn't think anything of it until about a month later and that doe kindles and a litter of four closed eye bunnies appear in her hutch. Well, Cody's Dad has a fit and smells a rat and just knows Cody had something to do with it. Cody finally squeals and tells him I did it. Cody tells me his Dad wants to talk to me so I go over there and face the music. Hell, he read me the riot act. I guess I'll never do that again. But I still have a chuckle over it whenever I think back on it. I could have sworn that buck never got to that doe, unless it happened while we we're laughing our brains out." Kipp grinned at me.

I laughed.

"Holy cow! Look over there, looks like the body of a Model A Ford."

"Where?"

"By those spruce trees are grown' in with the willows," he pointed, "Stop! Pull over let's go check it out."

I pulled off the track enough to let a vehicle pass if any came by. We get out and walked to the abandoned car. The mosquitoes and biting flies hit on us immediately. We both kept slapping our necks and coming up with dead bugs and blood.

"It's a '31 Ford," Kipp informed me.

The one side of the hood was open and it still had its four-cylinder *Huckster* engine in it. Radiator sported two large caliber bullet holes in it. The gauges were still in the dash, glass still unbroken. The tires on wire rims were sunk into the ground past the hubs.

"Fuckin' mosquitoes," Kipp cussed while slapping himself behind his neck.

"What's with the swearing?"

"Heck, like you never say fuck," he responded, aggravated by the torturous bugs.

"Ma ever hear you use the F word and she'll be all over you like blow flies on a dead heifer."

"Yeah, yeah, this roadster's in fair shape. Rusted a bunch, rumble seat rear deck is rusted shut, leather on the seats gone to crap in a hand basket, but I could get it upholstered in Naugahyde. Chop down the cab, sand, prime, paint it a cool color, pin striping and put new wheels on her. It would be a sharp lookin' Hot-rod," Kipp was saying, as if talking to himself.

"What? You planning to buy it, if it's for sale, or steal it?"

"Shit, buy it, dufus. It's been parked here forever. I don't see why they wouldn't sell it to me when I can come up with the money. Got seventy-five bucks saved up. Maybe they'll take twenty just to get it outta' here," he jabbered.

"How are you going to get it home, you don't have your driver's license yet?"

"Get you to pull it home on a flat bed. You can borrow one from the stock yard. Ol' Blast will let you use it. Won't he?"

"You're now planning all this with my truck, my time, my gas and Blast's flat bed after callin' me a dufus."

"Aw Gawd! Come on! I was just kiddin' about the name," he groaned, "Can't you take a little rankin'?"

It was five minutes to twelve when we pulled into the ranch headquarters.

*   *   *

ROLLING—U
CHAPTER FOUR

The ranch house, a two story white ship-clad sided house with an open front porch and turned columns plus a little ginger bread trim was for the most part similar to our house in town. A large barn and four other outbuildings, corrals, tall spruces and enormous antique cottonwood trees made up the nucleus of ranch headquarters. Here Canyon Creek ran narrower and deeper. A fenced in vegetable garden, irrigated by the creek, lay along the northeastern side of the house and looked to be four times larger than Ma's. Chickens ran or dusted themselves about the barn and property unbothered by the dogs.

Two curs ran barking towards us and an ancient black Labrador stood back, its white muzzle aimed up, joined the others' choir with a deep baritone bark. A big woman had just come out and added to the chorus by ringing the dinner triangle with vigor. Three riders rode at a walk towards the house, another came out from the barn and was walking at a fast pace, chickens squawked and scattered away from him as he passed close to them pecking in the gravel drive.

I pulled up near the corrals and stopped; the male dogs circled the vehicle one after the other and wet down the trailer and the International's tires.

"Howdy there!" called the woman, "Just in time to join us for dinner. You can go ahead and unload your horses, there's a stock tank over by the barn," she pointed, "Come on in when you're done unloading your horses and wash up. Here comes Dick and the hands. You must be Dakk, is it? And Kipp Lovett."

"Howdy, and yes'm. This here is Kipp and I'm Dakk."

After we took care of the horses, we walked into a large kitchen, dining area. At the table, that was a long affair covered with a red and white gingham oil cloth, sat all the men, dishing helpings of steaming beef stew and dumplings from a roasting pan being passed around. A heaping bowl of mashed potatoes, a platter of corn on the cob and fresh sour-dough bread were also being passed around. A performance of strawberry preserve, orange marmalade and butter sat at the center of the table. She had a choice of ice tea or hot coffee to drink. As the men passed each other food she introduced everyone and poured Butternut coffee into mugs for some while others helped themselves to cold sun tea. Everyone waited before diving into the noon chuck. Mr. Upton said a short prayer of thanks and I had to kick Kipp from under the table to keep him from grabbing the ear of corn off his plate before grace was said and finished.

As soon as the prayer ended Mrs. Upton stated, "Fingers before forks. Forks are for men, pitch in boys, eat all you can." And then added, "There's raisin-apple pie for dessert."

All engaged themselves with the chow before one of the men started to talk.

"So you two hopin' to find some airra-heads?" Mr. Upton asked.

"Yes sir. Kipp here's into collecting them."

"Well it's like I said on the telephone, they're here, just got to keep your eyes peeled to the ground. Mostly find them around the northwest section. Around the buff jump I told you about over the phone. Ground's pretty barren of grass and sage there. Good old campsite near a spring. Can't miss it. Further up but on the other side by the rock slide was where the Nez Perce fought it out with the army long before Colonel Samuel Sturgis caught up with them in ahh . . . September 1877 it was and just a few miles north of Laurel. Yeah, it happen' a year after the Custer massacre at Little Big Horn. Anyways, Chief Joseph's tribe got away from the Army. Wanted to live in Canada instead of the Res. in Idaho like the Government wanted them to do," he poured himself another glass of tea, added sugar, stirred and took a sip before he went on, "I'll have to show you the stuff that's been found by me and my dad when I was a boy. Got the best framed with cotton batting and glass over 'em. Hank, you ought to show these boys that rusted old gun you found up there."

"Everythin' welded by rust, no wood left in the grip. Looks to be a Colt .45 1873-ish my guess. Cylinder's still got loads in 'er," Hank informed us.

Kipp's eyes got larger with anticipation as he made a pig of himself with the stew. I was running a close second but wanted to save room for pie. Before everyone was finished with the meal she set a large rectangular pan pie and spatula on the table.

"Boarding house reach, help yourselves gentlemen," she stated.

Mrs. Upton was one good cook especially if she put out a spread like this every day. She beats Ma and our mother was the best there could be, was running through my head when I heard Kipp ask about the old Model A bogged down in the willows.

"Well," Mr. Upton replied, "She ain't in runnin' condition. But I reckon you figured that out by yourself. Engine cratered out a long time ago. Suppose you saw the bullet holes in the radiator."

"Yes sir, seen the holes and reckoned the motor was gone and the other runnin' parts also too rusted to make work again. But it's the body I really like," Kipp was saying, "I'd have to replace the running gears, motor, drive lines, new wheels and all from a junk yard. Rebuild it. Just need the body."

"Son, you capable of doin' all that?"

"He sure could," I put in, "He does all the mechanical work on my truck, dad's car and his buddy's vehicles. Has most of his own mechanic tools also."

"I'll be. What you think would be a fair price for that ol' Ford?"

"Got twenty-five bucks saved up. Course I'll need to buy all those other parts when I get more saved up."

"Tell you what, if you can get it out of the ground without my help or using my men to help you, then I'll sell you the ol' Ford for fifteen dollars payable the day you have her ready to move out. But you have to take the whole kit an' caboodle. Don't want you leavin' parts you don't need here."

"It's a deal!" Kipp almost shrieked and said, "We'll shake on it after lunch."

"It's none of my business but I'm kinda wonderin' how do you plan to get it done?"

"Dakk will help. Get a flat bed trailer. Jacks, shovels, planks, chains and a come-along. Plus my buddies to help. I can do it."

"Well you sure seem to have it figured out," he said as he turned to me, "He's got get up and go, your brother."

"Yes sir, he does." *Except when he's sleeping like a rock.*

After the meal Kipp and Mr. Upton shook hands on the agreement. Then he took us into his office to look at his collection of Indian artifacts. There on the wall were seven cases of perfect arrowheads. Ten of the points in one of the mounts were metal. He also had casings, lead bullets, military buttons and a rusted knife.

Kipp was now really jazzed. Around two o'clock we rode out heading northwest to set up camp.

* * *

We spent the afternoon riding around the areas near the bottom of the ridgeback and found an easy place to ascend to the top. From there, the ranch headquarters could be seen two miles away. Here we tied the horses to picket stakes on leads long enough for them to graze. Kipp slipped off the Acmes and put on his Keds sneakers. We hunted on foot for a mile. Found chipping here and there but nothing to get excited about. Then Kipp found a small, flint, corner notched point in a sandy blow out.

By seven the sun was hiding behind the west ridge and our camp was in its shadow. We were near the opposite eastern ridge by the spring seepage. I picketed Sioux and hobbled Jeep. He'd stick around and be in close proximity of Sioux. But as always, about the time you trust your horse, "Don't!" At least the hobbles would slow him down if he decided to find his way back and join the Rolling U horse string. Eight-thirty and we sat around our campfire cooking ground beef and onions in a skillet and elbow macaroni boiled in a pot. I sprinkled a little S and P on the beef. Using my belt knife, I cut cheese into bits and pieces for mixing it up with the macaroni and beef. Kipp gathered more firewood.

We ate out of tin plates, drank black coffee and cleaned our plates with Wonder Bread that had taken a beating, smashed in the saddlebags.

"Good meal, only wish we had some of Mrs. Upton's apple-raisin pie."

"Here, have a Hershey bar, it's somewhat melted," I offered, "You got a pretty good deal on bartering over the Model A junker. Thought you told me you had $75 saved up. Why you tell him $25."

"I didn't lie, I had saved up $25 as well as fifty more. But he didn't need to know that. I'm just a kid in his eyes. I didn't want him to think I was rich. Wanted to hold some of my cards back. Don't you ever play poker?'

"No. I'm not much at cards or gambling of any kind. You know that." I assured him, "My money's too hard to come by to piss it off thinking I can win at some game of chance."

"Remember Uncle Bob sayin', 'To be a good business man you've got to understand poker and chess because that's how business is played.' an' that's what I believe."

After turning in, wrapped in our blankets and manties, using our saddles for head rests, the air cooled and the wind came up. The combination of wood smoke from the campfire and the breeze coerced the mosquitoes to subside in their search for our blood.

"I bet we find some points tomorrow around here. If not, let's hunt the buffalo jump. Only the bottom. The top wasn't that good to try again." Kipp suggested.

"Yeah, the injured buffalo would be easy to kill off at the bottom, then butcher on the spot."

"Wonder where the soldiers were buried? You think close to where the battle took place?"

We lay in silence looking up at the millions of stars.

"There goes a fallin' star! See it?" Kipp noted.

"Yeah."

"You make a wish?"

"Nawh. Couldn't think of one fast enough. You?"

"Yeah."

"What?"

"If I tell you, it won't come true."

"Hey, what do you know about that explosion the other morning?" I asked.

"How do you figure I know anything about it? The paper said it was a sonic boom."

"You and the CC's were out catting around that morning. I'm putting two and two together and figure you are up to the usual shenanigans and may have the skinny on that blast."

"Shit! If I tell you, you're not going to run and tell Pa, are you?"

"No! Numbskull! I've never ratted on you before, why start now? You guys are wild shits but if no one asks me I'm not talking, you know that by now. So what you guys do?" I asked, as I reach for a burning stick from the fire to light my smoke. I cupped my hands around the cigarette in my mouth, protecting the red coals at the end the stick. Then I sat propped up on one elbow blowing smoke rings that blew apart as they rose and waited for Kipp to talk.

"Well, about a week ago Cooper and Cody were out driving around the day I was working on the neighbor's ol' Chevy, putting in new plugs and points, so I didn't hang out with them then. Anyways they're out on some old back dirt roads up north when they came upon this oil company's dynamite concrete shed."

"A magazine," I put in.

"It's got a padlock on the door but they can pull the door open enough on the sloppy big hasp to have a look see inside and there's cases and cases of Hercules TNT in there. So they leave and Cody gets hold of a crowbar and they go back that night and bust into the place and load it into the Pontiac and take it to that old shaft like cave out on the Rim. It takes them four trips to get all of the TNT and a couple of rolls of ignition wire to the cave. The next day they want to show it to me. We go up there and Cody brings along his .22 rifle, Cooper has a flashlight and into the cave we go. Hell, we're not into the shaft twenty feet and this rattlesnake starts to buzz up a storm and that dumb shit Cody takes a couple of shots at it before it's dead and we're yellin' at him not to shoot 'cause of the dynamite. All he can say is, 'I forgot,' the dumbass."

I just shake my head in disbelief.

"The rattler's still twistin' and rollin' around as we get by it and sure enough the back of the cave is full of fifty pound boxes, each filled with eight-inch sticks of red dynamite. So I asked them what the hell they plan to do with it. And they say shoot it off. I say how, we need blastin' caps and Cooper says he remembers his Granddad has some in his garage. So we head over there. Luckily no one was home there.

We go into the garage and Cooper shows me the can that says, 'Dupont Blasting caps' and I steal four out of the can."

"Dumb shits," I remark.

"So we make plans and did it the other mornin'. I meet them at the end of the street at around one that mornin'. When we get to the cave we remember we've got no way to set it off, no plunger but I remember the time Uncle Ed blew up that stump by settin' off the TNT with a blasting cap and the two wires runnin' to a battery and when he made the connection, kaboom!"

I'm shaking my head back and forth, in disbelief of this dangerous stupid act.

"I get this idea that if we run all of the wire on both spools we can use the car battery to set it off. It seems to take us forever to get the 250 feet of wire cords run out to where we parked the car behind some boulders."

I'm sure my jaw was dropped over these three idiots as he keeps telling me the story. The older the dynamite, the more unstable and powerful it becomes.

"I stick blastin' caps into the end of four sticks of dynamite while Cooper holds the flashlight at what I'm doin' and all this time my hands are shakin'. Then back at the car I'm ready to put the wires to the battery like Uncle did that time we were watching him. Remember?"

"A-haa!" I responded.

"We had all hid behind the Pontiac facing away from the blast. By now we're all scared shitless, Cooper's got the cold sweats. My throat is dry. Cody was shaking in his pants. We've got our ears covered with our hands. And I've got wads of cotton in my ears and my head and ear bent into my right shoulder when I put the wires to the battery terminals. What a bang. Shook the car so hard the hood fell on my arms. That's what these bruises are from," and he pulls his arms out from under his blankets, rolls up his shirt sleeves to show me in the fire light, "We couldn't hear a fuckin' thing for about an hour afterwards. Couldn't tell if the car had started when we jumped in to get the hell out of there. Jesus! I never thought it was goin' to be such a big blast. Cooper had his old car doing fifty miles an hour or more gettin' out of there an' that road had to be the worst track to drive over that I know of. We missed a curve once and come close to endin' up crashin' down a coulee by about a foot. Shit, we got scared all over again. But this time Cooper slowed down and we got back to town A-okay!"

"Son of a gun! You could have all been killed! I can't believe you guys. Where was your brain, for Pete's sake?" I groaned wishing I hadn't asked about the explosion to begin with.

"Yeah, I realize that now. I guess we all thought of it while we were settin' it up. But I was pretty careful."

"Well, it sure stirred up the town. The law will find out what happened one of these days, you know that," I warned.

"Yeah, but how they goin' to know we did it, unless someone blabs to the cops."

"Well it won't be me. But I sure had a gut feeling you and the CC's had something to do with it. Shit, the three of you are nuts."

We finally went to sleep to the sound of the horses munching grass and stomping on the ground.

*   *   *

After a breakfast of scrambled eggs, bacon and coffee, we decided to hunt around the spring. Jeep and Sioux were fine with a new place to forage once Kipp moved them to another location. Within a few minutes I'd found a broken arrowhead. The tip was missing. After a couple of hours Kipp had found a broken point, two side notched small arrowheads made of gray flint and a fair sized tan chert hide-scraper covered with lichen growth. Myself, I found nothing more than a jasper thumbnail scraper and a .44-.40 caliber casing, almost black in color and flattened by something stepping on it.

Around noon we saddled the horses, watered them at the creek and rode off back to the buffalo jump. At the old kill site Kipp and I dismounted, left the animals to graze with the reins tied up and the lead ropes dragging the ground. I felt pretty comfortable with them on their own now since they made no attempt during the night to escape. Green grass can keep hay fed horses interested in eating instead of taking off. They were enjoying fresh grass. And we hunted on foot.

The ground had been picked over very well in the past. I found another broken point. There was chipping everywhere. Kipp decided to check around the rock cliff. I stayed close to the horses.

A half hour later, I hear Kipp yelling down to me.

"Hey! Come on up! I just found an arrow back in a pack rat's nest!" Kipp was shouting.

When I finally made it to where he was, he held out a slightly bent arrow with a metal point attached by sinew. The shaft had the remnant of feather fletching also wrapped with sinew that had started to unravel.

"Looked up into the old rat's nest in that rock opening under that low overhang, had to crawl in on my belly and then wait for my eyes to adjust to the darkness so I could see before I reached over a snake and got bit. I could see the knock and what looked like feathers among the sticks, rat shit and bits of bone. Had to reach in as far as I could to get hold of it, but the minute I picked up the arrow I could feel the weight of the point at the end," Kipp raved.

I looked it over carefully, "It still has the ownership black stripes. They're faded but there's four of them and blood grooves on the shaft."

"Yeah, and the point is hardly rusted. Looks like the tip hit a rock or something hard, it's dinged."

"You are one lucky shit."

"I wonder how long it's been in there."

"Hard to say as dry as it is in there, could have been lying in there for maybe a hundred years. Who knows?"

Late that afternoon we rode back to the ranch and showed off our finds and then we took supper, soup and sandwiches with the Uptons and the ranch hands. I asked if I could use the telephone to call home and let Ma know we'd be late getting back to town. Mrs. Upton rang up the operator by cranking the handle on the wall phone, "Beatrice, this is Gail, I need to call Billings," and gave her our number. After talking to Ma for a minute, I told Kipp to drive the truck and trailer on up the road and that I would meet him at the old Model-A. I wanted to ride Jeep and would lead Sioux to give them a workout since we hadn't ridden them that much. And that way Kipp could check out how much of a job it would be to get the vehicle out of the ground.

* * *

We crossed the cattle guard of the Rolling U and turned east. It was now dusk and I turned on the headlights. Ahead of us by fifty feet, a coyote trotted across the road with a half eaten rabbit hanging from its mouth. It stopped and turned its head to watch us as we passed, then loped off into the sage as Kipp yelled out a "Cock-a-doodle-doo!" at him and laughed.

"Hey! You hear the one about the rooster talkin' to the hooker?" Kipp began.

"No."

"Rooster says, 'Cock-a-doodle-doo!' and the hooker says, 'Any cock will do.' Get it?" he chuckled.

"Where'd you pick up this stuff?" I asked chuckling.

"Cody heard his brother tell it to somebody and he told us. Want to hear another one?"

"You're on a roll. Go ahead."

"You want to hear it or not?"

"Yeah, spit it out."

"What did the good little girl say to the bad little girl?"

"I don't know, what?"

"The good little girl says to the bad little girl, 'Gee! It's hard to be good,' an' the bad little girl says to the good little girl, 'It's got to be hard to be good."

"You're growing up too fast. Cody's a bad influence on you and Cooper," I said shaking my head back and forth, "I'll have to ask Dwayne and George if they've heard those jokes."

"Dakk, you ever do it?"

"Do what?"

"You know get laid, get fucked?"

"That's none of your business whether I have or have not. That's personal. Besides it's the act of making love with someone you love, not get fucked!"

"Rabbits don't fall in love, they just want to do it. A little nooky."

"You'll find out one of these years. Besides you're not a rabbit. Till then keep guessing. And let's change the subject."

"Are you still a virgin?"

"No! And I said let's change the subject," I persisted and pulled a cigarette from the pack sitting on the dashboard and struck the head of a wood match on the dash. It sparked and hissed into flame and I lit a Lucky and sucked in a long deep drag of smoke.

"Hey, let me have a cigarette. I feel like a smoke too."

"It'll stunt your growth."

"I'll take my chances."

We rode in silence smoking. Kipp smoked acting like a big shot, coughing when he actually got a lung full of smoke. After he only had half-inhaled most of the time, he put out the cigarette in the ashtray and spit out the window.

"I don't think I'll ever get into this smoking stuff. Coop is into Copenhagen and looks like he always has a mouthful of shit."

I said nothing, but the comment brought the thought of Lee Pekhead to my mind and the animosity I had towards everything about him. The long sideburns, greasy hair combed back in a DA. DA stood for Duck's Ass because that's what it looked like. He was wearing a black motorcycle jacket, as always, and his teeth and gums covered with granules of black chew. The thought was only for a second before my mind wandered to Sue Palmer and our movie date Monday night.

"You think you'll like cowboyin' for the Milliron? Kipp asked out of the clear blue.

It kind of took me by surprise but I finally answered, "Well I don't know. It's got to be better than being a flunky feed lot cowboy. I hope."

*   *   *

When we got home it was around twelve-thirty, but not without a small problem. The truck ran out of gas only two miles from Billings. Luckily I had a gallon gas can in the pickup and Kipp said he'd walk into town and come back with gas. I asked where, since all the Billings gas stations closed early, especially on Sunday nights. He said he'd ask around. I suggested he take one of the horses and that he might be able to get gas out of Blast's truck at the stock yards and that there was a length of hose he could use to siphon with, hanging by the tack shed. He rode off on Sioux in the light of the quarter moon and I sat next to the road smoking as Jeep grazed nearby. I counted three falling stars and made three wishes, all of which involved Sue Palmer. Not another vehicle passed, coming or going while I waited.

A bat flew by erratically, emitting a high pitched squeal, and then disappeared into the ghostly night towards the black shadowed recesses of the coulees on the hillsides. In the distance there was a light glow from the city and refinery lights.

When I heard them coming back, a good hour and a half had passed before Kipp returned on Sioux at a walk. I put Jeep back in the trailer. When he reached the truck he was spitting every second.

"You swallow some gas?" I questioned.

"Yeah, I didn't pull away from the hose quick enough. Is there any water left in the canteen?"

"Some, I think."

"Gawd! Gas tastes horrible. Been spittin' all the way back."

He gargled with the water and spouted a stream of it onto the road. And kept spitting as we drove off. His breath smelled like a gas tank.

"Want a cigarette?"

"Think it'll get the taste out?"

"No, but you'll look like a fire eater once you light it and flames belch out of your nose and mouth," I sniggered.

"Screw you! Get your own gas next time," he opened the glove box.

"What you looking for in there?"

He pulled the Luger out and fumbled around in the box, "Trying to see if you got some gum in here."

"No! And put the gun away. You're making me nervous."

"Think I'll shoot you?"

"Hope not! I got a date tomorrow night. And I'd hate to miss it."

Kipp slipped the gun back into the glove box and slammed it shut.

Kipp kept spitting all the way home. He gargled with Listerine and went to bed after having taken a long pull on a bottle of whiskey Dad kept in the pantry. The next morning Kipp claimed to still taste the gas, no matter how much he gargled and washed out his mouth and brushed his teeth. The caustic gas taste stayed in his mouth for a couple of days.

* * *

VISTA VISION
CHAPTER FIVE

Monday was hell for me at work. Having gotten home and to bed late and then up at 5:30 in the morning, had me hoping I wouldn't fall asleep at the motion picture show. This was my first date with Sue and falling asleep on a date I knew would go over like a lead balloon as far as a first impression. I must admit a movie about people on the French Riviera was not a favorite theme. Give me a good Western like *Shane*, but dating Sue Palmer was a dream come true. I had been smitten with Sue for a long time. It was difficult for me to keep my mind on the job because the only thing I was thinking about was my movie date.

Sue Palmer obviously liked the thought of exotic places far beyond Billings, Montana, which was as farfetched for her as was my dream of owning a ten thousand acre ranch, with about as many cows roaming the land.

I remember Grandma saying, "We humans all have and need dreams. I believe a dream is what keeps people going. With dreams there are hopes." And Grandpa under his breath would mumble, "Hope is just a rope to hang on to for life or at other times hang yourself with."

Dad would say that Grandma always saw a glass as half full, while Grandpa saw the same glass as half empty. And that in life is why opposites almost always seem to attract one another.

Luckily I was able to talk Blast into letting me leave the yards at four and I drove straight home, told Ma I needed a short nap before supper and to wake me if I didn't come down on time. Kipp had just come into the house and overheard us talking.

"He's got a date tonight," he chuckled.

"Oh! You do? Who with? Where?" Ma inquired.

"Sue Palmer, she works at the Pronghorn Café. She's a waitress there. We're going to a movie at the Fox, to see To Catch a Thief."

"You just meet her? I don't recognize the name." she asked dubiously.

"She was a senior in high school when Dakk was. Same graduating class," Kipp put in, "She was that cute blonde Dakk was hoping to take to the prom. But he waited too long to get around to asking her. Guess she went with someone else," he snickered.

I side glanced at him with a pissed-off look, "I can answer my own questions. Thank you very much."

"Well go on up and rest. I'll call when Dad is home and we're ready to eat supper. I made meat loaf."

"I can smell it. It's making me hungry."

Kipp took two chocolate chip cookies out of the cookie jar and ran off to the porch with a new Dick Tracy comic book he'd just bought. I also took a cookie from the jar and headed up stairs.

"You boys are going to spoil your supper," Ma accused before we were out of earshot.

*　　*　　*

Sue looked good and smelled terrific, like lilacs in the spring. Her hair was braided at the back of her head, into one long braid. She had a light blue western shirt bordered by white piping, a full black skirt with a white petticoat and wore penny loafers and white socks. Sue arrived at the cafe and I bought her a pop. I was already drinking coffee, had gotten there fifteen minutes early. The short nap helped but caffeine would jack me up better than a four-hour siesta anytime. Sue lived only a street over from the Pronghorn Café with her mother and father.

She had walked to the cafe.

"Dad's worried about me. He said if you are going to date me he wants to meet you. I told him I'd have to get you first. Hope you don't mind," she blushed.

"No, I don't mind. I'd like to meet him also. But we'll have to make it quick if we're going to make the previews," I cautioned with a smile.

Meeting her father and mother was only a little intimidating for me. They were quite nice and he only asked a couple of questions, 'Where do you work? How old are you?' and the like. We talked for about fifteen minutes; his wife never asked a thing, just had a slight underlying look of concern.

"You will come home right after the show?" he asked in a tone that sounded somewhat commanding.

"We may stop at the cafe and have coffee or a Nehi and talk for a little," Sue suggested, "If Dakk wants to."

"I'll bring her home as soon as she wants, sir," I offered.

"Yes. Thank you," he replied. "You'd better get on now before you two miss the beginning of the show."

*   *   *

We arrived at the Fox a few minutes late. I bought tickets and the usher said the newsreel was about to begin, and that the cartoon and the two short movie serials were over. I bought large popcorn and we entered the dark theater, another usher lit the way with his flashlight to a couple of empty seats about center of the theater. When my eyes had adjusted to the dark, I could see only five or six other couples seated ahead of us. And no one was sitting behind us. Sue hadn't said anything about the movie not being a double feature on Monday nights. I wondered if her parents knew that.

We came in on the news, President Dwight D. Eisenhower playing golf somewhere and his plan to have four lane interstate roads built across the country so that if the time came, military convoys could make their way to any point in the country as expeditiously as possible was covered by the news announcer. The threat of a Communist invasion could come from any direction he warned. Then the preview of coming films was shown before the main feature started. The musical *Oklahoma* and the Wyatt Earp Western *Wichita* were coming to Billings soon, claimed the Fox Theater.

Sue leaned close, our shoulders touching and she took some of the popcorn out of the box I held. Her being so close made me feel great. Finally I got up the courage to up my arm around her shoulder and she nestled against my chest.

"Oklahoma looks like it would be fun to see," Sue suggested.

"I reckon. I wouldn't mind seeing Wichita myself," I whispered.

The sound became louder, "Vista Vision, in High Fidelity, A Paramount Picture, staring Cary Grant and Grace Kelly!"

After awhile and at one point in the film, Sue whispered into my ear, "There's Alfred Hitchcock sitting next to Cary Grant. He puts himself into all the films he makes,"

I nodded in the dark. Her breath, so close to my ear made me very warm. Her perfume made her delicious. I wanted to turn and kiss her.

In the film, Grace Kelly was her mother's fretting daughter. She worried about her wealthy mother's diamond jewelry, which she wore or kept in her room instead of the hotel safe. Grace Kelly also knew that Cary Grant was an ex-jewel thief.

"Isn't Grace Kelly just beautiful?" she whispered again.

I turned towards Sue and whispered back in her ear, letting out my warm breath slowly as I said, "She is."

Instantly Sue pushed herself towards me tighter and I felt my penis stir. I could feel my forehead get sweaty and my mouth getting dry.

"I'm thirsty. I'll get us a couple of soda pops," I pulled my arm out from around her, "What do you want?" I asked and I stood.

"A Nehi."

"Be right back."

The second feature wasn't anything either of us was much interested in watching.

Partway into the second movie I asked if she still wanted to go to the Pronghorn Café before I took her home.

"No, let's leave now and drive up on the rim for a little bit and park looking over the city. It's a beautiful night. Cool and refreshing. I'm getting awfully warm in this theater."

"Yeah, it sure was warm in there," I agreed as we left.

Again Sue Palmer sat close and leaned into me as I drove up Black Otter Trail and the top of the rim rock.

"Want a cigarette?" I offered. I need a smoke to calm my nerves as I shifted into a lower gear and brushed my arm against her breast. The truck climbed up the curving road and the headlights caught a coyote slinking quickly into the brush.

"Sure. I'll join you. I don't normally smoke. But with you it'll be fun," she cooed.

I shook the pack and worked a Lucky out and pointed it towards Sue. She pulled it from the pack with her lips. I shook another out and also took it by my lips, then began to fumble for a light.

"Here, I've got matches from the cafe."

She lit my cigarette, then hers and blew out the match and it went out with a puff of smoke. Sue settled back again against me.

On reaching the top of the plateau above the sandstone cliffs, varnished by time to the color of raw umber, I turned onto a dirt road. The cliff wall protected the city's northern perimeter and lay in a black darkness of night. Here above the Rim which overshadowed the city of Billings by its 300-foot plus elevation, I found a place to park and turned the headlights off, but kept the radio on with the volume low to a Country Western music station. The truck faced south, overlooking the city lights that shown white and gold while the Milky Way was muted by a full moon that brooded overhead. From this promontory point at the edge of the rim we could see the distant shimmering Yellowstone River sparkling among the cottonwood breaks that held shadows of marine and deep purple. Flames and plumes of steam jetted from stacks and pipes about the distant refinery with its hundreds of stark gleaming lights. It was a romantic vista even if it wasn't the Riviera.

We sat and smoked and Sue asked what I planned to do with my life. Was I going to work at the feedlots forever? I told her no, I was quitting in October and going to work for the Milliron slash B Ranch.

"Are you planning to be a cowboy all your life?" Sue asked.

"No. It's just something I've got to get out of my system. Dad says it's a dead end job and I know he's right. But he did it for a while, cowboying, that is, for the Running R Ranch in Wyoming if I remember right. I'll work for Archie Braddock until after spring round up and branding. Then get a job, I reckon. Maybe on turn-around at one of the refineries for the summer so I can save some more money for college come fall. What are you going to do with your life? Not stay a waitress at the Pronghorn Café forever?"

"No. Definitely not. In fact, waitressing is my way of saving up so I can start college in the fall of next year. That will give me time to save some more. I was accepted this year at Eastern but Dad hasn't enough money to carry me through the year even if I can waitress part time here. If I go to Eastern Montana College I'll still be living at home. But I'd love to get away."

"Yeah. That's the same reason I'm thinking of going to a college or university away from here. If I do I'll have to live in a dorm. But if I went to Eastern we'd at least be close. Maybe we could study together."

"Yes we could. And that way get to know each other better," she assured me as she snuggled under my arm and looked into my face.

I sat there holding her, sort of lost at what to say or do next. Then I blurted the question, "What's going to be your major?"

"Oh, Liberal Arts, until I can get into nursing in Missoula. Then I can come back here and work at the hospital or someplace like California. What about you? What are you thinking about as a major?"

"Liberal Arts also to start with I guess and then maybe English Literature. I'm thinking of trying to become a writer. Maybe work for the Billings Gazette, if they'll have me? But what I'm really hoping is to become a novelist. A Western novelist. Not like Louis L'Amour but good westerns about real people like Steinbeck, John Steinbeck. I don't believe I could ever be as worthy as he is. Have you ever read The Red Pony by him?"

"No, is it good?"

"It's a beautiful and moving book about a boy and a sorrel colt. Don't tell anyone, but I cried reading it. And normally I'm not that emotional about reading books or seeing movies."

She looked me straight into my eyes and kissed me. We kissed for what seemed a long time. And the passion in me was to a boiling point, and then I remembered promising her Dad I'd bring her home soon after the movie.

"I better get you home like I told your father I would," I said, somewhat panting. I wanted to hold her and kiss her all night. Then I said, "I'd like to take you out on another date sometime, if you're willing, that is?"

"That would be nice. I like you a lot. I think you're a man with soul," she admitted as she kissed me again while sliding her hand down on my inner thigh.

"I'll have to get The Red Pony from the library and read it." she cooed after we broke the luscious kiss.

I drove Sue home and gave her a long lingering kiss before we got out of the truck and walked her to the door.

"Good night." She whispered and gave me a flirty wink before she turned to enter the house. I could see her father through the open door sitting in the front room smoking his pipe and watching television as her mother looked towards us with concerned eyes. I said, "good night," then walked to the truck and drove on home. My heart wanted to explode.

*   *   *

The following days were hectic since other ranches started to bring in their cattle to sell and the Milliron slash B cows weren't being shipped out until Thursday, the feedlot pens began to fill up. Of course keeping my mind on the job was interrupted by thoughts of Sue Palmer. I was in love or sexually infatuated. I wasn't one hundred percent sure. Perhaps it was both at the same time.

Kipp razzed me now and again in front of Ma and Pa. One night he and I had a little talk about it. If he was hoping to have my help in getting that rusty jalopy of a Ford back from the Rolling U Ranch to Billings he'd have to shut up about my being in love. And he did. Except he called me Thumper once and lucky for him I missed with my swing. He's fast and ducked out of the way as my fist whizzed by his head.

"What's that for?" he asked sounding provoked.

"Because I know what you mean by calling me Thumper. No I'm not a rabbit and yes I reckon I'm in love with Sue, but anything else is none of your business. Got that?" I stared at him fuming.

He nodded and said, "Sorry, was just kidding. I got to go." And he ducked out of the barn and let me finish feeding the horses.

I remember Black Jack watching me sitting on the grain bin, the very tip of his tail moved ever so slowly back and forth. Then he gave me a wide yawn before jumping down and exiting the barn as if bored with me and my love sick attitude.

We kept the cattle separated into individual home holding-pens after receiving them, until it was time to ship them out by rail to Omaha or parts west. George and Dwayne worked feeding and odd jobs most of the time while Roy and I rode the densely packed pens. Riding the feed lots, you're on your toes looking for signs of potential problems. Cattle that are off their feed, that look listless, or isolate themselves from other stock. I watch their ears and noses and the way they walk trying to see if anything is out of the ordinary. Amigo was now my main work riding horse. A good sure-footed animal, with all the savvy of cows, he allowed me to open gates before moving in and automatically turn to let me shut the gate behind us all while mounted. He moved in a fluid motion sorting in the alleys. I brought Jeep in as my second riding work horse and alternated horses every other day or sometime every half day. I wanted Jeep to learn about cows long before I started to work for the Milliron slash B. This way, in the pens, he would also learn to manage doing his job, allowing me to work with my rope off him and build his confidence as well as mine. I kept my loop built and hanging close to Jeep and myself as I rode in the crowded pens. I'd roped off of him a bunch of times at the rodeo grounds practicing with cowboy buddies from the area, but Jeep never fully trusted having me rope. He seemed to have a slight apprehension of ropes in general.

* * *

I would stop in at the Pronghorn Café for coffee almost every night just to see Sue in hopes of having a couple of minutes to talk. We did get together at a Sunday afternoon church picnic at Riverfront Park. She and I strolled together down along the river's edge, leaving the church members behind, the men playing horse shoes in a true tournament fashion while the women took care of the food and passed local gossip. We stopped about a half mile from the group and sat in the shade of a cottonwood tree. It was quiet and peaceful watching the swallows dive and dip the river, catching insects over the water. Slow circular riffles made by fish rising to the surface of the sluggish flowing clear water added to the tranquility of the afternoon. Across the river, the south bank was almost bare of trees and the finger-like eroded scars ran from the top of the ridge, opened and funneled into the Yellowstone, one coulee after another.

After observing the beauty around us and talking for a while, Sue and I began kissing while lying in the cool grass. She was on her back and I was facing her. We kissed for what seemed hours. Our breathing became rapid and I could feel sweat running under my arms, I kept my pelvis facing the ground, I didn't want Sue to know I had an erection and it was pushing to get out of my Levis. Suddenly Sue took my hand and placed it on her breast. I could feel its firmness and the hard nipple bulging in her bra. She was now sucking on my neck and I was breathing heavy in her ear. I couldn't help myself; I turned towards her and was now humping her hip while she rubbed herself in a curricular motion through her pants. She finally stopped sucking my neck and shuddered letting out a pleasant fulfilled gasp. At the same time I found myself having ejaculated. We both lay looking up at the blue sky. Finally I fumbled in my shirt pocket and pulled out my pack of cigarettes, offered Sue one but she shook her head no and gave me another long kiss. We were both quiet for a long time, me lying on my stomach hiding the wet spot on my crotch while sitting on my elbows smoking and letting out long streams of smoke and watching as it dissipated into the air.

"What are you thinking about?" Sue wanted to know.

It took me a minute, I thought I'd lie and say, "Nothing." Instead I truthfully answered, "Us."

"What about us?"

"I don't know about you but I think I'm heads over tea kettle in love with you."

"You think?"

"I know I am! Do you love me?"

"Of course I love you, Dakk. I was in love with you since my freshman year in high school but was too bashful to tell you. I had a big fight with my friend Moraine for saying she was going to tell you."

"I wish she had," I smiled.

As we walked back to the picnic she brushed her hair on the way and I carried my hat off of my head and in both hands in front of me to cover the wet spot.

I wore my black silk neckerchief around my neck for the following couple of days to hide the purple hickey where Sue had sucked my neck like a vampire. Luckily the hickey was placed low. I checked its fading in the mirror every morning until it vanished out of sight.

*   *   *

One evening after dinner, Ma was out futzing around in her garden and Dad was reading the paper on the back porch, I was in my room reading and my gut was churning and grumbling. I must have eaten something that didn't agree with me. I had that sudden need to go to the can. The bathroom door was locked when I turned the knob.

"Kipp! You in there?"

"Yeah! Yeah!"

"Well shit or get off the pot! I really have to go! Come on, open up! I'm comin' down with the skitters."

The toilet flushed and Kipp came out, "It's all yours."

"What were you doing in there? Whacking your pud?" I said as I rushed in slamming the door behind me.

While I sat there going, I reached around to get some TP and that's when I noticed a playing card lying face down next to the toilet bowl. I picked the card up and looked at the face side of the card. Queen of hearts, only there wasn't a picture of a two headed queen holding up a flower but a black and white photograph of an Asiatic young woman, looking at me with her tongue sticking out of the corner of her mouth suggestively. She was naked except for black nylons and black garter belt. She had her small firm right breast cupped in one hand, the nipple erect and she was lying on a bed with her legs open and two fingers of her right hand at her privates holding herself apart exposing everything for your view. I sat there and felt myself get excited by the photograph. My mouth went dry. I put the card in my shirt pocket washed up. When I left the bathroom I went down stairs to check and see where the folks were. They were still outside. I went back upstairs and knocked on Kipp's bedroom door.

"What?" he answered.

"I think I found something that belongs to you in the bathroom," I half whispered.

Seconds went by, and then the door opened slowly.

"What you find?" Kipp muttered.

"This," I said, and I held up the card with the photo facing him.

"Shit!"

"You dropped it on the floor, asshole. Where the fuck you get it?"

"Ahh! Man, I got a whole deck of 'em," he offered as I passed into his room and closed the door behind me.

"Pa or Ma find out you've got this shit in the house, Dad will skin you alive. Asshole! You *pendejo*. Where'd you get them?"

"What's a pen-day-hoe?"

"That's what you are. Where'd you get them?"

"Cody's older brother, the one that was in the Navy during the Korean War picked them up in Hong Kong," and Kipp pulled out the deck and box they came in out from under some hot rod magazines lying on the bed.

"So what the hell are you doing with them?" I asked as I looked through the fifty-two cards. Photographs of couples having sex in every conceivable way anyone could imagine. Even some with three guys getting it on with one woman, had her in every orifice she had. Some pictured two couples having sex as if tied into a chain. My mind raced as I flipped through the cards slowly. I swallowed hard a couple of times.

"Cody's brother Zane went up to Helena to have the hood of his hot rod '49 Merc louvered in some shop up there. It's the only place in the state that has a machine to do the job. Cost fifty cents per louver."

"What's, that got to do with all the tea in China?" I demanded closing the deck and putting them back into the box they came in, noticing Hong Kong printed in English on the top of the box. I handed them back to him.

"I'm tryin' to tell you. Anyways, Cody found the deck in back of Zane's sock drawer sometime back. Zane's the guy that has that cherry red Mercury that's chopped, lowered, decked, bull nosed, chrome dual tail pipes and white pin striping on it," Kipp tried to divert the conversation again.

"I've seen that car parked around. Zane's got a DA, long sideburns wears peg pants. Car has those stupid big white fuzzy dice hanging from the rear view mirror and he's a friend of Lee Pekhead. They play pool in Jacob's Bar. Get to the point."

"Okay! Okay! Well Cody loaned them to me to look at, that's all. I'm goin' to give them back."

"You better get them out of the house before you're caught with them."

"Hey, you know they're marked cards," he said trying to change the subject.

I looked at him sideways, "How'd you know?"

"Cooper spotted that they were. He likes playing cards, poker, you know." He pulled the cards from the box, "Look here, all the face cards have little dots in white or red on the back corners so the dealer can tell what everyone's holding."

I looked closely to the upper right and lower left corner on the back of the cards and sure enough a sharp eye could make out the different tiny dot matrix incorporated in the design.

"You should see the switch blade knife Zane brought back also. Has a black horn handle and when you push the button the blade springs out faster than a rattler can strike. The blade locks up so it won't close on you until you unlock it," Kipp was on a nerves roll, "He's got another knife called a butterfly knife. The blade sits in a split pearl handle and you just flick the handle open, real fast so the blade comes out and the handle folds back into your palm. Zane showed us how it's done. Cody tried it and cut himself. Zane can flick it open with one hand so fast it would blow your mind."

"Big deal!" I replied.

"Give those cards back to Cody tonight," I ordered, "I just don't know what in Sam Hill you're thinking by bringing this smut home."

"Okay. I'll run over there now. Hey, Zane said he'd paint my Model A when I'm ready. He works at that auto body shop on Fifth South.

I must admit those photos had an effect on me for a long time.

* * *

Finally things at the yards died down a little. Many of the steers with shit caked hind legs had been shipped out on rail and an early frost seemed to have taken down the fly population to where they were tolerable. Kipp was back in school. The golden seas of wheat in the fields had been cut and the sugar beet harvest had ended. Billings was a beehive of activity, trucks brought the grain into town and most of it was stored in the many large silos to wait for a good price and then sold. Sugar beet trucks parked loaded, waiting to form a convoy. Many of the Mexican migrant workers and transient laborers that once had inundated the area now had relocated.

I borrowed Blastingame's flat bed trailer and the old boy even let me use his one-ton Dodge to go after Kipp's Model A. We went to the Rolling U on a Sunday afternoon. I had asked Sue if she wanted to come along with us. She did and I was glad as she sat next to me as I drove leaning forward on the large steering wheel while Sue shifted the gears when I told her to. She stole my hat and wore it cocked back on her head like Dale Evans in the Roy Rogers movies on TV. The KCC's all rode in back of the old truck along with the tools, chains, planks and wood blocks needed for doing the work.

The job went along without a hitch once the guys had dug under the Ford and jacked her out of the damp ground. I only had to tell them to cool it once while they were ranking one another as usual. Cody was giving Cooper some grief about the way he was doing something, called him an ass and Cooper remarked, pissed off, "I guess you're so smart because your father shot on a rock and the sun hatched you." Then I stepped in telling them there was a lady present and to watch their mouths. Cooper's face turned bright red and he uttered that he was sorry.

It was late when we got back to Billings. I dropped Sue at her house and said I'd see her Monday after work; we'd go for a drive. She agreed.

It didn't take long to unload the Model A even with the four flat and decomposing tires. I've got to give those boys credit when it came to ingenuity they had it. They put the "A" up on blocks on one side of the garage. The boys would be working on that old car after school every day until the snow came.

* * *

VAQUEROS, BUCKAROOS, BUCCANEERS

CHAPTER SIX

I had just sat down to my first cup of coffee at the Pronghorn, I had not ordered as yet; my mind wasn't made up whether or not to eat there. The place was busier than usual at that time of day and Sue was rushing about taking orders, pouring coffee, handing out water glasses and bringing hot plates of food to the customers.

She was too occupied at this time to talk to me, so I sat at a two-top table facing the door when George came in and as he looked about I waved to him and he came over to my table.

"Have a seat, George," I said, "Place is kicking butt for a Wednesday."

George sat, "Yeah, place is about packed. Thought I'd catch a meal in here. Don't feel like going home an' havin' to cook myself a burger. Ol' lady's out of town. Up to Helena with the kids. Some wedding comin' up on her side. An' I ain't all that fired up about it, 'specially since I've only maybe a week or two more workin' for Blast. Got ta make hay while the sun shines, like they say."

He sat back into the chair and pushed the sweat stained straw hat back on his head. There was a band impression deep on his white forehead at the tan line. The stubble of a dark beard showed, his brown eyes sparkled and his mouth seemed controlled but not set. George had on his khaki poplin work shirt, stained from oil or grease or both, the cuffs were frayed and the right breast pocket was torn off, leaving a darker shade of khaki where it once had been. There were small holes all over the sleeves, shoulders, and front made by spark burns from when he welded.

Most of George's clothes had spark holes in them, I thought to myself.

"Well, between me and you, I don't have much time left with ol' Blast. So if you can put up with Roy, you may fill my boots there maybe," I suggested.

"You quittin'?"

"Yeah, time I pulled up the picket pin and moved on. Archie Braddock offered me work on the Milliron slash B cowboying. Start in about two weeks. Just gave Blast my notice this afternoon."

"Shit, how'd he take it?"

"Didn't seem to take it one way or other. My guess he thinks Roy can take my place full-time now."

"Good luck! If he thinks that up-start can even blow snot out of his nose without help from his mama he's got another think comin'. I don't know if I want that turd to hand me out orders, since he's as useless as tits on a boar hog."

"Well, just thought I'd let you know."

"Thanks, but no thanks. Me an' Roy are like a coyote at a jackrabbit pow-wow. Besides I think I've got a job guiding elk hunters near Red Lodge. The outfitter also wants me to weld together some portable corral panels. He's picked up a load of galvanized pipe someplace. I'll tell you weldin' galvanized has to be done outside, 'cause of the poisonous gas come from it. That gas makes you sicker than a calf with the slobbers. I've got to eat, cut up bananas in cream before I weld galvanized. Sort of like eatin' bread to soak up the booze when you plan to drink hard an' heavy," George went on, "Then after that, who knows? Maybe by then Blast will have figured out how no good a hand Roy really is an' what a kiss-ass he is, an' get rid of the kid. Then I can ask him for a job. Ain't too worried, been livin' from paycheck to paycheck all my life.

An' if I ain't got the loot to pay all the bill collectors I just pull up the lucky ones name out of the hat that month an' the rest have to hang in there until I've got 'nough to dish out or they get lucky enough to get their name picked out of my hat next go-a-round."

Sue came to take our orders.

"I'll have a rib-eye, mash taters an' cup a coffee. Was goin' to get a cheeseburger but what the hay! It's only money," George said, putting the menu back in the little chrome rack that also held the salt, pepper and sugar shakers.

"How do you want your steak cooked?" Sue asked as she poured coffee into George's mug.

"Oh, medium's fine, thanks."

"More coffee, Dakk?" Sue asked me in an almost cooing tone.

"Please. And I'll have the same as George, rib-eye medium, but with fries. Ma's at her flower club and dinner's probably yesterdays leftover's," I said.

Sue left while still writing on the order pad. I watched her move to the cook station, tear the tickets from her pad and stick them on the cook's wheel and spin it around to face the cook as he stepped forward to snatch them. He was chewing on a toothpick as if it was a chicken bone he wanted to pull the marrow out of.

We sat drinking coffee. George pulled a battered pack of smokes out of his left shirt pocket and fished a bent cigarette from it, then leaned back to reach into his dungarees and brought out a book of matches. He lit the cigarette and let the smoke out of his mouth carelessly; it rose to the ceiling and mingled with the other smoke that hung in a blue pall. His hands were as brown as a migrant Mexican's, the fingers ingrained with permanent black lines from steel, rust and oil and all of his fingernails broken short and black. His thumbnail of the left hand was blue-black from having it caught in the release of the fence stretchers clamped on old wire he had just mended at the feedlot.

"So, you thinking' of becomin' a full-time cowboy, a vaquero, buckaroo like they say in Nevada an' Oregon, a buccaneer," George asked.

"A buccaneer? Hell, I don't plan to be a pirate," I put in.

"Well, let me tell you a buccaneer an' a cowboy is the same. An' most folks don't know it."

"How do you figure that?"

"The name buccaneer comes from the islands, Caribbean Islands about the time the pirate Morgan and the rest decided to rob the gold an' all from the Spanish Crown."

Just then Sue came with our orders and set the platters in front of us, "Here you go, men," she smiled, "Be back in a minute with more coffee and your bread."

"Holy cows," George muttered, "Hope this rib-eye didn't come off some ol' range bull. It's big. Sloppin' over the edge of the plate."

"It's the best cut we have here," said Sue as she set the bread down on the table and poured more coffee into our cups.

I cut into my first piece of bovine and put it into my mouth. "Tastes great to me," I commented.

George looked at me as I ate and swallowed, and I shook my head in approval with Sue.

"Real tender," I remarked.

"Fran, the morning cook, does all the meat buying. She likes it with good marble in the cuts. She knows how to pick the best."

By now George had dug into his rib-eye, "Yup, it's a keeper for sure," he said after his second bite.

We ate and drank in silence until the meal was done. Sue, bless her heart, kept our mugs of coffee full and brought George more bread.

Then I asked, "Well you can tell me the rest of the story now."

"Like I was sayin', buccaneers is an island term for men that went about in the jungle huntin' cattle, cattle-hunters. Anyways, these cowhands had a way of settin' meat, you know, smokin' it. They'd add bits of beef fat an' flesh to the fire as the cow was smoked, they called I think, ahh, was *boucan*, an' that's where their name buccaneers come from."

"So where does the pirate part come into play?" I questioned.

"You see the pirate ships needed hands 'cause they were in short supply. An' since cowboyin' was piss poor for pay, as always, they up an' quit to go to sea as sailors an' pirates, robbin' the Spanish Main under some pretty famous sea farin' captains as Laf-fitte, Morgan an' others."

"Well I'll be damn. Where'd you get this information?"

"Hell, read it someplace, maybe in a Jo Mora or in a Will James book. I like knowin' all these old facts and lies dealin' with the cowboy," he drank some coffee and went on, "I cowboyed for a bit myself. Liked it. Learned alot. Yup, cowboyed on the Hanging Y Ranch back in, what '38-'39, panhandle of Idaho. Ranch ran into Oregon. A 180 plus sections, somethin' like that. Had from time to time as many as 35 to 50 hands. Most of them buckaroos. Did nothin' unless it was off the horses back but sleep, an' a few slept real well mounted. All or most of those boys had the best trappin's for man an' beast. Rode thoroughbreds an' walkers in colors from bays to roans an' every other color in-between. Even had some twelve to fourteen hand tall Spanish and *Cayuse* ponies. Some of those was mustangs, that had spots an' others mousy, *gruello* or grullas as us northerners call'em, with striped legs an' a black dorsal stripe runnin' down their backs to the end of their tails."

"What made you give it up? Sounds like you had a love for it," I asked.

"WW-Two. Enlisted, had to fight the Krauts an' their Nazi idea of, we want the world for ourself atte-tude."

We talked some more about horses and cowboys. By now the Pronghorn had cleared out some and no one had come into the place for a while.

George had finished eating and as he pushed his plate away from himself said, "Guess I should make like a dog with worms an' drag-ass out of here." Then added, "Since mother an' the kids are off to Helena, think I'll slip down to the Golden Pheasant, have a few beers, play a little eight-ball. Wann'a come along?"

"Thanks, but I want to talk to Sue for a minute."

"Oh! Okay, see you in the morn'," he said standing and taking his billfold out of his pocket as Sue came over to hand him his countercheck and me mine. I stayed seated, while Sue and George went to the register, he handed her a tip after she gave him change. She smiled and he touched his hat and left as a couple with a small girl came in. He held the door open for them and tipped his hat to the lady.

I was out of coffee and sipping at my glass of water when Sue came to my table with the coffee pot, "More coffee, Dakk?"

"Sure, and I'd like to ask you something."

She glanced where the couple with the child sat, "Ask away, look's like the people that just came in are not ready to order yet."

"Can you get the weekend off? There's the end of the season rodeo Saturday and Sunday as you already know, but I thought we could go together. There's dancing Saturday evening, looks like a good band playing and it could be fun. Got to warn you I'm not too hot of a dancer, but I can get by on a dark night. What do you think?"

"Would love to but I'll have to ask Dory if she'd work for me that afternoon. Maybe we can swap shifts Saturday. I'll give her a call after I get these people's order in. I'll see what I can do."

She'd taken the folks' order and made her call. I watched her facial reaction to see if she could switch shifts with the morning waitress. Sue was all smiles as she came back to my table.

"She said it would be okay since she'd seen more rodeos than "Carter's got little liver pills" plus she wanted to make a cake for her grand-daughter's birthday on Saturday morning," Sue said gleefully, and added, "My folks are going to Sheridan Friday by bus, Dad is going to the artificial-ice plant about something, ice business. They're not coming home until late Sunday afternoon sometime."

"It's a date then! Rodeo, dancing, we'll have a good time!" I emphasized.

"With you I just know I will." Then added, "I've got an idea but I'll tell you later." she said and she winked at me and left to tend to her job before I could question her.

*   *   *

The end of September had turned to "Indian summer" warm comfortable days and cold nights. The cottonwoods along the river turned tawny and leaves parted from branches, fluttered to the ground or floated downstream with the low flowing river.

Yellowstone County Fairgrounds was a bustle of activity, horses, cows, bulls and people. All gathered with the usual civic pride for the two day entertaining event leading off with a parade, the kiddy calf and ram riding. Then the feature, the athletic bone—breaking, muscle pulling events of rough stock bareback riding, saddle bronc-riding, bull riding, bull-dogging, calf roping, team—roping. The barrel racing was as always fast moving with the girls and their horses decked out beautifully. This rodeo attracted circuit professional as well as competitive amateur cowboys filled with bravado and cowgirls entering for the sport, thrill, the competition and the hopes of winning the purse for the best in their event or events.

Sue and I had arrived at one o'clock just as the parade riders were riding out of the arena after the high school music teacher sang the Star Spangled Banner. I bought hot-dogs, a Nehi for Sue and a tall cold beer for myself from different concessionaires for our lunch. The place was packed with locals; ranchers with their families, ranch cowhands from spreads of 50 to 60 miles in radius, people from nearby towns, young Future Farmers of America in their emblem jackets and a few tourists were there. A dust cloud hung over the dirt roads as trucks and cars were driven around the fast filling parking lot. Pigeons flew about and landed nervously to pick up popcorn and other spilled edible finds.

The announcer called over the P.A. that the kids' rodeo was first to start with the younger children riding sheep, mutton busting. Fathers helped the youngsters get on the backs of the animals after a bit of confidence building. And off they went at a power take-off. The kids fell to the ground left and right onto the dusty sand. No one hurt; only tears and dirt hurt their pride. The announcer called out to the spectators to give the young riders a big hand. All received a ribbon for their try from the rodeo clowns, crying stopped and smiles appeared. The calf riding followed for the slightly older and bigger kids and it was a repeat of the past performance but lasted a second or two longer.

"Give 'em a big hand, folks! They're our next rodeo champions in the years to come!" came over the loud speaker.

I saw Blast and Roy talking to the stock contractor. Lee was there standing near the beer stand. Had on a white T-shirt with a pack of cigarettes rolled up in his left sleeve showing off his jailhouse tattoo of a knife made to look like a crucifix. Zane was smoking and drinking beer. He wore gray pegged pants and pointed shoes with toe and heel taps that clicked when he walked. Lee and Zane were joking around with their car club cronies along with a few of the town questionable females, one wearing a red poodle-skirt and another in tight pink pedal-pusher pants. I motioned Sue toward the holding pens where the stock waited to perform. There behind the white peeling wooden and welded pipe rust-stained chutes (all painted white,) were the cowboys, all making themselves ready for their particular events.

Everyone that had paid to participate in an event had an 8"x8" paper placard with their entree number on them, safety-pinned to the back of their shirts. Cowboys stretched their arms, legs and backs, limbering up for the coming ride. Entree cowboys were all busy putting on their chaps. The professionals all had fancy colorful fringed bat-wing chaps, showing off large oval engraved silver buckles on carved and tooled leather belts with their first or nick names embossed on the back.

While the participating ranch hands used their every-day stained and scratched work chaps, some cowboys tied the tops of their boots with latigo straps, their pants tucked into the boots. Others fastened nickel-plated spurs with short dropped-shanks, tinted blue to plum-brown from having been heat-treated and bent inwards at about 12 degrees, giving the rider a better hook when raking the bronc's shoulders. The bull and horse riders strapped the spurs to their boots, having also a baling wire or twisted leather strings from the setback band-studs under the heel and thus securing the spur to the boot. Most spurs having wide bands and five-pointed dulled star-shaped rowels, each rowel's center had been filed square so that they sung on the round rowel pin every time the rowel raked the shoulder of a bucking horse and spun hard. Some were still taping their wrists with wide adhesive tape or their elbows and knees wrapped with 4-inch elastic bandage hoping to save ligaments from tearing.

The bull riders rubbed pine rosin into their holding glove and the woven rope-twined handhold riggings, each rope cinch rig sporting one or two cowbells. Bareback riders and saddle bronc riders taped socks filled with powdered rosin against the inside area of their chaps for a better grip to animal or saddle. They even rosined the wide swells, fenders and jockeys of the horn-less rough-out leather saddle-forks, all this thought to be designed to help the rider stay in the saddle on a bucking bronc. Wooden oxbow stirrups held the rider's feet in them for balance. Bareback riders also worked rosin into their glove and handhold of their bucking-rigs.

In the back parking lot of trucks and horse trailers, mingled cowboys with callused hands that were the calf roping teams. They waited their time by riding their top horses in lazy circles and figure eights, sitting as if born in the saddle, the ropers with their extra pigging-string tucked into the back of their pants or chap belts. Both of the team ropers, heelers and headers built loops with their lariats and turning out an occasional throw then re-coiling their nylon ropes and again built another loop.

The women barrel racers in Dale Evans style colorful western hats and garb worked on last minute primping of themselves and their well-groomed mounts. They borrowed eye shadow and dipped into one of their jars of Vaseline to gloss over their lipstick.

Margaret Yellowhorse, a Crow Indian girl on a painted horse rode by them. Margaret was pretty looking except that she was on the heavy side of 200 pounds or so.

One of the barrel racers said to the others out of Margaret's ear shot, "Margaret should be called Crisco 'cause she has all her lard in her can."

The girls snickered and one laughed that had just taken a drink of soda and spit the liquid out onto the head of her horse. And the animal sidled and dipped his head up and down nervously.

Bull-doggers, mostly big men, stretched in the saddle aboard tall heavy-built quarter horses. They talked to one another and filled their lower lips or cheeks with chew, Copenhagen snuff or Redman cut-leaf tobacco. Occasionally a stream of tobacco juice was spit out at targets of flies sucking moisture and nutrients out of fresh green horse shit.

The smell of horse and cow manure combined with the scent of liniment, pine resin, all mixed with cigarette smoke and dust choked the air of its freshness. Stock handlers started to run the bareback stock into the chutes. Horses knocked about the metal posts and rails, nickered to one another bragging that they would jettison their rider in less than eight seconds and kick the living daylights out of him before the pickup men had a chance to save the daring cowboy from becoming lean hamburger.

In the back pens waited the near one ton bulls, all Brahma cross bred, with heavy horns on massive heads. Horns cut off at the tips and rounded blunt. Their testicles the size of grapefruits and hanging close to the ground, the massive animals pawed the ground and blew snot onto the dirt. Steers penned together milled and bellowed. Now and again one would attempt to mount another and be shaken off. Others cocked their tails and let loose a stream of watery manure.

"Dakk, why don't you enter an event in the rodeo?" Sue asked.

"I didn't think I've got what it takes. Most of these guys grew up on ranches and sat horses since they were knee high to grasshoppers. I was just a Billings city kid wanting to be a working cowboy not a rodeo cowboy," then I added, "Besides I like all my bones in one piece, not broken, if I can help it. If I break anything, it better be while I'm working a job, not playing around," I surmised.

We made our way back to the bleachers. I saw at a distance the KCC's in the parking lot hanging around a chopped hot-rod talking to the driver. Ma and Dad were sitting midway up the stands next to our neighbors. Sue and I made our way up to them and I introduced her to Ma and Dad. Sue sat next to Ma and I seated myself next to Sue.

"I brought some fried chicken and biscuits," Ma said, "Would the two of you like some? There's plenty."

We each helped ourselves to Ma's feed while Dad went for bottles of Nehi for all of us sitting together.

Ma and Sue were making small talk as the announcer boomed over the loud speaker, "Ladies and gentlemen we're about to start the bareback ridin' event of this end of the year row-day-o!

Please give the riders a healthy round of applause. They appreciate the recognition for their efforts as you do their entertainment. And now—number 31, here, all the way from Lovett, Texas, nineteen-year old, Billy Bob Murray ridin' Kick-a-poo! A red tornado! Originally out of the Oklahoma panhandle!"

The young Texas cowboy in the black Stetson with a golden eagle feather in his hatband set his hat hard and tight on his head. Climbed aboard the sorrel, his legs held high as the animal danced and knocked himself into the side panels of the chute. Both rider and horse settled down. The cowboy had a good grip on the rig handhold, nodded his head to 'let-er-rip.' Someone pulled the bucking cinch as another cowboy sprung open the chute gate. Kick-a-poo bulleted out and headed around and around the arena, kicking his back legs straight out and head down the whole time. The cowboy leaned way back, left arm high and back, raking the horse's shoulders, his spurs sang with a ringing buzz. But the horse never really bucked. The eight-second buzzer sounded and the pickup men rode on each side of him. The Texan grabbed the back of the rider to his left and swung over the pick-up horse's left and dropped to the ground. At the same time the second pick-up rider pulled Kick-a-poo's bucking cinch loose and let it fall to the sandy soil. The horse ran around the arena tossing his head up and down then suddenly bolted through an opened gate. He had done his job, but poorly.

I overheard our neighbor say to Dad, "Heck, that horse didn't buck. The closest he come to it was when he coughed."

"No score on that ride! This cowboy gets a re-ride! Folks, it looks like Kick-a-poo isn't in any buckin' mood. He's just runnin' around kickin' poo. Where's the stock contractor? Send that sorry hunk of horse flesh back to the pan, never mind the handle!"

Everyone laughed and jeered.

"Let's hope our next rider has a better buckin' horse than that sorry sorrel, he's no tornado! Folks, I've got a cat that can buck better than that, an' his name's Puss-n-boots!"

Again, there was laughter and whistling.

"Number 31 gets a re-ride if he wants."

From then on things got better. The horses came out bucking like a wildfire out of a volcano in a lighting storm. Only a few rode out the full eight seconds as the buzzer struck. One cowboy had to be taken to the hospital after having been kicked in the head. He had managed to walk out of the arena while spitting out blood and teeth before he passed out. Sue hung on to my waist every time things got close to going out of hand in the arena with the stock and rider. I felt good being Sue's security post.

"You know I'm glad you've got the good sense not to compete in rodeos, Dakk," she whispered in my ear during a lull in the excitement.

During the short intermission while the rodeo clowns entertained, the kids sitting in the bleachers, with their antics and tomfoolery, Sue and I decided to walk around to the contestants' waiting area. I wanted to look over the competing working cow horses. Rodeos generally had some of the best ranch horse stock on hand.

As we passed by a stock trailer we heard some young bronc riders chatting or mostly ranking one another.

"I thought he'd stomp yuh into the ground so deep you'd take root an' sprout," one joked.

"Yeah, you and Waldo know how to pick 'em. Number 21, Grease Ball. Shit, that horse bolted like a jackrabbit with his ass on fire. That dipstick make a hell of a race horse but not worth a damn as buckin' stock. Damn horse only bucked a couple times. He was as bad as that first horse Kick-a-poo."

"Yeah, hope my re-ride has some bounce to him this time," he said as he dipped Copenhagen, "My luck I always get a knot head," Waldo professed.

We were passing the barrel racer groupies sitting on fancy tooled saddles aboard their beautiful mounts. All the horses had slick coats wearing sliver plated and studded trappings.

"Oh! Connie, Pretty Boy wants you," said the racer with the red-fringed silk shirt. The others snickered. Connie's horse had an erection.

"Pretty Boy's proud cut," she stated, and she moved him out and into a tight figure eight to get his mind off studding.

"I bet he still could buck you out of bed." another said, giggling.

Sue was looking at the barrel racer's horses. She had given Pretty Boy a glance at his long erection that bobbed toward the ground. Embarrassed, she turned and looked off to the palazzo, the auditorium with the Quonset architectural styled roof.

The announcer called over the P.A., "No score! For number 34, Rick Johnson out of Fargo, North Dakota! Ladies and gentlemen! Looks like we have a lost child here. Won't give us his name 'cause he too busy bawlin' to beat Hell! He's got on a blue plaid shirt an' dungarees an' he's sportin' a head of red hair under that straw hat."

The public address system squealed. "Whoa! Sorry 'bout that, folks. Ahh! Here comes the boy's mother, folks. He's saved now."

By late afternoon Sue and I had decided to leave the rodeo.

*   *   *

GOO GOO
CHAPTER SEVEN

The early evening had cooled some once the sun had dropped and settled over into Idaho and California. Sue and I had decided to take a drive before heading to The Spur for supper and dancing to a western band. The Spur bar had a sizable dance floor. I'd asked Sue if she wished to have supper at The Spur, Bella Vista, Wango Village Restaurant, or The Beacon Club.

"Definitely not The Beacon Club, that's where all the hotrod and car nuts hang out and there's a good chance we'd run into Lee Pekhead and that bunch he's always with," Sue said curtly.

"They don't bother me," I said in case she had thoughts of my being troubled by that gang.

"That's not the point. I don't want to chance having our evening spoiled by them or anyone else. That's all," she cautioned and added, "I've been to the Bella Vista before but if we're going dancing at The Spur, then maybe we should just eat there, I've never been in that place. Have you?"

"Once sometime ago with company my folks had visiting. It's okay."

I decided to take Sue on a drive before we went to dinner and drove up to Airport Road past Boot Hill with the graves and cobblestone obelisk on which there is a plaque that reads poetically;

> *"In memory—of those who blazed the trail and showed to us our west in boots and spurs they lie and on this hill find rest."*

The International, in second gear fussed up the road and onto the top of the bluff over the Rim. We passed the airport with its striated runway lights and a few miles later drove down the steep, narrow, and winding Zimmerman Trail back into the city. The old truck griped and backfired twice, giving Sue a start both times.

The Zimmerman Trail, named after the businessman Joseph Zimmerman, who sometime in the 1890's had decided to get supplies and water to his herders and 2200 sheep in a more expedient way than the 32-mile round trip that took two days by horse or mule wagon teams. He contracted his brother to cut and blast the face of the sandstone cliff and build a trail to the top at the west end of the city. In the 1930's the WPA (Works Progress Administration) widened and paved the trail so automobiles could use it.

We had dinner about 8:30. The Spur wasn't the best eatery in town but they served beef and in just about every cut: T-bone, prime rib, New York, rounds, BBQ ribs, tenderloin, Rocky Mountain oysters, and hamburgers the size of saucers.

We both settled on the prime rib special, salad, green beans, and our choice of spuds. I had fries and Sue a baked potato which she couldn't finish because when it came to the table it looked like a small football.

For it being a rodeo night the place wasn't crowded. I did recognize some of the OVO Ranch cowboys having dinner. Sometimes kidding, they were called the lollipop cowboys because the ranch's brand looked like two lollipops that were connected at the base of the sticks which formed the V. We sat at a table towards the back, the lighting was minimal, a small shaded lamp with a black vignette of a cowboy roping a steer, ran around the outside of the rawhide looking paper shade. All the tables had similar lamps. The lamp held a Christmas tree light bulb no brighter than a candle.

Sue said, "It gives the dining room ambiance, it's romantic."

I felt like saying, "If any critter crawls over my food I wouldn't be able to identify it let alone stab it with the steak knife." But I thought better of it and just agreed with her.

"Yes it is," I admitted in a congenial tone, as I smiled at her under the dim light.

We could hear the band tuning and trying their instruments and from my vantage point could see the band members setting up on the small back stage. They checked the mikes for sound from which an occasional piercing squeal issued; the spot lighting when turned on smeared the center of the stage in a blazed white circle. Someone cut the stage lights, but after some fuss the lighting came back on and it was a significant improvement over the first attempt.

One of the OVO cowboys walked by our table on the way to the men's room and nodded at me and touched the tip of his Stetson at Sue. He walked stiff on legs bowed like bent cedar staves.

"That's Frosty West, he's been with the OVO forever," I whispered to Sue, "They say he killed the man that stole his horse after tracking him down for two years. Found him and his horse in Holbrook, Arizona."

We ate, drank and we talked. We both declined dessert but I ordered another glass of wine for Sue and a third beer for myself.

"I'm looking forward to dancing together," Sue stated lovingly.

I leaned towards her and in an apologizing whisper told Sue, "I'm looking to the slow dances with you but I must warn you I'm not much at that jitterbug stuff. But if you can put up with my two left feet I'll give it a try. But I'm not makin' any promises."

"I'd rather slow dance with you anytime. That fast stuff isn't all that romantic to me."

I felt myself feeling warm and electrified.

"Do you want to come over to the house after the dance? You know my folks won't be back in Billings until late tomorrow afternoon or evening," she toyed.

It caught me by surprise and I took a minute before I answered, "Sure, if you think its okay?"

"What they don't know won't hurt them."

"Suppose one of the neighbors sees me going into your house?"

"Old Miss Powers is out of town and the Reynolds always go to bed by nine o'clock. At least the lights are always out by then and every shade in the house is closed up before eight. Just park your truck on the next block and walk over after you let me off at home."

It sounded to me like she had given this evening a lot of thought after finding out that her folks would be out of town.

"I suppose I could come over for awhile," I said stupidly.

"A while? How about the night?" she urged.

"Are you sure?"

"I'm sure," She whispered with a wanting look at me.

I could feel myself sweating under my arms, my heart seemed to have quickened and my whole body seemed to be pulsating. I thought for sure Sue would see me shake with this intrigue.

"I've never done this before but it's you I want to be with tonight." Which I later learned was a lie—she wasn't a virgin.

I didn't know what to say so I just looked at her.

She smiled back.

We finished and I paid the bill and left our waiter a generous tip.

We went into the bar. I saw into the side room where the poker table was and most of the tables had a card game going and the room was suffused by the blue smog of cigarette and cigar smoke. The bar was starting to fill up. I found a table at a booth. I ordered Sue a ginger ale and I had a beer. We danced the slow ones and watched those that danced the fast ones. I nursed my beers. Just three beers for the whole night, I didn't want to get drunk.

It felt great holding Sue against me while we danced very slowly. I was no Fred Astaire but in slow dancing I could get by on a dark night. The smell of her perfume, her hair, her breathing at my neck was almost too much for me, repeatedly I'd kept getting aroused and tried to dance so she could feel the bulge in my jeans. But I know she had though acted as if she had not.

When the band stop playing and went on their break Sue asked, "Do you have to work tomorrow? It being Sunday and all."

"Yes. Suppose to be there by at least seven, have to feed the stock. Most have been shipped out on Friday, but the OVO Ranch brought in 26 of their shells late on Friday afternoon. Plus I've got to get home and feed our horses. Wish I had asked Kipp to feed them for me."

"Shells?" Sue asked with a baffled expression.

"Yeah, that's what these old ranchers call the old, weak, or skinny cows and bulls that they wanted to cull from their herd."

"Oh. Why shells?"

"I guess in the old days these animals were nothing more than a bag of bones. In other words just shells, a hide covering and little meat left on the bones."

She seemed to think about what I told her for a minute. Then said, "Well if you've got to feed these shells in the early morning maybe we ought to leave."

At first I thought she was going to say we ought to call it a night. Which meant we shouldn't go to her house and I not spend the night there?

We left the Spur just as the band was getting back on the stage.

"This is a good band," Sue mentioned as we walked to the truck.

"I like them too. The played a lot of slow dance music," I added.

Sue looked at me and smiled.

* * *

At the front of her house I stopped but didn't shut the motor or headlights off. We just sat there for a couple of minutes. Then she said, "Go up the street and park. Then come back and come in by the back door. I'll say good night loud enough for the neighbors to hear if they're up. You do the same." Then she got out of the International and said, "Good night! Stop by the restaurant tomorrow. Sunday the cook will have made some Boston Cream Pies."

"Okay! I will!" I replied as loud as she had in case the neighbors happened to be listening.

After Sue had waved at the door and entered the house and closed it behind herself, I drove off and parked a block away on the next street. Locked my truck, lit a cigarette and walked towards Sue's house. When I saw a car coming down the street I stood in the shadows beside someone's house until they had passed and then I went on.

When I got to the house all the other houses were unlit except for one and the front hall light in Sue's house. I made my way to the back of her house and knocked lightly on the door while holding the screen door open. The adrenaline in me made me feel like a thief in the night.

Sue opened the back door quietly and I slipped inside, making sure the spring screen door didn't slam shut with a bang.

She took my hand and led me upstairs as I tried to be quiet while walking as if sneaking around. She turned the lights off in the front hall from the top of the stairs. She was barefoot. There was a small light on in her room on top of her bureau. All the shades and curtains were closed. She turned and pulled me into the room and wrapped her arms around me. We kissed for a long time just standing there in the room. I was hard and I no longer tried to hide the fact from her. She had moved her pelvis into mine and I could feel her moving slowly up and down against me. *God, I hope I don't cum before I get my clothes off,* I thought to myself. Just then Sue moved away from me and unsnapped my shirt and pulled it out of my pants and off of me and dropped it on the floor. She then took off her blouse as she turned away from me and threw it on the bedroom chair. She slipped out of her skirt and petticoat and tossed them on the chair also. I stood there transfixed. She reached behind her back and unsnapped her bra, let it fall to the floor then slithered out of her underpants and stepped out of them and walked to the bed and pulled the covers back, climbed in, then pulled the covers over herself.

I was still just standing there like an idiot.

"You've got to be up early tomorrow. Won't you come to bed?" she urged in a whisper.

I walked to the bed before I realized I still had my boots and pants still on. I sat on the bed and pulled my boots off with some difficulty. My second problem was my hard-on. It made bending over tougher even with my belt undone and my fly opened. But I managed finally. Then dropped my jeans and underpants next to the boots and pulled off my T-shirt. Dropped it also to the pile of my clothes on the floor and stood as Sue moved the covers aside so I could get under them and in bed with her. I was still erect. And she moved the bedding off of her chest so I could see her erect nipples centered on firm ample breasts. She was smiling and then bit her lower lip as I slipped next to her, my hat still on my head. She flipped it off and it landed on the floor.

Immediately she sidled towards me and lifted her head so I could put my arm in back of her neck and then she rolled around onto her side and kissed me and I kissed her back hungrily. After a point I found my tongue slipping between her teeth and she allowed it to enter her open mouth. It just happened sort of unplanned and involuntary. Then I felt her tongue hitting mine forcefully and I backed out of her mouth and her tongue entered my mouth and in so doing she rolled over and on top of my chest. We exchanged kissing with each other's tongues wildly trading places. I cupped my hand over a breast as we continued kissing. She moaned softly and I felt her hand on my penis. Then giving it light squeezes, she pumping slowly, milking me. I thought I'd explode. I wanted to explode. But I knew I'd have to wait. My mind raced to forget what was happening; forcing myself to think of something other than what was happening. I thought of Aunt Bernadette burning the corn bread while we were at her house for a Sunday dinner and all the smoke and everyone opening doors and windows trying to get the smoke out of the house before all the other family members got there. I thought of Kipp and the rattlesnake and Ma yelling to kill it! I held off. Sue slid off of me, pulling me to her. I rolled over on top of her, bent down and began kissing then sucking her left nipple. She moaned; her breathing was rapid as I felt between her thighs and she opened her legs to let me in. I was about to enter her when she said, "I hope you have some protection?"

The question was like putting the brakes on.

"Oh! Yeah. Yeah, in my wallet."

"We better be careful."

I pulled myself away from her and reached down off the bed and grabbed my pants, found the wallet and pulled the foiled wrapped condom out. I'd had the thing in there for what seemed forever. Fumbling, I opened it while leaning on one elbow over the bedside.

If you got a girl pregnant, you only had two choices one, marry her, or two, join the military.

Then I swung off the side of the bed to roll the thing on. Of course I almost tried to put it on backwards but thank God the light was on so I could see what I was doing. I turned it around, rolled it down and secured it on right. I couldn't remember ever having been this hard before. Kipp referred to any dog or horse with an erection as a "Woody." Now I knew why he called it a Woody, but had no idea where he'd picked up that expression.

I now remembered the box of condoms in back of the truck's glove box under the Luger. *Why hadn't I grabbed them before coming here?* Hindsight, the mind works very slowly sometimes.

I tumbled back into bed. Sue had moved the covers to the foot of the bed. She flung herself at me, we kissed some more. I rolled over her and between her spread legs. She helped put me into the wet warmth of herself. We both humped at one another and I could feel her sucking on my neck. Then she groaned, "Yes, Oh yes!" and shuddered. Just as suddenly I felt that I was to ejaculate and I thrust myself forward and exploded with a wave of ecstasy. I moaned and fell wilted on Sue. She held me tight while I lay there on her and panted like a dog. She loosened her grip and I slid to her side. I felt transformed from boy to a man.

Sue went into the bathroom. I lay there and after she came back into the room she turned off the light and everything was thrown into total blackness. I got out of bed and slowly felt my way to the bathroom, almost tripping over my boots.

"Sorry about the light. You can turn it back on," she apologized.

In the bathroom I found it somewhat lit by the streetlight. I shed the condom into the toilet and flushed it, making sure it disappeared. I ran the cold water in the sink and washed my face and elsewhere with a face towel, dried and by now my eyes had adjusted to the dark.

Moments later I was back in bed. Sue had pulled up the covers and I crawled under them and next to her.

We talked for a while. We kissed some more. Then we eventually fell asleep in each other's arms.

Around three o'clock I woke and didn't recall where I was. Then Sue said something in her sleep; she had rolled to her side. Then I remembered where I was.

"What?" I asked.

But she didn't respond.

I thought of waking her; then remembered I had no more protection.

Dakk, you're such a dumb shit sometimes, I assessed myself.

I wanted more of Sue but didn't want to chance knocking her up. I wasn't ready for the long haul of marriage and raising kids just yet. Besides I remembered what Dwayne once said, "Why buy the cow if you get the milk for free?" Yeah, I was pretty sure I was in love. Hell, I knew I was in love. But was I ready for so much responsibility? Finally I drifted back to sleep.

I awoke suddenly to a dog with a baritone bark giving warning down the street. It was a little after five. Sue lay there on her side pressed to me, her breathing was shallow. It felt great. I had another hard-on. I sat up from the bed and Sue moved, opened her eyes for a second and fell back to sleep. The bedroom had the aroma of sex. I took a deep breath, kissed Sue on her shoulder lightly so as not to wake her. I didn't want to get things going again, though I would have liked to. Grabbing all my clothes and boots I followed my erection to the bathroom. I jumped in the shower and pissed straight out before Dakk junior settled down. After showering I looked in the mirror, a shave would have to wait but I'd have to button my top shirt button to hide the purple hickey on my neck. Borrowing the toothpaste I brushed my teeth with my finger.

After having dressed I went back to the bed and woke Sue.

"What time is it?" she questioned.

"Six thirty-ish. I've got to go."

She rose up bare breasted to kiss me. My jeans got tight. We kissed long.

"I'll see you this afternoon. I'll call," I said as I pulled away.

"I hope so. I don't want to go to the rodeo this afternoon. Maybe we could go for a ride in the country. I'll bring a blanket and pack us a picnic."

"Yeah, I've had enough rodeo also, but I want more of you."

"I want more of you too," she said as she climbed out of bed and kissed me once again long and soft as I held her warm naked body to me.

I left as she went into the bathroom.

"See you around one," I told her.

Outside everything was quiet. No one around as I slipped to the front of the house and hurried down the street and to my truck.

* * *

Monday morning, Kipp gave me one of his smart-ass looks but kept his mouth shut. Ma and Dad normally went to bed about a couple of hours after it became dark. Dad generally fell asleep in front of the TV and Mom would wake him, turn the television off and they'd head to bed. Kipp on the other hand stayed up until eleven or twelve reading car magazines, comics or Popular Mechanics. He knew I hadn't been home Saturday night. Ma and Dad thought I'd come into the house after feeding the horses, grabbed a cup of coffee and headed out the door to work before anyone came down stairs on Sunday.

"Dakk, you look haggard this morning. Are you okay? You're not getting sick are you? I hear there's something going around. Hope you're not catching it," Ma said as I drank my coffee at the kitchen counter.

Dad was sitting at the table reading what he had not already read of the Sunday paper and Kipp had just came downstairs as Ma set bowls of hot Cream of Wheat cereal on the table.

I sat and poured milk and sugar onto my cereal and when I looked up that's when Kipp gave me "that look." I looked back at him with my "that look" just as Ma put toast in front of me and Dad.

"You want toast, Kipp?" she asked.

"Sure, Ma. Please."

"Dakk, I don't want to be harping on you, but you look like you need a haircut," Ma declared.

Dad put the paper away and poured milk on his Cream of Wheat. "You still go to Mr. Lewis for your haircuts? What's he charge? Still a quarter like when you were a kid?"

"No, fifty cents now days," I replied.

Just then Kipp put in the question to me, "Why you wearing your neck rag? Is it cold out there?"

"Yeah! There's frost on everything," I said not looking at him.

I'd wrapped my black silk neck scarf around my neck twice and knotted it in front. Wearing it was more for hiding the hickey more than the cold. It was customary at that time of year for most cowboys to switch from summer straw hats to their winter felts and start wearing their neck rags to keep their body heat in while working out in the cold.

Taking a pause after swallowing a piece of toast, Dad continued, "I remember when Mr. Lewis was married to his wife. She was nothing more than skin and bones. I don't think she ever put on weight. Nine months after they'd been married and was pregnant with Goo Goo she look like a rope with a knot in the middle."

"Dad, that's not nice!" Ma protested. "Some folks are just unable to gain weight while others put on weight just by looking at food. Most can't help it. It's in their genes or something."

"Yes, well, she still looked real unnatural when pregnant and all."

Roland Lewis had been nicknamed Goo Goo and was called that even by his folks. As a three year old he had repeated goo goo for over an hour and they were the first words he'd ever said.

At the time it was thought that Roland "Goo Goo" was mentally retarded. He was far behind in school and only passed ahead as teachers became tired of seeing him in their classes for two years. Back then there were no "Special Ed" schools or classes. So if you had problems learning you were just pushed along until you dropped out at sixteen or graduated at the bottom of the barrel and shoved out in to the world to see if you could survive.

Goo Goo didn't have that retarded look. No strange-shaped head or body parts or protruding lips, only his eyes had that spaced out look as if he was staring beyond the beyond. But he was not ever considered the town pariah. He had sandy hair and hazel eyes. Goo Goo in classes would always be put to sit in back of the classroom and most times just sat and probed at something with a finger at the edge of his desk or looked out the window or the inkwell hole on his desk. The teachers didn't allow him a bottle of ink for the inkwell. In fact inkwells were removed in the desks of most of the boys until they had to use ink to write with and only then were they placed in the desk holes. After classes the teacher would collect and store the inkwells in the classroom closet. The reason for the removal of the wells was that boys didn't always use them as intended; they'd carefully catch a long pigtail of the girl in front of them and plunge the tip of the long braid into it. And other times as class ended one smart-ass would put a broken piece of Alka-Seltzer into the inkwell of one desk as he passed by and after everyone had left the room the ink would bubble up and out of the well creating a staining black mess. Teachers thought ballpoint pens to be the mother of all inventions. No more inkwells. No more ink spots on clothing or fingers.

It wasn't that people didn't like Goo Goo, it's just that he was hard to deal with most of the time.

At times Goo Goo would sit on the floor and endlessly study a spot or crack the whole day. Other times he'd draw a circle with a pencil on paper repetitively but when he wanted to he could draw something he had only seen once for a very short time in its exactness. If he saw the photo of an elephant or a camel then he could remember it as if the thing was a model sitting in front of him.

There were the times he'd interrupt the class and just blurt out something or screech like a feral dog. Goo Goo had to be taken out of the class on those days and his mother had to come take him home. Most often he wasn't in school. He was very shy, fidgety, avoided looking you in the eyes, and rarely spoke when you spoke to him. Other times he was a fluent talker and showed signs of being smart.

Dad use to say, "That poor boy brain's short a couple of bales to make a full ton. He just isn't firing on all cylinders."

It wasn't until many years later that Goo Goo was diagnosed by a psychiatrist that he was autistic. In his adult life he was able to receive some treatment for his affliction and became able to work as an illustrator of animals for children's books.

The Lewises lived in a white clapboard house with a small back yard that skirted a set of spur railroad tracks that were used periodically by the refinery. Mr. Lewis had his barbershop on his front porch until he was able to find a ground floor room near the railroad depot on Montana Avenue in which he had his barber chair and effects. Mrs. Lewis was a seamstress and worked on the clothing of some of the wealthiest people in Billings.

One summer day Kipp and I, age ten and twelve, were walking down the railroad tracks, among the greasy weeds, cinders and creosote ties on our way to Cooper's house when we saw and heard Goo Goo up ahead sitting next to the rails at the back of his house. He was whacking on the tracks with what looked like a knife. When we reached him he had the remnant of what looked like a snake, maybe a garter snake that he had hacked into little pieces with a beet knife. We stopped to watch Goo Goo and he just kept up whacking this snake into oblivion on the rusty rail with felicity.

"What you doing with that beet knife, Goo Goo? Trying to cut the track in half?" I inquired.

But he never answered, only kept hitting the track making a dull pinging sound.

I remember Kipp had piped up out of the blue, "Hey! Goo Goo! A peanut sat on the railroad track. Its heart all a flutter. A train came down the railroad tracks. Toot! Toot! Peanut butter."

And Kipp had laughed at his own saying. It was a saying Ma used on us real young kids and we'd laugh, mostly because we liked the "Toot, toot" part.

Goo Goo went on whacking the tracks and his mother came out of the house and called Goo Goo but had to come and get him.

We said, "Hello, Mrs. Lewis. Looks like Goo Goo's having a good time."

She smiled when she recognized us, "Oh! You're the Lovett boys. Dakk and Kipp."

"Yes ma'am."

She grabbed Goo Goo's arm gently and got him up as we started to walk away.

"Nooo!" Goo Goo yowled as if he was being tortured.

We looked back to see Goo Goo stumble towards their house lead on by his mother. Goo Goo had dropped the beet knife. Kipp ran back and picked it up out of the weeds once Goo Goo and his mother had disappeared into the house and raced back after me.

Beet knives were almost as common around Billings as the daily paper. They were used to harvest the sugar beets from the fields by the migrant workers. The knives are a bit longer than the average butcher knife but with a wide straight blade that has a pointed spike hook on top and at the end of the blade. The hook was used to pick at the beet and the blade to chop off the leafy tops. Goo Goo's beet knife blade had been pounded so badly that there was no longer an edge on it and the beet hook was bent and the point had been peen.

"What you need that thing for?" I asked.

"Don' know. I thought he'd maybe cut himself with it one day if I didn't get it away. Guess his mother didn't see what he was hammering with."

Down the tracks, Kipp gave it a toss into a vacant lot and it sailed in and among the litter of weeds, oilcans, worn out discarded tires, and broken and empty cheap wine and liquor bottles.

As kids we loved walking the tracks, sometimes balancing on them like a tight rope walker, seeing how long a distance we could go without losing our balance or running on the ties two at a time which was most challenging when we did this on the trestle over the Yellowstone River. Now and again you'd find a dead dog or some other critter cut in half lying next to the rail. And we'd hold our snot rags to our noses to abate the stench and examine the remains with a stick and watched hundreds of orange and black carrion beetles and white maggots milling in the carcass. Once we set a couple of pennies on the rail and hid in the weeds and watched as a slow moving freight lumbered over them, sending the flattened pennies flying out and onto the trap rock between the ties. Then after the cars had passed we'd go find them and keep them as copper oblong good luck pieces.

*   *   *

I was by now totally confused yet filled with amatory ecstasy. I was infected by sex. Sue was not my first experience with fornication anymore than it was her first time either.

My first time came about when at seventeen, a few of us high school guys decided to take a road trip up to Butte that Fourth of July. No one knew us up there and we had decided not to shave for a few weeks so we'd all look older than seventeen with what whiskers we may have had at the time. We generally shaved maybe once a week anyway.

We were planning to get drunk, raise Hell, and party. Well that night we found a bar that didn't ask us any questions, got drunk and stumbled into a party after we left the bar. They had some quarts of beer there but no hard liquor so after pooling money together, I went back to the bar and purchased a fifth of Old Grand Dad, a pint of vodka and a screw top bottle of white wine for the girls. The party went on all night at this girl's house whose folks were out of town. In the morning I found myself in bed with this young brunet with a very nice body naked and passed out next to me. When I stumbled out of bed and hunted for my clothes I discovered I still had on the rubber I don't remember putting on let alone having used. So the whole sexual affair was nothing more than a blur with a hangover the next day.

Sue on the other hand, I discovered later had been deflowered when she was fourteen by a high school senior after a dance and in the back seat of a car. The senior had left Billings after high school and gone to college in Fort Collins, Colorado, for veterinary medicine. But the whole incident between Sue and him was no more than a one-night-stand borderline rape. Later she had become infatuated with a bohemian poet from Boston who sported a goatee that lived for a time in Billings while writing poems about the land, wheat fields, big skies, and lost art of hunting buffalo with a bow and arrow.

Sue thought he was wonderful and filled with a passion for life and he made love to her while reciting some erotic poems he'd written. She believed him when he had promised to take her with him to California where there it was all the world of the "Beat." He disappeared after she had told him she had missed her period. He'd left Billings and his bartending job at Casey's with what few possessions he had, "Lock-stock an' barrel" leaving behind Sue and his last week's pay check and no forwarding address.

Sue was only a few days late getting her period and was not pregnant. After finding that her poet lover, teacher, and mentor had left town, she believed it was the beginning of the end of the world for her. Her father, on the other hand who had no idea she was seeing an older man, and if he had he would have thrown her out of the house and disowned her and the baby if it had come to pass.

"How old was this guy?" I'd asked her.

"I think he was twenty-two or three at that time," Sue confessed.

"And you how old?"

"Sixteen," she admitted, "I was going to be a junior that Fall. And I believed he really loved me and I thought I loved him."

"Do you still love him?'

"No. I know he just wanted sex. But then so did I at that time. I now wish I had not met him."

My mother's expression at that time came to my mind, "If wishes were horses, beggars would ride."

Abortions were nearly non-existent in Billings and all of Montana for the most part. What few there may have been were hushed up or were done out of the state. Most pregnant girls would be sent off to have the baby, and then it was put up for adoption.

Sue by now knew what she was doing sexually as she led me into our courtship. Which at the time was that, we would go at it full throttle whenever we could.

*   *   *

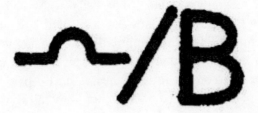

MILLIRON SLASH B
CHAPTER 8

The following week before I was to start working for the Milliron slash B became torture. I was thinking of buying Sue Palmer an engagement ring with what little money I had saved. All I could think about was the two of us and how wonderful it was. I didn't want to leave her and go to work on the Milliron Ranch some miles away, south of Musselshell, a one horse town. Not seeing her for months at a time would drive me nuts I thought. I would drop in at the Pronghorn Café every afternoon to see her and talk when she wasn't too busy with customers. We'd make plans for dates that al-ways involved making mad and passionate love.

One Sunday night we had a date and that's when I noticed that Sue wasn't quite herself. We'd spent four hours that afternoon at the Rio Movie Theater to see "East of Eden" and a re-run of "Shane."

We watched James Dean as the rebellious Cal whose confusion and intrusiveness nearly ruins his family into shreds. Then seeing the second movie, "Shane" played by Alan Ladd and the young blonde-headed Brandon De Wilde as Joey Starrett, a story of a Wyoming homesteader's dilemma of aversion between him the little guy and the large ranchers set in Jackson Hole's Teton country.

At first I thought Sue's languid mood was due to the combination of the two films' intensities.

We had gone to the A & W for fries and a couple of root beers served in cold frosty glass steins. I'd parked toward the back end of the lot and pushed the speaker button and a garbled voice asked, "Can I take your order now?" I gave the unintelligible speaker voice our order. Moments later the car-hop delivered our order by coming to an abrupt stop beside the truck on her roller skates. After I'd paid her and given her a quarter tip, she then sped off with her pony tail flying in the wind to another customer.

"Are you okay? You don't seem yourself today," I interjected as we sipped the root beers through straws.

"Oh! I guess I should tell you now as never," Sue shrugged.

"What? What's the matter?"

"Dad is taking a job in Sheridan. He's quitting Pierce; he's got a new job for a fridge company. So we have to move. Both Mother and Dad are not happy about the move but because my mother's mother had apoplexy. That's what they call it. It's a stroke. She had it while they were staying at her house when Dad and Mother had gone down to Sheridan. Grandma is all alone since Gramps died last February. She's in a wheel chair now and Mother is taking care of her until Dad and I move there in two weeks. We have to move because Grandma refuses to move out of her house."

She paused then went on, "I had to give my two weeks' notice at the Pronghorn. Dad is putting the house here up for sale. The realtor is going to put up a sign in the front yard sometime today. Dad has been with Pierce Packing forever. Well at least 15 years now. He's gonna lose his retirement from the plant. I know Grandma needs someone to look after her but why don't they have her move in with us and sell her house? I don't understand why she won't leave Sheridan. She has no friends there left alive."

Sue rambled on, "Besides I'll be going off to college next fall. She can even have my room for now. I'll sleep in the basement. It's not bad down there. Dad put a bathroom in a year ago. I could fix it up nice, there's lots more room than my bedroom. Just smaller windows down there that's all."

I didn't know what to say and I just sat there staring out the bug-splattered windshield for a while. Sue was silent. Finally I turned to her and said, assuring, "I'll come to Sheridan and visit you when I get time off from the Milliron. I guess we're both leaving Billings."

"Yeah," Sue agreed as tears began to form and she turned her head away. Her hand shook and I took the root beer stein from her and placed both of them and the fries back on the window tray, then turned and put my arm around her and pulled her to me as she shook sobbing.

"Maybe it's meant that we both move out of Billings for awhile," I offered as a weak consolation.

"But I'll miss you so much. We were having a great time together."

"Yeah, and I'm going to miss you also. I was about to call Archie Braddock and tell him that I'd changed my mind about cowboying and was thinking of going to work at the refinery so I would be closer to you."

Sue cried harder and I held her harder and kissed her on her forehead. She grabbed me and we kissed.

"I love you, Dakk," she whispered.

"I-I love you too, hon." I sort of stammered.

"Will you come and see me when you can. I'll write you every day."

"I'll write you also," I said feeling hopeless.

Sue wiped her tears, "I think you're right, maybe this move is meant to test our love for one another. Next fall we can be in college together, maybe rent a place together to live in."

"Yeah, I'd like that." I said hesitantly.

She smiled, "Me too."

* * *

I now had no other choice but to keep my word to Mr. Braddock and work for him on the Milliron.

Sue and I spent every possible chance we had together. We managed to make love on more occasions than we had since we first started dating. It was as if we were love starved. We knew that this craving was soon to be disrupted by our separate departures from Billings.

Their house was bought and the moving van was being loaded of all the household and personal belongings the day I headed to the

Milliron. I stopped by with my two horses riding in the trailer behind my truck. My saddles, tack, bedroll, slicker, two new hemp lariats, and duffel bag of clean clothes lay under a canvas tarp. I had weighed down everything with a long logging chain in the truck bed to keep the wind from blowing the tarp away. Grandpa's old Winchester .30-.30 in its scabbard sat on the gun-rack at the truck's rear window.

Sue cried as we sat on the old glider on the porch. It squeaked as I rocked it back and forwards more out of nervousness than wanting to swing. I consoled Sue with the promise of going to Sheridan whenever I could and that I'd write at least weekly. She said she'd write me every day. She gave me her grandmother's telephone number and said to call once in awhile, that she wanted to hear my voice.

I left with a heavy heart and the road to Musselshell seemed long and the fall air was still keen even at that time of the morning. Mealy tendrils of clouds washed across the sky. I drove on. Reaching Musselshell I turned the truck south on the macadam road that eventually turned to dirt. Stopping at a river I unloaded Jeep and Sioux, led them to the water's edge and let them drink. A blue-slate colored heron flushed from the shores rushes having fished from a placid eddy on the opposite bank. It rose and flew on, it's great wings flapping away slowly rising upwards above the shores willows and on downstream, a fish speared by its beak. The horses' heads came up to watch the majestic bird fly off, their muzzles dripping water back into the current. I let them eat the nearby grass dragging their halter ropes as I lay with my back to a tree, lost in thought of Sue, my life, the beginning of sexual abstinence for me, my wants, fears and doubts of why I was doing what I was doing. My mind was muddled and my enthusiasm about the cowboy job mired. A few trout broke the water snatching at the late hatch of tiny flies with clear pinnate wings dancing in the sun's warmth above the rippling water. Swallows flew by erratically from their rook of mud nests built under the bridge and they dove to feed on the multitude of insects.

After loading the horses I drove on down the dirt road with a light pale dust growing and falling behind me. This was beautiful cow country with endless meadows of good grass, dirt ponds, sandstone outcroppings and ledges with fragmentary tall pines. It was open range once I drove over a cattle guard. Yearling cows grazed on each side of the newly widened lane. A few miles further a county grader sat at the edge of the road. The operator sat drinking coffee while the machine idled and the grader's exhaust pipes puffed a blue smoke from under the flapping rain guards that capped the top of the exhaust pipes. Another two miles down the road there was a metal sign nailed to the trunk of a lofty pine that read **Milliron / B,** 7 miles. At a bend in the road stood two deer, both young does that suddenly turned back from where they were coming. They bounded off towards the nearby shrubbery, with tails flagged and disappeared in the brushy entanglement.

To my left seven miles from the first mileage sign was a drive with a ranch entrance of large upright poles buttressed by fieldstone and above, a cross pole bar supported a black cut out metal **Milliron / B Ranch** sign. I found out later that the ranch had been in existence since 1899, founded by a cowman, Everest T. Braddock from Wichita.

I drove on and now the drive had on each side a four-strand barbwire fence made of cedar posts and split cedar staves. Far ahead I could see a grove of large trees already in their fall yellow that shaded the surrounding outbuildings and the white two-story house. A large barn sat away from the grove and as I got closer could see a corral with a well worn snubbing post, pens, drives, and the chutes that surround it. A sizeable round pen stood off from these structures, its sides leaning out made from stout poles buried into the ground and wide rough sawed planks made up the seven foot inside walls. The gate sat ajar. A low long log building with a hitching post in front sat a short distance from the main house, *the bunkhouse*, I thought. Some distance near the equipment shed and another outbuilding that looked like a shop alongside which sat five small buildings also of rough cut planks posed in a line, like roadside cabins. Each had a stove pipe protruding out of the roofs and electricity was going to them as well.

Numerous dogs ran to greet me with Sylvia, the old red heeler poking along as drag, also barking. Slowly I drove to the main house and stopped as an older woman with long gray hair pulled back into a single braid opened the front door and came out.

I stopped and got out of the truck and walked towards her.

She was a tall woman, long legged, and dressed in tan gabardine riding pants, ox-blood cavalry riding boots with blunt nickel spurs. A starched white blouse made her tanned face and hands standout; she obviously spent time with outside work. By all appearances she was a woman of distinction.

"You dogs be quiet!" she chastised in a feminine but yet throaty voice. And the dogs ran around my truck and trailer, their tails high, still barking, not one heeding to her order except Sylvia and Misty. A hound gave out one long howl after sniffing my leg. Then the males sniffed and squirted the truck and trailer tires while Sylvia sniffed where the males had just hosed. All the dogs belonged to Archie Braddock, with Sylvia his favorite and Misty his second and the three black and tan hounds, Chuck, Wally and Dusty. The hounds had been used at one time to hunt bears and mountain lions. The old black and white Border collie called Misty, kept circling around the truck and trailer waiting for the horses to be unloaded.

"Howdy! You must be Dakk Lovett?" Mrs. Braddock inquired.

Doffing my hat. I replied, "Yes, ma'am. I am." We shook hands and she had a solid grip.

"Archie said he had hired a new man to replace the hand that left for Hollywood," and she added with a touch of skepticism, "Hope he does well there."

"Yes, ma'am," I replied not knowing what else to say.

"Archie is in his office you can unload your horses by the barn. Someone there will show you where you can put and water them for the time being. The bunkhouse is over there." And she pointed to a long low log building that looked like the original homestead ranch house. The old ranch house had been white-washed over the weathered gray notched logs that had for years sat weathering there. The chinking was of mortar held up on the curve of the logs by lengths of willow saplings tacked at the base of each chinking course. The old adobe mud had been replaced a long time ago with cement mortar. Green rolled roofing covered the low-pitched roof from which a stovepipe protruded.

"Then come in. You missed noon chuck but Little Raven, the cook will fix you up a bite if you're hungry?" she continued.

"That's okay ma'am, thank you anyways. I ate a couple of sandwiches my mom had made for me on the road."

"Well there's always coffee cookin' and cold lemonade if you're thirsty. Little Raven will show you where things are. I'll tell Archie you're here. Kitchen's around the back."

"Thank you ma'am."

I parked near the huge unpainted board and bat sided barn with its New England cedar shingled gambrel roof. On the front gable end were the large white symbols of the ⌒/B and I went in through the open sliding doors to see if someone would tell me where to put Jeep and Sioux. The barn smelled of fresh cut hay. It was a large post and beam structure built around the same time as the main house. Horse stalls lined either sides of the central alley and above was the hayloft. A few of the horses housed in the stable poked their heads over the stall doors to see who the intruder was. One nickered as I passed. All had their ears perked up.

Coming from the back of the barn I could hear someone singing. I stopped to listen,

> *"When it's round-up time in Texas and the bloom is on the sage . . .*
> *How I longs to be in Texas, just a ridin' on the range . . .*
> *I can hear the breakfast a fryin', hear it sizzlin' in the pan . . .*
> *Hear the breakfast horn in the early morn, drinking coffee from a can . . .*
> *Just a ridin', rockin', ropin', poundin' leather all day long . . .*
> *Though I know I'll never go there, I would work for any wage . . .*
> *To be again, be free again, where the bloom is on the sage."*

The voice was anything but pretty, somewhat more like a gut-gored buffalo, a deep baritone. I could tell that whoever was singing was happy in the thought that he was alone with only the horses in their stalls. He was enjoying his own singing even though he sounded very much off key.

I called out, "Hello! Is anyone here?"

The singing came to an abrupt stop.

As I moved down the alleyway someone came out of a back room.

"Howdy!" I stated to the man that looked to be about the same age as my dad.

"Howdy. Didn't know anyone was here. What can I do for you?"

"I was told by the Missus to come in here to see if someone could tell me where I can put up my horses. I'm Dakk Lovett, Mr. Braddock hired me to replace one of the men that quit."

"Oh, yeah," he shook his head, "There's always someone thinkin' the grass is greener on the other side of the fence. Well good luck to him. Hell, he might make it as far as I know. He went to Hollywood. Gonna become a new Tom Mix he thinks. Hell, here he was just a mixed Tom. You go 'head an' use those two end stalls on the right for now. There's water at the hydrant at that end of the barn with a hose an' there are buckets in the stalls. I'm Jed McRae," and he extended his hand to me.

We shook hands, "Thanks. I'm much obliged."

"The bunkhouse is the long cabin with the rail hitch in front. Grab any empty bed you want in there."

"Okay. Thanks," I replied.

Jed stood six feet plus. A lanky man looked to be in his late thirties. He was clean shaven, pale emerald eyes in a chiseled and tanned face with an aquiline nose. He dressed like a cowboy with a well-used black felt hat on his head, a vest and fading Lee dungarees with rolled up cuffs. His boots had sharp undercut heels.

"I'll be in the tack room if you need any help," he suggested.

On my way out I noticed that the horses that had stuck their heads out over the stall doors were all tall and looked like thoroughbreds.

"Nice looking horses," I called back as we both headed in two different directions.

"They all belong to Missus Braddock," he said.

After taking care of my horses and unhooking the trailer next to a stock trailer I drove to the bunkhouse and there I parked next to a couple of pick-up trucks, one with Nevada license plates on it. The dogs didn't bother with me anymore. Sylvia had disappeared back into the house and the other five lay in the shade unaffected by my comings and goings.

Inside the bunkhouse, the beds were lined apart spaciously. Large spikes nailed to the logs on the wall held coats, chaps, shirts, and some personal trappings. Each bed had a plywood army footlocker painted slicker yellow and the hasps had a variety of padlocks hanging from or off them on a small chain. None were locked. Most of the beds, also army surplus, were iron and held rolled out canvas bed rolls or blankets and striped ticked pillows. A few boots lay under some of the beds. And above or next to several beds, pictures of girlfriends or favorite horses were tacked to the log wall. Coffee cans with sand in them were on the floor near the beds and served as ashtrays for the smokers. Next to one bed and on the window ledge with a plank shelf sat a Zenith Oceanic radio with its many worldwide short wave bands, which I soon discovered belonged to J.W. Each bed had a certain orderliness or lack of it depending on the individual using that space.

The floor was marbled pattern linoleum, scuffed and worn down showing the burlap at the doorway where the heaviest traffic took its toll on the floor as well as by the large wood stove. The stove was originated from the iron tank from what looked like that of a hot water heater. It had hinges on a fashioned loading door and a stove pipe elbowing from the back and on up through the ceiling. A large crate adjacent to the stove was filled with cordwood and a cardboard box held kindling with old newspapers.

I took an empty bed on the east side of the bunkhouse. The mattress was rolled up with blankets, linens, and a feather pillow in the center. I unrolled the mattress and laid my duffle bag on the bed. I stowed my bedroll under the bed until I needed it on the range. Opening the footlocker at the end of my bed I found a battered paperback copy of a twenty-five cent, "***Texas Rangers***, *A thrilling publication.*" Another old ten-cent paperback book with a green cover, Ripley's "***Believe It Or Not***" with the face of Abraham Lincoln with the byline reading: Lincoln was wrong! The book was printed in 1933. I flipped through the Ripley's and my eyes fell on the story of, THE CRUISE OF THE DEAD. I quickly read through it. The schooner "Jenny" had just been released from its 37 years captivity in an ice barrier was encountered by the schooner "Hope," that was sailing in the Southern Ocean south of Drake Straits on September 22, 1860. On board the Jenny were the dead, seven crewmembers including the captain and one woman and a dog all frozen to death that had been found aboard the ship. The article sent a chill up my spine. I dropped the book back into the locker.

At one end of the bunkhouse was a bathroom with three stall toilets, four sinks, and three showers. Everything in there looked almost new. The floor was concrete painted a slate gray color. After washing my hands and running a comb through my hair I headed for the main house to report in with my new boss. As I was about to exit I noticed over the door inside the bunkhouse there was nailed the upper section of a buffalo skull with the horn caps missing. The center of the skull had a gaping hole in it and the bone was weathered gray and the whole skull was encrusted with a green lichen growth. It reminded me of a geode. *An old Indian kill*, I thought to myself, seeing the cavity from which the brains had been taken out.

Walking around to the back porch of the house I found myself faced with Sylvia lying under the shade of clothes hanging on the clotheslines. She raised her head as I walked by, then laid it back lazily on her forepaws, stretched a back leg out, and closed her eyes with a slight moan.

I knocked on the screen door and there was no response. I knocked again and called, "Is anybody home?"

A heavyset Indian woman wearing a long-sleeved flower—printed gingham dress that extended to her ankles came to the door. She wore plain elk-skin moccasins on her feet. She had no jewelry on, not even earrings. Her long hair was white and gray and braided in two long braids that hung down her back.

Leslie Little Raven's face was a road map of wrinkled trails; cheek bones pronounced and a bit puffy, with skin the beautiful color of a used penny. She smiled slightly as she opened the door.

"Come in. Door's always open. Emma told me you were here."

"Thank you," I said as I entered and held my hat in hand.

"Want coffee?"

"No, thanks, I'm fine. It smells good though," I remarked.

"You need to see Archie?"

"Yes, ma'am, I'm here to report in," I said, finding it strange that she would call her employer by his first name.

"You come. I show you where his office is," she stated. "He sits in there for hours. He's writin' a book about the ranch and this Crow country his granddad stole from us," She said with a slight smirk.

I didn't know what to say. So I kept my mouth shut.

She looked at me to see if there was a response in my facial expression. I did my best at a poker face.

Then she gave me that half smile again. "Well, they won the war against us so you could argue that they didn't steal it. That's how Archie sees it. He calls it waived an' I guess he's right, we did give up."

Again I just stood there not saying anything and not knowing what she meant by the word waive. I'd have to look it up.

"I better take him some coffee. You sure you don't want any?" Little Raven suggested.

"No ma'am."

"You can call me Little Raven like everyone else on this ranch," she urged.

I thought it sort of odd that she called Archie Braddock by his first name while she insisted that everyone else call her by her Indian last name, Little Raven. Perhaps she was trying to keep the fact that she was Indian and that the aboriginals had been here in Montana long before us whites. Her way of pointing out, "Who's who."

"I'll just bring an extra cup along with the coffee pot in case you change your mind. Follow me," she insisted.

She chaperoned me through the house to Mr. Braddock's office. It was a fair-size room for an office, at least compared to Ben Blastingame's hole in the wall over the Hoof and Horn Diner. A large window looked towards the east and the rangeland with a distant buff colored sandstone butte. I could see by the long tree-line that there must be a stream or river out there.

On one wall hung a substantially large Charlie Russell oil painting set in a gold frame of Indians hunting off of painted ponies with bows and arrows killing milling buffalo. Below it was an eight foot long weathered barn board with what looked like a six-foot or more, diamondback rattlesnake skin with rattles longer than my trigger finger that had buttons on the rattles as big as .45 caliber bullets. The whole reptile was stretched and tacked to the wood.

Another wall was nothing but bookcases filled with books. There was a glass-framed Will James pen-line drawing of a cowboy smoking while sitting his horse. A few black and white photographs of people, horses, prize bulls, and one of Archie and Little Raven when they were both much younger and Little Raven much lighter in weight wearing a hide dress with elk teeth sewed all over it and long dangly dentalium earrings. Her hair hung in two braids in front of her. Archie was wearing a Buffalo Bill style fringed buckskin jacket with his arm around Little Raven's shoulders and both had smiles on their faces. On opposite walls displays of Indian trappings, old rifles, a stuffed bull buffalo head. A black longhorn cow's head also hung on the opposite wall.

Archie's desk was a large mahogany affair, carved and polished. On it was a bronze sculpture of longhorn cow and calf, books of Montana history; some lay opened on the desk along with letters and fading newspaper clippings. Archie was at a side-typing table hammering away at the keys with two fingers, one from each hand. The new highly lacquered Blouponk radio and record player console was on low with Bing Crosby singing, "On the Sunny Side of the Street."

"Mr. Lovett is here to see you, Archie. An' I brought you a fresh pot of coffee. I'll set it on the hot plate for you," Little Raven said as she poured him coffee into the mug on his desk before putting down the pot on a small electric burner and turned it to low. She sat the empty mug next to it.

I stood by the door.

"Well! Come on in! Dakk, isn't it?" he asked.

"Yes, sir, it is."

He rose and we shook hands.

"Sit down. I've got to finish this paragraph before it escapes me. Then we'll talk." And he sat back down and commenced to type again.

Little Raven left the room.

I sat in the green leather chair next to his desk and looked about the office some more.

This was the first time I'd seen Archie without a hat on and he had a full head of white hair which is surprising since so many men that wear cowboy hats all the time seem to end up bald sooner or later.

When he stopped typing he looked over the paragraph before turning his attention to me. He rolled the paper back into place and pecked out another sentence while looking at the keys.

"I use the Biblical system. Seek and ye shall find," he admitted as he typed.

"That's pretty much my way of typing also," I said.

"You type?" he asked, swinging around in his swivel chair somewhat surprised, as he had finished what he wanted to type for the moment.

"Yes sir, I do once in a while on an old Underwood."

He took a drink of coffee. Then said, "I don't keep a full crew around anymore. I use waddies to cut and put up hay and a few at branding time. But I like having at least two or three cowboys around to feed through the winter and a couple of horse wranglers. I've been using the same Mexicans for the past 13-14 years now during the summer and into fall to irrigate and do much of the hayin'. They left to work in Idaho. Pickin' spuds I guess. You'll work under Tom Huffman, he's been the ranch ramrod for the cowboys goin' on fifteen years now. Anyway you'll take orders from him unless Jed needs to use you to wrangle," he said as he pulled a cigarette from a pack of Chesterfields and lit it with his lighter. He let the first drag of smoke escape from his nose and continued, "You can learn a lot about horses and horse sense from Jed. Can you operate a tractor?"

"Yes sir, had to at the feed lot," I put in.

"Good. We have model H 1952 Farmall that's a hell of a workhorse. Last one International made. There's a six-cylinder Ford tractor, we use both in the summer for farming. You can use the Farmall to pull the wagon or hay sled. I want you to feed the bulls in the winter bull pasture twice a day until we turn them out in the spring. We use the draft horses to pull the sled when the snow gets too deep. After your morning feeding, you're Jed's for work until the afternoon feeding."

"Yes sir," I interjected as he talked to me.

"Since I made you a horse wrangler for now there'll be a time or two that you'll be asked by Emma to work with her thoroughbreds. They're her hobby. Me, I'll stick to quarter horses. Which reminds me, the big 16 hand sorrel with the white star on his forehead, well is my riding horse. Names *Rojo,* means red in Spanish."

I nodded.

"Well that 'bout sums it up. Oh! We normally give the men Saturday an' Sundays off but you have to take turns having one of you stay at the ranch on those days. The hands decide the rotation. There will be weekends when we all have to work, especially during round up, calving, branding, weaning an' the rest that goes with ranching. I don't mind if one of you gets drunk while off an' in town as long as you're sober by Monday morning. An' that means getting here to work by five A.M. in the spring, summer and seven in the fall and winter. No drinking on duty an' that means no booze on the premises an' that includes beer. Saturday an' Sundays your days to do what you wish as long as you're not the one cowboy working on that weekend."

He took a sip of coffee and took another puff on the cigarette then went on, "You want a cup of coffee? I see Little Raven left an extra cup."

"No, sir, she has already asked me if I wanted some. Thanks."

He took another sip of coffee and a drag on the cigarette and then stated, "You know the pay and all. So if there's any questions, shoot!"

"Can't think of any at this time."

"Well if you do and Tom, Jed or Little Raven can't answer you, you just come an' ask me. I've got to get back to my typin'. Little Raven will have supper out about seven. Sandwiches and leftovers at night, big meals at noon around here. Jed will show you around."

He stood and put out his hand and I stood and shook his.

"An' by the way everybody calls me by my first name, Archie. None of this Mister Braddock business. After all we live in the west an' there's no need for all that uppity eastern protocol," Archie said.

"Yes, sir, Archie," I said.

I found my way back to the kitchen and back out to the barn.

*   *   *

Sunday night Jed and I went to the main house for supper. The kitchen was large and the table stretched a good seven feet long. A red and white gingham oilcloth table cover was stretched and tacked under the tabletop. On the table were three crockery pots, each filled with separated flatware, knives, spoons and forks. A sugar bowl and green glass salt and pepper shakers sat next to the "eatin'—irons" also. Ten bent-bow and spindle-back chairs sat on each side and at the two ends of the table. The place was well lit and the stove was a large iron cook stove and by the pantry stood a Frigidaire with a freezer. Next to the kitchen worktable, above which hung pots and pans, stood a heavy butcher's chopping block and at one wall was a deep double white porcelain sink. The place had the look of a restaurant kitchen. On a sidewall hung a John Deere tractor sales calendar and a few small-framed works of western cowboy art. They were pen and ink drawings of cowboys moving some longhorns, three pencil drawings of cowboys and horses, cowboy, his dog and horse, cowboy chuck wagon and cook working over an open fire. Then between these was a watercolor painting of a big foreboding brindle bull. From the kitchen windows you could see the barn and horse corrals. The shiny white painted plastered walls made the place seem more spacious than it actually was.

The both of us were the only ones eating in the kitchen. Little Raven, the Braddocks and the other winter hired hands were not present for the sandwiches, coffee and a fresh baked peach pie.

"Little Raven must of seen something in you she liked to bother making a pie for us," Jed said gingerly, "She normally doesn't go to such a fuss on a Sunday."

Back at the bunkhouse I read one of the Texas Rangers books before turning in. Jed was playing solitaire at the plank table with benches. No one had come in from their days off as yet and I could have sat in one of the two beat up stuffed chairs but decided to read in bed. I was trying to get my mind off of Sue Palmer by spending my time reading. I read through Blood at Bent Fork when my eyes got tired, then I started chapter one of Outlaw Brand and soon dozed to sleep as Jed kept up his game of solitaire.

Around midnight one of the hands came into the bunkhouse and immediately went to bed. He was asleep within minutes and was snoring. What had awakened me was his pickup truck with a hole in the muffler sounding externally clamorous in the stillness of that time of night. Also the hounds had welcomed the truck with their bark. Jed had also hit the sack after giving up on the cards and shut off the lights. I soon fell back to sleep.

Again at 3:30 two more cowboys came in and went to bed by just flopping on their beds fully clothed.

At five in the morning, I awoke out of habit and noticed the bathroom light was on and the door ajar. When I entered the lit bathroom I found Jed shaving. I had also noticed that one of the late arrivals had never bothered to pull his boots off before falling to sleep on his bunk. His hat lay on the floor.

By six a.m., we were all in the kitchen eating breakfast, myself, Jed, Clint, a big man in his late forties with deep wrinkles around his dark eyes, a hook hawkish nose and hands the size of skillets. Tom looked to be in his thirties. He wore round wire framed glasses and had a silver dollar sized purple wine stain birthmark high on his left cheek. He seemed to have an unassuming demeanor, an easy going kind of guy. J.W. blonde haired, blue eyed, Nevada buckaroo twenty something, sported a handlebar mustache that looked like a couple of hay hooks when he'd wax the ends and shape them out. This morning they drooped some, as did his enthusiasm for working after having been on a drunk. He looked as though he had a bit of panache by the way and style he was dressed.

We all sat eating hatless since we'd hung our hats on the peg hat-rack by the door. Little Raven had made the men hot cakes, eggs and bacon and coffee strong, the color of coal. She knew how to soak up and kill a hangover.

I sat next to Jed since he was the only confederate I had from the bunkhouse since I had arrived. I hadn't been introduced to the other hands as yet.

"I reckon now's a good a time to have you make your acquaintance with the rest of the bunkhouse immigrants," Jed admitted.

I looked up from my meal as Jed started the introductions.

"This here is Clint," pointing a fork in the direction of the man, "Clint, meet Dakk."

Clint raised his coffee mug in a salute.

"An' that's Tom, he's the ramrod here. The ol' man gives him the orders and he passes them on. And the guy with the 'stache is J.W. out of Nevada."

Tom reached across the table with his hand out to shake and I met it while rising from my seat.

"Howdy," I said.

"Howdy back," he replied.

J.W. gave a salute after putting a fork full of food in his mouth, nodding and muttered, "Hi."

"J.W.'s a tad under the weather this mornin'," Tom interjected.

I smiled knowingly, "I've been there myself a time or two."

"You boys get your pipes clean last night?" Jed asked somewhat dubiously.

"Tom found himself in a tangle with a bar fly," J.W. volunteered with a big grin on his face and continued, "That gal looked like a real mud fence, a dog, a swing bag ol' cow."

Tom tried to hide his face behind his mug of coffee as he glanced towards the stove to see if Little Raven was listening but she had left the kitchen.

J.W. went on, "He took her out to the pickup while I ordered another beer and waited for them to come back into the bar. I'll tell you," he said lowering his voice while looking at Jed, "I wouldn't have nailed her even with your dick if you paid me a hundred dollars."

Tom flipped J.W. the "Bird," and Jed raised his mug of coffee and replied out of the corner of his mouth, "I wouldn't let you."

I did my best to keep from laughing.

We then kept to the business of the breakfast meal for awhile, and as I ate the thought of the milliron mark came to mind and that I hadn't a clue of what a milliron was. I knew what it looked like drawn out but what it was as compared to a slash, bench, quarter circle, or rafter I had no idea.

"Jed, can I ask you a stupid question?" I inquired.

"Sure. It won't be the first time someone has asked me one," he accused unforgiving while looking at J.W. with a smirk.

Everyone looked up while eating, curious to hear what my question was.

"What exactly is a milliron?" then I added, "I can't figure it out. I even asked the brand inspector once but he couldn't tell me. He said that he took it for granted that it was just a mark."

"Well let's see, a milliron is basically a yoke or C-clamp used to hold some sort of axle in place. They're used a lot with mining machinery back when belts operated or drove the many wheels for crushers and such. You can find small millirons holdin' axles on the wood benches of them old sandstone grindin' wheels or holdin' the axle on a wheelbarrow. Some early rancher probably had to come up with a brand to register his cattle or horses an' went to his iron scrap pile an' found a milliron there, an' turned the already shaped piece of iron into part of his brand. An' later others took it up as part of their brands also. That would be my guess," Jed explained.

"Hell I didn't know that. Just took it for granted myself. Never even gave it a second thought," Clint declared.

"Hum," mumbled Tom.

J.W. just looked at Jed with a glazed and sheep like expression.

Archie came into the kitchen carrying his mug of coffee followed by Sylvia at his heels.

"Mornin', men. Looks like a beautiful day out there!" he bellowed.

"Mornin' sir," everyone replied in varying tones of enthusiasm.

"More coffee, Archie?" Little Raven suggested as she returned into the kitchen.

"No, not just this minute. I've got half a cup here and it's cooled off enough for Sylvia. Just need a dab of milk or cream in it."

Little Raven went to the frig and pulled out a bottle of milk, "Here you go."

I watched as Archie put the spot of milk into the cup then after stirring it poured it into Sylvia's dog dish. The dog lapped it up in two shakes and then watched Archie as if to say, "Got anymore?" She watched Archie go to the stove and pick up the coffee pot, then pour hot coffee into his empty mug. Her stub tail wagged with anticipation.

"Coffee's pretty strong this morning." He said casually.

"Strong is heap good. Need much sugar." She said in pidgin Indian, grinning.

"Heap black too!" Archie mimicked.

And Little Raven chuckled as she poured more pancake batter on the grill.

"You want breakfast now also?" she asked.

"No. Maybe in a while when Emma gets up."

Little Raven gave him a wondering look.

Archie and Sylvia left the room and I leaned over to Jeff and said, "I've never known a dog to drink coffee in all my life. Can't believe Sylvia likes it."

"When Sylvia was a pup Archie started to give her milk with a drop or two of coffee in it an' eventually cut back the milk and added more coffee. But she won't ever drink her coffee black. Always has to have at least a couple drops of milk in it before she'll drink it."

The other men looked at me and smiled.

"Wish I'd trained my dog Arnold to drink coffee," J.W. put in, "She was the best mutt I ever had until an eighteen wheeler got her one day. I buried her in a tree Indian style, wrapped in an Army blanket."

Arnold a she? I thought but didn't want to ask as I glanced out of the window and could see the other dogs at the barn hunting around. The Border collie lay in wait as she kept her eyes on Jed's horse tied near the corral.

In my later years I discovered that caffeine is very toxic to dogs and will shorten the animal's lifetime considerably.

*   *   *

HOOLIHAN
CHAPTER 9

Jeep and Sioux and the rest of the horses spent most of their days and nights roaming a large pasture with plenty of grass to eat and a stream, to drink from when they were not needed to work off of. Normally the remuda horses were rounded up when necessary and brought into the big corral, where we caught them either by just walking up to one and haltering it. Or at times J.W. would rope each of the day horses to work with. J.W. was also generally the one that worked the three and four year old horses. It was his job to turn them into good smart cow ponies.

After saddling the animals we began work. I was told that in the spring, sometimes Archie bought a few rough stock horses, which would be worked into working cow horses. Archie would retire one or two of his older horses at auction as good kid's horses because they were very much "bomb-proof" to everything under the sun. But according to Tom, Archie hadn't invested in rough stock for some years now.

My first day was mainly helping Jed with feeding, mucking, watering and grooming the thoroughbreds. One of the horses had managed to tear up a back leg and Jed did the vetting while I held the horse. After which I was to find where the horse had caught himself in the stall. A T-hinge had come loose from the bottom of the stall gate. I found two of the screws in the saw shavings and fixed the hinge using carriage bolts in place of the screws.

That afternoon I saddled and exercised the thoroughbreds in a back paddock. That took most of the afternoon. I'd groom one, saddle and bridle it. With the first horse, Jed had to show me how to saddle him since I'd never used an English saddle before. Then I'd ride the horse at a lope, canter, and a gallop for a time; cool the horse down at a walk. And repeat the process on the next horse. The one with the injury I only groomed in the stall. By the end of the day I felt more like a jockey than a cowboy. I had caught Archie and Emma Braddock watching me with the binoculars from a window in the main house. Archie had later come out to see me exercising one of the mares.

That afternoon Jed told me that Emma wanted to see if I could handle her horses.

"Think I passed?" I asked dubiously.

"I believe so," Jed cautioned.

"I'm no jockey."

"Maybe not, but you're light enough and did good for your first time on an English saddle."

"I sure would have rather had a western saddle on those horses but by the end, it felt okay with that postage stamp saddle. Almost like riding bareback if it wasn't for the stirrups."

"Well it looks like you may be Mrs. Braddock's new horseman. Tom, Clint and especially J.W. won't ride English. If forced to they'd quit first," Jed confided, then added as if I might be thinking the same as Tom, Clint and J.W., "But come spring Archie will have you cowboyin' and Emma will have to hire her own groom and rider. She's into all that horse paper stuff, you know, like who's the dam and what stud sired whom. All that fancy bloodline and looks. Archie and I mostly like a horse that works cattle good. Don't matter who his or her daddy or mom was or if he looks like he belonged to the queen of England."

I nodded my agreement though I liked having been able to have the opportunity to ride such fine horseflesh.

"Don't get me wrong, there's some great thoroughbred cow horses between the Mississippi and the Pacific. J.W. loves thoroughbred horses, just can't stand those English saddles. In fact he said that while he worked on the Cross Heart Ranch in northeastern Nevada most of the horses working cows were thoroughbreds, not quarter horses." Then added as an afterthought, "That's buckaroo country, everything is done only off a horse. If it can't be done off a horse, it don't get done by a buckaroo. Hell, he even will ride his horse from the bunkhouse to the kitchen for mess."

"That's what I've heard," I replied, then added, "For just a cowboy, he sure has the best looking trappings for himself and the horse I'd ever seen."

"Find trappings comes with the ol' buckaroo tradition," Jed responded.

J. W. was always dressed to the "nines" in the vaquero custom. He wore a vest, pocket watch with horse hair braided chain with two bull elk tusks as fobs, red or black silk scarf around his neck, leather sleeve cuffs to protect his wrists, a flat crowned and straight wide brimmed black hat and his custom made high topped Paul Bond boots that must have set him back over a hundred dollars or more. He had told me that the boots were style number 13, made of wax French calf leather. They, like Jed's had sharp undercut heels. When riding J.W. had on his Adolph Biancani silver mounted spurs with two inch rowels including jingle-bobs that hung at the shank of the spurs and when he walked or rode chimed against the rowels. Man and horse always knew when J.W. was coming or going by the ringing of the jingle-bobs.

* * *

Jed and Tom would play a few games of dominos or checkers at night then turn in as late evening darkness gripped Montana. Clint was an avid reader and Archie had given him the right to borrow books from his private library to read and at times spent occasions after dinner with Archie talking politics or world affairs or playing chess on the front screened-in veranda. J.W. was either drawing horses in pencil or plaiting split rawhide strings into hondos with a turk's head, button reins, bosals and other tack. With different color horsehair he would make *mecates*. Which is Spanish that we pronounced "McCardy" that is a twisted horsehair rope used with the bosal to make a hackamore. The mecate became a combination of rein and lead rope.

J.W. had decided to hang at the ranch instead of heading for town one Sunday that I was on weekend duty at the Milliron while the others had the day off. I was watching him practice throwing a hoolihan using his braided *reata* in the corral. Roping from the ground he held his loop on his left side and then swung it with one revolution over his head and throws it over the snubbing post in one fluid movement. He worked at this skill all afternoon between breaks of rolling and smoking a cigarette.

I never saw him spill a loop or miss a catch with that rawhide rope. He had traded a set of silver mounted Garcia spurs for the 60 foot rope with another buckaroo in Elko, Nevada. He bought or traded for the best of trapping for himself and his horse.

After the weekend chores I would read or write Sue or Ma and Dad. There was no use in dropping a line to Kipp because the little shit was always busier than 'a one legged man in a shit kickin' contest' getting himself and his two confederates into some mischief.

I had received four letters from Sue in the first week of our separation all at one time since the mail wasn't picked up from town at the Musselshell P.O. but once a week. Generally the mail was picked up on Friday, by Archie, or occasionally Little Raven on her way back from her monthly food shopping trek to Billings with Jed as her driver. She could drive but didn't, she did not care for it and so Archie gave her Jed as her chauffeur for that day. This gave Jed the opportunity to get a haircut and a carton of cigarettes or on a whim a tin of thin cigars called In-between the Acts. To me that first week was the toughest when the evenings came because there wasn't much to think about except missing Sue and wishing I was in bed with her instead of lying around in a bunkhouse with a bunch of cow hands that snored, farted and groaned a good part of the night while in their sleep.

Sue had told of the move, the new house and her new job as a waitress at the Sheridan Hotel where she was making very good tips from wealthy customers and how great everyone there was to work with. She said she missed me and wished that I were working a ranch closer by.

I wrote her back telling her about this and that, such as how bad the gadflies had been, driving the cattle and horses nuts while they were at some parts of the creek. I also wrote about J.W. the buckaroo and how deft he was at throwing a hoolihan over the horses and never missed.

I wrote about how I missed her very much. I didn't dare say anything about how horny I was thinking about her. I had a fear that her folks might find and read my letters that I sent to her. But as always I signed off with I miss you, Love Dakk.

As weeks passed and time became a bit more limited because of work, both Sue and I found that letter writing had become less often on both our parts.

* * *

One morning I went into the can for my three S's (shit, shave and shower) as Jed was coming out with just a towel wrapped around his middle and still a bit of shaving cream by one ear. And that was the first time I'd seen that much of his hide on him before this. As he passed me and turned towards his bunk I noticed that one arm and part of his back was covered in large rough shaped old scars, some of which looked rather deep.

"Mornin'," I had said as we passed each other and he replied, "Yup!"

I didn't dare ask him what caused the old wounds, though I had a feeling that he knew what I was thinking at the time that I saw him. He'd tell me in his own time at a right occasion, if he wished.

A few days later while working with Clint, we were riding out to the bull pasture to check on them. While we stood and sat overlooking some cows on our way, I kind of casually asked him if he'd ever seen the scars on Jed's back.

"Yup, I saw them once an' couldn't get my mind off of them and just up and asked him what caused his injuries," and Clint just leaned forward, looked down at his hands that lay folded one on top of the other over the saddle horn while we sat on our horses, but he wasn't saying anything more.

"And!" I said staring at him.

"Well, Jed was in the second World War, Army Air Corps. Flew in a B-17 Bomber with the 100th Bomber Group. Said his plane was called "Miss Irish." You see he was a belly gunner in that plane. Stuck in that Plexiglas rotating turret bubble with two fifty caliber machine guns. An' one time while flying a mission over I don't recall where. Anyway the B-17 was hit by flak in the fuselage just behind the wings an' the belly turret. That's when he also got hit with the flak by God. Plane made it back to their landing field an' he ended up in a hospital. Lucky his pilot was good at the controls," he explained.

"He's lucky to be alive," I stated.

"Yeah, lucky. Well if you're ever with him some place an' there's a juke box you'll see him plunk in a dime an' press B-17 no matter what. One time we were in this café and he played B-17 an' some odd music started to play. One day after he played B-17 I asked him why he picked that awful song an' he says, 'Don't care about the music, just like playin' B-17.' Wanted to ask why, but figured he say if he wanted to tell me. You watch, he will do it every time. He hasn't said why he does that as yet. An' I'm still waitin' for the why. Must be for luck? Hell, ain't it like the Army," Clint went on, "to stick some guy that's as tall as Jed into a gun turret as small as a baby's crib? I'd be what's called, what? Closter . . . phobic I guess and scared to Hell while shittin' my pants."

I had never seen a B-17 Bomber let alone a gunner's turret, so I couldn't imagine what he meant by the last statement but knew it must have been Hell for not only Jed but all the airmen being shot at.

I set my horse to a walk and we rode quietly the rest of the way to the bull pasture. I'd watch to see if Jed would play B-17 if we were in town together someday and near a juke box.

*　　*　　*

A weekend had arrived and I had a chance to get away for awhile. I left the ranch before supper. Little Raven had been kind enough to put a couple of sandwiches wrapped in waxed paper and an apple in a bag for me and I had filled my thermos with hot black coffee. Little Raven knew I was going to see my gal. As I drove off Misty sprinted full bore ahead of me trying to cut me off and herd me back. I could hear the black and tans bay behind me. Misty finally gave up and raced back to the other dogs that waited at the barn.

I was now heading for Sheridan and my heart-throb Sue Palmer. I'd stop and call her in Musselshell at the pay phone. I didn't want to use the ranch phone because it was hard to have any privacy unless you asked if you could use the phone in Archie's office if he wasn't in there working.

It was dark by the time I parked the International by the phone booth. After fishing out my change from my pocket I went into the booth only to discover that the overhead light didn't work, so I went back in the truck and unlocked the glove box, got my flashlight out next to the Luger and box of Trojans. I called Sue's number but misdialed and quickly hung up before it rang having caught myself putting my finer in one wrong number and dialed; only my money didn't drop down into the chance pan even after I pushed the change button repeatedly.

"Son of a bitch!" I swore.

Then I remembered how the KCC's had discovered that if you crammed a ball of cotton up into the change redeemer it would not let the money fall back out and into the pan if the number the person was calling didn't answer or the line was busy. Most people would figure the phone was screwed-up and walk away indignant at the telephone company. Then every few days one of the KCC's would go into the phone booth, make believe he was making a call and while doing so, stick a hook made of baling wire up into the change compartment, pull out the cotton out and change would drop down and they'd go buy pops or cigarettes. They did this to about five or six telephones booths around town and near the trails they most traveled.

I reached a finger up the change receiver and sure enough it was clogged. Someone locally must have come to the same idea as the KCC's. But I managed to unclog it with my pocket knife and a dollar ten cents in change dropped down.

It took the telephone company awhile to figure out what was going on and awhile longer before they installed the little trap doors that kept kids like the KCC's from stealing the profits from Ma Bell out of the change receiver.

I finally got my call through. "Hello," said the familiar sweet voice.

"Hi Sue, it's me. How are you?" I blurted out.

"Oh, Dakk. I never expected you to be calling tonight. Well, yeah, I'm fine. How are you? Are you calling from the ranch?" she said with a hint of a subdued tone.

"Well I've got this weekend off, so I thought I'd come down to Sheridan and we could spend a bit of time together," I suggested. There was sudden a stillness over the phone.

Then she asked, "Are you calling from the ranch or Billings?"

"Neither. I'm at Musselshell. Heading your way as soon as I hang up." I went on, "Just wanted to make sure you were home so we could be together when I got there."

"Oh great," she said, paused and then continued, "Mussel-shell is a long way from Sheridan. How long is it before you get here?

"It's a good hundred and fifty miles maybe," I said, "How do I find where you're living when I get there?"

"You'll be on North Main when you enter Sheridan. Then just go west until you're on West Seventh Street and you'll see the house with a tall spruce tree in the front yard. It's easy to find. I'll be up waiting for you."

"I'll find it. It's going to take me hours to get there. I miss you, Sue."

"I miss you too, Dakk. Drive carefully," She almost whispered and hung up as I was about to say, "I love you."

I poured myself a cup of coffee while sitting behind the steering wheel thinking of what had been said on the telephone. I drove with my high beams on towards Forsyth and south. It would take me maybe three or four hours to get there, if I didn't hit a deer crossing the road in this pitch darkness. I saw six old Burma Shave signs in the headlights one after the other that read;

"Your shaving brush . . . . Has had its day . . . . So why not . . . . Shave the modern way . . . . With . . . . BURMA SHAVE."

The two-way highway south had a thousand mended frost heave cracks, repaired by the county workers pouring hot asphalt into them and then topping them with sand that the International tires chattered over the route.

There was no moon and slight cloud cover with only a few stars pinpointed in the sky. Moths and other night flying insects splattered the windshield leaving snotty splotches.

*   *   *

It was sometime after ten that I pulled into Sheridan, Wyoming. I had drunk all the coffee and devoured the lunch Little Raven had given me and smoked almost half a pack of Luckies. The only thing big I had hit on the way down was a jackrabbit that had darted across the highway a little too soon. I had seen one single deer next to the road, her golden fluorescent eyes mesmerized by the headlights, but she bounded away back into the fields as I passed slowly by.

On reaching Sheridan I had no trouble finding where Sue lived. The towering spruce was a dead giveaway of Sue's new residence on West Seventh Street. A light came on the porch as I pulled up to the curb and parked. Sue came out wearing a sweater draped over her shoulders and her purse in her hand. I could feel the coolness of the night once I got out of the truck.

She walked to me as I hurried towards her and pulled her to me and kissed her. At first her kiss felt bland, but changed and suddenly became more passionate.

"I sure miss you," I said.

"I miss-ed you—too," She stammered, "We've got to get away from this house before Dad or Mama wakeup. Grandma's deaf so she's no worry. Let's go," She insisted.

She pulled me towards the truck and got in and I rushed around to the driver's side and I drove off slowly without me slamming the door or racing the motor.

"Where do you want to go?" I asked lamely as soon as we were down the street a ways.

"I should have had you reserve a room at the inn."

"Well let's go on to the Sheridan and I'll get one, I've got money," I suggested excitedly.

"Okay. I don't know the night clerk and he doesn't know me so that will be alright. But we don't have any luggage?"

"I've got my war-bag with a change of clothing and shavin' stuff that should pass," I assumed. War-bag was what we cowboys called our traveling bag.

"I hope that works. I don't want to lose my job over this," she forewarned.

"You want to try one of the tourist cabins on the outskirts of town instead?"

"Only if it looks like getting a room at the inn won't work."

The Sheridan Inn opened in 1893 and had electric power from the start; it is a three story building with a gambrel roof with a total of 69 gables protruding from each side of it and a grandiose white—columned porch that ran the length of the building. This historic inn once was partly owned by William F. "Buffalo Bill" Cody. The historic Sheridan had been advertised as "the finest hotel between Chicago and San Francisco" and it had been visited over time by numerous dignitaries and some royalty.

We entered the lobby of the Sheridan. The place was empty; devoid of humanity, not even the desk clerk was to be seen at the front desk. It was understandable that no guests were around; after all it wasn't the height of tourist travel at this time of year. But no desk clerk?

We looked at each other confused. "Maybe he's in the restroom," Sue whispered to me.

Yeah, I thought. *Maybe masturbating or drinking cheap wine.*

We walked up to the front desk and Sue was about to ring the bell for service but I stopped her and put my finger to my lips so she'd stay quiet.

No sense lollygagging around here, I figured.

Quickly I slipped behind the desk and took a key from one of the top floor pigeon holes that held room keys and mail drops. Then I hurried Sue up the staircase and on up to the top floor. I looked at the brass key tag's room number, found the room and we entered it. I turned on the light as we entered and I closed the door and locked it. It was a very nice room, big bed, nice sitting chairs, table and wonderful bathroom with a big bath tub and shower.

"We'll get caught being in here," she objected.

"I don't think so, but if we do I'll just lie and say we needed a room but there was no desk clerk even after we rang the bell and we being tired didn't think of signing the guest book. I just grabbed a key and we went to the room to sleep, planning to square everything up in the morning. Simple as that," I told her.

"Well, I've got to be downstairs at the restaurant by ten to six in the morning to work. I couldn't get time off on such short notice," she explained, "I'll just sneak down and no one will know I was here all night." And she went on, "You can come into the restaurant and have breakfast after you shower."

"We'll shower together before you leave," I suggested.

Sue smiled and began to take her blouse off. I stepped up to her and we kissed as she undid my belt to my jeans. She took my hat off and tossed it on the bed. As soon as she did that I remembered my mother having said that setting one's hat on the bed was bad luck. *Just an old wives tale*, I thought to myself, like always leaving someplace by the same door you came in by.

Within seconds I had managed yanking off my cowboy boots with some difficulty, wishing that there was a boot jack around. Sue was already naked and in bed hiding herself under the sheet after having thrown the covers on the floor along with my hat and our clothes.

By now the whole idea of doing something basically unlawful had her adrenalin up and she was very sexually excited as I was myself. Within minutes we were both in the bed going at it like Tarzan and Jane.

The night was long on sex and short on sleep. But as usual, I awoke at five, we played some more, then showered together. Sue, after dressing, snuck out of the room and down to the restaurant to change into her waitress outfit and begin work.

A bit later I nonchalantly walked down stairs carrying my overnight bag and in the lobby saw the hotel clerk who looked more wasted than me having played with Sue most of the night. He was talking to an old lady and man, so I passed on by to the restaurant, hung my hat at the hat rack, set my war-bag down on a bench there after which I was seated by a hostess.

Sue was the only waitress in the restaurant and she came to take my order and acted as though she didn't know who I was. I ordered a steak and eggs OE, coffee and orange juice.

When Sue came to my table to present me with my bill she also slipped me a note and said, "I hope everything was to your satisfaction sir."

"More than I could have ever imagined," I said quietly and smiling. By now there were more customers in for breakfast. After she left the table I looked at the note, it read:

I get off work about 2:00. Come by we have to talk.

She hadn't signed it. I put it in my pocket. Left a two dollar tip and went to the cashier and paid my bill, put my hat on grabbed my bag and left the Sheridan Inn.

I drove around the town. Wondered why she hadn't signed her note, "Love Sue" but let it pass; she might have had to cut it short for some reason.

I spent some time at a saddle shop, lunch at a café, read the Sheridan Press paper and browsed a bookstore with a nice collection of arrowheads in cases on the wall behind the cashier. The cashier allowed me to inspect the arrowhead cases after I bought a book by Hemingway called, "The Old Man and the Sea." I sat at a table in the bookshop and began reading and found myself yawning, not because the book was anyway boring but that it had been a very short night. By one thirty I needed some coffee and it was about time to meet Sue at the Sheridan Restaurant at two.

I sat at a table and kept my hat on. A waitress coming on the new shift came to take my order.

"What can I get you this afternoon, cowboy?" she said with a smile.

"Just coffee, please. I'm waiting for someone."

"Black?" she asked, knowing it was most likely a lame question since most cowboy types drank their coffee black.

I could see Sue in the back at the waitress station going through her ticket receipts and tips. She disappeared from my sight as the new waitress came with the coffee pot and filled my cup.

Ten minutes later Sue came into the dining room with her regular clothes on her, the same as she had on when she greeted me the night before. It was a full black skirt with a carved Ranger belt and silver buckle, her white blouse and penny loafers. She was carrying her sweater and the clutch purse.

The new waitress had now gone back into the kitchen.

I was about to jump up and kiss her right there and then.

"Come on, let's get out of here before Dottie comes back out. I don't want her to see us together," she urged.

I tossed fifty cents on the table, *a dime for the coffee and a forty cent tip for the waitress, that should make her happy*, ran in my mind.

We walked quickly out and to my truck.

"Can we go for a drive? I don't want to go home just yet," she said sounding a bit miserable.

We drove around until we were by the cemetery. No one was around. So I parked.

Sue had been quiet all this time and I couldn't figure out what was wrong or if I had screwed up somehow.

"You're awfully quiet. What's going on? Did I . . . .," I was saying when she burst into tears.

"I'm pregnant," she blurted out between sobs.

*   *   *

Sue was now in a family way. She had been having sex with the chef from the Sheridan Inn. He was in his early thirties, divorced with two kids that his ex-wife had custody of. She and the kids had gone back to live with her parents in Buffalo, Wyoming, who owned a small sheep ranch south of town.

He and Sue planned to get married right after the holidays once things had settled down at the restaurant.

Saturday afternoon I headed back north to Montana, the border only a few miles away. I felt totally disillusioned by this new situation. My love for Sue, plans I had made in my head about the two of us, the future, now all hope was heading for the crapper and my life seemed on its way to being flushed into the sewer. I guess I should head for Billings and home.

Fifty miles into the state and just passing the Black Angus Cross Heart Ranch, I saw two coyotes lumbering across a wheat field checking between the stubble rows the swather had cut, hunting for an unsuspecting mouse or mole, when a rabbit spooked and the chase was on. The rabbit lost and the coyotes trotted off, one carrying the hare, head held high as the other coyote tried to steal it and did.

Son-of-a-bitch. Well ain't that the fuckin' way life is some times. Hope! Yeah. Well shit maybe there is hope, Dakk. Pull your boots on one foot at a time and keep on goin', and as Dad would say, life's short with many bumps on the way, I thought in my mind as I drove the highway north and listened to the truck tires thump over the pavement's frost rifts.

My life right now is cowboying. I pulled the pack of Luckies from my pocket and lit a cigarette, letting the smoke weep from my nostrils slowly.

I accelerated back to the Milliron slash B. The beauty of the countryside soon fell to the shadows of evening and the Montana coulees became deep royal purple scars.

*   *   *

GETTING BOOT
CHAPTER 10

The fall horse sales were being held in Billings and the paper had advertised that there were some fine horses from the Boot X horse ranch out of Jordan Valley, Oregon.

Archie and Emma Braddock loved going to the horse sales every year. But this year Emma didn't care to go. It may have been because of an argument she and Archie had but Archie was going no matter what. Emma knew that Archie would flirt with the women at the sales and in town which usually made him feel better knowing he still had it in him as a ladies' man and things would be great around the ranch for some time. Archie's flirtations never seemed to annoy Emma. She just took the whole thing in stride.

J. W. had received a check from his father for a grand which was yearly interest from stocks his father had invested for him and he had told Jed about it that day, "They just send me money so I won't come home. Personally I haven't the slightest interest in ever going east of the Mississippi River; it's too crowded back there. I like people well enough as long as they're scattered." It was as we all suspected: J.W. came from a family with money.

We considered that J.W. would trade in his 1950 Ford pickup for a new one. But when Clint asked him, he said no, the Ford was just fine, it ran good. What he was planning to do was buy himself a nice colt. That was if he could get to the horses sales that weekend. Clint said he'd work while we went to the Billings horse sales; he wasn't all that interested in going. Archie said he would meet us there. He liked the comfort of the Coupe de Ville rather than piling into a pickup with J.W., Tom and me. Jed would go with Archie.

We had moved all of the cows down from the hills to the lower pastures the week before and let them feed on the mowed hay fields after the bales had been pulled and stowed in the main barn. Once the snow fell, we'd have to feed them baled hay until spring. The cavvy, except Emma's thoroughbred horses, were in another pasture. The thoroughbreds wintered in the barn. Now that the gathering was over there was less to do until winter weather blanketed the ground white. So a two day weekend off was possible.

Working long hours and seven days a week had helped take the edge off of having Sue break up with me. The life I thought we would have together was now problematic. I just didn't want to take time off. By now the folks had heard from me about our breaking up. Ma had called the ranch one evening and Little Raven sent Jed to the bunk house to get me.

"You've got a phone call at the house. It's your Ma." Jed informed me.

"Thanks," and I headed for the ranch house and took the call in the office. Emma was making small talk to my mother, "Here he is now," she said, "Nice talking to you." And she handed me the phone with a smile of concern and left the office.

Instantly I thought something was wrong, someone was sick or Kipp had gotten himself in trouble or worse, hurt.

"Ma, is something wrong? Dad, Kipp okay?"

"Yes, everybody's fine. We just got your letter today. And I just wanted to say I'm sorry to hear that things went bad between you and Sue. I'm sorry, I know how much you liked her."

I could hear dad in the background saying, "Tell him life goes on. When I was his age girls were like missing a bus, there would soon be another one coming around the corner at any minute."

"I hope you didn't hear what your father just said because he's full of it. I was the only gal in his life back then and still am." She paused, and added, "I think?" And the conversation went on for awhile and we said our goodbyes. After which I thought of Dad's statement and he was probably right, but at this time waiting for another bus would have to definitely wait for some time.

Like Jed had said to me, "The heart is a slow healer but sex will keep it alive. You know, when I was your age, I was young and dumb and full of cum. Bet I've got a few bastard French or Italian kids runnin' around askin', 'Where's papa?'"

We met outside of Billings near the auction arena and grounds and had lunch at a diner, across the street from Letcher's Feed Store. The waitress sat us at the curved corner booth so all five of us could sit together.

"This booth okay for you gentlemen? Coffee all around?" she asked.

"I reckon this will do just fine. Much obliged. An' you bet, coffee all around," Archie answered as we all slid onto the curved red Naugahyde vinyl booth.

Jed sat across from J.W. and me and automatically plunked a dime into the juke box coin slot and punched B-17 on the selector and after the song that was already playing ended, Dean Martin began singing *"Memories are made of this."* J.W. had elbowed me so I would watch Jed's lure to play B-17.

Archie sitting next to Jed said, "You picked a good song for a change," as he pulled his Zippo out to light his cigarette. Jed just nodded. We ordered lunch and afterwards we all headed back to the sales.

*   *   *

The killer sales had been the first and all the horses and two ponies went to a slaughterhouse broker to become dog food. None of these horses were much good. They were old and mostly borderline "bear bait." A couple of them were blind, a pie-bald bay and a flea-bitten white. Another horse had horrible feet, she had never been shod or had her hooves trimmed and her hooves had grown out into paddles, causing her legs to become deformed. She must have been a yard horse that was obviously badly neglected. There was even one broke-dick draft horse that may have been one Hell of a stallion in his heyday. Thirty-three of these animals were headed for feeding dogs instead of bears and coyotes. That afternoon most of the horses that came up for sale were of no interest to any of us.

Archie, having become bored with what horses he had seen, looked around and found a ranch lady friend he knew that was with two other women from town. With no husbands to be seen there with them, he had instantly settled into his flirtatious big smile repertoire with this fine group of good looking women. One of which had her claws into him already by hanging onto his arm. He looked as though he was in his full glory, glancing at their breasts and shapely bodies. He was all smiles and acting very debonair in his fine suit, tie and 6x silver-belly Stetson.

After awhile he came over to us and said that he was going to town and would meet us at Casey's Golden Pheasant around eight that evening said, "Tell the club doorman you're with me, I'll be inside and maybe at the poker tables." He mumbled something about buying us drinks. I noticed him leaving with the blond that had her hooks into him.

Poker tables my ass, poking that bee-hived blond more likely I mused.

By four-thirty things at the sale were winding down, so we looked at the horses which would go on sale the following day, of which only one really caught J.W.'s eye, as well as the rest of our attention, it was a young stallion. He looked good, stood about fifteen hands, weighed maybe around a thousand pounds and was iron gray with a black mane, long black tail that almost touched the ground. He had a good head with bright eyes, with a confirmation that was almost perfect. He wore a few old battle scars from running with the wild herds and was definitely, as often wild horses are called, "a broom-tail." He had come in with the Boot X horses to be auctioned off on Sunday.

J.W. was all excited over the animal, "Did you ever see a color like that on a horse? He's a beaut'. I've got to bid on him. Got too!"

He had gotten his auction paddle with the number 77 and program at the same time that Archie had. Archie had number 76.

As Tom and I were walking back to the parking lot and while J.W. was out of earshot Tom said to me, "Well, you know what they say, 'a good horse is never a bad color.' If J.W. ends up with that stallion, I sure hope a good color doesn't become a bad horse. That horse could be a real wassup."

"You really think he's an outlaw?" I asked.

"Could be," he said shrugging.

Before leaving the sales I had called the folks from the pay phone at lunch time to let them know I was in Billings and would come home for the night. Ma had said that I could bring the boys home for supper and they could stay the night. There's the bed in the basement, the sofa and one could sleep in Kipp's room since he was going to be at Cooper's for the night. And I could hear Dad in the background say, "He's gone over there to watch '*Kemosabe*' and Silver on the TV."

Kipp, Cooper and Cody more likely were out finding some mischief to get into, and something that only the Lone Ranger and Tonto might be able to get them out of if they got caught.

I told her that Archie was staying in the hotel and the guys were staying at the new YMCA. The old YMCA having been on 29th Street since1905 had moved some years ago to 23rd Street. I said that I would come home for dinner but would be meeting Archie and the cowboys for a while and have a couple of drinks at Casey's that night. But that I'd come home after that to sleep in my bed.

"Casey's, oh, well, okay. Hope Mr. Braddock is buying, that's a pretty fancy club I hear. I'll make you and Dad some sour-dough pancakes Sunday morning," she declared.

Dinner conversation with the folks was all questions about the ranch, Archie, the other cowboys and, of course Sue. Ma had made lasagna that afternoon as soon as she knew I was coming home for supper since I just happen to like it and garlic toast. Ice cream was dessert.

I picked the guys up at the Y. We all again squeezed into the cab with J.W. sitting on Tom's lap and headed for Casey's Golden Pheasant. I parked my truck in the alley and we went around to the front door. Archie had shed himself of the blond and was at one of the poker tables being dealt his last hand which he lost graciously but not intentionally to the other players. Together we all went and had steaks in the Roundroom, with me as the exception since I had already eaten. But I sat at the table with the guys and drank beer. The place was packed with most of the large tables holding 15 and 20 patrons. I nursed a couple of beers while the others ate. J.W. was all jacked up over the gray stallion. And that horse was what most of the dinner conversation was centered on. After supper we had more drinks that Archie paid for and we listened to the band and by ten-thirty I drove the guys back to the Y and I went home to bed. Our big night at Casey's was enjoyable but uneventful.

Dad had gone to bed but Ma was still up knitting while watching television. We talked a little before we said our good nights and I went to bed feeling border-line drunk. I'd hook up my horse trailer to the truck in the morning.

Sunday, we all met in the same diner by the sale barn. The place was crowded with potential auction horse buyers. Eventually we were seated at a six top table and everyone ordered breakfast except me, I just had coffee, having had breakfast earlier at home.

By nine-thirty we were at the sales. Archie made his way around talking to other ranchers he knew and acknowledging good looking women with a smile and sometimes a wink.

Finally the auction started and most people sat in the bleachers with their assigned numbered paddle waiting for the horse they wanted to bid on. Most of the Boot X horses brought two to three hundred dollars and one came up for auction and finally sold for five hundred bucks. That was a lot of money for a wild one that they claimed was saddle broke. Which they demonstrated in the arena as a cowboy saddled and bridled him with a snaffle bit and rode him around, putting the animal through the paces in front of the potential buyers.

"This five year old is broke to ride and should become one good cow horse with a bit more work under his girth!" the lanky auctioneer barked over the P.A., "He sure is one pretty color bay, folks. Get him settled out and he'd make a handsome parade horse. Let's start the biddin' at three hundred dollars, folks!"

The auctioneer had to drop the beginning bidding to two hundred to start with but as soon as one bidder raised his number the bidding war began and at five-hundred dollars the auctioneer called, "Goin' once! Goin' twice! Sold! To number . . . thirty-seven!"

After lunch the iron gray stallion came up for bid and started at three hundred dollars and four bidders were at war against each other, one being J.W. The bidding moved up by fifty dollar increments and by the time the bids reached seven hundred two bidders had dropped out. When the horse's bid hit eight hundred, number ninety-two gave up and J.W. won the gray horse for eight-fifty. He sure was jazzed, even jumped up and down a few times shouting, "He's mine! He's mine! Yahoo!" and ran off to pay for the stud and collect the paper work and bill of sale.

"I wonder if that guy that ran the price of the gray to eight hundred was a shill for the auctioneer. The horse might be even be a snide," Tom ventured to me.

I didn't know how to answer Tom's question, so I said nothing as we walked to my truck.

I dug around in behind the truck seat and found an old lead rope and halter for J.W.'s new horse. I always carry these items as well as an extra catch-rope that I kept hanging from the rifle rack in the vehicle.

By now it was two o'clock and the sky outside was gray with the hint of snow falling a flake every couple of seconds.

I pulled the International to the gate and J.W. lead the gray into my horse trailer without any problem. If this horse is a snide he sure loads easy and seems to have a good head on him so far.

Jed and Archie had already left for the ranch and we soon followed, about a half hour behind them. What was looking like a possible snow storm by now had abated from Billings and the dark clouds had proceeded south-easterly.

*   *   *

At the end of October, most mornings were cold, your breath and that of the animals showed in the air and frost carpeted the ground. The horse herd was now growing their thick winter hair and their long whiskers began to show.

Early in November we had two snow storms, neither of much circumstance. Finally one good storm laid down a foot of snow that lasted on the ground, especially in places it had drifted three or four feet. The ranch and county roads stayed clear with the exception of some icy spots. Fortunately we had finished weaning out the yearling calves from their mothers. The calves kept their bawling continuously for days and nights for what seemed forever. Though the weaning pens were a good distance from the mother cows that mooed some for their calves, they still could be heard at the bunkhouse all night. It is always surprising how fast the calves grow in just such a short time. The spring-born suckling calves would be eating grass by the time they were three to four weeks old. It had been a good calving year with a loss of only 18 calves to a variety of mishaps and coyotes during calving time out of 847 bred cows. The calf count this year was up by eight percent from the year before, according to Archie Braddock.

Though the days were short on daylight, J.W. found time to work the gray stallion on most days. He often talked to the horse in a plaintive voice that was almost a whisper. The animal was fine under saddle and J.W. was riding him in the corral teaching him to rein properly and to respond to the commands of backing up, walking, trotting and loping. The day before he was about to saddle the gray, he rigged a night latch by using an old belt he cut down and punched a few new holes in it. Then he ran it through the gullet of the fork and over to the off side and buckled it like that on a suitcase in case the gray went to bucking thus giving J.W. a good handhold. Grabbing the saddle horn for support would be a useless hand hold if the bucking was fast and hard.

"You've got to have something more secure than the horn to grab. I'm no bronc rider," J.W. told me.

Now that he had the gray, he spent his weekends working the horse. I would ride Jeep or sometimes Sioux and J.W. on the gray would ride out together and get the gray used to working around the beeves. The horse was a quick learner once he had conquered his first fear of the cows. The first time he was ushered close to a cow, he buggered up and tried to make for the high country but J.W. got him settled down by disengaging the animal's back legs and feet by pulling the horse's head around to one side until its nose was at the saddle and he was headed in the direction J.W. wanted him to head. Then he walked him off towards the cow. As soon as the gray learned that the cows or steers feared him more, he began to enjoy the sport of making them move and being driven. J.W. was hoping to soon teach his horse how to cut out a certain steer or cow from the rest of the herd. The gray seemed to be a very savvy horse.

J.W. wanted to name his horse but was having a hard time coming up with one that fit the animal. Tom said to call him Gun Barrel or

Cannon Ball. Jed said, "Just give him a human name because he could change color as he gets older."

I suggested he should be called "Pot-Luck." Because to me it was like pot-luck he ended up getting the gray. This was a name J.W. kind of liked. Then one day he awoke all excited and said he had a name for his horse but he wasn't going to tell us until we next went to town and could drink to the gray's name and make it official.

* * *

The weekend came; Tom hung at the ranch while Jed, J.W., Clint and I headed for Billings. We arrived after dark and decided to have a few beers at a bar not far from the Pronghorn Café before having dinner there. Jacob's Bar was a dingy hole, nothing like the Golden Pheasant but the alcohol and beer was sold cheap in this establishment. It was a very large barroom, poorly lit; walls wainscoted in dark wood with everything a dismal veneer by years of cigarette and cigar smoke. Pool tables, a poker table in the back of the pub, cigarette machine, two pinball machines, shuffleboard and a jukebox that Jed fed a dime into and played B-17 as soon as he saw it. While the rest of us walked straight to the bar at which there was only one old drunk sitting at the far end, J.W. ordered beers and a shot of Jack Daniel's for all of us as Jed sat on a stool next to me.

"The wayward wind is a restless wind, a restless wind that yearns to wander . . ." filled the bar as the bartender set four beers in tall glasses in front of each of us along with a shot glass and began pouring J.D. into them.

The old drunk with droopy eyes looked our way expecting J.W. to include him in our celebration. J.W. feeling in good spirits pipes up to the bar man, "Give that ol' boy a drink same as we're havin'."

"This here drink is to celebrate the naming of my new horse. May he become my partner for as many good years that God will allow him on this earth. I name him *Llano*!"

"To Yeah no!" we all piped up and saluted our beer glasses into the air. Took a swig then picked up the J.D. and shot that down our throats in one fell swoop. The drunk only shot the whisky down and would nurse his beer until the next free drink came his way.

"*. . . and he was born the next of kin to the wayward wind . . . the next of kin to the wayward wind.*"

As B-17 ended we all shouted, "Here, here!"

"What's Yeah—no?" Clint wanted to know as much as the rest of us. We had never heard that word.

"*Llano* is Spanish, spelled L-l-a-n-o. The double L is pronounced like Y," J.W. enlightened us, "an' it means prairie, open plain. In eastern New Mexico, Texas and Oklahoma pan-handles is the plateau called the 'Staked Plain.' Some 40,000 square miles. That the Spaniards set wood stakes in the ground to measure the land with."

"Well I'll be dipped" said Jed.

"Well I sure like the sound of it. It fits him a Hell of a lot better than Pot Luck," I admitted.

"That sounds like the staked plains could be part of the XIT Ranch. A syndicate ranch in the western Texas panhandle," Clint put in.

"Didn't the XIT have a ranch here in Montana? North of Miles City?" Jed asked Clint.

"Yeah, sure did," Clint went on, "the Texas ranch was three million acres and they were all fenced in by 'bob-wire' like they say in Texas instead of barb-wire. Railroad car after railroad car filled with wire spools of barb-wire, I can't imagine, how many rolls of wire in them. An' they built 6,000 miles of fence. Shit! That's pretty much got the west all tied into wire from then on. My dad told me once that his father as a young man worked for the XIT in the late 1890's at the time the syndicate was starting to sell out some of the XIT property near Delhart, Oklahoma."

"Those must have been the days to cowboy in." I commented.

"Yeah, but after that all the dirt farmers came into that country and ripped up the land which eventually caused the Dust Bowl in 1930." Clint put in, "An' that's when the shit hit the fan: dust blew clear to the east coast."

The bartender poured another round of beers and J.W. paid the tab.

I was with the cowboys so I would be having dinner with them at the Pronghorn Café. I had to face the fact that just because Sue once worked in the place shouldn't make it an 86 for me. Eighty-six is generally the number used in kitchen and restaurant work as something being finished with or thrown out and even someone told not to come back into the establishment.

I had come in my own truck because I wanted to see my folks and the guys would most likely go out drinking before heading to the Y. I'd call Ma from the pay phone at the café and let her know that I'd be there tonight and not worry about me missing supper there.

Jed was riding with me to the Pronghorn and when we got there J.W.'s truck was parked across the street and I parked behind a familiar looking chopped hot rod Mercury, with a fancy metallic paint job that looked cherry red in the street light and I knew it was Zane's car. When Jed and I entered the café I saw Lee Pekhead at the back wall near the restrooms playing at the pinball machine with Zane Rhodes, Cody's big brother, watching him play. Zane nodded a hello to me as I sat down at a table with the other guys and I nodded back to Zane. Both had on black leather motorcycle jackets emblazoned on the back with the name "Rod Bandits," with a skull and crossed pistons under it. The two had enough Palmade in their D.A. hair styles to grease the hubs on a wagon wheel. Lee didn't see me. Jed was about to play B-17 but the juke box was out of order. The sound of the pinball bell was the only music in the place. We all ordered cheese burgers, fries and coffee with Jed being the exception, he ordered the special Salisbury steak, mashed potatoes and green beans.

We sat around eating and talking for almost an hour. Lee and Zane had quit playing pinball and sat at a table drinking coffee and smoking. I happened to look their way and Lee, after blowing a smoke ring into the air, put the cigarette back in his mouth and, as I was about to look away, he flips me off. Zane gives him a, what the fuck you do that for look. I just turned away and ignored Lee Pekhead for the pecker-head he was. They finally left the Pronghorn.

Minutes later, the old waitress comes by with a pot of coffee and our receipts and asks, "More coffee for you cowpokes?" as she hands out the bills for our meals. Calling us cowpokes is a derogatory name for cowboys. Cowpokes is a term used on rail—road men that used to use poles with sharp metal points to poke cattle on up the chute ramps and into cattle cars in the days before hot shots. Her tips dwindled down to next to nothing after that statement. We don't mind being called boys but being called pokes didn't cut it in any shape or form with us.

We walked outside and the air was cold. I buttoned up my coat and thought that I'd better take my long johns, sheep skin vest and that red plaid wool Mackinaw jacket Dad had handed down to me and my winter wool railroad cap with earflaps back to the ranch when leaving Billings this time.

J.W, Jed and Clint headed across the street to J.W.'s truck and I was about to get into my truck when I saw that the Mercury parked in front of me was idling and just then the passenger door of the Merc opened up and Lee stepped out as J.W. and the guys drove off.

"Hey! Shit stomper, I hear from Jolene that Suzie the slut got herself knocked up. Are you the daddy?" Lee asked curtly.

"For your info. Peckerhead! No! Not that that's any of your fuckin' business, asshole!" I warned.

"Who you callin' an asshole?" Lee said as he came at me, his fist clenched.

"If the shoe fits wear it, pendejo," I insisted. And he swung and I moved back but his fist caught me on the right eye and I swung back, nailing him in the nose. It gushed with blood. He came at me again this time missing altogether and I hit him in his side but ended up just bruising my fist because he had on the leather jacket. He grabbed at me and was trying to knee me in the groin and I got a hold of his throat and managed to knock him to the ground. I began pounding him in the face when someone pulled me off of him. It was Zane yelling, "Okay! That's enough, Dakk!"

I was going to swing at Zane also but he let go and backed off saying, "Hey! It's not my fuckin' fight but Lee's had enough."

I turned to see Lee still on the ground with his face bloody.

"You had enough, asshole?" I asked him.

He shook his head yes and was wiping the blood from his nose with his arm. Blood smeared the sleeve of the leather jacket.

I picked up my hat from the street, got into my truck, started it, backed away from the Merc and pulled out into the street and drove off.

"I'll kill that fuckin' cowboy asshole!' Lee ranted.

"Let it be, Lee. I mean after all you did say some real shitty stuff to him and you swung first." Zane remarked.

"Fuck him!" Lee swore.

*   *   *

At the house everyone was asleep. I pulled the ice cube tray out of the fridge freezer and cracked it open, sending a few cubes scattering onto the floor. After wrapping some into a dish towel I went up to bed. I could see a light on under the door of Kipp's room and suddenly he opened the door, "Thought I heard you," Kipp whispered, "what's a matter with your eye?"

I entered his room and closed the door behind me.

"Got into a fight with Peckerhead. We locked horns that's all," I stated.

"What happened? Why? Where?" he wanted to know and I told him the whole story including that Sue was getting married to some chef and that she was in a family way.

"You've got to watch out for Lee. He could do anything when he fights," Kipp warned, "You know, pull a knife or a gun. I wouldn't trust him. He's bad news."

"He's just a punk," I said.

"Punks can be dangerous."

"Yeah," I said and we left it at that.

To change the subject I asked, "How's the Model A coming along?"

"Show you in the morning. Got it chopped and welded, hood's off to be louvered. Got her decked and mostly all primed," he said all excited.

It was the wrong thing to ask at that time. It would have Kipp up all night looking through hot rod magazines for new ideas and making new plans.

"Love to see it even if I only have one eye to see out of in the morning," I joked and left for my bedroom.

My eye still blackened even though I had iced it and I had to replay what had transpired the night before to the folks at the breakfast table.

"Will you be coming home for Thanksgiving?" mother asked as I was leaving.

"If I don't have to work on that Thursday maybe. We'll see."

I had gotten back to the ranch before dark and was unpacking my winter stuff when Tom came into the bunkhouse.

"Well what's the stallion's name?" Tom wanted to know before he spotted my black eye.

"Llano, it means the plain," I said looking up at him.

"Nice shiner you got there," he said.

I just nodded in agreement, "Yep. Sure 'nough."

"I've had a couple now an' again over the years. Hope the other guy looks worse than you."

"He does, I'm sure," I promised.

"Did J.W. and Jed get into the same bar fight?"

"It wasn't a bar fight and they had left before it happened."

* * *

Little Raven had seen my black eye as soon as I had come into the kitchen that morning. Being the first one to arrive early I would catch her attention. But she never asked about it. She just went back to cooking again. I poured myself some coffee, sat down and lit up a Lucky Strike as the other guys came into the kitchen for their breakfast. I then iterated what had encountered to the rest of the group after J.W. said, "Nice shiner. How'd that happen?"

After breakfast we headed for the barn while Tom went to see Archie for our daily orders. Clint and J.W. went to the tack-room while Jed fed the barn horses and I started mucking out the stalls. When Tom got to the barn he gave out the day's work orders. J.W. and I jingled all the remuda into the corral to have their shoes removed by Jed before winter really set in. Tom, Clint and J.W. rode out checking the cows and then the weaners while Jed and I would exercise Emma's thoroughbreds. Then he and I would ride circle to the line shacks, inspecting fences on the way, checking the one room shacks as we went, since no one had lived in them from the end of calving last spring. Each cabin had to have a supply of firewood and some dry goods, coffee, flour, sugar, salt, beans, oatmeal, some dried fruit and a box of wooden matches, all kept in a couple of large tin containers to keep out the mice and bugs.

Having packed up by eleven thirty and after having eaten the noon chuck and gulping down a fast cup of coffee with a slice of newly baked pie, Jed and I saddled and rode out around one o'clock. The black and tans seeing the rifles thought we were on a hunt and started to head out with us when Archie called, "Chuck, Wally, Dusty! Here!" Reluctantly the hounds obeyed, their tails between their legs. Misty was helping Emma and watching the thoroughbred as Emma put one through its paces in the arena.

I rode Jeep and we had packed Sioux with two panniers of supplies including three cans of kerosene, one for each shack for the lamps. We had a thermos of coffee and sandwiches Little Raven had made. Each of us had rifles in our saddle scabbards in case we came across coyotes which we were to shoot. Coyotes would kill and carry off new born calves. They would hunt in pairs or more. One would divert the mother cow while another attacked the new calf and drag it off. It was two o'clock, that gray afternoon when we reached the first of the shacks; snow had started to pelt us with granules instead of flakes.

The cabin was a stone-walled affair, small with a bunk, table, an apple box for a chair and sheep herders stove. Another apple box shelf with a cook kit, metal dish, tin cup, frying pan, a cook pot, a set of eating irons missing a spoon and an enamel coffee pot, all covered with a coat of fine dust. There was a Prince Albert tobacco can with tobacco, cigarette papers and wood matches in it on a window sill with a kerosene lamp, the chimney needing to be cleaned and the wick trimmed. A book called A Field Guide to Animal Tracks by Murie, that one corner of the cover and dust jacket had been chewed up by a mouse; sat on the table, aside from the chewed corner, the book looked new.

There was an old Collier and Saturday Evening Post magazine in the wood box. The Collier with a few pages missing from it I tore out more and started a fire going in the stove. The cover of the 1950 Post had the illustration of a young cowboy bottle feeding a fawn on the cover. I looked to see who the artist was that had done the painting. It was someone called James Bama.

Outside the wood pile had to be restacked after lunch because a badger had hunted out some rodent or something and scattered wood everywhere. We covered the pile with some corrugated metal found near the dirt tank which was leftover tin from the cabin's original construction. The gray ghost of a cottonwood stood out naked with a raptor's nest high up against a sky of light falling snow.

At lunch in the shack, Jed and I ate, drank our coffee, smoked and talked. My curiosity having always been as they say 'the best of me' I turned the conversation to Little Raven and Archie. I wanted to know about their relationship.

"Well," Jed began, "from what I've once been told by Little Raven, her first name is Leslie, don't know if you know that? But she has always been called Little Raven, her Indian name."

"I figured as much. She's Crow, isn't she? Or is she Northern Cheyenne?" I asked.

"Yeah, she's a Crow, one of Plenty Coup's people through the generations," he ventured, "We were alone at the ranch one day an' I had come in for some coffee an' she sat down with me. Had coffee also an' we had ourselves a leisurely talk about each other's lives. You know, about parents, growin' up an' so on."

I offered Jed a Lucky and he took one, we smoked and Jed went on, "Come to find out her father was called Buffalo Bull Facing the Wind, or something like that. She told me she was a River Crow on her father's side an' her mother was a Kick in the Belly Crow. That's the clans. Which reminds me, do you know the real name for the Crows?"

"Yeah, I do its *Ab'saarokee*. Means 'Children of the Large Beaked Bird,' I'm not too sure if I'm pronouncing the name right but pretty sure on the meaning." I explained.

"Believe you're right, some say it's *Aps'aalooke*. Either way it's a mouthful," Jed theorized and added, "Looks like the snow stopped for a minute. We better move on."

Outside the three horses had been sleeping. We had un-loaded the store earlier for this cabin and I tightened the cinches on Jeep and also readjusted Sioux's britchen, and moved the rest of the stuff around in the canvas panniers to equalize the weight. Once that was done I hung one back on the sawbuck pack saddle while Jed hung the other one on the off side. With no top load I hadn't needed to bring a latch rope, only a cotton lead rope. The sun was making an attempt at shining but we knew it wouldn't last. To our west the sky was dark and hostile. We pulled our draped slickers that had kept the snow from building up on our saddle seats off, put the slickers on, mounted and rode off at a trot to the next line shack.

I knew Jed would start his story about Little Raven once we had a chance again.

By the time we made it to the third line shack it was snowing again and it came at us horizontally. Already there was a foot of it on the ground. The squeak from the old windmill was barely audible in the wind and snow. Its blades turning very slowly and the broken sucker rod swung in the wind as it rose and fell.

"Think we ought to camp here the night?" I cautioned Jed.

"Sure is lookin' like the best thing to do. Hope you remembered to bring some grain for the horses."

"Yeah, I did. Enough for a couple of days."

"Let's unload them an' put them up in the makeshift corral in back."

We unpacked and pulled the saddles off the horses and carried everything into or under the cabin overhang and I covered everything with a couple of pack covers and snow to keep the canvases from blowing away. Jed built a fire in the stove and made coffee while I hung nose bags of feed on the horses.

This small eight foot by twelve foot log cabin was no bigger than the other two line shacks, and all were furnished similarly. I brought in another load of firewood and dumped it near the stove. "Shit, it's getting cold out there." I said.

Supper was candy bars I'd brought and coffee.

"Look like we've got a bit of baking powder and soda in both these tins," I said, nodding towards the shelf on the wall. "We brought salt and flour we could make skillet bread, only wish we had some lard or bacon fat," I said.

Jed was moving things around so the two of us had a bit more room. "Hell I'm fine. Maybe in the mornin' if you're up to tryin' to bake some then." Jed said.

"Yeah, you're right; we'll need something in the morning besides coffee."

Jed made himself as comfortable as he could on the spring bunk. He'd laid out his chaps and slicker over the springs as a makeshift mattress and used his saddle blanket for a pillow. The mattresses were part of our bedrolls which we didn't have with us since we hadn't planned to have to camp in the line shack. We each had brought with us wool blankets tied to the back of our cantles. It would be a long night. A few snowflakes blew in-between some of the openings in the log chinking each time a breeze blustered from the west and Jed wrapped and twisted some paper to stuff into the chinking cracks. Now the place made a very good shelter.

I had melted snow in a pail on the stove until there was enough to make a pot of coffee. After my first cup of scalding coffee I went back out to check on the animals and pulled their feed bags off. All three had their tail ends to the wind and snow was piling on their backs. I went back into the shack after stomping my boots off of snow at the door. By now the place was warm and the lamp threw a golden glow throughout the shack. Jed was smoking another cigarette and had taken his jacket and shirt off. He sat on the bed in his stocking feet and long-johns; he'd hung his blue jeans up on a nail near the stove. The log walls had spikes strategically driven into them to hang whatever needed to be hung up.

"They okay out there?" he asked, as I hung my coat up to and pulled my chaps off and suspended my wool gloves on a wire that had clothespins on it to dry near the stove.

"Yeah, they're fine," I said as poured myself another cup of coffee and then sat on the only chair at the table with a wobbly leg and worked my boots off.

"Too bad we don't have a deck of cards," I said as I poured myself another cup of coffee and sat back down.

"We don't, besides I like playin' dominos better. Tom an' me both love dominos," he paused and then said as if out of the clear blue, "You know the expression, to boot?"

"Yeah, it means something extra to trade, a plus. It's like a baker's dozen, thirteen, where he throws in an extra to sweeten the deal."

"Well, you see that's what Leslie Little Raven was. She was boot in a trade."

"You're kidding me!" I said, astonished by what I had just heard Jed say.

"No, that's the truth as I was told by Little Raven herself."

"How . . . What happened? That she was boot . . . I mean?"

"Archie's father had money, was an attorney and Little Raven's father wanted him to buy some of his horses. But he wasn't interested in buyin' more horses at the time. You see Little Raven's mother had died some time back an' her father had a chance to go to work off the rez in California on building of the Golden Gate Bridge. He didn't want her to go to the Indian boardin' school. Plus he didn't want to take

Leslie with him, so Archie's father, seein' that Raven's father was in dire straits, bought the horses anyway an' got the kid as boot an' he an' his wife took in Little Raven an' raised her along with Archie. She was twelve an' Archie was ten at the time. She was educated here on the ranch by Archie's mother."

"Why didn't he want her in boarding school?"

"I guess he hoped she'd be better off livin' with them than in boardin' school. You see Archie's dad knew how to speak Crow an' had been instrumental in helpin' the tribe get legal representation now an' again. He was big in their cultural affairs as well. You see he had been taken into the tribe as one of their own. I've even heard Archie speak to Little Raven in her native tongue."

"So Archie speaks Crow? Didn't she want to go back to her father and the tribe after the bridge was built?" I asked.

"Well from what I was told he had some sort of accident while workin' that killed him. You see they liked havin' Indians workin' up high because they don't have a fear of heights like most of us do. They've got a name for bein' scared of heights, but I don't remember what it is."

"Acrophobia," I said.

"Yeah, that's it. Little Raven had no direct family left in the tribe after her father died. So she has been one of the Braddock family ever since."

"Does she ever go back to the reservation?" I quizzed.

"Yeah, she's got friends there an' goes to the annual pow-wows every once in awhile. But I guess she always felt more at home here on the ranch. She never got married that I know of. She lives, works and just maybe has always had a thing for Archie. But she has always gotten along very well with Emma as far as I know."

I made a makeshift bed on the plank floor with my saddle blanket, my jacket and used my sheepskin vest for a pillow, added wood to the stove and closed down the damper some. As Jed turned down the lamp's wick to let the light burn out, I could see the glow of his cigarette die as he extinguished it against the side of the metal leg on the bed and watched the smoke curl up to the ceiling and expire in the old boards as the lamp faded out. The line shack became pitch-black.

I finally went to sleep. Woke once and added another chunk of wood on top of the coals and went back to sleep while the out-side stillness bore no sounds in the cold of night.

*   *   *

TWO HEADED CALF
CHAPTER 11

Christmas and New Year's Day had come and gone and so had the months of January, February, and March. During which time I spent a part of the day feeding the bulls and other stock. Early every morning started out the same. I'd been taught by Clint how to harness the two draft horses. What was the proper way to put the collars on and where to attach the traces to the hames. I learned about stay-chains and how to hook them to the front axle then to the double-tree and adjust the length so there is a proper pull on whatever horse.

We used the wheeled wagon at first. Then as the snow built up we changed to the sled wagon, which had skids, wide runners that slid over the packed snow and ice. From it we fed baled hay to the cattle and horse string out in the winter pastures. Sometimes I drove the team while J.W., Clint or Jed fed out flakes of hay in a line as the sled moved through the snow at which time the animals would come to eat. When the temperature plummeted well below minus twenty degrees the cows wouldn't move to eat. They would just stand humped up covered with heavy frost with steam vapors escaping from their nostrils.

Most days we wore just about everything we owned to keep warm. We didn't exactly look like any Hollywood cowboys in winter; then again none of us ever look like Roy Rogers, Hopalong Cassidy, Gene Autry or the Cisco Kid at any time. Knitted wool watch caps covered our head and ears, heavy canvas sheepskin lined coats with high collars or wool lumberjack coats, wool and flannel shirts, flannel-lined denim dungarees or duck-canvas coveralls, long johns we all called our long handles, gloves, neck scarves and old boots a couple of sizes larger so you could wear two pairs of wool socks on our feet in them. This was the cowboy dress for the winter days.

Jeb was the only one of us that was always warm in winter; he wore his well used Army Air Corps B-3 bomber flight jacket and sheepskin cap. Both had kept him from freezing in the unpressurized B-17 when they flew at high altitudes where the temperature would be 60 degrees below zero. He said more than once that he wished he still had the RAF flight boots that were sheepskin lined. It was his second sheepskin jacket issued to him while he was still in the service he had told us. He looked like a bomber pilot on horseback.

J.W. wore white wooly chaps that kept his legs warm and had also lined the tapaderos of his stirrups with sheepskin to keep his toes from freezing. Luckily the sub-zero days didn't linger as long as in some other parts of the country because we'd get a good Chinook wind that kicked the temperature up to fifty or sixty degrees and the snow would rapidly melt off.

When driving the sled team we'd take turns, one would drive while the other fed out. Driving was no effort since the Belgium's knew the drill from years of having worked pulling the hay wagon or sleigh. Once in the fields, if we were in a big hurry the driver would just wrap the leads to the sleigh's post and we'd both pitch out hay to the stock while the horses moved ahead at their usual slow plodding and carefree walk, kicking up snow and frozen clods as they moved forwards.

In April came signs of spring. The grasses greened, the willows budded, most of the snow had melted and the creek ran cold, roiled brown, high and fast. In a week they would clear and still run very cold.

The veterinarian had come on the ranch to check the mother cows. We had run them into a holding pen and sent one at a time down the alleyway and into the squeeze chute. There the vet would reach up into the cow and say, "She's good," meaning she was pregnant and she would be turned out with the rest of the mother cows. If the vet said, "Open," it meant she was not pregnant and would stay separated from the pregnant cows in another pen.

All of the mother cows had been moved up pasture, on to eight sections of new grass that would soon be the calving grounds. This was one of the most important times of the year with the anticipation of a good crop of calves with a low mortality count. Mortality came to a calf in a number of ways, first if the mother cow couldn't birth the calf because it wasn't facing head out with the front feet first, then you had a problem, or it was a large calf and it had to be pulled out, sometimes the calf would end up frozen on the ground because the mother cow would ignore it and if not found in the nick-of-time would die, on occasions it was stillborn and then there was the perpetual danger of coyotes attacking the newborn babies. Though coyotes generally made it through the winter months hunting mice and an occasional winter kill of a sick or aged deer, elk or other types of carrion to survive, calves and lambs became Christmas and Thanksgiving all rolled into one great feed in the spring for them. The cowboys had their hands full night and day checking the mothers and their newborn.

You pretty much knew if the cow was in labor, she would act restless, lie down and then get up and walk with an outstretched tail behind her. If a cow had retention of afterbirth and after which the fetal membranes are expelled, it could take anywhere from three to six hours after parturition for it to revert into the cow. This meant you had to keep an eye on her. You had to watch out for calves showing signs of scours, a diarrhea that is treatable with scours pills and antibiotics.

Anything and everything that could go wrong, at calving time would during the twenty-four hours of the day and night.

I was stationed at line shack number three through the calving season. It was called and known to us as the Jackrabbit Line Camp. It was the same log shack that Jed and I had holed up in for the night months ago. I'd have no time off and limited sleep until maybe just before branding.

Having arrived at the line camp fully equipped with bedroll, groceries, reading material and two notebooks, one small one to keep a record of ranch work and a larger one for a personal log, I made the place my new home. The place had water, plenty of stove wood and an outhouse by the corral that had a fair share of cob webs and a Sears catalog missing pages. I was glad to have brought along my own TP.

It would be sometime before I would be visiting 'The Magic City,' as Billings was called or see the folks and Kipp. Frederick Billings of the Northern Pacific Railroad had his name stamped to the town's location and because it grew so fast due to the railroad as if by magic, it became known as 'The Magic City' and the nickname stayed to this day.

Jackrabbit Line Camp is situated in a knoll with an early style of Aeromotor windmill that dated back to the beginning of the 1900's. It had taken a beating from nature and neglect over the years. It was missing some of its blades while others had been bent out of order and the vane had a few bullet holes ventilating it. The windmill no longer was used, it had been abandoned for some time, the blades spun in the wind and the motor squeaked and groaned. The broken sucker rod was wearing thin where it rubbed on the edge of the platform which looked like it had once been occupied by some large nesting bird. I had climbed up it and wired the vane to one side to keep the blades from running and squeaking. The storage drink tank still held water and was fed by a pipe that ran from a cistern tank that collected water from a new spring a fair distance away. The spring was located in a coulee overgrown by willows, tall sage and choke cherry bushes.

One spring day in camp I thought I had heard a coyote yelp a couple of times. I grabbed the .30-30, cranked a round into the chamber and slowly opened the cabin door. There it stood looking at something I couldn't make out in the shrubbery and tall brown grass. The coyote danced around and was bouncing to and fro from whatever it had encountered. I took aim and shot him. Suddenly I knew what he was after as the scent of a skunk registered with my nose.

Damn! Dumbass, I thought, *should have waited. Now I'd be smelling skunk for the next month.*

Luckily the coyote hadn't had a direct hit from the skunk. I hung him up on a fence post downwind and hoped what skunk scent that was on him would soon dissipate from the carcass.

"I smell a pole-cat," Tom said as he got off his horse who danced some, wanting to get away from the malodorous scent. He then added as he tied his horse to a post, "That galoot's smell will sure clear your sinuses."

"Yeah, it got into it with a coyote I shot today," I said as I began to explain the situation to him.

"Want some coffee?" I offered as I set the axe into the chopping block after having split kindling.

"No thanks, had some while at Little Sandy. J.W. says hi," Tom said, "I got a letter for you." And he pulled it from his inside coat pocket and handed it to me.

I looked at the envelope and saw it was Sue's handwriting and it had a Sheridan, Wyoming, post mark.

"Come on in. Had two calves born. One yesterday and another during the night. Both are doing well. The mamas are taking good care of them," I said, "How are things at White Rock and Little Sandy?"

White Rock was line cabin number one where Jed was and line shack number two was called Little Sand; J.W. occupied it.

I pulled my tally book out and went over the facts I had entered. I had tossed Sue's letter on my bunk. But I was in no hurry to know what she had written me. *She must be close to having her baby. She must look like she swallowed a watermelon by now,* I pondered.

* * *

That night I still hadn't opened Sue's letter.

Why she writing to me? She made it pretty clear that it was over between us.

I let the letter rest on the table. I needed to sleep on it, it could wait. Outside a light rain was falling. I lay in my bunk thinking I'd better check the cows during the night. I'd ride out every four or five hours to make sure any newborn were not in danger of dying from the wet weather or neglected by their mothers.

By three in the morning the rain had stopped, the sky had become clear and the stars shone but there wasn't any moon out. My flashlight was starting to get dim as it needed new batteries. I had lucked out, no newborn calves that night and none of the cows looked as though they would give birth soon. I was whipped and needed a few more hours of sleep. I returned to my cabin by six and crashed on my bunk fully clothed after I had unsaddled Sioux.

Sleep came to me until nine when I awoke from a dream or rather a nightmare. I dreamt that I was driving my truck down a country road when I heard a hissing sound and when I looked on the seat next to me there was a large rattler and it suddenly started to rattle vigorously. It was coiled and its head was ready to strike, only it had two heads with two long forked tongues flicking at me. I sat there in bed wondering why I had had such a dream. I hadn't seen a snake in months.

I had just saddled Jeep, leaving Sioux behind and a chance to rest. Mounted, I was headed back out to check on the stock when I saw Tom riding at a lope towards me. I put Jeep forward at a walk to meet Tom.

"No babies in the past twenty-four," I remarked as we each stopped side by side. "I was just heading back out when I saw you."

"Well. It was a wet one last night," he said matter-of-factly. Then he pulled a cigarette from his shirt pocket, lit it and dismounted, dropping the horse's reins to the ground. Tom walked off a few feet with his back to me and pissed. His horse being a good cow horse never moved, once the reins hit the ground. It stood and waited. I lit up a Lucky and shifted in the saddle to make sure my cinch was right and Sioux sidled to one side and bent its head to graze.

He came back to his horse buttoning up and puffing on his cigarette out of the side of his mouth.

"Sure had to piss like a race horse," he sniggered.

Tom gathered his reins and mounted again.

"You've got to ride to J.W. and give him a hand, he's got a cow that's in trouble and he may need your help. I'm headed back to the ranch to call the vet. I don't think we can pull this calf," he informed me. "I'll let Jed know when I get to White Rock and he'll join you." We both rode off at a lope. At Little Sandy, J.W.'s line shack, Tom told me I'd find J.W. a mile north, near the sandstone ridges. We rode off in different directions.

When I showed up the cow was humped up, her tail straight out and mooing. J.W. had her roped by the horns and tied her to a tree. Every time he walked too close she'd kick at him, then moo in pain.

I got off my horse and hobbled him, loosened the cinch and pulled the head stall off of him and let him graze along with Llano who was also hobbled and eating the new grass, withdrawn from near the cow and her distress.

"I don't think she's goin' to make it," J.W. observed.

"Want to see if we can pull it for her?" I said, getting the obstetrical chain and burlap bags from my saddle bags to use in case I had to wipe off a newborn.

"She won't let me near."

"I can rope a hind leg so she can't kick at you," I said.

"We can try."

I got my rope and building a small loop managed to catch hold of a hind foot and was about to tie it to her front leg when Jed rode up carrying a calf puller. With J.W.'s help we got her tied.

Seeing the predicament and looking the cow over, he says, "I think we ought to wait for the vet on this one. Hopefully he can save the cow. Tryin' to pull that calf looks more like a real problem. She's real big. Things just don't look right. Let's let her try to relax some."

After awhile Jed was able to get a hand in the cow now that she couldn't kick out.

"Yep, this surely goin' to be a problem," Jed vowed, shaking his head from side to side then said, "Vet's going to have to be the midwife on this one."

We heard a couple of trucks coming. It was Tom and Archie in Tom's truck and the vet in his pickup.

The vet was able to give the cow a sedative and he tried to reach up in her and then he finally pulled his arm out and shook his head as Jed had.

"What's wrong?" Tom asked.

"Calf's got two heads," he said point blank.

"What?" Archie said.

"Calf has two freaking heads."

"Shit!" Archie swore.

"It's polycephaly, more than one head, monocephalic is what it should be. Sometimes it's parasitic twin heads joined at the skull. But this one has two heads joined at the shoulder by two necks," the vet said.

We just looked at each other. I don't think even Archie really understood the vet's medical jargon.

"Can you get her to birth?" Tom asked.

"I'll have to cut it out. Do a Cesarean section. I don't know if I can save the cow. The calf won't live long, though."

Archie just shook his head and said, "Well Hell. Just give it a try. Don't mind losing a calf but not a cow. Hell, after you bill me the damn cow will have more papers as those high lineage thoroughbreds of Emma's."

The vet worked and sure enough it was a two headed calf with one body. Both heads looked alike in color and each head had one nose, two ears and two eyes. It was the strangest thing any of us had ever seen. The vet said that he had seen pictures of two headed cows, pigs and cats. But he had never seen one in person until now.

"Well this is for sure a phenomenon," Jed said, using the first ten dollar word I'd ever heard him speak before.

The vet was going to euthanize the calf but Archie stopped him, "Your bill will be high enough with the delivery and taking care of the cow. The calf we'll take care of."

"Okay then I'll finish and close up the cow."

"Tom, get your rifle and end it for this sorry-looking freak, will you?" Archie said miserably.

Tom dispatched the calf still covered with placenta by having put a bullet to its heart and then we helped load it into Tom's pickup to later be thrown into the old kill pile dump of one of the coulees used for that purpose.

"She'll come out of it here in a bit," the vet said about the cow, "You'll have to check on her every day. Let Archie know how she's doing and Archie, give me a jingle and keep me abreast of her condition."

"What I should do, is get this two headed freak calf to a taxidermist and have it stuffed so I can hang it on my office wall," Archie grumbled, "It should make for a good conversation piece."

I thought to myself, *wouldn't Fouche the snake museum man just love it for his museum. It would make a great tourist draw.*

*   *   *

That evening I was dog tired and hungry. My stomach had been growling most of the afternoon; none of us cowboys had eaten since the early morning. I decided to face the music and see what Sue had to say in her letter. But first I was going to eat. Canned beans, fried Spam and a scrap of skillet bread I had left over that was close to being brick hard which I used to soak up the bean juice in my plate. I had brought some Postum from home and made a cup of it to drink along with a can of peaches to finish the meal with.

Once my belly was satisfied, I propped myself with my back on the wall sitting on my bunk. Sue's letter had no return address on it. I opened the envelope by the glow of the lamp and began reading:

Dear Dakk,

I'm sorry that I've made such a mess of the relationship we had. I'm also sorry to have not gotten around to writing you after I broke up with you before now.

As you know Stuart and I were married so now I have a new last name. I'm no longer

Sue Palmer, I'm Sue Long.

Stuart is wonderful to me. That is not to say you were not. But things sometimes go deferent ways than we think they will.

Again I'm sorry.

I know I said I loved you and I did and still do but getting pregnant changed things in my life.

The baby is due next mouth. I hope it's a

Girl but a boy would be nice also. If it's a girl we'll name her Sandra or if it's a boy we'll call him

Jacob.

I hope we can still stay friends.

L . . . . Sue

I crumpled the letter as well as the white envelop and threw them into the stove and watch them burst into flames and burn up. In less than a few seconds the letter had gone up in smoke. I shut the stove door gently though I really wanted to slam it. *She couldn't even spell out the word love. L . . . Sue.*

*   *   *

The next morning I looked at myself in the mirror. I needed a shave. I hadn't shaved in three days and I couldn't remember the last time I'd taken a shower or a bath. The morning was beautiful, sunny and a very light breeze. *I'll shave and bathe after I make my circle and after Tom has been here and left.* I was thinking as I got Sioux, saddled and rode off, leaving Jeep to rest in the corral from the evening and early morning circle.

Sue was still on my mind but so was that two-headed calf when I saw one of the cows standing watching me approach and a short distance from her was something on the ground. I rode up to it and saw that it was a dead calf. She had cleaned it but it must have been stillborn. As soon as Sioux and I got too close she charged us. I swung Sioux around and hit with my spurs and we bolted away. The cow went back to her calf and stood guard. We rode back towards her again and once more she charged and we out-maneuvered her again.

If I roped her I'd have to dally her to my saddle horn. There is no tree around to snub her to and I'm not sure Sioux wouldn't get horned. To take away that calf from her isn't worth the effort right now. I pondered.

"Well, Sioux, there's nothing we can do for her. The coyotes get a free meal of veal on us this time," I said to the horse and we rode on.

I was back at Jackrabbit and had just heated some water and began shaving and heard Tom ride up.

"This must be shaving day for all you guys," he said, "When I got to Jed he was scraping the whiskers off his hide. Then when I rode into Big Sandy J.W. was drinking coffee an' had shaving cream still clinging to his face and that mustache of his all waxed an' curved up."

"Mine was starting to itch, figured I'd take it off since it's a pretty day. You know sun's warm, birds are singing and I'm thinking of baking some skillet bread because I'm out of bread," I told him. I didn't want to tell him I was planning a swim in the stock tank.

"I guess that's a for sure sign of spring around here."

"Yep, you bet," I conceded.

"I came across one of your cows stuck up this real narrow coulee, you know out by that bad land area. Why in Hell she was trying to climb up there is beyond my wildest guess. Had to rope her and pull her out. Damn cows don't back up like horses. Anyway, I almost had to pull her over backwards but then she turned in a wider spot in that cut-bank and just about run my horse and me over.

"I caught one up that same coulee two days ago only I got off my horse and with my rope, was trying to persuade her to back out. She finally spun around and bee lined out and as she did one of her horns caught my shirt and ripped it just about off me. Don't know what the fascination is to her for trying to climb up that coulee," I said.

"Fickle headed S.O.B." Tom ventured.

"I guess."

"Well that mother cow that had the two headed calf seems to be holding her own right now. We'll see." Tom speculated.

"Good," I said, then told him of the dead calf and the two new ones just born that were doing well.

"Jed has himself a poddy, the mother died. He's stuck bottle feeding until I get it back to the barn, then Clint can take care of it there. So you're better off losing a calf than the cow."

"Never heard the word poddy for an orphan before," I said.

"Is it just like the term little doggies but for the motherless calves?" Tom said then added, "Oh, that's an old term. It's what my dad called them. He worked in South Dakota on the Bent Arrow Ranch for some years before he got married.

"Is the Bent Arrow near the Pine Ridge and Standing Rock or the Rosebud?" I asked. With a name like Bent Arrow I thought it might have been a ranch close to one of the Indian Reservations.

"No. Farther to the east. Nearer to Abilene, Kansas."

I lit a cigarette while Tom loosened the cinch on his horse and let him graze with the rein ends dallied to the saddle horn.

"Still, sure hate losing calves," I said to Tom.

"It happens," he said, "You know when that cow of yours finally realizes she is protecting a losing case, she'll give up the ghost and move on. Might as well use that calf for coyote bait." Then he asked, "Do you have any number four or five Victor traps here someplace?" he asked.

"I haven't seen any traps around here."

"Jed's got some traps at White Rock. I'll bring a couple with me tomorrow." Then he asked, "You know how to trap?"

"My kid brother and I ran a trap line for a couple of winters and we did okay," I said, "We used both Victor and Newhouse traps. We caught twenty-eight weasels on aught size traps. Had to build trapping boxes and used chicken livers for bait. We found an ad in Field and Stream and ordered a 'how to' trap book."

"Good," he said then added, "Little Raven packed a bunch of roast beef sandwiches for my lunch. I'll share with you if you've got coffee."

"You bet! I'll put some more on."

After Tom left I took a bath in the stock tank and the water must have been forty degrees. I jumped in and was out faster than when I went in. I then soaped up and jumped in the cold water again to rinse off. This time I was in the water for maybe ten seconds and then out to dry myself off. But I felt great to be clean again, if only for a while.

Jeep and I made our afternoon circle. I watched a hawk plummet from the sky with great speed, brake with wings outspread, talons out, catch a young rabbit and take it into the air and land at a distant tree. I pondered what it would be like to fly. I had never flown in an airplane. I thought of Jed flying all those missions over Europe squeezed in that belly gun turret constantly surveying his surroundings for danger. That thought diminished the joy of wishing to fly, even as a bird.

That night the moon bleached the landscape as I rode out to check on the cows. I heard a war party of coyotes yelping, barking and crooning at the moon and stars as in a celebration.

*   *   *

As Jeep plodded along one afternoon heading back to Jackrabbit, my mind wandered to the ranch Tom's dad had worked, the Bent Arrow and it made me reminisce to when Kipp and I were just kids.

When Kipp and I were about eight and ten years old and playing Indians we had made bows and arrows to hunt with. I had done most of the construction of the weapons. The arrows were a deadly affair with points made from cracked open turkey and chicken leg bones we had sharpened on the sidewalk. The turkey and chicken bones we had dug out of the burn barrel. The sharpened bones became the arrowheads and using slit chicken feathers to make fletching I had built five or six good willow arrows. We practiced shooting at hay bales with a makeshift paper target on it. Then one day after reading a *Classic* comic book called 'Last of the Mohicans' we decided that we should get Goo Goo's dad to give us Mohawk haircuts. So we went to him and told him what we wanted and how it should look. He was very skeptical about it and asked if it was alright with our folks for him to give us Mohawk haircuts. We lied or rather evaded his question by answering that it was summer time, we didn't have school and that our hair would be grown out by the time school started.

"School starts in September and I'm not sure it will be all grown out by then," said Mr. Lewis the barber, with a tone of reluctance.

"We'll get crew cuts before school starts," I said.

"Did you bring a note from your parents for me, saying that it's okay to give you two Mohawk haircuts?"

"No, but it's okay," I insisted.

"Well I better call them and make sure."

"Dad's at work!" Kipp put in.

"Fine, I'll ask your mother," he said and rang up mom.

We didn't get Mohawks, just crew cuts.

Kipp, Cody, Cooper and I dressed up as Indians with war paint on our faces and bodies. We had on our bathing suits and made breechclouts from rags. We put turkey feathers in our hair held there with ribbon headbands. Cody had made a tomahawk using a piece of slate that had fallen from a roof in town. Cooper made himself a spear. The four of us were now fearless Mohicans, warriors ready to go on the warpath.

Not far from our house was an old two story Victorian home in a somewhat derelict state, we called it 'The Haunted House.' Ninety year old Mr. Walker, a long time widower, lived there with his old hound that had a baritone bark. Mr. Walker also had a multitude of Rhode Island Red chickens that were free range birds. The house was grayed from loss of the old white paint, had a few broken window panes, some covered with stained cardboard. One of the dormer windows was totally broken out and that part of the house had become a roost for white and slate colored pigeons. The house stood on two acres of overgrown weed-infested land. It had a few decaying outbuildings, one that looked like it had housed a milk cow, a dead apple tree orchard, and one ancient cottonwood giant that still sported a rope-tire swing that hung silent. The Walker property had a mesh fence around it, with aged 'No Trespassing' signs every twenty-five feet, along which grew a thicket of blackberry bushes that the chickens frequented to forage under for feed and cover.

We had determined that this was the place we would attack and the chickens were the enemy. We found a place in old man Walker's fence to crawl under, right below one of the no trespassing signs. Kipp and I crept on our bellies through the fence and bushes with our bows at the ready. We left Cooper and Cody at the fence as lookout guards on the house. I kept getting scratched by the blackberry branches but I could see some of the chickens scratching and dusting themselves in the dirt. I saw one fairly close to where I was laying, took aim and fired. It was a lucky shot but the chicken wasn't totally dead, she started up a real fuss that got all the others to scrabble out of the brambles complaining up a blue storm. Just then the old man's hound came bounding though the bottom torn out screen door barking and charging like a buffalo. I crawled to the floundering chicken I'd shot while not heeding to Cody and Cooper's warning for us to get out. I grabbed the dying bird, her wings flapping me in the face but I wouldn't let go. The screen door slammed shut at the house.

"What you damn kids doin' to my chick-ins!" yelled old man Walker at the top of his corky voice.

Kipp had gone back and was on the other side of the fence with Cooper and Cody now.

"He's got his shotgun!" yelled Cody, "Get out!"

I was almost at the fence, my arms and back bleeding from the scratches and the chicken in my hand with the arrow through it while she kept flapping her wings, when I heard the twelve gauge blast and felt some of the pellets cut through the foliage. Kipp, Cody and Cooper were already headed for the woods. Cody had dropped his tomahawk and left it where it lay. Once I was on the other side of the fence I ran after them. Another blast was heard from the second barrel of the shotgun above the barking dog coming closer to me at the fence.

"Don't you little shit-ass kids ever come back here!" Walker yelled at us as we disappeared in the timber.

None of us were hit by the shotgun blasts but once in the woods with our hearts pounding we stopped for a minute to see if any of us had been hit. The blood on Kipp's and my body was from the blackberry brambles only. Once we thought we were safe, Cody and Cooper dug a fire pit and started a fire using a magnifying glass he'd found in his dad's shop. I had to wring the chicken's neck but she was pretty much a goner by then. I gutted and plucked her and we roasted her on a stick. We ate her after I figured it was finished cooking and we all thought she tasted real good once I cut the areas of burnt skin off with Cody's jackknife. Even though the chicken was a little on the pink side and somewhat tough, we finished her off, tossed the bones into the embers, added wood and did a war dance around the fire until the stink of burning chicken bones made us put out the fire. That night both Kipp and I had the skitters and we fought for the toilet.

Never again did any of us go on the warpath or trespass onto Mr. Walker's property.

*   *   *

THE CHIEF AND THE GOLDEN PHEASANT
CHAPTER 12

We finally got a couple of days off in May mainly because Archie had hired some waddies, a few drifter cowboys but most of them were ranch workers and vaqueros from Mexico as well as a Mexican cow camp cook.

The calf crop had grown tremendously and the loss of cows and calves not substantial. We lucked out only having a few orphans or poddies as Tom's dad would have called them. Thirteen calves in all had not made it into the world of the living. First-time mothers sometimes had the hardest times with delivery or acceptance of the newborn calf.

It was nice to be home for a couple of days and be able to sleep a full night's sleep and awake to a breakfast of eggs and bacon, juice, fresh coffee and sliced bread. How I loved Ma's pancakes with homemade berry syrup and butter, lots of butter. Ma thought I had been starving. She kept cooking and I kept eating. Butter, eggs and milk were items that were nonexistent in line camps. Lard and Pet Milk in a can suffice and occasionally Tom would bring some beef steaks, eggs and slab bacon to us along with whatever else we might need.

Jed wouldn't eat Spam at all. Said he has had his fill of Spam while in the Army Air Corps to last him the rest of his life even if he lived to be a hundred years old. He'd shoot himself rabbits when he was in the mood for fresh meat.

"Best time to get a couple of rabbits is at dawn and dusk at a watering hole. That's when they come in to drink," Jed had told me, to which I didn't reply because I knew it to be true from my experience hunting cottontails.

I most often slept fully clothed at night since I'd have to make my rounds every three or four hours. To dress and undress every time was more trouble that it was worth. Lighting a cigarette, pulling on your boots and putting your hat on your head was as much work you wanted to do at those times. And there were a couple of times I didn't even bother to remove my boots and spurs. I'd just flop down cover myself with the blanket and slept.

The coffee pot never got scrubbed out; you just dumped the grounds out now and then but most times just added to the old ones and got the pot to boiling again. The coffee pot was a standard fixture on the stove. My eating habits became nil or just plain horrible. I had lost fifteen pounds during that time. But with no time off I had saved some money, but the way the pay was, it wasn't a great deal of cash.

Kipp had come into my room that first morning that I was home, to wake me up and excitedly said he had something to tell me but it would have to wait until after breakfast, mother had it ready.

I went out to the garage after breakfast with Kipp so he could show me what he was doing on his hotrod Model-A, and in there we could talk freely without Dad or Ma overhearing us.

He and I uncovered the Model-A which was being protected with a canvas tarpaulin. The rod was really coming along; the hood had been louvered on top in two rows on each side, the side panels removed so when the new motor was installed it would stand out. The seats had been reupholstered in a tuck and rolled brilliant red Naugahyde.

"I'm hoping to get a Ford V-8 motor one of these days," Kipp said.

"Where did you get the money to do all this?" I asked.

"I did some trading with the upholstery guy that has that small shop on 24th Street. His name is Martin Thayer. Anyway he had car troubles one day and Cody and I helped him get his Chevy home by pushing it down the street. I did some work on it on weekends. I just had to buy the Naugahyde." Kipp explained, "It took him forever because he worked on the seats in-between paying jobs. He finally got them done last week. After I bolted them back in place I keep a blanket over them to keep then clean."

"Well its sure coming along well," I said, noticing that the floor boards had also been redone.

"Yeah it is. It's slow but I'm in no hurry. Besides if I get on turnaround this summer I'll have some money to buy parts and do more work on it."

"So this is what you were so excited about to tell me?" I asked.

"No," he said and went and looked out the garage door to see if anyone was close enough to hear us talk.

"Well, so what's the big secret?"

"Did you hear about what happened at the Dairy Queen?" Kipp asked.

"No, what?"

"I guess you didn't read about it in the paper," he realized.

"No. I was in line camp. We don't get the Billings Gazette delivered out there," I rebuffed.

"Well, someone sent one of those old iron freight wagon wheel tires down the hill and it went through the door and smashed into the ice cream maker," Kipp sniggered. "The place was closed up for a month after that."

"And I suppose that someone was you three. The KCC's," I said.

"It was just me and Cody. You ain't goin' to tell on us, are you?"

"Somebody could have been hurt or killed. Those old wheel tires weigh close to fifty pounds!" I exploded.

"Dakk, keep your voice down. Dad will hear you," he whispered in all seriousness. "We did it in the middle of the night. There was a full moon and the place was closed up. Nobody was around."

"Where you find the wheel?" I asked, shaking my head and added scolding, "You guys are going to end up in jail if you keep pulling this kind of stuff."

"If you'd been with us you'd of seen how scared we were. The damn tire just went out of control and we ran like Hell down the hill after it but it was going like a bat out of Hell."

Then he added, "We took the wheel from behind the Yellowstone Museum. It was just leaning there. It must have come off one of the old freight wagon wheels they had collected." He went on, "Anyway, Cody and me rolled it down the road and when we got to where it really drops down, we let it go and it ran straight. Then it hit a pot hole and only bounced a couple times but kept its course until it slammed into curb and jumped into the air and flew through the glass door and smashed into the stainless steel ice-cream machine. We could hear it hit and when we got there and saw what happened we took off and hid until the cops in the prowl car left the place. They kept going up and down the streets with the search lights looking for us. Cody was scared shitless and I was too!"

"Hope that taught you guys a lesson," I said, and then added, "but I doubt it."

"We just did it on a whim. It's not that we did it on purpose," he mumbled, "I mean we didn't figure on it running into the Dairy Queen. But when we told Cooper about it he started to laugh and we all got to laughing about it too. And then when we saw the picture in the paper of the wheel stuck in the ice cream maker we laughed again. I saved the picture. Want to see it?"

He showed me the Gazette photo and I laughed. Then I warned, "Sometimes you have to think ahead. Of what could happen, not just do it and hope for the best. You're just lucky no one was hurt and just as lucky the cops didn't catch you."

*   *   *

Branding time was the busiest time for us. We started early and ended late in the day only to repeat the same tasks the following days until all the calves wore the Milliron slash B brands on their left sides.

All the cowboys were camped at Buffalo Grass cow camp. There we had the chuck wagon and the men's tents set up. Nearby was the rope corral that the wranglers used to hold the cavvy and where the remuda was kept until a cowboy needed a new mount during the day.

By now all the mother cows and their calves had been driven and strung together in one large mass. They were kept in a half mile fenced area we called Buffalo Grass Meadows. The area still had some of the indigenous buffalo grass growing there where the other grasses hadn't as yet overtaken them. Here also were some large stock pens used to separate the animals before and after they were branded.

The branding crew was made up of basically three teams, the ropers that went out and caught the calves and brought them to the branding fire, the two sets of rastlers that held down the calf that worked in turns and the iron men who stay busy doing the branding and kept the fire hot as well as the marker men who worked with their sharp pocket knives and vaccine syringes.

Ropers either lead or drag a calf to the fire and this depends on the size of the calf. If the calf is a big one it is heel roped and dragged to the fire, while little calves are usually roped around the neck and led to the fire and the rastlers.

The calves being led are then flanked by two rastlers who throw them down and hold them. The rope is removed so the rider can ride back to catch another calf. While one rastler holds the calf's head down with his knee on the neck and holds one of the front legs to the calf's chin. The rear rastler, while sitting on the ground catches hold of the top hind leg of the calf and pulls it towards him stretched out while using his right foot to brace the other leg of the calf away from him with his foot. It is not too uncommon for a rastler to get kicked by the struggling calf if he isn't fast enough to hold the calf down. Once the calf is down in this position it is helpless; then it is branded, marked, vaccinated and if the calf is a male it is castrated.

Sometimes, if the ranch is in the mindset that the cows should be without horns, the branders also will dehorn the calf. Dehorning was at one time thought to enhance the price of the cattle at market but it actually didn't, and often the calves had to then be doctored for screwworms because of it. Screwworms are maggots from flies which attacked the wound where the horns had been abolished. Screwworm is mostly found in the southern and southwestern states. The practice of dehorning was stopped and became one less step for the hands to have to accomplish at branding. It is better to have range cows with horns because it is the only defense tool it has to protect itself and their young against potential predators aside from its hooves. Additionally, a cow with horns is easier to handle when rope work is necessary. Horned cattle can be roped and lead out of rough country, bogs, and tied to a tree when they need doctoring, all of which is better than being roped around the neck for a fully grown cow.

Mixed cattle branding, that is if cattle from two or more different ranches or owned by other family members with different brands are gathered together; then the calves have to be identified to the branders. This being the case, the roper first has to identify which cow the particular calf belongs to before he ropes it and brings it in to the rastlers. At this time the roper bringing in the calf calls to the rastlers, first the brand and then the marks that belong to that ranch. The rastlers repeat the calls to the branders and these iron men pull the proper heated branding irons from the fire to mark the calf with.

The iron men that do the branding have to keep the fire going at a temperature that will insure that the irons are hot enough to sufficiently burn deep so that the scab will later peel off. The iron men don't want the iron to be too hot so that when they brand with little pressure it will not burn a hole through the calf's hide. It is vital that the iron man be careful not to allow the branding iron to slip. If the iron does slip it may result in a blotched and unreadable brand.

Cowboys that are designated as markers are men who know how to use a sharp jackknife when it comes to castrating, cutting wattles, dewlaps, ear marks and cutting jug handles as other means of identification on the calf. Ear marks make identifying beeves possible when they're held together in a closed area and a rider can't see the brand or in winter when the cattle's hair has grown long over the brand. When cutting an ear, the right ear is first cut and then the left. There are almost fifty different ways to mark the cow's ears and those not marked are called slick-ears. These additional marks make it difficult for rustlers to work over a brand and keep from having the cow identified by its true owner.

When the male calves are castrated the testicles are thrown into a pail so that the cook has them to prepare as prairie or Rocky Mountain oysters to eat at meal time.

The cook, cookie or in the old days he was sometimes called coosie, would first remove the surplus tissue on the oysters and then split them open, wash them and then fry them in a hot deep Dutch oven or skillet with fat until they are thoroughly cooked; after which he removes them from the fat. The prairie oysters are then salted and replaced into the skillet and kept warm before serving them to the hands which consider them as a very special and tasty delicacy.

The first day of branding I became a rastler and was quickly taught the tricks of the trade. But I still managed to get kicked twice, once in my inner thigh very near my groin and once in the face but only grazing my cheek which bled until the cook patted the scratch with some white pepper and the bleeding stopped.

The stench of burning hair was at first a bit much but I soon got over it as well as having a panicking calf spray shit on me. I worked on and watched the iron men and the cutters do their work with the efficiency of professional surgeons.

We broke for the noon meal around two o'clock. There was an abundance of food: beef, oysters, mashed potatoes, cooked carrots and onions, beans, tortillas, plenty of hot coffee and cobbler made from canned peaches to end the meal.

I sat cross legged on the ground next to Jed and J.W. and we chatted some between working our eating irons, eating the noon chuck and drinking coffee out of tin cups.

Jed noticed how beat I was looking and said, "You look like some one-legged guy that's been in a shit kickin' contest," and he added, "Matter of fact you smell like it."

"Sorry. Guess I should move so you guys can enjoy your meals without me stinking you out," I mumbled.

"Hell, don't take Jed to heart. This whole place smells like cow shit," J.W. put in, "Besides if we couldn't put up with the smell of cow or horse shit, we'd be workin' some other occupation like a ball bearing factory or coal mine. Wouldn't you like that better, Jed?"

"Only maybe the money but the boredom would drive me plum nuts in an hour or less," Jed admitted.

"I think you're both right, I love the open air, the space and like they say, 'this big sky country," I stated smiling with a mouthful of mashed potato.

"Have you had your chance at ironing out any of these calves yet or you just rastlerin' the babies?" Clint questioned as he sat down next to us while balancing his plate of food in one hand and hot cup of coffee in the other, trying not to spill anything.

"Yeah, I had my chance. And I guess I'm okay with it so far."

"Well, Tom will probably have you ropin' tomorrow as a break and one of the Mexicans will take your place," then Clint remarked, "Bet he doesn't end up lookin' like he's been put through a wringer like you have by the end of the day."

"Probably not." I said, "at least I hope he doesn't, these knocks do hurt some. Especially the kick I received next to my nuts. Bet I'll be black and blue there for a month."

"So one of the babies almost got you in the family jewels?" said J.W. with a facial grimace.

"Too close. It's throbbing some. I should have kept my chaps on. They might have helped some."

"Not if the little shit got you in the crotch," Jed stated.

And he was right; chaps are opened crotched with no protection whatsoever.

*　*　*

Every newly-branded calf was hazed back to its mother and they were then turned out to another area away from those not yet branded and would eventually be moved to new pastures. The ropers kept us rastlers and branders busy until seven that first day. I was exhausted to the point of just wanting to not eat but fall down onto my bedroll and die.

I did manage to eat but had nothing to say to anyone and as a whole there wasn't much talk at all between the men. Everyone was beat. After I ate I wandered over to where Manuel had the tub of soapy water for our dirty dishes and plunked my dish and eatin' irons into it.

"Thanks Manuel, you sure put out some good chuck," I told him.

"You look tired, vaquero. How *hi-is* dah cut on your face, *amigo*?" he asked.

"It's fine. No more bleeding since you fixed me up. Good night," I said and headed for the comforts of my bedroll and I didn't care if I didn't wash my face which I knew was covered with dust or bother to brush my teeth. Sleep is what I wanted as the daylight had now turned from long shadows to darkness.

The stars were out and the Milky Way trailed across the heavens. The cows were bedded down for the night and as I lay in my blankets and listened to a cow moo for her calf, the clanging of pots and pans coming from the camp-jack washing the evening dishes, I could hear someone start to strum a guitar and sing in a low voice something in Spanish. I fell asleep almost instantly even with the throbbing pain in my leg.

The next morning we were wakened at five as daylight was easing up and the morning star and a billion other stars began to fade in the Montana sky.

In the morning after I quit my blankets I was still dressed in my shirt, pants and socks but found it difficult to pull on my boots. My leg had stiffened up considerably and was hurting. I found myself hobbling with the bad leg as I walked towards the chuck-wagon.

Tom, seeing me walking in pain, asked what had happened and I told him about the kick the calf had blessed me with.

He just chuckled and said, "Well, live an' learn cowboy. Got to be faster than those babies." Then he added, "Think you can ride and rope? If so I'll replace you as rastler."

"It's my right leg so I think I can still get a leg up and fork a horse."

"Have J.W. rope you a mount out of the cavvy and throw your saddle on him and see how it goes. Hate to lose a man during branding."

After eating breakfast and drinking coffee at the wagon I headed to the remuda and saw J.W. had the cavvy lined out against the rope corral. He had his rope under his arm and was in the process of lighting a smoke when he saw me limping towards him.

"Leg hurtin' this mornin'?" he asked as he inhaled and blew out a double smoke ring.

"Sure does. But I think I'll be okay. It sure is black and blue. Had a bitch of a time trying to put on my boots." I told him.

"So you ridin' today?"

"Yeah, Tom hopes I can. I'm sure I can. Fuck the pain," I guffawed trying to sound tough.

"Okay, bad ass," he responded, "Want one that's as frisky an' as hot as a pistol? If you do, I'll rope that flea-bitten one over there on the end."

"No, I'm just hoping I can pull my own weight with this bum leg. Believe me, it hurts a bunch." I said miserably.

"See that little buckskin? Well, she's sweet and is an easy ride. She's as good a cow horse as any of the geldings in the cavvy. She'll do all the work. All you got to do is point her where you want her and then rope. She'll do the rest. I've ridden her so I know what I'm takin' about."

He swung his rope and let it fly over the buckskin's head as all the horses were lined up with their back ends to him, and the lasso loop fell over her neck. As soon as she was caught she moved away from the others and came towards J.W. while the other horses held to the rope fence facing away from J.W. some whisking their tails violently chasing away pesky horse flies.

I haltered her and J.W. took the noose off of her and we both headed back to where my saddle was. After she was saddled I turned her head to the saddle, grabbed the reins and a lock of her mane, set a foot in the stirrup, took hold of the cantle and swung up onto the saddle, found my off stirrup and tried standing up off the seat. The damn leg throbbed more when I had my weight on it. I hoped my chaps would help protect my leg some as I rode away and to the day's work.

That day I had held my own for the most part. At the noon chuck, I only ate halfheartedly and that was only a tortilla and some beef for me. Everything Manuel had prepared looked great and all the boys had heaped their plates to the max. But my leg had cut my appetite. Clint had given me a couple aspirins and they seemed to help some that afternoon.

I did end up working with two waddies, Jimmy Catch'um Horse, a Crow from the rez, perhaps in his mid thirties. He dressed and looked pretty much like the rest of us, jeans, plaid western shirt, boots, and sweat-stained felt cowboy hat. His hair was cut short and his right little finger looked as though it must have been broken in his younger days and the tip never reset because it was always bent up. It didn't seem to ever interfere with whatever he was doing such as roping or rolling a cigarette.

The other waddy was Ramon Marietta, a vaquero from the state of Chihuahua, near Casas Grandes, Mexico. He looked to be maybe in his late twenties and had the appearance of having Indian blood in him also. He stood about five feet ten inches high in his cowboy boots. He, as well as many of the other cowboys, had on a summer straw hat. In a sheath at the back of his belt he wore a Mexican fixed curved blade knife with a brass hilt and a cow horn handle that looked as though it was turned round on a lathe. The knife was one of the tools used daily by cowboys and we all carried one, though most of us used jackknives rather than fixed bladed hunting style knives.

My morning horse that day, the little buckskin, was as J.W. had said, a great working horse. She almost knew what to do before I had time to think about it. She was doing all the work for me. It was as if I had put her on automatic pilot. My afternoon horse was a pretty good cow horse but he wasn't anything overly spectacular compared to that little buckskin. She sure was special.

The waddy, Jimmy, was a jovial jokester, always looking to play a prank on someone and loved to have a good laugh whenever someone screwed up or even when he screwed up himself. A waddy from Billings was always mooching cigarettes from everyone so one day Jimmy rolled a cigarette with a hair from his horse's tail in it and trimmed it off so you couldn't tell it was in the cigarette. And when the waddy asked Jimmy for a smoke, Jimmy gave him that one. After smoking it the waddy got sick as a dog and had lost his lunch to the point of even having the dry heaves.

Having worked with Jimmy Catch'um Horse for a time, I got wise to his pulling jokes and kept on the lookout for any possible practical joke he might play on me again. He already had snuck up on me as I had fallen asleep on my stomach with my face buried in my hat one noon after eating. Jimmy had tied my spurs' shanks together with a piece of string. When I awoke with a start to the noise of everyone going back to work, I tried to get to my feet only to find out my spurs were tied together. I had a Hell of a time trying to cut the string off with my knife, never mind the fact that bending my bad leg was painful. Needless to say Mr. Catch'um Horse had a really good laugh at my expense.

Jimmy Catch'um Horse and his practical jokes reminded me of the time Kipp and I played a practical joke one day on an old Indian that would come to town after he received his monthly reservation government check and cash it at Casey's Golden Pheasant Bar and Lounge, then with some of the money buy a half gallon of cheap red wine. Billy Young Buck, who must have been in his seventies or older, would then sit in his old beat up Dodge pickup truck in the alley behind Casey's and drink until he fell asleep.

One day I asked Jimmy if he happened to know Billy Young Buck.

"You bet I know Young Buck, he's a distant cousin on my mother's side." Jimmy said.

"Was or is he really a chief?" I asked.

"No, he's never been a chief or medicine man. Billy Young Buck was in the Warrior Lodge but they threw him out after a short time. He's one of those dreamers, thinks he was a warrior but he never was. He was born on the reservation sometime around 1880 something. His father and grandfather were most likely warriors or at least scouts for the army working against our enemies the Sioux, Arapaho, and Cheyenne. Chief is what the cops in Billings call old Billy Young Buck. It's their way of putting him down as well as the rest of us Indians. They call every one of us chief and our women squaws. You know it's like us calling you white eyes."

I had nothing to add to what he had said and I'd wished I hadn't asked him that stupid question to begin with. To apologize would add insult to injury. So I kept my mouth shut and went back to work.

Billy Young Buck still wore his gray hair in two long skinny braids. Atop his head he'd have on an old brown felt hat with the crown not dented and the flat brim sagging all around. When he smiled at you, you could see that he had only a couple of upper front teeth left in his mouth. His eyesight must have been going bad because most times he wore dark sunglasses. Billy was a happy-go-lucky drunk who had spent many times behind bars after being picked up on the street. They'd haul him off in the paddy wagon to jail. Eventually they would let him out and he'd go back to the reservation. Until his next government relief check and he'd be driving back to Billings in the old jalopy Dodge truck that spewed a cloud of black smoke from the tailpipe for another go around of drunkenness. But once he learned that if he stayed parked in his truck to drink and sleep it off and not end up flopped down in the street or some doorway, the cops wouldn't bother with him unless he started to drive off still drunk. Besides they were tired of dragging him to jail every month.

A few years back one morning Kipp and I happened to be walking down the alley where Billy was parked and saw he was fast asleep in his truck.

"Hey! Let's pull a joke on Billy," Kipp urged.

"Like what?" I asked.

"Let's get some black paint an' paint all of the windows on the truck so that when Billy wakes up he'll think it's the middle of the night and try to drive home."

"You are going to stick around until he does wake up after the windows are painted?"

"No. We can make a bunch of noise and wake him and watch what happens," Kipp suggested.

Like a fool I went along with Kipp's brainless scheme. We went to the hardware store and purchased some black paint and two brushes and went back to the alley. Billy was sound asleep lying on the seat. His bottle of wine sat on the floor with a good deal of it having been consumed.

No one was around and we began painting the windows black. Then we left for sometime after tossing the empty can and brushes into one of the trash cans in the alley.

When we got back with Kipp's buddies, Cody and Cooper, we started up a racket and shook the old Dodge until we knew Billy was awake. We could hear him jabbering in the cab and then he started up the truck and turned the head lights on and drove off. Still being drunk and not being able to see where he was headed Billy drove into the alley trash cans but didn't stop until he had wiped out about eight or more galvanized trash barrels and covers as well as spilled trash throughout the alleyway. The truck finally came to an abrupt stop when it hit a phone pole. Billy opened the door and discovered it was still daylight and just stood next to his truck squinting in the sunlight trying to figure out what had just happened. That's when we all took off around the corner laughing our brains out.

Later my conscience got to me and I felt bad for Billy. Billy's Dodge was taken to the gas station just down the street from the alley and parked there until he got out of jail. Billy spent a bit of time in jail for drunkenness and damaging property. But when he got out and found his truck he saw that it was in as good a shape as it had been before we pulled the joke on him. We had cleaned off the paint with lacquer thinner and straightened out the front bumper which hadn't been too badly misshapen and had the gas station attendant put two bucks worth of gas in Billy's truck which gave him eight gallons of gas. Plus Kipp checked all the truck fluids and I made him change the oil in the Dodge which was blacker than coal and put in new plugs that I had bought.

Billy drove off back to the Crow Reservation and next month he'd be back to Billings and get drunk once again.

* * *

By the end of the week the branding was finished and all the cattle and their calves moved to new grass on open range. Branding time was the most labor-intensive time for all of us and I was happy that it was over for this year. I had learned a lot during these past months and my roping had much improved. It was like my mother used to say, "Practice makes perfect."

J.W. had let me use Llano to work off of a couple of times after my leg had healed up some. Manuel had taught me how to make and roll out flour tortillas using a cut-off broom handle or bottle as a rolling pin.

Jimmy Catch'um Horse taught me humility towards his people. He and I got along real well. He even invited me to come visit him on the rez and do the sweats with him in the sweat lodge and said that I sure should come to their annual pow-wow ceremony.

* * *

COULEE

Chapter 13

Things at the ranch had pretty much gone back to their normal routine and we had some time off again. I even got a week off, a vacation of sorts.

As soon as I got home, one of the first things Dad wanted to know when he came into the kitchen from watching television was if I was going to try to get a job during 'turn around' and that I better check it out because it was harder to get on these days. And he told me that Kipp was not able to get hired on as he had hoped.

Sitting at the table drinking coffee, I could hear the loud shoe commercial on the television in the front room, "That's my dog Tige, he lives in a shoe, I'm Buster Brown, look for me in there, too."

"Dad, the ranch is treating me well and I like the job and the people I work with. Besides I've put some money, away and I'd like to stick it out until after the next branding. I'm in no hurry to go back to school," I implored, and added as an afterthought, "It's like you once said, you ride for the brand, until the brand does you wrong."

"Well it's your life, but every year you let go by the harder it gets to get your mind back to formal education," Dad retorted.

"Why do you think that? I've heard that many G. I.'s that fought in Korea have now gone back to further their education with the G.I. Bill,"

"Yeah, well many had been drafted or enlisted because there was a cause to," he said, "It wasn't procrastination like you're doing. They were fighting the North Korean Communists in another crappy war."

"Well weren't they 'Riding for the brand,' the U.S.A. brand, Dad?" I asked. He just shook his head and that ended the discussion. The television resumed its program and the volume had muted some and Dad went back to his TV watching.

I looked through the want ads in the Sunday morning paper but there wasn't anything I would want to spend time working at just to make a buck or two more than working on the Milliron slash B ranch.

The three of us watched TV that night. Ma had made us some popcorn to eat while watching the Ed Sullivan show. Kipp and his two buddies had headed up to Yellowstone National Park, camping and seeing the sights. Cooper, just turned eighteen, had had his driver's license for a while and graduated from high school ahead of Kipp and Cody. Cooper had his old 1938 four-door Pontiac sedan to make the trip in. They took an old canvas umbrella tent and camping stuff from Dad and had left the day before I got back home, otherwise I would have most likely gone along with them, which Ma would have liked, just to make sure they kept out of trouble.

"When are the KCC's coming back from cavorting in Yellowstone?" I asked Ma.

"They should be back in a few days but not later than the weekend. They left Saturday. Kipp said that they would spend time at the Buffalo Bill Museum in Cody. He wanted to look at all the Indian stuff in there. You know how he loves all that Indian stuff."

"Yeah, I know. Which reminds me, I'll have to tell him that I've been invited to the big pow-wow on the Crow rez. And if I go I'll see if he wants to come along for kicks."

"I'm sure he'd love it. Who invited you?"

"Oh, this cowboy that worked with us during branding. His name is Jimmy Catchum or rather Jimmy Catch'um Horse, which is his

Indian name," I said as a matter of fact then added, "That's the obscure meaning of his name from Crow, Catch'um Horse."

"They have such interesting names, almost poetic," she remarked.

I continued, "He invited me to go and I probably will. He's more cowboy than Indian. He's a real card, a jokester. Loves to tell and play jokes on anyone. He and I became friends working together."

"What kind of jokes does he play on people? Did he play any on you?" she urged.

"Yes he did. I fell asleep at lunch break and he tied the back of my spurs together and when I woke up to go back to work, well I just tripped over myself and everyone had a big kick out of it. Anyway, he was always doing stuff like that. He's as bad as Kipp when it comes to being a joker."

"Yes, Kipp is a clown sometimes. I just hope he doesn't get into any big trouble because of it," Ma worried out loud.

*   *   *

When Monday came around I decided to go over to the Hoof and Horn to have a cup of coffee. I also wanted to talk to old Blastingame at the stock yards out of curiosity and to see how things were working out there since I hadn't been by because I started working for the Milliron last fall.

Everything in the Hoof and Horn looked pretty much as it did the year before. Donna had changed her hair style. It was now somewhat flamboyant, a permanent wave that made her looks glamorous. Cliff was now sporting a Clark Gable mustache that would have looked better on someone else but everyone said it looked good on him to inflate his ego.

When I walked into the café around ten o'clock, the jukebox was playing, '*Why do fools fall in love?*' Dwayne was the only customer in there sitting at the counter. At first I didn't recognize him in his Marine uniform with a crew-cut hair style until he turned to me and said, "Dakk, how's the cowboy life treating you?"

"Dwayne! I'll be damned, is that you?" I bellowed.

"Well I ain't the queen of England. How the Hell are you?" We shook hands and he had a grip of steel.

"Damn, you look great! You home on leave?" I inquired.

"Well I'm not AWOL. Just got out of boot camp three days ago. Came back to Billings from boot camp. Camp Lejeune, North Carolina. Flew into Billings yesterday. Thought I might find George in here but Doris here says she hasn't seen him in months."

"My name is Donna, Dwayne," she interjected as she poured me coffee.

"It was meant as a compliment. That new hairdo makes you look like you're Doris Day," Dwayne chimed.

"Why thank you, Dwayne," then she added, "If I wasn't married to Cliff I believe I'd fall in love with you the way you look so good in that Marine uniform."

Just then the Frankie Lymon song, 'Why do fools fall in love?' ended.

For over an hour Dwayne and I smoked and drank coffee and talked about the Marines, boot camp, the training and his sharp shooters medal that he had qualified as. He had become an Expert with M-1 rifle, carbine and the forty-five pistol and made Marksman with the B.A.R. He told me that a B.A.R. stood for Browning automatic rifle and he didn't want to be too good with it because in a fire fight, his life expectancy would be extremely short.

We ate lunch at the diner and as people came in for their noon lunch and coffee some came over to us and talked to Dwayne and said they were proud that he was a Marine and wished him all the luck in the world and hoped he wouldn't have to fight any Commies in the near future.

When Roy Blastingame came into the café for lunch he never acknowledged Dwayne's or my presence. I know he had seen us sitting at the counter. And that's when I decided not to go see Ben today. I'd try again some other day when I might not have to see Roy around.

*   *   *

Thursday night, sometime after ten, Kipp and his buddies came home while I was out on the back steps smoking. They were all full of themselves while unpacking the camping stuff and always breaking up into laughter over nothing. They would just look at each other and start having a good laugh. When I asked what they were laughing about Kipp would say, "I'll tell you later." Of course that made me suspicious that once again they had pulled some shenanigan on someone or something. So I waited for him to tell me what was so damn funny to all of them.

Around the middle of the morning the following day, my curiosity was at its pitch and I asked Kipp if he wanted to go to the Pronghorn Café for a piece of pie or ice cream sundae so he could tell me what he, Cooper and Cody had been laughing about. He had been acting a bit fidgety while dinking on something he had started with on his hot rod.

"How about both?" he chortled.

"It'll cost you," I said.

"Thought you were buying,"

"I am. I just want to know what all the laughing was about yesterday."

"Okay, let's go. I'm not in the mood to work on the car today. Besides all I had for breakfast was a bowl of Cheerios."

He cleaned his hands with solvent and wiped them on a rag and we jumped in my truck and drove to the café.

I pulled in behind a Federal truck with a stock-rack loaded full of steers parked in front of the Pronghorn. The truck had Wyoming, Park County license plates with the famous logo of a bronco bucking horse known as 'Steamboat' and rider on it. On the red truck's doors was painted, Jarratt Ranch, Cody, Wyoming, and the brand, a lazy B and upright J.

We went into the Pronghorn and saw only two men and a boy, all with straw cowboy hats on, sitting in a corner booth drinking coffee, smoking and reading the paper. The boy was having a glass of milk and pie. As we sat in a booth behind the cowboys the waitress walked up to us. She was a new girl and said, "Good morning," handed us lunch menus and asked, "What would you like to drink?"

"I'll have coffee," I said.

"A Coke," Kipp put in. And she went off to get our drinks.

One of the Lazy BJ cowboys said to the other, "Well I'll be dipped. Listen to this," and he read what was surprising to him; in the newspaper; "It says here that a black bear was seen in an alley here in Billings and was discovered when the trash men came down the alley in the early hours of the morning. The bear had found refuge in some cardboard boxes between trash cans. The trash man that discovered the bear was so surprised that he froze where he stood as the bear ambled off."

Kipp, overhearing the cowboy reading the paper out loud, started to snicker behind his menu.

"What's with you now?" I quizzed in a whisper.

He looked from behind the menu and whispered back with a grin, "I'll tell you later."

The waitress came and asked if we had decided on what we wanted.

"What you got for pies?" Kipp asked.

"Apple, cherry, blueberry, chocolate cream and lemon meringue," she rattled off.

"I'll have apple pie with a scoop of vanilla ice cream," I said.

And she looked at Kipp as she scribbled on her pad.

"I guess I'll have the same but I want chocolate ice cream on mine," Kipp ordered.

"Chocolate with apple pie," she winced, "never heard of that."

"Why not, it tastes real good," Kipp chimed.

"Okay," she said and walked off briskly, writing on her pad.

The cowboy reading the paper in the booth behind me said to the boy, "Wyatt, listen to this. 'By the afternoon a Mrs. Wheeler happened to look out of her kitchen window and sees the bear rampaging though her vegetable garden eating everything in sight. She then went and got her rifle out of her closet which had belonged to her father's father, an old Henry .44 caliber lever action rifle, and shot the bear twice. When asked what she was going to do with the young bear she said, 'What do you think? Eat it; after all he's full of my vegetables. Besides bear grease makes the best and flakiest pie crust.' And it goes on sayin' that her son was coming over to butcher the bear for her." And they all laugh.

"That .44 rim-fire ammo she had musta been old as dirt. I'm surprised it fired at all," commented the older cowboy.

Kipp was now in hysterics as the waitress came with our pies a-la-mode and poured me more coffee.

"Is he alright?" she asked me, looking a bit bewildered.

"He's fine, something just tickled his funny bone. He's not berserk," I said gingerly.

The Jarratt Ranch cowboys paid their bill, left and drove off in the old Federal stock truck.

"All right, what's the joke? What's gotten into you?" I wanted to know once and for all. Also I had a feeling that today's laughter had something to do with yesterday's. I just knew it, but couldn't figure out what the KCC's and the bear story in the paper had to do with each other.

"Okay, okay I'll tell you," he muttered through a mouthful of pie and a grin.

"Well?"

He swallowed and leaned towards me and said, "That black bear yearling is one we brought back from Yellowstone the other day."

"No! How? You guys are out of your God damn minds," I asked and accused at the same time. I was flabbergasted. *These three guys are really all berserk.*

"Keep your voice down," Kipp said in a whisper with a sudden worried look as the laughter and smile diminished from his face. He quickly looked to see if the waitress was looking our way. But she was in the kitchen and we could see her arguing about something with the cook through the serving window.

"Well," Kipp started to tell, "We had a great time in Yellowstone. An' by the way, if you're ever in Cody check out the Buffalo Bill Museum. It's got all of his stuff from when he had his Wild West Show in there."

"Yeah," I said, "Go on."

"We drove all over Yellowstone Park and counted 164 black bears as we drove around the loop while we were there. Saw buffalo, elk and a couple of river otters. Got to see all the geysers, Old Faithful and it spouts up to 185 feet they say. We saw the hot springs and pools, they're all over the place. Boilin' mud pots, spray geysers, terraces. There's got to be hundreds of them and the place smells like rotten eggs. You know, sulfur."

"Yeah, I know all about that. I just haven't seen it for myself yet. But what makes all this so freaking funny to you guys?" I wanted to know.

"The last mornin' we were in Yellowstone we had camped near the east end of Yellowstone Lake. There wasn't anyone else camped where we were and this young lookin' black bear, a yearling, comes along lookin' for a handout. Well Cody has this box of cookies he had bought at Mammoth Hot Springs. They got a store there, they sell food and tourist stuff. Anyway Cody tosses the bear a couple of cookies and after he eats them he's looking at Cody for more. Well we've got the trunk on the Pontiac open ready to pack up camp and Cody keeps tossin' the bear cookies and he's getting closer to us and I'm thinkin' let's take this bear back home with us. So when the bear is real close to the car I grab the box of cookies from Cody and toss it in the trunk and the bear climbs in and starts to eat the rest of the cookies and I slam the trunk lid closed," he says, starting to laugh again, then goes on with the story. "Cooper's going fuckin' nuts about the bear being in his car. Anyway Cody and me start loading all our campin' shit in the back seat while Cooper is swearin' at us. Just then a tourist pulls into the area we're in and lets his family out to go look at the lake. And I say to Cooper, 'Let's get out of here,' and we all jump in the car and drive off."

"I can't believe you guys. What the bear do to the trunk of the car?" I wanted to know.

"Not much, he just took a crap in there. And when we let him out he ran down the alley and hid behind some big boxes and we got out of there. It was dark by then."

All I could do was shake my head. Think of that poor bear and all he had gone through just by coming across the infamous trio, the KCC's, and I had to laugh and laughed even harder when I thought of that old lady blasting the bear in her garden. As well as how good a pie crust bear fat made. The pie crust on the pie Kipp and I were eating certainly wasn't exceptional, just okay.

I paid for the pie and drinks and noticed Kipp digging into his jeans pocket. He pulled out some change and from it took a couple of dimes out and put them in the March of Dimes can next to the register. I used my change for the waitress's tip.

In 1954 a Doctor Salk had discovered a vaccine that immunized people from the terror of polio. Prior to this find, the March of Dimes helped provide research funding for poliomyelitis, the most dreaded affliction of the twentieth century.

Kipp must be feeling reprehensible because of what he had done, causing trouble and having brought on the death of the yearling bear by putting it into an unnatural environment.

On the way home I thought as the big brother I'd better try to tell Kipp the facts of life and read him the riot act.

"You know that if you guys had been caught taking that bear from Yellowstone, which by the way is under federal laws and restrictions, you could have had a bit of a long prison term to face," I said sort of matter of fact even though I knew only Cooper of the KCC's was over eighteen years old, "You might end up in a federal prison like Alcatraz. You know that's where Al Capone and all the real bad asses end up. Besides, once you turn eighteen and get caught screwing up doing something illegal you'll be judged as an adult and that means, if not the Billings jail then the state pen, Deer Lodge where you might learn to hitch horse hair belts and head stalls," I surmised, hoping to get him scared.

Then to really scare him I added, "You'll end up in prison at a young age. And there is good possibility that your lewd horny cell mate might rape you in the still of the night. You'll for sure become this rump-rider's girlfriend and get yourself corn-holed every night."

Kipp's face went white and I knew this did instill some serious fear not to get his ass into anything that would get him or his buddies in jail. At least I hoped so.

*　*　*

Kipp's little trip to Yellowstone Park had given me the itch to see the countryside so Saturday morning I decided to head back to the ranch by taking a drive towards Harlowton, Judith Gap to Lewiston and then meander back down to Roundup and then east to the Milliron and back to work.

I took my time driving the two lane roads, enjoying the scenery. Kipp had given my old truck a tune up and it now purred like a kitten over the tarmac as I watched horses and cattle grazing. And the endless coulees that appeared just about everywhere in Montana. Nature's erosion had for thousands of years moved and changed the landscape. Coulees, the result of natures carving, could be seen throughout the northwestern states.

I had been brought up with the term coulee whereas in the south Jed told me they were called arroyos. I looked up the word coulee in the Encyclopedia Britannica and discovered it was a Quebec Canadian French word, *Coulée,* meaning to flow. A coulee is a valley, gulch, ravine, drainage that is often dry in summer. Coulees are areas that are for the most part scablands or badlands.

The largest coulee in the United States is The Grand Coulee which is on the Columbia River and has The Grand Coulee Dam built across it which is a hydroelectric dam. Its construction began in 1933 as one of President Franklin D. Roosevelt's depression Public Works Project. The dam was completed in 1942.

Coulees to me have had a certain mystery, or rather fascination. They are great places for discovery. The discovery of the earth's and even man's past. They are to me little Grand Canyons, where you can read the strata, sometimes find fossils of plants, fish, reptiles, exposed old hunting grounds or mineral deposits that are only a few feet below the prairie's grasses.

Kipp and I have found fossil shells: Crinoid stems that look like beads, snail-shaped fossils, worm tubes, turtle shell fossil parts and many more. We had found a buffalo jump coulee with old crumbling bones with obsidian, flint and jasper points among them. Coulees were our treasure chests of natures wonders and some of mans artifacts.

In places, coulees became trash dumps with everything in them from sheep, cow and horse carcasses, bed springs, junk trucks, cars, even un-repairable farm machinery and household rubbish.

Coulees were homes to rabbits, birds, coyotes, foxes, snakes, other reptiles and insects. Some coulees sprout springs or seeps of water which are covered in rich vegetation.

Just outside of Judith Gap I saw a large coulee, with what looked like the bones of an old Ford rusting in the hot sun. It looked to me to be the same vintage as Kipp's hot-rod. No one else was on this road but me, I hadn't seen another vehicle coming or going for the last thirty miles. There were no signs that said 'No Trespassing' so I parked off the road and climbed over the barb wire fence to have a look. The car was pretty much cannibalized already and there wasn't anything left on it that Kipp could use so I left. But walking back to the truck I found a small arrowhead made from red jasper only five feet from the carcass of a road killed antelope that was crawling with black and red carrion beetles. I heard a "*Quork, Quork,! Touk!*" coming from above, it was a raven on the cross bar of a telephone pole. He spread his wings as if to take flight but settled back down and watched me. Two more ravens wheeled in flight above me and cried at my interference with their smorgasbord.

"He's all yours," I said to the ravens as I drove off. I would give the arrowhead to Kipp next time I was home knowing it would make his whole day.

I stopped in Lewiston for coffee. An anorexic old bleached blonde waitress came to the table I'm sitting at and she asked me what I want to drink as she handed me a menu and eating irons. "Coffee," I told her.

Over the cook's serving window hangs an American flag, its corners nailed to the wall and showing its thirteen red and white stripes and the blue field with forty-eight stars.

I ordered a barbeque roast beef sandwich that comes with potato salad when she took my order. The coffee was as stout as anything most cowboys will drink. I thought it must have been sitting in the coffee maker since breakfast. At a back table a couple of farmers in well worn grease-stained overalls, plaid and light denim shirts with railroad caps on their heads were playing cards.

Some ranch hands came in for their afternoon coffee break and all nod at me as they passed to the counter stools to sit, smoke and drink coffee. All have on their spurs and sweat stained straw cowboy hats on their heads. One is still wearing his chaps. I looked outside and saw a Ford pickup parked with an open top stock trailer, inside which were standing three saddled horses, all at rest and eyes closed while napping.

Outside, I found the sun was blinding but was now on it's descent into the western sky. I drove on east; the few windmills I saw were still, the blades at ease. The green endless rows of wheat fields winnowed in places by previous micro bursts of winds now laid flat to the ground. The fields I had passed await the coming of the fall harvest. This is dry land farm country. Newer Harvester combines sat idle in the farm yards awaiting action while old ones sit parked in tall weeds and rust along with other unserviceable farm machinery. Every town I passed had a white church, their steeples with an apex cross aimed to the sky. Nearby, cemeteries with old and new grave stones sat silent. Tall galvanized co-op grain elevators wait to become choked with wheat. At Grassrange, I turned towards the south, heading for the town of Roundup and then on to the Milliron slash B Ranch.

*   *   *

AERMOTOR &
RAVEN

CHAPTER 14

There was this ad in Western Horseman magazine that Jed was reading that advertised:

HORSESHOERS WANTED
(HELP!)

Rugged individualists as strong as Samson,
   As patient as Job, as wise as Solomon, but gentle and understanding.
   Must be willing to travel long distances, work steady and hard, take kicks, wounds and bruises; and be falsely accused of making horses lame.
   Candidates will be expected to cure in several minutes what it took Nature years to cause, Those who are weak-backed and weak-minded need not apply as they can be kicked out of business overnight.

Pay is excellent for the actual hours worked.

Services of competent, dependable, and highly-skilled craftsmen are in short supply.

Job satisfaction guaranteed for properly suited and trained horseshoers in soul-rewarding occuppation which provides life preserving services to sensitive animals which mean so much to their appreciative owners.

APPLY TO THE HORSESHOEING SCHOOL MOST HIGHLY RECOMMENDED TO YOU

He read it aloud so we could all hear what it said one evening as we sat around in the bunkhouse.

"There you go, Jed. That's a good job an' right up your alley," Tom joked as he and I played dominos.

"Yeah, I like the part, 'take kicks, wounds and bruises,' and how's that different from a working cowboy?" J.W. retorted.

"Not much. Just pays better," Jed stated, and then added, "but it sure gets hard on your back as you get to be long on tooth in later years."

"It's not like you don't have the experience. How long have you been shoeing horses?" I asked.

"Oh, I don't know. Years! You've got to know that I understand that it's a job where you work with your head below your ass most times," he said. Then went on, "Use to watch the blacksmith when I was a kid an' he showed me how to forge horse and mule shoes. It sure was an art back then. Now they've got these readymade, store bought cold-shoes, come in all sizes. An' that's what everybody is usin' these days. An' that's what put the blacksmith out of a job. You don't see blacksmiths much anymore, it's a dead trade. A guy that likes workin' with iron now is a welder," Jed stated.

"Welding is a pretty good payin' job these days and there's a demand for them more than ever," Tom ventured.

'Yeah, there's a Miller or Lincoln welder on every farm and ranch these days along with acetylene torches. It's the all around tool now an' all the old forges are rusting in the dumps. Use to be a guy would make all his own tools with a forge, now you just go to the hardware store and buy it. Presto!" Jed grumbled.

"I guess we live in a time that there isn't time enough to make anything anymore. We got all this junk comin' over here from Japan made of pot metal an' none of it holds up worth a shit. If I see it's got made in Japan on it I won't touch it with a ten foot pole. You're just pissin' your money away buyin' that crap," Jed protested.

"Well, I don't buy anything that's not handmade as far as trappings and I want it made by the best of the best in craftsmen and made here in the good old U.S. of A.," J.W. announced.

Well before you know it the Japs will be sellin' us cars an trucks an' all kinds of stuff an' puttin' guys out of work here in the states," Jed theorized.

"Who'll buy cars or trucks that are made like crap?" I asked.

"We'll see, people here are already buyin' German made cars like Volkswagens. Beetles, they call them," Tom went on, "I've only seen one on the road, damn ugly looking thing. Don't think it can do over fifty miles an hour on a flat road or downhill. Read someplace that they're not worth a damn when it comes to going up long steep hills."

The conversation died after that last statement and everybody went back to what they were doing. Jed went on reading his magazine, J. W. fiddled with his radio trying to get a Country Western station and Tom and I kept at our seventh game of dominos for the evening before calling it a day.

* * *

By now all the cows and calves we called 'little doggies' and bulls had been run together and sent up country to breed and summer graze. Gestation for a cow is the same as humans, nine months, and so you want to have the bulls seed your cows at a time that will mean that your calf crop will be born in the spring. Calving then would begin at a time that the weather is hopefully considerably improved from the perils of winter.

Manuel Daez, who was our cook, moved his operation to the cow camp up in the hills. We cowboys, Jed, J.W., Ramon, Clint and I would work from here during the summer months keeping an eye on things until the fall round up started.

The cattle would pretty much stay together but you had to ride the circle to make sure that some didn't skedaddle off to areas from the rest of the herd. So we were always looking out for trouble when riding the loop.

Cow camp was located in the high country among a pine and aspen forest with cool air, not many biting insects and lots of scattered meadows that all had a profusion of colorful wild flowers that included blue lupine, fire red Indian paintbrush, white daisies, yellow balsam root, purple fireweed and countless other blooms.

The high country cow camp was made up of corrals for the horses and a one room building made of sandstone and mortared walls, about 20 feet wide by 40 feet long with a pitched roof of corrugated metal. Inside was Manuel's kitchen with an old Monarch coal-wood burning stove built by Malleable Iron Range Company, a long table, a bench and a few chairs, bunk beds and a stuffed leather cushion chair that had seen better days. The place housed the bare necessities. Outside some thirty feet away were two privies. And we got our water from a nearby creek. All our drinking, cooking and wash water had to be boiled before we used it to keep any of us from getting giardia. Giardia is a disease that is a bacterium, caused by drinking water that has the bacterium living it. This bacterium is found in animal feces and animals that have died near water. Because this bacterium is known to have a hard outer shell it is able to even be found living in ice during winter.

Jed had a case of it a few years back and that was why Archie mandated that all the drinking and dish water be boiled before we used it.

Never having had giardia I once asked Jed how he knew he had it.

"Yup, I sure had a real bad case of it. Sick as a dog I was. Was stove-up or rather under the weather for what seemed like a month or more. Lost twenty pounds. I had the skitters bad. Farted like a bull dog an' every time I did, I thought I'd crap myself. I stayed close to the crapper the whole time. Had gut cramps an' grumbles that made me want to puke. It was the worst sick I can remember havin' been my whole life. Never want to get it again," Jed explained, then added, "Archie, Emma an' Little Raven wanted to drive me into Billings an' the hospital. But I didn't let 'em. Though there was a time in the beginnin' I thought I was goin' to be a goner because of it an' half considered goin' to the hospital. But I hung tuff."

At night the day horses were turned out with the others except for two that we kept in the corral as our morning jingle mounts. We'd bell the lead horses so we could locate the herd in the dark of the morning when we went looking for them and then wrangle them together back to the camp. After picking out the day mounts we'd turn out the rest back towards the wooded meadows.

These were for the most part long but leisurely working days of riding in different directions and occasionally meeting one another on circle at which time we'd exchange conversation dealing with the cows or just plain talk and a smoke before moving on.

Tom or Archie would come up in a pickup or send one of the Mexicans up with supplies. Once a month two of us would get a weekend off and head for Billings or Sheridan to 'paint the town' and get the stench of city life out of our periodical whims of needing something we could just as well do without. Most times it was something as simple as a yearning for ice cream or a particular candy bar or visiting a bar your friends hung out in. Then there was the need of female companionship for a night or two just to, as the saying goes, 'Get your pipes cleaned out.' After which you couldn't wait to get back out in the high country and away from civilization with its bad smells, noise and what seemed like perpetual commotion.

* * *

One day as I was riding out of a patch of aspens I spotted J.W. galloping Llano across this meadow when he suddenly leaped from the horse while holding onto the saddle horn, his feet hit the ground and with that momentum swung back up into the saddle. He did this three times before he realized that I was watching him.

He reined in Llano to a walk and headed towards me with a grin on his face.

"That was some fancy riding," I told him, "Where did you learn how to do that?"

"It's easy as long as the horse isn't too tall for you."

"Well I'm impressed," I said.

"I saw it done on some western movie when I was a kid," J.W. said, "And one day I was out riding with some buddies back home and we all tried it and believe it or not it was easier than you'd think. We all did it on our first try."

"It looks like it would take a lot of practice," I said.

"Not really. You see, if the horse is runnin' all you have to do is jump off while still hanging onto the saddle horn or mane an' when your feet hit the ground an' if you're aimed forward, it springs you back on the horse in one fell swoop."

"Well I'll be dipped," I declared.

We rode together on up the big coulee to the sandstone ridge in an area we called the hoodoos because of the weird land and stone formations. Hoodoo is considered an evil supernatural force. In Blackfoot mythology the hoodoo shapes had once been giants whom the Great Sprit had turned to stone because of their evil deeds. This was an area with a few pillars, each with a capstone as crown. The whole area covered only a couple of acres. When this area becomes wet the bentonite or clay is like grease and impossible to negotiate on foot or horseback.

We got off on top and while J.W. looked the lower area over for cows, I dropped the reins and walked around reading the ground as my horse stood and watched me.

"What you lookin' for?" J.W. asked.

"Oh, not much. I'm just checking for chipping to see if Indians had once been camped in the area." I said.

"See any chippings?" he asked.

"No, must have been a place they didn't like."

"So what if you did find chipping, what does that mean to you asides that maybe they had camped here?" he wanted to know, "An' if there was a camp here, then so what?"

"Nothing much except there's a chance they hunted something around here and there's a possibility that I could find an arrowhead, point, blade, drill or scraper," I pointed out.

"You collect arrowheads?"

"Yeah, if I find one I give it to my kid brother; he's the one that's always collecting them."

"I've got a few I picked up in Oregon from when I worked on the Seven Forty-three Ranch. They're someplace in my war-bag. You can have them and give them to your brother. If I hang on to them I'll end up just havin' them get lost. What's your brother's name?" J.W. inquired.

"Kipp with two p's," I told him, "And yeah, I'm sure he'd love them. He mounts them in cases and knows all about them, the types, their names and what period they're from. He's a real nut when it comes to Indian culture and artifacts," I explained.

"Sounds like a good kid."

"He's a hot rod nut also and a pretty good mechanic. He works on people's cars and trucks from time to time. But he and his buddies are always getting into some trouble. Luckily he and the others haven't been caught at any mischievousness yet."

"Trouble like what?" J.W. wanted to know.

"Oh, more like just mischief rather than trouble. Like the time they got hold of some TNT and set it off one morning. They blew out this cave on the Rim and woke up all of Billings bright and early."

"That happened last year. I remember talk about it. The paper said it was a jet breaking the sound barrier," J.W. said.

"Yep, it was my brother and his pals, Cody and Cooper the KCC's we call them, real mischief misfits."

Then we headed back into the low land making plans to go to Sheridan together on our next time off.

*　　*　　*

A few days later J.W. gave me three points, all arrowheads for Kipp. The Oregon points had been found on a ranch J.W. had worked for as a buckaroo in what is known as 'The Great Basin,' that the **743** Ranch was in. One of the points was made of agate and was missing one of its tangs but the rest of were in perfect condition and made of obsidian.

"These Oregon points are sure nice, real humdingers," I said.

"Found them in a dry playa one day. Got off my horse to take a piss an' there they were. If I'd been more interested in them I bet I could have picked up a dozen more just like those.

"These are known as 'gem points' because of their size, material, colors and how well they are made. Kipp will go nuts over these. Hell,

I bet next time we're in Billings he'll tune up your truck for you if you want!" I exclaimed.

"Well good, it's a trade then. I'll buy the plugs and anything else he needs to do the job."

I rewrapped them in the tissue and placed them back into the envelope J.W. had them in and set them into my shaving kit so I'd have them with me next time I went home. Kipp would be one happy camper when I gave him these points.

*   *   *

At noon chuck, J.W. was telling us about the time when he was just beginning to cowboy and how he worked in Louisiana and the trouble they had with the cattle there coming down with hoof rot from time to time.

"Where they ran cows down there, there is a lot of swamp. Wet, full of bugs tryin' to suck the blood out of you an', of course, snakes. Water moccasins, cotton mouths, copperheads an' also gators," J.W. started to say. Then went on, "Anyway it's an awful place to work. High humidity. You're always sweating like a boiler feeder. You didn't dare get off your horse 'cause you'd sink in the mud to your knees or some snake might bite you. You know what they call a cowboy down there? They call 'em crackers because those southeastern guys use bull whips an' crack them at the stock to move 'em along. The place was no place for any self respecting cowboy young or old. I only worked there a short time an' headed for Texas an' good cow country right quick."

No one had any questions or comments to make so J.W. went on, "The place was kind of pretty in some respects, had some nice really big trees, lots of Spanish moss hanging off of every branch. You'd be lookin' for cows in the thickest jungle-like swamp until you found a place they called 'stomping grounds' an' that's where the cattle hung out. High ground an' dry. What I mean by high ground there is maybe two, three feet or more above swamp level. The place was stomped by hundreds of foot prints from the cows. Only place they could lay down to chew their cud without drowning. Seemed to be fewer bugs there also. Don't know why but it was. I reckon that's where the term, 'this here is my stomping grounds' comes from."

"I've heard some of the stories about cowboys working in southern Arizona's brush country, an' that kind of place havin' to chase maverick cattle in which doesn't sound any better," Clint put in, "All that cactus, thorns on everything that grows in the desert and dozens of kinds of venomous snakes also, Gila monsters that will chew poison into you and when it rains, it's like bein' hit by a waterfall. An' from what I hear, if you're caught in some coulee they call arroyos after a rain like I just described, you're a drowned rat for sure. Few men or beasts ever make it out alive. They say it will come at you as a wall of water that's on you before you got time to scramble out of its way. Damn water could wash away a full grown elephant. An' after a rain like that you can find water for a few days in what they call *tinajas*, which are just puddles in the rock or clay basins until it evaporates."

"Cowboyin' has always been a job with risks but I must admit I'm not much anxious to buckaroo in those places. I think I might like workin' in chaparral hill country like in southern California," J.W. put in, "Where the worst thing is gettin' poison oak."

Ramon then put his two cents worth into the evening's conversation in his broken English about hunting cows in an area that was also pure Hell.

"One time, I *trabajo* . . . you say work, rancho in Mexico. *Rancho Sagrada* in *Sonora* very close to *Chihuahua*. *Vaqueros* have to go in place called *el malpais, mocho tierras baldias*. How you say valcan . . . . Volcano, *merer negro* . . . black rock to look for cows. Very bad place. No good for cattle. No good for *caballeros* . . . horses," he tried to make his point.

I later found out that the *malpais* is a twisted cinder like jagged volcanic lava flow that can extend for many miles and is some of the toughest terrain to navigate on foot and impossible on a horse. The rock can cut up your shoes or boots in no time if you're on foot walking around in there. It is worse than a prairie dog town of holes that a horse can easily break a leg in if you try to cross the *malpais* on horseback.

"What's *sagrada*, mean Ramon?" I asked.

"Sacred," he said as he made the sign of the cross, blessing himself, "but can also mean how you say . . . cursed."

Ramon told of how the Yaquis Indians would hide out in these lava flows and conceal themselves in the caves and survive by eating lizards, snakes, insects and collect water within *tinajas* of the *malpais* until their enemies had tired of waiting for them to come out and since they didn't dare go into the cursed and extremely rugged terrain for fear of getting lost, cut up or breaking a leg, they left. The four-legged limber coyotes and a few rabbits were the only mammals that lived and crossed the awful land.

He told of a young boy having gone into the *malpais* to look for lost cattle after being told not to and he and his burro both perishing in there. But days later the boy's body and burro were found by men on foot going in the *malpais* because they saw the activity of vultures and ravens in the sky and had become suspicious that was where the boy was.

Cow camp evenings were full of stories, discussions, laughter, guitar music, good comradeship that often ended with the melodious yowls of distant coyotes crooning at the moon.

*   *   *

I rode to Jackrabbit line camp to check on things. I also wanted to see if I could find my pocketknife, if I'd left it there. I had missplaced it some time ago. It was an old Case jackknife with a stag-horn handled, that had two blades. It once had belonged to Grandpa Lovett and Dad had passed it on to me. So I felt not only bad but also stupid for losing it.

That afternoon the sky to the west had darkened and the wind was up and I had a feeling I'd get dumped on with precipitation before I made it to the shelter of the cabin.

I hurried the old horse we called Henry to a lope in hopes of getting out of the oncoming weather. The harder the wind blew the darker the sky above me looked.

Suddenly I was being pelted by sizeable hail and that put Henry in a more hurried move. I could see the shack ahead of me by a quarter mile and as the hail grew stronger and larger I spurred Henry into a gallop for shelter. The ground we crossed was now solid white, the air freezing and I was wet and cold in a matter of only a minute or two.

Reaching the cabin I jumped off Henry and pulled him under cover of the overhanging roof and opened the cabin door after tying Henry to an O-ring-tie in the wall. Now the hail was the size of quarters and made an intense racket.

Inside I started a fire to get dried off. I was becoming hypothermic and began to shiver almost violently and it seemed to take forever to get the cabin heated. I had pulled my wet clothes off and hung them near the stove. Steam began to rise from my clothes and the stove's warmth and the old gunny sacks wrapped around my body reduced the shivering. Henry stood still under the porch after having shaken himself off. As quickly as the hail had started it stopped and the sun eased out from behind the gray clouds as they moved steadily on east with haste.

A half hour later my shirt and pants had dried off and I put everything back on and the warmth felt ever so good. Everything outside was solid white. I had managed to make some coffee as soon as I had stopped shivering. I gave Henry a noise bag with a bit of grain in it after loosening the saddle cinch. And we both knew we had lucked out by making it to Jackrabbit when we did.

My slicker was still tied to the back of the saddle. There had been no time to put it on as the weather had hit us so fast and with such velocity that all I wanted to do was find shelter.

As I looked around and up at the Aermotor windmill with the folded tail and stagnant blades that I had secured fast with wire earlier when I first started to live in the cabin, I saw that on the platform the old nest of sticks and wire had grown larger since I had last been here. And now with all the hail covering the surface it looked to be the formation of an igloo.

"Cr-r-ruck!" The metallic squawk of a raven was heard lacerating the chilly air. I looked up and there were four ravens gliding on outstretched wings. Two and two the ravens were flying in close proximity to one another yet apart. One raven was missing a couple of wing feathers which made no difference in its flying ability. *"Prrruk!"* one of the others answered and one after another they banked and flew over the windmill and then the cabin, eyeing me and Henry as they passed overhead. Away they flew farther to the east and then out of sight.

The sun was now melting the hail so fast that rivulets of water ran down slope, carving the ground with channels of cold water.

Now once again warm and with fully dried clothes plus having found my jackknife I was ready to head back to the cow camp.

"*Cra-a-wk!*" came a cry from above and as a shadow passed over me, I looked up to see the same ravens chasing a raptor. On slow wing beats with alternative flapping and then soaring the ravens kept close to the hawk. Occasionally a raven swooped down at the raptor and pecked it and the hawk would fold its wings and drop some before flying on. This battle and harassment of the *Buteo* was kept up by the ravens until they had driven it from their territory and air space.

Three days later I rode upon a deer carcass that a coyote was busy eating. The ravens walked around him, one occasionally grabbing at a bit of the deer and the coyote would lunge at the raven to chase it away and then return to his meal. The other raven would then sneak up behind the coyote, pull at the tail or nipping a rear leg at which time the coyote turned to attack the pest and chase it, while the other raven jumped in to steal a meal.

I sat my horse and watched at a good distance. Again and again the brazen ravens took turns in badgering the coyote, robbing a meal and flying off to eat it. Nearby magpies walked around at a safe distance twitching their tails, fluttering and hopping closer to the carcass.

Finally I rode up to the carcass and the coyote slinked away at a trot and into the sage. Not having my rifle all I could do was interfere with the coyote's meal. Shooting at him with the Luger I kept in my saddle bag would most likely have made me waste ammunition, since I was a poor pistol shot even at close range. The ravens and magpies also moved off to nearby trees, landed and watched me.

I got off Sioux and examined the deer's remains. It was an old doe; her eyes had been plucked out, most likely by the ravens. The coyote had torn open her abdomen and eaten what it wanted. I could tell that the deer had been dead for a few days by the amount of activity that was around the carcass and the fact that beetles and maggots were busy within the animal.

"*C-r-r-r-u-u-k!*" croaked one of the ravens as I mounted Sioux and rode off a short distance and turned Henry around so I could watch the carcass. The ravens flew back to the deer and fed some more. A turkey vulture was now circling high over the marauding ravens and lifeless doe. As the shadow of the vulture passed over the deer corpse, one of the ravens looked up.

"*Tok-tok-tok*," he told the others.

The vulture with its broad six foot wing span, fanned at landing then folded them and began to tear the hide off the deer. The ravens had backed off, but now came back in to share more of the meal.

To me there was a great comparison between the carrion eaters: the buzzards with their naked red heads and curved beaks looked morbid, whereas the ravens with their Roman-nose beaks and obsidian eyes and polished jet plumage had a royal and intelligent look to them.

Ravens are bright birds with uncanny wits as sharp as a razor. I remember watching one unbuckling the two strings on a saddle bag and stealing a sandwich out of it. I once saw one that hung upside down looking into Ma's clothes-pin bag fastened on the clothes line, to see if there was something to eat or steal in there. I've heard of people raising a young raven and teaching it to talk like a parrot. Tom said he had one steal his key out of his truck's ignition and fly off with it. He wouldn't have believed it if he hadn't seen the thief hop out of the truck's open window with a shiny thing in its beak and fly off with it.

When telling the story, Tom ended it by commenting that ravens and jay are all camp robbers and worse than any pack rat and smarter than most average dogs.

It seems that if you ask someone in the west about ravens, each will have a tale to tell about their experiences while watching these regal black birds.

The Aermotor windmill with the raven's nest of sticks, turning to the wind with quiet blades, now still had a purpose, if not to draw water from the depths of the ground, then to the tenants that raised their young in the nest there from year to year. The Aermotor would be their home until time would rust and rot the old windmill to the ground and the family of ravens would need to move on.

* * *

TWO CACKLES
& A GRUNT
CHAPTER 15

Manuel was a good camp cook but the only bread he made was tortillas
and on occasion attempted biscuits which were passable if you soaked
them in your gravy or coffee before biting into one.

We all missed Little Raven's sour dough pancakes, breads and
baking powder biscuits which she had learned to perfect over time.
No one ever complained to Manuel about his cooking, as it was one
of those unwritten rules. Cowboys had more names for cooks than, as
the saying goes, "Carter has Little Liver Pills." He was known by such
names as cookie, coosie, bean master, biscuit shooter, dough puncher,
hash slinger, sizzler, sourdough, star chief and occasionally someone
would call him 'Dutch' because of the Dutch ovens he did most of his
cooking in. Cooks with bad reputations were called, behind their backs
that is, belly cheater, grub spoiler, gut burglar, gut robber, hash burner,
lizard scorcher and numerous other names. And as another saying

goes, any and all crackerjack range cooks were "Worth their weight in gold."

The cook was the pride of any cow outfit no matter where. He had to be resourceful, was depended upon to have three hot meals a day, no matter what the weather was, and had to have enough grub to feed what company might happen to drop in. In the old cattle drive days, if an unemployed cowboy or anyone for that matter was riding the range and came across a cow outfit they would head for the chuck wagon for a free meal. No one was turned down. But it was understood that if you were one that was riding the grub line, after you ate your meal and the men went back to work it was your inherent responsibility to help the cook with washing the pots, pans and dishes. If you did, often the cook would then send you on your way with leftovers and at times a meager amount of coffee beans.

Cowboys knew that if they were working for an outfit that had a bad cook they only had three options: one; quit the brand, two; put up with the bad vittles or three; kill the son of a bitch cook in which case even though the act could be described as justifiable homicide, you then had the responsibility of now cooking for the whole outfit, in which case you better be a better cook than the one you had just murdered.

The other thing we all wished was that Manuel would lay off the chili spice once in awhile. Though I'm sure he had our best intentions in mind.

He'd say, "Chili, she's good. Keels de worms en you. You no get sick. You see."

One day while Manuel was away from his kitchen Clint got hold of the can of chili powder and quickly emptied most of it into one of his boots before the cook came back into the building, thinking that Manuel, after running out of the chili would have no choice but to do without. Once outside Clint dumped out the chili from his boot but had a hot foot for the rest of the day.

When Manuel was out of chili powder he asked Tom to get him some more next time he was in town and bring it back to cow camp. But Tom had a hundred excuses of why he had forgotten the chili and so we had a break from the spice and no more heartburn.

None of us got giardia. But whether it was the chili or having the water boiled remained to be known.

* * *

Finally J.W. and I had a couple of days off together. We decided to spend the two days in Sheridan, Wyoming, instead of going to Billings.

J.W. was suffering from a toothache and was hoping to see a dentist there. He had a small cavity that was troublesome to him. Jed had said that what his grandmother did for a toothache was to burn a small piece of paper on a plate and with a bit of cotton wad wipe up the sweat residue off the plate and plug it into the cavity of the tooth. J.W. tried this old fashion method and said it seemed to help and was able to put up with the toothache for awhile. Jed admitted that though his father had this method used on him as a boy, it had never been tried on him and he believed it to be just one of those old wives tale remedies. I said that it might just be a placebo effect.

"What's a placebo?" J.W. wanted to know.

I realized that if I told him, the placebo effect would not work and he'd be back with a damn tooth ache. So I wasn't going to open that can of worms and I answered, "I'll tell you after you get your tooth fixed."

J.W. insisted in driving his truck, so I left mine at the ranch. We took off toward Sheridan as soon as we had showered and put on clean clothes. J.W. was an extremely fast driver. He only slowed down whenever we came to a town and did the town's speed limit. When it came to curves he would straighten them out if no other vehicle was heading our way by driving in the oncoming lane. By the time the sun had melted into the western horizon, a full moon had risen over the eastern plain and the night sky was illuminated, casting black shadows in the deep coulees that trenched their way towards the river. The two lane country roads back then didn't have much traffic on them even on a Friday night. I thought for sure we'd end up getting a speeding ticket but luckily we never saw a county cop car all the way to Sheridan.

I had to ask J.W. why he was driving so fast and he said he just liked speed when he was behind the steering wheel of a car or truck.

"Why do you think the speedometer goes up to a hundred? Why that's what cars are made to do, otherwise the speedometer would only go up to fifty or maybe sixty miles per hour an' that's as fast as your car could go an' no faster," he reasoned. "Besides, we've got places to go an' people to piss off. So let's get 'er done."

He then had the truck up to ninety on all of the straight away two-lane blacktop.

"I sure hope we get there in one piece," I stated.

"Hell, I know this road better than the one to Billings. Besides I've been driving since I was twelve," he said with an assuring tone.

"Always this fast?" I asked.

"No!' he said, giving me an exasperated glance.

*   *   *

Friday night we stayed in a place called the 'Why Go By? Motor Court' on the outskirts of Sheridan and kept the cabin for the following night also. The place was cheap and only two other cabins had been rented out when we pulled in. After we dumped our war bags off in the room we locked up and headed to town for a meal.

We found a diner that was open until midnight and reopened at six in the morning even on weekends. Doty's Diner was an actual dining railroad car sitting on a foundation and without its wheels or rather 'trucks' as they are called. The converted eatery had a long counter with chrome pedestal bar stools and a few booths all in chrome and yellow Naugahyde. The diner seemed to cater to mostly local clientele. We both ate steaks with the fixings and lots of coffee. The waitress never wrote down our orders, she just yelled it to the cook at which time he'd just nod and begin cooking what she had asked for. The kitchen was in a separate add-on to the dining car. The steaks were as large as the dinner plates with mashed potatoes and gravy along with cut green beans all slopped on an oval white plate.

Famished as we were, we commenced eating in silence and speed.

"It ain't none of my 'Peas an' Q's' but you cowboys eat like you're starvin'. It's not good to gulp down your food. You got to chew it some," she told us in a motherly way as she poured us each another cup of coffee. The bill came to four dollars and twenty seven cents. We split the bill and each left the waitress a fifty cent tip which was a very rewarding tip in those days.

We then headed for a bar with a Friday night dance. J.W.'s tooth was bothering him again and I could see that he was always poking at it with his tongue. "Freakin' tooth is a pain in the ass," he said at one point.

We found a bar called the Silver Spur that had a sizeable dance floor and a good western band called The Swing Riders. The three members consisted of a lead female guitarist singer, a well-proportioned blonde with a good twang of a western voice; a backup bass player; and guitarist that also played the fiddle and mandolin, all dressed in western clothing, boots and cowboy hats.

The place was full but not overcrowded with mostly cowboys, all wearing their hats. Most of the men seemed to be enjoying drinking at the bar or playing pool at one of the four tables. Around the bar's back mirror's wide frame, local ranchers had burned their Wyoming brands into the wood and at the center of the frame was the Rocking Wine Cup brand, a wine glass with a curved rocker base.

Couples were dancing to the western music. There were single women sitting at tables looking for some brave cowboy to ask them to dance. It didn't take J.W. long to find a dance partner. After which we were invited to sit with the three gals at their table.

J.W. bought a round of drinks. The pretty brunette that J.W. had just danced with was Maxine and her two girl friends were Donna and Sharon. All were in their early twenties. Donna was a blonde with a long braid down her back and freckles that added to her cuteness. Sharon with black hair was nothing to write home about except she had a good set of lungs, 'nice tits.' She never smiled or even laughed when one of us said something funny. She had a sour face and only drank Coca-Cola. Why the three girls hung out together was a mystery to me except that they all attended college here in Sheridan.

Maxine and J.W. had hit it off right away. Thinking I'd be a nice guy I asked Sharon if she would like to dance, hoping that it might raise her spirits.

"No, thank you very much. I do not dance!" she pointed out rather curtly, in a southern accent, as she turned her head away and watched the band and ignored me.

"Okay," I said, wishing I hadn't asked her since she seemed so repulsed by my doing so.

Looking at Donna with what I'm sure was a confused look I asked her somewhat hesitantly, "Would you like to dance?"

"You bet, cowboy. Let's polish our buckles together," she said, smiling at me as she rose and we headed to the dance floor and a waltz. Donna was a good ranch stock kind of gal that had been a barrel racer in high school and was now furthering her education to become a nurse.

After the second dance Donna wrapped herself around me, making sure our buckles were rubbing and after that dance we danced four more times before the band stopped for a break. She smelled good and felt good to be holding onto. It had been a long time since I had had a female to be close to since Sue Parker had split up our relationship.

Walking back to the table I asked Donna what the story was with Sharon since she seemed so incompatible with her friends.

"Honey," she said, "She's a WASP and thinks she's better than any of us."

"What's a wasp?" I asked.

"White Anglo Saxon Protestant," she chimed, "You know, she being from the Maryland and from some uppity family, thinks she's something special like an aristocrat," she told me as we approached our table, "Tell you more later."

"This is a pretty good band. She's got a wonderful voice," Maxine said, "They're here this whole weekend. Next week some group called the Range Riders are coming. I've heard them before an' they're okay but this group should make it to Nashville."

Sharon gave her an exasperated glance.

At which Maxine smiled and stuck her tongue out at Sharon.

"I like this band. How about you guys?" Donna asked.

"You bet!" piped up J.W., "Besides, they play a lot of slow songs an' I can dance close to Maxine."

Sharon just gave Maxine a glaring look as she held her unlit cigarette out for one of us to light it for her.

I lit a match and she put the cigarette to her mouth as I lit it and she took in some smoke, poised the cigarette to the side and blew a small smoke ring in the air.

J. W. was already smoking and seeing this act of Sharon's, he took in a big drag on his cigarette and exhaled out three consecutive large smoke rings up into the already clouded ceiling and smiled at her.

Sharon leaned over to Donna and whispered, "It behooves me to want to leave. May we go?"

"Dear, Maxine and I are having fun," she emphasized. "So if you wish to go, go! Skedaddle! It behooves Maxine and me that we stay."

Indignantly Sharon rose and asked, "Am I supposed to walk back to the campus without being chaperoned?" and added, "This late at night especially."

"Here, take the keys to my car and go. These gentlemen will drive us back after the bar closes." Maxine handed her the keys with a pink rabbit's foot key chain holder.

"Thanks," Sharon said and made her way out of the place as the band started up again.

"What's her problem?" J.W. wondered.

"She's uppity, thinks she's a Rockefeller," Maxine said.

"She's not smart enough to go to a college like Wellesley and her parents thought going out west to a junior college would make her more human before they bought her a good liberal education. But she just loves being a bitch," Donna said.

"We only asked her to come with us because I felt sorry for her never getting out. But now I know that was a big mistake. She's so obviously pretentious," Maxine laughed.

We went back to dancing and having a real good time until two o'clock and we all climbed into J.W.'s truck. Donna sat on my lap and Maxine sat in the middle and hung onto J.W.'s arm while pressing against him and kissing his neck while he drove to the college campus.

At the campus the girls said that they would meet us at the Silver Spur Saturday night and promised not to bring Sharon with them this time.

J.W. stayed in the truck with Maxine while I walked Donna to her dorm. Donna gave me a long tongue-twisted kiss when we stopped at the door after which she whispered, "I want you, cowboy, so be ready to ride tomorrow night." That made me so damn horny I thought I'd explode.

When I got back to the truck I could see that J.W. was at it in the front seat. So I went for a stroll, smoked my last Lucky Strike thinking of Donna and Saturday night. By the time I got back to the truck J.W. was coming back from having taken Maxine to her dorm. Now all the beers I had consumed were beginning to affect me and I noticed J.W. was walking a bit unsteady.

"What a gal that Maxine is," J.W. exclaimed, "Whoopee!"

I drove to the Why Go By and as tired and drunk as I was all I could do was to think of Saturday night and holding Donna and getting lucky.

Saturday morning, around eleven J.W. and I walked into Doty's Diner and sat at the counter. The place was full of customers. A flaming red-headed waitress behind the counter with a name tag that said her name was "Pumpkin" put two mugs in front of us and started to pour coffee into them.

"You guys want coffee?" she asked us after the fact.

"I guess we do," I said, "Thanks."

"You need the cow?" she asked, making a wry face at us, knowing that cowboys as a rule never used milk or cream in their coffee.

"Nope, we're okay. Black's the way we like it. Just keep 'er comin'," J.W. put in as Pumpkin handed us menus from the condiment rack in front of us. She went on down the counter refilling coffee mugs as she went.

Soon she came back to take our orders.

"You all figured what you want to eat?" Pumpkin asked.

"Yeah," I said, "I reckon I'll have eggs over easy and bacon."

"And you, cowboy?" she asked J. W.

"I'm still undecided," J.W. said.

"You guys want separate checks?"

"Sure." J.W. said.

Pumpkin turned to the kitchen window and yelled at the cook, "Two cackles an' a grunt, o. e." as she put toast in the toaster.

"I'll be back for your order in a minute, hun," she said to J.W. as she took plates of food from the cook's window to a customer down the counter.

J.W. ordered pancakes, scrambled eggs and link sausage.

We left Doty's Diner floating in coffee and satisfied with the breakfast meal and headed into town to check it out.

J. W. and I stopped at a dentist located on the fourth floor of an office building. I hung out in the waiting room and looked through some magazines while J.W had dental work done.

"What he end up doing to you?" I asked after we got down to the street from the dentist.

"Drilled and filled. Shot me full of Novocain an' I'm still numb. If you hit me in the face I wouldn't feel it," J.W. vowed. "He said not to eat on that side of my mouth for awhile so let's get somethin' to drink. A little Jack Daniel's, maybe? An' by the way, what's a placebo?" J.W. asked suddenly.

I answered his question as we drove around a bit. At one point we drove past the Sheridan Inn and I thought of Sue Palmer, now Missus Sue Long and I knew I was over her for good and wished her the best in my thought.

By mid afternoon we went into a small bar and had a couple of drinks before wandering around until we saw a barber shop. We both went in for haircuts so we'd look good and smelled good for our dates that night, especially after the barber doused us with some aftershave that wasn't witch-hazel but Old Spice. I hadn't packed an extra shirt and so only had the one I was wearing and if I was going out on a date I thought it best to have on a clean shirt. So we stopped by a mercantile and I bought a new western shirt, plaid with piping and square pearl snaps.

"You plannin' to be the belle of the ball tonight?" J.W. asked with a smile.

"Well I'm not planning to go dancing with a shirt that smells like a hog pen after dancing with it on last night. Besides look who's talking. Where did you get that fancy striped shirt and silk rag you're wearing?"

"Elko, Nevada, two years ago."

Then we headed for a pharmacy to buy some rubbers, knowing that our chance in getting lucky that night was a good possibility. I had decided to rent a cabin for myself next to the one we had already. I had told the clerk in the motor court office that I need my own room because J.W. snored too loud. He had smiled as I paid him eight dollars for the cabin and he handed me the receipt and room key.

*   *   *

Saturday night at the Silver Spur was hopping just as the night before. We had told the girls we'd meet them there around nine but J.W. and I got to the Spur just before eight and secured a good table near the dance floor and band. We drank beers and watched the band come in and set up and make sure everything was in working order and the lead singer sang a couple of practice songs before starting their show at nine.

Maxine and Donna arrived before nine and both looked great and dressed to the nines.

"Evenin', ladies," J.W. said as he stood up, tipped the brim of his hat and pulled out a chair for Maxine.

I had also stood up, doffed my hat to them and had Donna sit in the chair next to me.

"Well fancy meeting you gentlemen here tonight," Maxine crooned as she looked at J.W., smiling and licking her upper lip suggestively.

Donna, having seen Maxine lick her lips, then looked at me and blew me a kiss. I in turn puckered up and kissed back.

"You ladies look great," I said.

"Thank you, Dakk," they both chimed.

A tall barmaid came to our table, "What would you ladies like to drink?"

"I'll have a brandy Alexander. I need something chocolaty to start off with," Maxine said.

"A vodka sour with a couple of cherries with stems," Donna said.

"You fellers need another beer?"

"You bet we do," J.W. insisted.

I looked at her, wondering what was with the two cherries.

The band lead singer spoke into her microphone, "Ladies and gentlemen, I'm Deedee Harmon and we're 'The Swing Riders'. To my left is David on the bass and here to my right is Justin, who once played in Nashville alongside Hank Williams as a stand-in for awhile. Thank you all for being here tonight. I'll begin with a slow number."

The drinks came and J.W. asked the barmaid to run a tab.

"Want a sip?" Maxine asked J.W.

"No thanks, I'll stick to the beer."

Donna plucked the two maraschino cherries out of her drink and put one in her mouth, stem and all and dangled the other for me to take. Of course I did and pulled the stem off the cherry and set it on the table. Smiling while looking at me she seemed to be working her tongue around in her mouth for a minute after eating the cheery and when she extracted the stem she had managed to tie a knot in it.

"Bet you can't do that again," I said.

"How much?" she teased.

"I'll buy you another drink," I said.

Donna picked up my cherry stem from the table and put it in her mouth and produced another knotted stem.

"How did you do that?" I said.

"With my tongue," she laughed.

"Can you do that, too?" I asked Maxine.

"No. I've tried a bunch of times. I almost got it once," she admitted.

J.W. just shook his head, "What will people come up with next? The only trick I know how to do is balance a salt shaker on its edge an' that's easy."

"I can balance two forks on a match stick on the edge of a glass of water," I declared.

"Can you float a needle in a glass of water?" Donna asked.

"Never tried it, you?" Maxine put in.

After a few dances the barmaid brought us another round of drinks, one of which was vodka sour with two cherries. I tried to tie a knot in the stem with my tongue with no luck. And Donna took my stem and popped out another knotted cherry stem. Then Maxine attempted to do the same but couldn't.

The girls nursed their drinks and we did the same but spent most of the time dancing the night away. When the band took a break we all stepped outside into the evening air to cool down. We had danced too many fast dances. During the slow dances both Maxine and Donna let us know with their bodies what they wanted.

Outside, Maxine asked J.W. in a whisper where we were staying and he told her we each had a cabin at the Why Go By Motor Court.

"Oh, those are such cute cabins," Maxine exclaimed.

"They're okay. Got a bed in them and a bathroom." J.W. said as he gave Maxine a smirking smile.

"Donna, these gentlemen are staying at the Why Go By and each has their own cabin."

"Gee, maybe they'll show us the cabins. Won't you, Dakk?"

"Let's have a couple more dances an' pay the tab and we can give you a cook's tour of our abodes," J.W. said and pulled Maxine to him and kissed her.

"I can't wait," Donna said as we could hear the band start playing again.

By one o'clock we quit the Silver Spur and J.W. went in Maxine's car and Donna and I drove the truck to the Why Go By.

We awoke the next morning around ten and after showering we all went to Doty's Diner for breakfast.

Together we sat at a booth and I was real tempted to play B-17 but when I saw what the song was changed my mind. B-17 was "Why Do Fools Fall in Love?" by Frankie Lymon.

* * *

Sunday afternoon J.W. and I left Sheridan and headed back to the Milliron slash B. The late afternoon sunlight spread golden over the landscape, creating drawn-out purple shadows. Everything around us was dreamlike as if utterly renewed. The distant clouds became flames of orange and red.

We had just passed the one horse town Garryowen on the Crow Indian Reservation and the Custer Battlefield to the east of us. A few miles after the Crow Agency I glanced at the speedometer and saw that J.W. wasn't speeding as much as he had when we had come down to Sheridan. Finally I said, "That was one Hell of a weekend."

"You bet. If they were all like that I'd want every weekend off."

"Don't tell me you're in love with Maxine," I muttered.

"Look, just because she rode me hard an' put me away wet don't mean I'm head over heels about her. You know there's no need to buy the cow if the milk is free," he protested.

"Got a point, and like they say, 'Don't go lookin' a gift horse in the mouth.' Free is free."

"Yeah!"

"Think we'll ever see them again?"

"Maybe an' maybe not. That's a fifty—fifty chance. Why, you fall in love with Donna?"

"No, but I sure enjoyed the time we had together."

"Hey, I enjoyed the time I had with Maxine too, but I'm not dreamin' of becomin' double harnessed with her or any other women at this time of my life. I got the life I love for now an' maybe always. Who knows? I like easy women an' booze once in a while an' that's all I need from time to time, not marriage, family an' responsibility. But my guess is that if I ever decide to get hitched then I'll probably go for it, lock, stock an' barrel."

"I come close . . . but you're right, I am not ready to cross that bridge either," I confided.

At Harding we headed on north along the Little Bighorn River known to the Indians as *The Greasy Grass* and on to its confluence with the Yellowstone River. The air became cooler and the aroma of new cut hay laying in windrows came through the open windows. Swarms of dark birds flew sporadically across the highway ahead of us; they frayed in all directions as the truck entered their airspace. A few antelope stood on hilltops grazing in the now dissolving light and the long cast shadows from telephone poles and trees grew lengthier across the highway. J. W. sped on; the radio played "Bye Bye Love."

* * *

RED HANDED
CHAPTER 16

Fall was close now with the beginning of September. The rigorous task of haying was complete. The mowed wide windrows of hay had been spared from rain and the New Holland baling machine Archie had bought made the field hand's job a bit easier. The Milliron hay was made up of wild grasses and Timothy grasses while the irrigated fields were a good mixture of Timothy and leguminous; alfalfa and clover. The bales were then picked up by men in the field and handed to the catchers on the wagon pulled by the tractor and transported to the big barn and hay shed. But now with the new baler you only needed a catcher or two to stack the bales on the wagon because the machine innovation did all the work men in the field used to do. Gone were the days of the horse drawn rakes, beaver slides and large hay cribs or the hand feed horse-operated hay baling machines. Machines versus labor was becoming more and more the thing of the future and less expensive than hiring men in the long run. I wondered when they'd invent some machine to replace the cowboy and his horse. It seemed to be a complete impossibility even in the distant future that the working cowboy and his horse would vanish from such lousy pay and abuse only to be replaced by some new fangled high dollar piece of ultra modern machinery. That was my way of thinking at that time anyhow.

As I came out of Little Raven's kitchen eating an apple heading back to the bunkhouse, I saw that all the dogs were lying about enjoying the sun. Sylvia lying on the porch snapped at a fly, missed and snapped again, caught it, chewed it with her head up in the air, swallowed and set her head back down on her paws. Her eyes wandered around looking for another pesky fly to venture close. The hounds lay on their sides near one another while the Border collie followed me to my horse Jeep that was saddled and tied to the hitching rail at the bunkhouse along with J.W.'s horse Llano. Biting off a chunk of apple, I offered it to Llano; he sniffed at it, pulled his head back and snorted as I held it out to him.

"So you don't like apples. Well Jeep does." I handed the piece of apple to Jeep and he ate it and looked at me with great anticipation of also getting the core which I gave him after I had eaten around it.

J.W. came out of the bunkhouse.

"Llano refused my giving him apple. Wouldn't eat the piece I gave him."

"He likes carrots."

"Horses are as picky eaters as humans sometimes. I once saw a women feed her horse a banana. She'd peel it and feed it to the horse an' then gave it the damn peel an' it ate it also. I asked her if her horse was part monkey at which she got a bit perturbed."

"I've seen plenty of horses that like drinkin' beer an' gettin' drunk but I'll be damned if I ever heard of a horse eatin' bananas. Wonder if horses in the tropical countries learned to eat bananas?" J.W. remarked as we both mounted and rode off at a walk with Misty pacing back and forth at our heels.

Rojo, Archie's horse, whinnied at us as we passed by.

Jed was getting ready to put new shoes on Rojo and was busy banging one on the anvil forming it to fit one of Rojo's back feet. He was shoeing Rojo just out of habit since Archie hardly ever rode the old horse much these days. Emma Braddock was working one of her thoroughbreds in the arena dressed in her eastern riding clothes and helmet.

Once Misty knew what we were going to do she would assist in the operation of moving the yearling steers into the pens by circling them and keeping them together and would chase any steer that broke from the group. All we had to do was keep driving the steers on and occasionally give Misty a command that she followed like a Marine.

Aside from the usual dog commands like sit, down, off, here and heel that most dogs obey, working stock dogs know more commands. If you wanted Misty to move the bunched up steers forward you would say, "Walk up." If you wished for her to move them clockwise you just called out, "Come by!" If you wanted the stock to move counter clockwise to you the command was, "Away to me!" To slow the dog you'd say, "Steady." To move the dog away from the stock, "Get out!" If you saw that the dog didn't see behind itself or there was a straggler you'd call out to her, "Look back!" Finally, to release Misty from working the stock you would call out as one word, "That-el-do!" and she would stop, back off and lay down panting with tongue lolling out but eyes on the stock until you called her to you.

"If I ever have a dog it's going to be a border collie like Misty," I said.

"Border collies are great dogs when it comes to working stock. In Idaho, Nevada, eastern Oregon and Wyoming there are lots of Basque sheep herders, you know the guys livin' in sheep-wagons an' wearin' those black berets instead of cowboy hats. Anyway one herder on horseback with two or three dogs can work three, four hundred or more sheep from range to range. The dogs can even cut out a certain sheep from the herd. They're incredible to watch them work," commented J.W., then he added, "They're smarter than most humans I've met an' horses I've known."

"I can't argue that point." I said.

We had moved the steers into the pen and then rode circle for ten miles looking for any steers that may have been missed with Misty following and helping bring in seven elusive ones. At times the steers hid among the heifers or in the brush as if having the intuition that we were out to move them to a new location.

We drove them slowly back to the ranch headquarters, and at a time or two had to run cows back from following us.

The day was cloudless and as blue as mountain blue-birds. Small lizards ran for cover as we advanced. Now and again we flushed sage chickens that sprang from in front of the steers and caused the beeves to scatter until Misty herded them back together and on the right path. The chickens would blast out of the sage at the last second and fly up and out, then glide on and land some hundred yards away. In the distance a flicker could be heard drumming on a tree trunk with its beak drilling in the bark grubbing.

When we got back to the ranch Tom needed someone to go to town and pick up tractor parts that morning. Everyone had their morning job already set and he didn't want to send one of the Mexicans for the part because there had been talk that immigration was in Billings looking for illegal workers, according to what Archie had been told through the grapevine.

"Well which one of you wants to make a run to town? I'd go but I have to go to the Hash Knife Ranch on business for Archie," asked Tom, "So you guys can flip a coin to see who goes if you want."

As we three stood near each other I reached in my pocket and found a nickel.

"You call it," I said to J.W.

"Heads!" he said.

I flipped it into the air and Tom caught it in the air and slapped it on the back of his other hand.

The Indian head or as it was better known, 'the buffalo nickel,' showed tails with the buffalo. I had won the toss and showed the buffalo to Tom.

"This is a 1938 nickel. I bet you guys didn't know this but the buffalo that was the model for the design on this nickel was killed right here in the Musselshell Valley near the Phillips Ranch," stated Tom. "Shot here in Montana by some guy called Hornaday I think, that's what Archie had told me and the buff was such a fantastic specimen that Hornaday had it sent back east to be mounted for some museum and that it later became the nickel model for some sculptor."

*   *   *

The tractor distributorship and shop in Billings had the part Tom wanted so one of the Mexicans that did mechanical work around the ranch could fix it. It was waiting for me to pick up since Archie had called ahead and ordered it and had them send him a bill.

Sending a cowboy to town at anytime generally meant it would be an all day affair, besides cowboying isn't a time clock kind of job. So my second stop was the Pronghorn Café for a mid morning cup of coffee and see if there might be a new cute waitress working there before I dropped by the house to see how the folks were. I discovered that Cooper had a dish washer's job at the Pronghorn and that the cook was teaching him how to cook and having him help at the stove when he got busy with to many orders at one time. Cooper came out to sit with me on his morning break and that's when I found out that the Texaco Station had hired Kipp to pump gas, check oil, wash the windows and fix flats for a buck per hour which had just become the new minimum wage since March and that was real good money. He told me that Cody had a job at the Five and Dime working as a soda jerk part time. And that on his first day Cody, thinking that the pressurized can of whipping cream was almost empty, had shaken it vigorously to insure he got an ample amount of whip cream to top off this older couple's sundaes that he was making in front of them while they sat at the counter watching him. What Cody had not known was that the other fellow working with him had replaced the container with a new one so that when Cody went to top off the sundaes it gushed and sprayed everyone, including himself. It was such a sudden error of comedy that Cody got to laughing uncontrollably while handing out paper napkins and tried to say he was sorry to the whip cream splattered customers, who took it all in good humor and he didn't get fired.

I got home and visited with Ma and had lunch there of left over tuna casserole and hearing about what was what around the house. Dad had come down with a bout of walking pneumonia but was healthy now. She talked about the garden, the chickens and that a new feral cat that had found its way to our barn but you rarely saw it because it was very elusive so no one had named it as yet.

"Thanks for lunch, Ma, it was great," I said, "Wish I could see Dad before I go but I've got to get some gas and then skedaddle back to the ranch."

"When do you reckon you'll be home for a day or two?" she asked.

"Don't know," I said, kissing her on the forehead and leaving.

I drove to the Texaco to get gas and see Kipp.

"Hey! Give me a couple of bucks' worth of regular, Dipstick," I said.

"Hey! Yourself. Want me to check the air in your tires too, or just puncture them? Big brother." Kipp said low enough so his boss wouldn't hear him.

I got out of the truck and shook his greasy hand and whispered in his ear, "Asshole, pendejo." And we laughed. While gassing the International and going about his usual attendant routine we talked.

"Did you hear that Lee Pekhead got the gumption to join the Marines? He's in basic training now. An' you know that *Pachuco* cross tattoo he had in-between his thumb an' forefinger, well he burned it off with a big freakin' cigar. Just branded himself before he enlisted."

"What for? The moron," I said curtly.

"Because you can't have any tattoos on your body that show when you're in uniform. Anyway that's what Cody was told by Zane who's been in the Navy so I guess he knows."

"I don't know why Pekhead had that on his hand to begin with."

"Well I saw his hand after he burnt it and it was a mess, but the Marine recruiter swore him into the corps and they shipped him off just last Friday."

"Here's the two bucks for gas," I said as I handed him the money and added, "I for one won't miss that *Pachuco pendajo*. Maybe the Marines will turn him into something more than the dickhead that he is."

"You know Lee, Zane an' all those guys that hang out with the Rod Bandits Hot Rod Club?"

"Yeah, what about them?"

"Well Cody told me they do tea, you know, Mary Jane," he whispered to me.

"What are you talking about? Who's Mary Jane?" I whispered back.

"Mary Jane, tea, that's marijuana. They smoke it an' get high. Cody said he heard Zane say it's better than booze."

"Tell you what, I sure hope you and the CC's don't get the idea to do that stuff. Besides where did they get it? If you get caught you'll for sure end up in jail," I scolded.

I had heard about the *pachuco*, a Mexican-Spanish slang for Mexican Americans living in El Paso and Los Angeles; gangs of young men mostly, that dressed in the zoot suits with pants that were peg legged, long hanging gold watch chains. They had metal taps nailed at the heels and toes of their shoes so you could hear them coming and they greased back their hair back slick. Later white gangs and *Pachuco* wannabes, bad-asses adopted the fashion as well as the homemade tattoo of the cross in quotation marks between their thumb and forefinger.

In the nineteen fifties movies like "Rebel Without a Cause," "Blackboard Jungle and "Wild One," became subculture films that many teens idolized in cities across the United States adding to change in young culture's dress, looks and music, much to the dismay of the older generations.

*   *   *

Tawny eruptions of dust rose each time the horse's hooves' hit the ground as we rode loose down the dirt track side by side. The sky was mottled with cumulus clouds that dotted the landscape with patches of broken shadows. Jed and I were riding circle together and moved in and out of the sunshine as we rode, looking for any cows we may have missed during roundup. As we reached the crest of a hill overlooking Miller's coulee that stretched out for a half mile from the northeast we could see Miller's old homestead a couple of miles off. Deserted years ago due to the aridity of the land, the Millers had moved on and now the buildings were only the home to spiders, snakes and packrats to name a few of nature's year round inhabitants. The old gardens now grew sage, prickly pear and yucca as did the rest of the surrounding landscape on this part of the rolling prairie. The land was extremely sparse of grass so that the few rabbits that lived there survived on eating mostly cactus pads, while sand and wind would sweep the area into a dun colored desert. Archie had toyed with the idea of buying the old place but the acreage wasn't much good as grass goes and so it sat owned by some failed bank someplace.

Montana had gained statehood in 1889 but prior to that had been hit by numerous hardships over the years of its settling into a conquering civilization. In 1886 the roughest winter in recorded Montana history had killed off thousands of cows, bankrupting homesteaders and ranches. Then again in 1929, at which time the 'Great Depression" was beginning, and by 1930 to 1936 the 'Dust Bowl' hit the west, causing people to lose the whole kit and caboodle of their property to banks and therefore abandoning them. All over the west stood decaying houses, barns and other outbuildings. All sitting in the scorching sun, summer after summer and the harsh countless winters they all now stood with blown out windows and doors, some with caved in roofs, their boards turning gray. They stood in the fields as ancient ghosts awaiting nature to turn them to dust, leaving only stone or spalling concrete foundations.

"You see that?" Jed said.

"See what, where?"

"I could swear I think I saw something reflecting from the old Miller place."

"I don't see anything," I said, scanning the homestead.

"Wish I had my binoculars."

"Maybe it's just the sun reflecting off a piece of window glass or bottle."

"Could be but my gut feelin' says no."

"What you think it is?"

"Don't know. Maybe I reckon we ought to ride there an' take a gander."

"Okay with me," I said.

We rode to the fence line and I got off my horse and took the fencing pliers out of my saddle bag. At the cedar post I pulled the staples off of each barbwire strand and put the staples in the pocket of my chaps. With my foot I held down the four strands to the ground while Jed crossed over on his horse and led mine as the clouds moved away and left us in sunshine once again. After letting the wire spring back up I mounted. I looked down the fence line and noticed that a section of fence was already down.

"Jed!" I called.

"What?"

"Look down there, the fence was down already."

"I see it now. Didn't spot it in the shade. We better go check it out."

We rode at a walk to the downed fence and it had been cut. From there we headed to the rim of Miller Coulee and then sauntered down one side, following the new steer tracks that looked as though he was on the run.

We traversed the incline in file and at a walk; reaching the bottom, we skirted a prairie dog village and as we passed it a burrowing owl flew out of one of the holes. Jed's horse sidled with a hop side-ways making Jeep spooky and I brought him back under control. We rode on not talking.

Suddenly I saw a flash of light as did Jed and we set the horses foreword at a lope.

"You see that?" Jed asked.

"Yup, sure did."

"Sonuvabitch! Wish I'd brought a gun," Jed muttered.

"I've got my Dad's Luger in the saddle bag," I said, "And it's loaded."

"Good. Get it out and keep it in your waistband. We may need it."

I reached around and fished it out of the bag. It was wrapped in an oily neckerchief. I took it out and stuck it in the waistband of my pants at the small of my back that held it to me by my belt. The holster I kept in the truck's glove box.

As we got closer we slowed the horses to a walk again. I knew Jed saw the vehicle tracks that had been recently made to the Miller house.

"Shit!" we heard someone say.

Rounding the corner, there stood two guys and a dead steer that had just been butchered into quarters. Seeing the saddle gun they had leaning against the truck, I reached around and pulled the Luger out and held it loose over my rein hand that rested on the saddle horn. Jed dismounted. The two guys were really just teenage boys with red blood-covered hands, both looking like two deer caught and frozen by the headlights of an oncoming truck.

"Looks like you boys have been busy," Jed said as he went to the .30-.30 picked it up and levered out the cartridges onto the dusty ground.

Then Jed said sarcastically, "Looks like you two nimrods had a successful hunt."

He took the rifle and with the barrel poked the steer's hide hair side out to see the brand. It was a Milliron slash B brand. The steer's gut pile was already swarming with flies and the head had been cut off and was already in the truck bed, along with two front quarters. The ground was covered in a dark congealing puddle of blood. A cloud passed over and its shade instantly dropped the temperature by a few degrees.

Neither of the boys spoke; they just stood there looking scared to death, their red hands at their sides, their Levis and overalls smeared with blood. The one with the knee-patched overalls had on shoes that had the sole taped up and around with electrical tape. The other boy in the faded Levis, also with patches, on patches, wore downright beat-up cowboy boots, one with the heel missing. Both were a sorry looking lot.

"This here steer you just butchered is a Milliron slash B animal and we're Milliron cowboys. An' I'm puttin' the two of you under a citizen's arrest for rustlin' our steer," Jed addressed them. Jed then picked up their butcher knife and axe off the ground and threw them into the bed of their pickup.

"Where did you boys get this rifle?" Jed asked them.

Finally the older boy spoke, "It belonged to our Papa but he up an' died two years ago, so it's mine now!"

"Aw shucks, mister, we didn't think you'd miss just one ol' steer," said the younger one as he brushed away a pesky fly from his face then stuck his bloodstained hands in the pockets of the bib overalls.

"We knew you musta had missed this here one at round up an' we was huntin' an' ain't seen nothin' to shoot, not even one of them antelope goats an' we got to have food," the other said in desperation.

"Huntin' food is one thing an' stealin' it is another," Jed declared.

The younger boy started up crying.

"Quit you blubberin'," the older one snapped.

But the boy kept crying to the point that he just sat down in the dirt and bawled. Finally he quieted down and looked up with a dusty tear-streaked face and asked, "Are you goin' to put us in jail?" And the older boy kicked him and told him to shut up.

The cloud that had covered us in shadow moved off and the sun bathed us again. I noticed that the sudden brilliance made a flash off of the open wing window on the old rusty junker. The truck looked as though it was held together by a prayer and the tires showed the beginnings of becoming threadbare.

"What's you boys' names?" Jed asked.

"Joel—Joel Wah-waters," the younger stuttered.

"An' yours?" demanded Jed.

"Mathew! Same last name!" the older boy barked, looking pissed-off at his younger brother.

"Your Mama know you're out here rustling?" asked Jed.

"No sir!" they said in unison and the older boy added, "We wasn't plannin' to shoot this here beef. We was huntin' wild game but we didn't see none. Then we see this here cow up top, so we snuck up there an' cut the fence an' circled around an' drove it down here an' I's shot him dead. I reckons you can figures out the rest," Mathew admitted.

Jed walked to the truck and taking the ancient lever action rifle and tossed it on the seat through the open window. "Keep your eye on them," Jed said to me while he rolled a cigarette and smoked, looking at the two sorry kids. After he finished smoking he mounted his horse and said, "This is what's goin' to take place now," as he uncoiled his rope.

Panic stricken the older boy yells, "You's not goanna hang us, mister, are you?"

"Well you're rustlers an' this here cow belongs to our outfit an' you been caught red-handed. You reckon hangin' too good for you?"

"We want a trial," Mathew demanded as Joel started to cry again.

"Now just hold on a minute!" Jed exclaimed, "This is what's goin' to happen now."

"What?" Mathew asked with some bravado.

"You two are going up that hill an' goin' to fix that fence back up so no more cows can get out. Got it?" he said.

"Yes sir," they said in unison sheepishly while fear was in their eyes.

"Good. Give 'em our fencing pliers, Dakk."

I tossed the pliers at them and Mathew picked them up once they hit the ground.

"Now get on up there an' get 'er done," Jed said.

"But we ain't got no extra wire or staples," Joel said.

"I've got a tobacco tin full an' you most likely find extra wire at corner up there. That's where the fencing crew usually leaves extra in case we cowboys need some," Jed said. As we followed them up the hill I put the Luger back in my belt and was glad that I hadn't chambered a round in the pistol. I don't think Jed knew I hadn't since he most likely was just a wheel gun man.

We watched the two boys work up a sweat while fixing the fence for awhile.

"What are we going to do with these guys?" I asked Jed in a low voice when they were out of earshot.

"You'll see," Jed said as he rolled another smoke.

I lit a Lucky Strike and we sat our horses and watched.

When they finished, Mathew gave Jed back the tin of staples and handed me the pliers.

"Now back to your truck," Jed ordered.

At the truck Jed told them to load up the rest of the steer and skedaddle before he changed his mind and hung them.

"Can I pick up the bullets you ejected on the ground, Mister?' Mathew asked.

"Yes! You do that an' hand them to me. I'll take them as pay for the steer," Jed said.

The boys picked up the .30-.30 bullets out of the dirt and dust and Mathew handed them to Jed.

"Now get in your truck an' hightail it out-ta here an' I don't ever want to see hide nor hair of the two of you around here ever agin. Go on thataway as you came."

They got in the truck and after it coughed a couple of times it started and they backed around, face back down the same trak and took off with the steer. We watched as their dust faded in and out of the shadows and the truck disappeared over a knoll.

"What we going to do with that hide?" I asked.

"Bury it in back of that fallen down shed. There's an old shovel head next to that outhouse."

We buried the hide and rode back the way we had come and I stapled the fence wire back up to the cedar post after we crossed over and as I mounted Jed looked at me and said, "Let's keep this a secret to ourselves." and winked.

He then he added, "They'll never rustle another cow or steer again. You know as well as I do those boys needed the meat. Chances are they have a few more mouths to feed besides just their mother. They're poor as dirt. The whole family probably ain't got a pot to piss in, they're destitute. Poor as church mice. An' by the way, I noticed you hadn't chambered a round in that Luger unless you're careless and keep one in the chamber all the time."

"You're right, I hadn't. Didn't think you'd notice," I said.

"I was in the Army an' had to qualify with a forty-five. So I reckon I know about semi auto handguns and we had fired a Luger a few times on a range so we'd be familiar with the enemy's hand gun and other weapons."

Neither he nor I ever told about the red-handed boys to anyone at the ranch.

*   *   *

Around the end of October I went home for a couple of days. Things at home hadn't changed much except that Kipp was all excited because he finally got himself a Ford V-8 motor for the hot rod. He had it in the garage and all apart with everything organized, parts had been cleaned, motor painted, new chrome header covers, red spark plug wires, and new chrome this and that parts. He was just elated with how, as he said, 'cool' his project was coming along. He was still working at the Texaco part time and loved the fact that he was able to get parts at the dealer's discount through the gas station which saved him a few bucks.

"Where did you find the V-8?" I asked.

"Got it from Arnold's Junk Yard. Lee Pekhead works there now and Cody was tellin' Zane about my rod and he came over to see it and had Lee keep an eye out for a V-8 for me. Got it for fifty bucks. So now I've got a motor for 'Betsy'."

"What's Peckerhead doing working at the junk yard? I thought he was in the Marines," I said. Naming his hot rod Betsy had gone right over my head at the time.

"He got kicked out in basic training as what they call an undesirable. Couldn't cut the mustard as Ma would say."

"You're shitting me? Here I thought he was such a badass punk that he'd make a tough Marine."

"According to Cody and what he heard Lee tell Zane, Lee went to hit his D.I. with his fist and the D.I. grabbed his arm and did some jujitsu move that tossed him to the ground an' knocked Lee out. The reason he tried to hit him was because the D.I. was yelling at him an' called his mama a slutty whore while Lee was in company formation. Later he shot the N.C.O. with his M-1 in the foot with a blank and called him a mother-fucker. Just missed a bit or would have blown the sarg's foot off. Zane says he was lucky that he didn't end up in the brig for attempting to kill the N.C.O."

"What's a D.I. and what's N.C.O?"

"A drill instructor. N.C.O. is a non commissioned officer. A sergeant."

"So now he's back for good?" I asked,

"I guess. He got himself a job at Arnold's an' the Marines must'a done him some good 'cause he seems to have changed a bunch," Kipp said.

"Hum," came out of my mouth.

"He has. If it wasn't for him I would still be lookin' for a good Ford V-8 and Arnold wanted sixty bucks for it an' Lee got him to sell it to me for fifty."

"Well good for you. Life is full of surprises. Hey, who's Betsy?"

"That's what I call my car. Betsy."

I didn't question the name of his hot rod because it then dawned on me that Grandpa Lovett called his car Betsy when we were just kids. So Kipp picked up the name for his car.

When a week later I ran into Lee at the Dairy Queen, he had on his Rod Bandits motorcycle jacket and was wearing pegged chino pants and he looked like he'd bulked up, his hair was cut real short but he had started to grow out his long side-burns again. And I couldn't believe it, he was even civil to me by just saying "Hi" and asking, "How's Kipp's rod coming along?" He had bought himself a car. A 49 Ford coupe, which he had already lowered, bull-nosed, decked and it had been primed a rusty red plus was sporting four new white wall tires on it.

"Hey, you want to see my dog?" Lee asked me as we stood next to his car.

Cautiously I said sure. He pointed to the rear window of his Ford and in a box on the back seat was a young black and white pit bull pup. Lee opened the door and pulled the car seat forwards and reached into the box and brought out the black and white pup for me to see up close.

"Ain't she just a doll? Got her from Arnold at the yard. His bitch had four puppies an' I picked this one. I call her Holly," Lee smiled and gave the pup the last of his cone. While he held the pup up for me to see I noticed the cigar brand on his hand. Just then a man and woman were walking by, saw the puppy and the man said to Lee, "Nice looking pit bull pup you've got there. I used to have one myself and she was a very good dog."

"Yes sir! Thank you sir!" Lee responded.

This type of answer from Lee "Peckerhead" I would have never believed. The old Lee would have likely told the guy to fuck off and mind his own P's and Q's.

"Good looking dog, Lee," I said, "Thanks for all you've done to help out my brother. See you around," I said as I was walking away in disbelief and headed to the Dairy Queen for a cone myself.

"Tell Kipp I found a set of pipes for that V-8 if he wants them," Lee called out to me.

I turned around as I was about to open the door and said, "I will. Thanks!"

* * *

At the ranch we were getting things prepared for another winter. I wasn't sure I wanted to go another year on the Milliron. I felt the itch that cowboys get of wandering to another ranch and seeing some new country even if it was still here in Montana. I had saved up some money but again I was in denial about attending college anytime soon and there wasn't anything job related in Billings that had much appeal to me. This would be my second year with the Milliron but already I knew every hill, coulee, bog, timbered area and grassland as the proverbial saying, "Like the back of my hand." Would this be a long cabin fever winter for me? I didn't know. I wished I had a girlfriend but I didn't. J.W. and I had had a few good run-ins with the ladies as he liked to call them. We tried to get time off together and go find loose women or whores wherever we could as one night stands but most times we would just get drunk.

J.W. was always talking about places he had buckarooed at and the good times he'd had in Elko, Nevada, and hanging out at the Stockman's Bar, chasing the wild mustangs across large playas, all kinds of gambling, and prostitution being legal in that state made me want to leave Big Sky Country and see some new ground like Nevada the "Silver State" or Oregon's Jordan Valley country. I knew J.W. was also thinking of moving on because he had bought a stock rack for his truck in Billings to transport Llano in, and had asked me if he could store it at my folks' place. He didn't want to keep it at the ranch for fear that someone would figure that he was about to quit the brand and he and Llano would be history after being canned, until he found his way back in a few years of drifting cowboy work and rehired once again by the Milliron slash B.

Over the months that went by and the times J.W. and I had hung out together I finally discovered what J.W. stood for. The J was for Jeremiah, the W for William and his last name was Ramsey. I don't think that anyone else knew what the J.W. stood for, except Archie and maybe Tom since he was privy to some of Archie's paperwork and books that dealt with hired hands and the payroll.

The others, myself included, always went by our first or nick names and it was rare that we ever knew each other's last name unless you saw it on a piece of correspondence that they had left around and you happened to read the envelope and see the name written on it. As time had passed I learned that Tom was Tomas Huffman, Jed was Jed McRae and Clint's last name was Twitchell.

Where a cowhand hailed from was sometimes as much of a mystery as their last names. You might be able to get a pretty good idea by the individual's accent of where he was from but rarely exactly.

Jed McRae was from Augusta, Montana. Clint Twitchell, Saskatchewan, Canada; J.W. Ramsey from Huntington, West Virginia, but had no southern accent any of us could discern. J.W. had been known to have moved around many ranches and came highly recommended. Tom Huffman was born in South Dakota but his father had moved to Pinedale, Wyoming, and Tom had cowboyed as a young man in the Kendall Valley and the Wind River Range near Cora since he was sixteen. That's the way it was with most of the cowboys, all from different parts of the country and always moving from job to job all over the place. Unless you were born to a particular ranch family and your legacy was molded there, a cowboy moved on. Even the Mexican vaqueros wandered from ranch to ranch on both sides of the border, chasing everything from the wild mustangs, Corriente cattle to maverick Longhorns and Brahmans.

A few cowboys that had the talent, ability and the hopes of making it to the big time traveled around the country from rodeo to rodeo until they finally made it or lost it with the circuit.

We were all drifters in a way of life following the lore of the west and its hundred year heritage. We all loved the horses, the many varieties of cow breeds: the Texas Longhorns, Red and Gray Brahmans, Charolais, Brangus, Black and Red Angus, Herefords, Simmental, Beef Masters, Hotlanders, Santa Gertrudis, Senepol and the many variety of cross breeds or *corriente*. Horses and cattle together will always be a cowboy's life, but the horse is his heart and always will be.

Charles M. Russell the renown Western artist was quoted to have said, "The West is dead . . . you may lose a sweetheart but you won't forget her." And as cowboys you live that life so that the West, your sweetheart, is not forgotten but is endeared in its history for the many years to come.

* * *

ꗯG

WHOLE KIT AN' CABOODLE
CHAPTER 17

Archie Braddock had lost weight and was coughing all the time and when he wasn't hacking, he wheezed. Emma had taken Archie to the doctors and, though nothing was said to any of us hands, we all had a pretty good idea that Archie's doctor's prognosis was bad. Archie kept smoking Chesterfields and worked long hours at night writing his memoirs while Sylvia slept nearby. She would wake and watched Archie every time he started up his hacking cough, then lay back down and drifted back into a catnap.

"My thinking is he's got lung cancer," cautioned Jed to me one day in the barn as we were feeding Emma's horses.

"How long you figure he's got?" I whispered.

"Don't know, but he sure sounds bad," he said and added, "Damn coffin nails these smokes." He pulled the makings from his shirt pocket and threw them in the muck wheelbarrow and forked a load of fresh horse shit on top.

"You're young enough now that if you quit those Lucky Strikes you stand a good chance you could live a good long life. Hell, Archie is only sixty-seven; he should have a bunch more good years in him. I reckon he's known for some time his days were numbered because he started to write his life history awhile back," Jed accused, unforgiving.

"You're probably right but I like smoking anyway. Everybody smokes."

"Well I for one, am gonna give not smokin' a stab. We'll see. I know it won't be easy," Jed said, "What I'll miss most is building a smoke. Like when I take a break from shoein' a horse and just lean back on him and hand roll a cigarette. In the old days we all rolled our own or smoked a pipe. Only a few of the folks back then could afford a two cent cigar. Now it costs you a quarter for a pack of cigarettes an' most of that quarter goes to government as taxes. Hell, back then you could buy a pair of socks for three cents or get two pairs for a nickel. I guess that's why they call it, The Good Old Days. Your money was worth its weight in gold back then."

Thanksgiving had come and gone and I hadn't gone home for it. Little Raven had made us all a wonderful meal of turkey, mashed potatoes, fresh corn on the cob, green beans, cranberries and two pies for dessert. Mincemeat and pumpkin with whip cream. Little Raven's cooking bible was 'The American Woman's Cook Book,' that she had bought mail-ordered for a dollar in 1942, published for the Culinary Arts Institute. Everything around the ranch that day was easy going with not much work aside from the normal chores. We even played a game of catch ball and had a few beers that Archie had bought us, which was a big surprise to us all.

When Tom brought the beers out to us playing ball he asked if any of us had a church key because Little Raven couldn't find the kitchen one.

"I've got an opener in my glove box," I said and went and got it.

We sat around outside the bunkhouse and drank after saluting our open bottles to Archie's health. He had not come into the kitchen dining room for Thanksgiving and we hadn't seen him or Sylvia for a couple of days. Emma had told Little Raven he wasn't feeling up to eating and just wanted to rest in bed since he had had a fitful night's rest.

Thanksgiving had been a beautiful fall sunny day but that night it had clouded over and the following day the sky was the color of lead and the daytime temperature cooler by thirty-five degrees. Jed, having been the first one up that morning, found the bunkhouse cold enough to start a fire in the stove to take the chill out of the place.

A week later I got a chance to go home for a weekend. There seemed to be some sort of temperature inversion and all of Billings was covered in a low pall of ice crystals and smog. The smell from the refineries was pungent in the air. It was after seven o'clock at night and most folks were home from work and in for the night as cold as it was. The International's windshield kept icing up as the defroster wasn't working well on the driver's side of the cab. So I kept running the wipers in hopes of scraping the frost off while I kept rubbing the interior of the windshield with my bandana.

Everybody was home and surprised to see me and they were full of questions about my not coming home for Thanksgiving.

"Cold enough for you out there?" Dad had asked as I had come in.

"Yup!" I answered, "Sure is."

After I took off my hat and coat Ma asked if I wanted her to make me some Ovaltine or hot chocolate to drink.

"Sure, a cup of hot Ovaltine would be great."

"I can make you some supper if you want?" Ma asked.

"No thanks. I ate at the ranch before leaving."

Kipp had been reading his latest Hot Rod magazine when I came into the living room and after some small talk with him and Dad, Ma brought me a cup of Ovaltine.

"I'll bet you haven't heard about the fire here in town?" Dad said.

"What fire? Where?"

"The Pronghorn Café caught fire an' burnt to the ground last week," Kipp blurted out, "Cooper was out of a job but he got one at Casey's since then."

"They know how it happened?"

"They think it may have been a grease fire, the paper said. But in today's local news they said that the fire marshal thought it had started in an upstairs bedroom," Dad said.

"Wally the cook who was teaching Cooper how to cook died in the fire," Kipp said, "The whole kit an' caboodle went up in flames. Burnt to the ground. Fire department could only save the building next door."

"That was such a shame, that poor man dying like that," Ma said.

"He was addicted to cough medicine, codeine. Cooper would see him drink it all the time. Had the waitresses go to the drugstore and get it for him an' anybody else that could buy it besides him," Kipp said, "Cooper said his stomach was always bothering him an' the codeine gave him relief."

"I bet the old boy was smoking in bed an' he fell asleep because of the codeine makin' him sleepy," Dad surmised.

"That's too bad. I liked that little café. I'll miss not having it around anymore," I said.

"Well, now Cooper is working as prep cook and the chef has him working at the stove from time to time. Cooper loves cookin' an' says he wants to go to some chef school once he gets out of high school next spring," Kipp said.

"The good news around here," Dad said, "is that Kipp has the hot rod runnin' now."

"I got the engine in an' I drove it around the block a couple of times but I don't have plates for it yet. Besides I want to get her painted before I register her."

"I told him not to drive it without plates but he did," Dad said sort of indignantly.

"I almost got busted one day. A cop in his prowl-car was coming up the street as I was turning back into the driveway and in the garage and he saw me an' turned on his gumball light and pulled into the driveway. But he didn't bust me, he read me the 'riot act' an' gave me a warnin'," Kipp grumbled.

"Glad you have Betsy running. That was a project and a half," I said. "Let's go out to the garage and see her and you can start the engine for me so I can hear it run."

When we were in the garage Kipp sat in the car and started the hotrod and it roared to life. But suddenly I smelled something rotten.

"Kipp, what have you been eating? You're stinking up the garage," I complained.

"Cabbage farts, we had corn beef an' cabbage for supper tonight," he said while smirking.

"I believe you. I better not light up a Lucky in here, the whole place will go up in smoke," I said as he let another one loose while he revved the engine again. He shut the motor off as I walked back to the house getting, away from his smelly cabbage farts. He trailed behind me and caught up. "I suppose your shit don't stink," he said.

"When you get plates on the car I'll drag race you." I challenged, changing the subject.

"It's a bet. How much?" he asked.

"We'll see. Ten bucks maybe."

"Make it twenty an' you're on."

"Okay, twenty," I said knowing I would probably lose.

*   *   *

Winter came early and with a bang. It started with snowflakes as large as quarters floating to earth, and then they turned to normal size. The night was dark, without stars, the moon hid somewhere else. The snow piled high, cold and soft. Steadily it snowed more that morning and on into the night. It was a total whiteout. The wind that battered the landscape had heightened drifts in places of six and eight feet. When it finally settled down the following day the sun shone through the chrome sky and the temperature plummeted to a minus forty degrees. If it was this cold on the plains it had to be minus sixty degrees on the river bottoms.

Frost had crawled over everything. The window panes became opaque in crackled crystal motifs. The outhouse by the barn that we used if we didn't want to go back to the bunkhouse while working in the area had had a path shoveled to it so you could get in. Its shed roof was crowned with a three foot mushroom cap of snow. No one would think of using it for any reason since it had one inch of frost built up on the toilet seat as well as the walls. At the bunkhouse the windows stayed opaque with frost even with a roaring fire in the wood stove that we kept going all night.

With this much snow, power lines had failed so we were without electricity, which was just an inconvenience. We used kerosene lights and J.W. had batteries for his Zenith radio.

The vehicles wouldn't start unless you pulled out the batteries and warmed them up in the house. Once you had the truck or tractor running it was Hell trying to get things to shift into gears, because all the fluids were also frozen.

Tom had us run ropes from each and every building we needed to go to so that when we had to venture out in the blinding snow we could find our way by holding the rope as we went. In a whiteout it is easy to become disoriented and lost. Many a person has frozen to death in the west only a few feet from shelter because he couldn't see it in front of him.

Jed was busy all day on the Ford tractor, using the front loading bucket for plowing and removing snow and creating high mounds of it away from everything we needed to get around to. Three days later things had been cleared of snow to a degree including the road to the county highway.

J.W., Clint and I had been shoveling walkways around the place as well as the roofs of all the buildings that had too much snow piled on them or just breaking off the snow cornices the wind had constructed that would play havoc with their weight on the overhangs. The evenings after retiring to the bunkhouse the smell of Absorbine, Sloan's Liniment and Ben Gay was strong. Everyone was bathing in the stuff trying to ease the pain of aching muscles. Everybody but Tom and Jed crawled into their bunks and began snoring within minutes. Tom, being the ramrod, hadn't put in as much muscle power as the rest of us and he managed to talk Jed into a few games of dominos before they decided to call it a night.

It took awhile for the electric power to come back on and Emma was glad Archie had the TV to watch in the evenings once again. We hadn't seen him in a long time but Tom said he was doing okay and that Archie's book was going to be sent out for editing. Archie was now going through the albums and shoe boxes of all the old ranch and family photographs, picking out which he thought should go in the publication. Archie titled the book, "Braddock's Ranch, the Milliron slash B Family History." We all wanted a copy of the book once it had been published because we were part of that book in some respects even if we had just ridden for the brand for a short time—it was a segment of our history as well.

As soon as the county roads had opened Jed took Little Raven to town for groceries and mail. He had to place a piece of cardboard in front of the truck's radiator. We all did this to our vehicles so that the heater and defroster worked in the cab, otherwise the water even with antifreeze wouldn't allow the fluid to become hot enough to do a proper job because of the frigid air.

Thing warmed up during the days after awhile and two and three foot long icicles hung towards the ground off of the eaves of the buildings that weren't well insulated. Every morning we had to chop ice out of the drink tanks for the cows and horses. Next to every tank was an ice palace built up from what we had tossed in a pile out of the water troughs. One of the pipes to Little Raven's kitchen had frozen and broke, which Clint was able to fix after much swearing and banging around in the crawl space under the kitchen. Little Raven made him a chocolate cake with chocolate frosting for all his hard work and being one that loved chocolate, all the agonies of the day disappeared once he sat down to a healthy slice of cake and hot coffee.

We had snowshoes on the ranch that we used to get around in deep snow. If there was any real distance we had to go, then we'd saddle a horse and let him plow his way there. The horse's bits, we would put under our coats at our arm pit to heat the mouth piece before placing it in the animal's mouth. Even on those real cold days a horse pushing his way through the high snow would work up a sweat and icicles would form off his long hairs and nose. Each time rider and horse let out their breath a cloud of heavy mist billowed out. Most times the rider covered his nose and mouth with a bandana or scarf; otherwise his facial hair grew frost and icicles like the horse. The saddle leather creaked in the cold.

In the very end of February a Chinook hit Montana. Now everyone grumbled to a different tune.

"This fickle effin' weather is like we use to say when I was in the Army Air Corps; it's like red-tape, a 'catch twenty-two.' It's damned if you do, an' damned if you don't. Good in the respect for the warmth and getting rid of too much snow but bad because of the mud it had created, a real double bind," Jed theorized.

Chinook winds are warm dry winds that come over the Rocky Mountains and can melt one foot of snow a day, creating rivers of water, ponds and mud everywhere. Everything became caked with mud and was a new ordeal to bargain with for the next few days. The temperature rose to fifty-two degrees and we all walked about in the mud working around the ranch in our shirt-sleeves and wore no gloves for the next few days. At night a Chinook arch hung over the plains, keeping everything above freezing and we didn't need to fire up the stove in the bunkhouse and the drink tanks were ice free for awhile.

J.W. was in a funk. He had a bad case of cabin fever. Shoveling snow wasn't part of his buckaroo adopted heritage. He bemoaned about wishing he had moved on, to a ranch where the winters were a bit more mild and pleasant for man and horse.

In March things began to look up with spring just around the corner. Jed was putting new shoes on all the working cavvyard and the dogs, especially the hounds, hung out and watched him trim the hooves and toss them the clippings to eat. Misty, on the other hand, would crouch down behind the horse being shod and wait for it to make a wrong move. Her eyes going from horse to Jed then back again in anticipation of any forthcoming needed command. Eating hoof clippings was for hounds, work was for her.

Calving would soon start and once again the New Year's ranching cycle would begin. The repetitious bachelor cowboy life at Jack rabbit line camp had become home to me again during calving. Now I was making better and more entries into my diary in which I made myself notes of the guys' conversations and experiences. I made observations of my own as well as watching the others working around me. Though most nights I didn't have as much time as I had in winter at ranch headquarters, I still managed to edit some of the short stories I had put together that winter. I made changes and additions to the narratives. I had Christmas time off and borrowed Dad's Brownie Hawkeye camera to take back to the Milliron with me. With the camera I would sneak photos of the guys working or of the horses, cows and calves, the bulls, the landscape, rusting junk and old buildings. Everything I saw was becoming a fascination and my imagination was nearing full throttle. I thought to myself that perhaps Ma was right, I should write short stories and submit them to magazines like Field and Steam, Boy's Life, Collier's or Reader's Digest. After all, people in the east were becoming more fascinated with the west and tourism was on an upturn. Dude ranches began springing up with whole families vacationing in the "Wild West." Just maybe I'd start going back to school and take English Literature. After all I had a good bit of money saved up from working for over a year now at the Milliron. I had written a short story about cow camp, the cowboys, their horses and the cows and calves and I thought that one of these days I would send it out to see if some magazine might want to print a Western tale about one aspect of ranching in Montana's "Big Sky Country." Of course I'd have to type it out next time I was home for a couple of days. The beeves and their young would be my priority until caving was finished. The short story would have to wait

*   *   *

Archie Braddock was now and again seen outside of the ranch house with winter gone. With a warm sun and Spring in the air there came the cooing of doves and meadow larks singing love songs. This gave Archie new strength inside but from the outside he looked older, tired, a lot slimmer and pale. He'd walk to the barn and check on the thoroughbreds and find Rojo and spend time talking to the old horse, giving him a carrot or two from Little Raven's kitchen. Jed said that he saw Archie hanging onto Rojo's head one day and whispering in the animal's ear. And when he heard Jed coming Archie walked out of the barn with tears running from his eyes.

The day we all were to head out and move the pregnant cows to the calving fields, Archie came out of the house looking like he was going riding. He had on his spurs and was headed for the barn with Sylvia following him. When he saw Jed he called, "Jed!"

"Yes sir, Archie," Jed said as he walked toward him.

"Would you saddle Rojo for me? I don't have the strength to toss my saddle on the ol' boy. I feel like goin' for a ride today."

"You betcha. I'll get 'er done, Archie,"

"I'm goin' to sit right here on this chopping block with Sylvia an' wait," he said as he wiped his eyes with his bandanna. His eyes were constantly rheumy these days.

The rest of us got ready to move out. We thought we'd wait for Jed and when we saw him leading Rojo saddled to Archie we all assumed that Archie was going to join us. Tom rode towards Jed and Archie. Archie saddled up with a little difficulty but once seated on Rojo he looked and was elite. We all turned and headed north towards the mother cows' paddocks riding loose in twos side by side with no one saying anything. The hounds raced ahead with their tails in the air and noses to the ground. Sylvia ran at Rojo's heels and Misty paced back and forth, left to right behind us. Clint and J.W. were in the lead and Archie and Tom brought up the rear with Sylvia and Misty coming along behind everyone.

Tom looked at Archie and saw that he was sweating and had a gray clammy look.

"You doin' okay, Archie?' Tom asked dubiously.

"Yeah, it'll pass," Archie said.

We were just about to the paddocks when Archie gave out a groan and fell slumped over his saddle horn, spilling his hat to the ground.

"Jed!" Tom called.

Jed looked back as did I and saw that Tom had stopped and was holding Archie from falling off of Rojo.

Jed turned his horse back to Tom and dismounted and pulled Archie out of the saddle and to the ground as Rojo shied and sidled away from the men. Jed laid Archie down. Tom had gotten off his horse also and was now feeling Archie's neck for a pulse.

"There's no pulse!" Tom said.

Jed slapped Archie's face, "Archie!" he said. But Archie wasn't breathing or moving and his face was pallid.

"Damn it to Hell, he's dead!" Tom said. And the hounds, as though on cue, started to bay.

Sylvia licked Archie's face once. Misty was a nervous wreck as she paced back and forth, making little whining noises.

"Shit!" someone said.

"Let's get him back to the ranch." Tom said, looking at us all sitting our horses in shock. He added, "We'll all go back. We'll move the cows later. Jed, let's put him back up on Rojo."

As they lifted Archie back on Rojo I got off my horse and picked up Archie's Stetson off the ground, dusted it with the sleeve of my shirt and mounted back up and followed.

We all rode quiet; the only sound was that of the horses' hooves hitting the ground as we slowly accompanied Tom and Jed as they rode on each side of Archie, holding his limp and slump body in the saddle, the dogs all pacing close behind, periodically sniffing the air, all trotting with their tails down.

*   *   *

The funeral was held on the following Sunday at ten o'clock as the quarter moon swung low to the west and the sun hung high overhead. The Milliron Ranch cemetery was at a distance on a small knoll behind the house. Enclosed by an iron ornamental picket fence, the cemetery awaited with an open grave near the only distinctive and somewhat conspicuous headstone, that of a tree stump. Sometime back, out of curiosity I had visited the cemetery and read the names and dates on the various headstones. The marble stump, now stained by time was the largest of all the stones. It belonged to William Braddock, Archie's father. The chiseled stump had an embellished circular seal that depicted a maul, axe and wedge, around which it read, 'WOODMEN OF THE WORLD, Memorial, Dum Tacet Clamat.' The latter in Latin meaning, 'Though silent, He speaks.' I had asked Dad one day while at home if he knew about the Woodmen of the World. He told me it was an organization like the Freemasons, started by a man called Root, who had heard a sermon about the pioneer woodsmen clearing away the dense forest so that they could have fields to grow food in order to support their families. After which Mr. Root started a society that would insure or rather clear away problems of financial insecurity for its members once the head of the family had died. Over a hundred doleful people came to pay their respects to the deceased Archie Braddock and the bereaved family members. I saw my old skinflint boss, Ben Blastingame with his wife there but he didn't see me alongside the multitude of Archie's family and friends. The only cowboys that were included as pallbearers were Tom and Jed.

Emma was dressed in black, as was Little Raven who stood by her the whole time of the funeral, both in tears throughout most of the ceremony. All the men, ranch cowboys included, held their hats in front of themselves and had their heads bowed and the women held white laced handkerchiefs to their eyes wiping tears and kept up sobbing. The casket was covered with flowers and Archie's silver belly Stetson also crowned the top of coffin.

The sermon was short, starting with a prayer, the reading of Psalm 23, Then the singing 'Precious Lord, Take My Hand' and 'When the Roll Is Called Up Yonder,' fallowed by a benediction, after which the casket was lowered into the grave and the long line of mourners passed by and tossed a bit of dirt from the grave pile onto the coffin. The women all wept as the dirt hit the casket and moved away quickly and down the path back to the house.

I heard Jed say in a low tone to Tom, "At least Archie died with his boots on and mounted. When it's my time to go, I hope that's how I go."

"He must have known it was his day and that's why he rode out with us and had the dogs follow," Tom interjected as he shook his head slowly from side to side.

"He was a real good man," someone said, consoling a tearful friend.

"We're all just passin' thru this great life on earth" another man said.

"He had a pretty good sixty-eight years here, born an' raised in Montana an' now buried here at his end," a friend of Archie's said, then spat a chew of tobacco juice onto the ground.

"He'll be missed by one and all here in his beloved Montana," somebody else said as they began to head for the house and the food Little Raven had prepared as well as the food other women had brought for the occasion. Tom, J.W. and Clint, still all holding their hats in their hands, went on ahead, escorting the two distraught women back to the house along with the other mourners that trailed behind.

Before everyone was to share in the nourishments there was the eulogies, sharing memories of the well like cowman were expressed that brought forth at times laughter and at other times more tears.

A couple of the hands from the reverse C G Ranch stayed at the grave site as people had left and would finish burying Archie and placing the flowers on the grave.

Emma had ordered a gray granite headstone with an epitaph,

> *"He died with his boots on.*
> *He loved life, his family,*
> *his horses, and his dogs."*

It also included Archie's date of birth and death and the carving of his favorite horse Rojo. The headstone would be set in place at a later date, once it was delivered to the ranch. Jed and I stayed behind to help.

The following morning cows were moved to the new grass and calving grounds. Already there were seventeen newborns among the mother cows. I was again stationed at Jackrabbit for my second year. My first day there was like 'old home week,' I was alone and for the most part totally independent. It was as if I was stepping back in time. It felt good and had my mind flowing with imagination. I could hear nature without any distraction and hear the distant cows occasionally moo in the spring air.

Tom had promised me time off to go to Kipp's high school graduation and I was looking forward to it. I had brought Dad's Brownie camera home so we could get pictures of Kipp in his cap and gown receiving his high school diploma and all the activities afterwards. Kipp hadn't wanted to go to the school prom but peer pressure and Ma had forced his hand and he found enough nerve to ask a pretty sophomore girl to go with him to the prom dance and she was thrilled to go. Ma had taken pictures of the two of them all dressed to the nines and Gretchen in a light blue satin gown wearing a carnation corsage and Kipp in his dark blue suit with a carnation boutonnière looking uncomfortable wearing a tie.

By now Kipp had the engine block of his coupe painted bright red with chrome valve covers and air filter plus anything else he could get in chrome for the engine compartment. All the new spark plug wires were also red and the Ford's body was now painted in an electric blue. The tire rims were also chrome. With the red Naugahyde interior the coupe was a prize that was finally street legal with Montana license plates.

"I'm getting her pin-striped when this friend of Zane's comes down from Butte. He's real good, has been doin' pin-stripin' since he was, as

Zane put it, 'knee high to a grasshopper.' He just goes around doing cars all over the state and other places," Kipp declared.

He used Betsy to take Gretchen to the prom and she felt special to be seen in such a 'cool car.' Kipp was no Fred Astaire when it came to dancing and Gretchen was no Ginger Rogers but both managed to fake it with the slow dances.

After the prom Kipp drove Gretchen up to the rim and parked among some of the other graduates that had come up there to make out and grab a few cheap feels in hopes of maybe getting lucky after trying to get the girls tipsy on a little booze. They had talked some local wino into buying them the alcohol; in exchange they gave the guy money for a bottle of Ripple or Thunderbird wine. All the boys parked on the rim only wanted one thing and that was to fornicate in celebration of having graduated from high school and on to manhood.

Later Kipp told me that his date must have been told by her mother that if she kissed a boy open mouthed she'd become pregnant.

"It was like she had lockjaw, no way could I get her to loosen up but she let me feel her up all over and I got her to jerk me off after I fingered her an' she came," he told me, then added, "I think I'll ask her out again."

"Next time you go on a date you better have some rubbers because if you knock her up, it's either you get married and start a family or you end up in the military with child support until the kid is old enough to vote," I preached to him.

"Shit, I'd have to get them from the druggist an' he'd know," Kipp grimaced.

"So what, moron, he doesn't know you and all he gives a fucking damn about is making a profit anyway. And you are best off not knocking your girlfriend up. Believe me I know. If you do you'll be sweating more than bullets," I scorned.

Then to lighten things up I said, "You want to hear a joke?"

"Sure, you bet! What?"

"This guy goes into the drug store and tells the pharmacist he wants to buy some condoms. So the pharmacist says to him after putting the package of three rubbers on the counter, "That will be seventy-five cents plus tax." And the guy buying the rubbers says, "I don't need the tacks, they'll stay on okay." Kipp laughed and so did I.

Then he said, "Want to hear a poem I read on the crapper wall at school on the subject?"

"Sure,"

"It goes like this," and he sing-songed it, "In days of old when knights were bold and rubbers weren't invented, they use to tie a sock around their cocks an' that way babies were prevented."

I chuckled, "Don't believe everything you read, especially if it's written on the wall of a crapper.

Needless to say I bought Kipp condoms just to make sure he'd have them.

*   *   *

Now that calving and branding was over, one day J.W. and I rode out to check on the stock. We rode side by side, he was on Llano and I on Jeep and he says to me, "You heard the rumor that Emma wants to sell the Milliron to the Kendrick and Rumford Land and Cattle conglomerate back east an' she plans to live in California with her sister who owns a thoroughbred outfit there."

"Yeah, I heard rumor," I said.

"I'm thinking of movin' on myself, seen all this country three-four times over. It's time I quit the brand an' find some new territory to work in."

"You thinking of Oregon, Nevada or south?"

"I'm thinking of getting away from cows for awhile. You know, a little dude ranching and fall hunting camps."

"You're kidding me? Thought you were a diehard buckaroo?"

"It's like this, I love being a buckaroo but once in awhile you've got to try some other aspect of cowboy life."

"I guess you're right, everybody needs change in their life. I guess that's why Emma is thinking of selling out now that Archie is gone."

"I reckon. A friend of mine is working near Moose, Wyoming. He grew up in that country before he moved around an' cowboyed with me while I was in Nevada. It's a dude ranch he's workin' at in the summer. They take out hunters in the fall. Have a huntin' camp in the mountains. I got a letter from him a week ago an' said I should come down an' check it out, get hired on. He's been there two summers and falls. Come winter he heads for Arizona and works," J.W. explained.

"Think that's your cup of tea?" I jibed.

"Tell you what, when he and I worked in Nevada every chance he had, he'd be chasin' pussy. He was an' still is a fornicating fool, a real stud. Anyway he says that workin' the dude ranch he's gotten more nookie from dudes' wives, daughters an' town girls than he can handle plus he says he gets great tips. Got five sawbucks off of one hunter for finding him a nice big bull elk to shoot, plus he gets most of the ivories. You know, tusks from the elk because those eastern hunters don't know anything about them. He digs them out of the elk's jaws when the guy's not lookin' and keeps them," J.W. sniggered.

"So you're going down there and check it out?"

"You bet! Why not? I can bring my own horse. Besides they've got some Hereford cow ranches there, except they use the local cowboys mostly. An' Bernie's painted a good picture of the place in his letters. You ought to come along, see if you could get hired on."

"Where's Moose, Wyoming?"

"Jackson Hole Country is south of Yellowstone Park. High mountains, lots of real pretty country, all kinds of wild game, good fishin'. The real plus is that they have a couple of good party towns that a guy can carouse around in with lots of college gals working there. An' there's tourist women lookin' to make a cowboy while passin' through. It's like heaven for a cowhand."

"Well if you get hired on and see that there is an opening for another hand send me a line at my folks' house and I'll for sure make it to Jackson Hole in hopes of gettin' on."

"Hell, I'll just give you a jingle at home. Not much into writin', you know that."

"Yeah, but maybe I'll still be here working at the ranch. Who knows?" I said, "Besides if I get a letter my mother will call me here to let me know that you wrote me. So watch what you say in it in case I ask her to open it and read it to me over the phone."

* * *

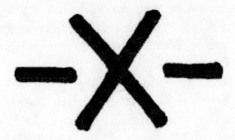

YELLOW SLICKER
CHAPTER 18

With the Milliron branding complete, J.W. had collected his wages and gave his goodbyes after loading Llano in the new stock rack he had bought some time ago. The cab of his truck was a bit cramped with saddle, bedroll and other belongings stacked on the passenger side.

"I don't know what I was thinkin' gettin' a stock rack instead of a horse trailer," J.W. said to me, "Here's the P.O. Box numbers in Moose where the ranch gets their mail. If you write, put in care of the Bar X Bar Ranch. Hope to run into you there. Think about it. The Milliron won't need you one of these days an' it's better to quit than get fired."

"Thanks for the address. I want to talk to Jed and get his take on the ranch here. If the Milliron is up for sale things will probably change a bunch. New bosses and ways of doing things. I night as well move on. Besides I'm pretty sure that I need a change. It's time I got out of Dodge as the old saying goes," I said.

"Well, see you down the trail one of these days," J.W. said.

"Good times to you, J.W., and ride at a lope." I said.

I could now for sure see the handwriting on the wall as J.W. much earlier had than I did. I thought Emma would keep the Milliron going but when she had her thoroughbreds shipped off to California I knew she would follow. Jed had said that Emma was packing her things and would be leaving the ranch for Tom to run and that she was going to find a private publisher to print Archie's memoirs of the family and the Milliron slash B in California and then once it was printed into a book she would return to Montana to promote it and sign autographs on behalf of Archie Braddock.

The syndicated outfit that was buying the Milliron Ranch wanted Tom to keep all the cows and heifers as well as those that had lost their calves to mishaps during calving this spring and all the seed bulls at the ranch. The rest would be sold off. Most of the horses went to the sale barn, the ranch only keeping a cavvy of ten. Old Rojo was sold off also. The draft horses stayed on, they'd be needed in the winter to pull the hay sleigh.

Rojo died a short time after being bought as a kid's horse by a family living in Huntley. One morning they went to his paddock to feed him and he had managed to get a fore leg hung up high in a fork in the only tree that existed on the place and had struggled until he died. Maybe he just committed suicide was my thought. Sylvia stayed at the ranch but was no longer her old self. She always stayed very close to Jed to the point of always being under foot. She lived for another year after Archie's death and died at the age of ten.

So came the day at the end of July that Tom laid the bad news on me as I was saddling Sioux out by the corrals.

"Dakk . . . I guess you know what's goin' on around here now?" Tom said as more of a statement than a question

"Yeah," I said.

"Emma's leaving for her sister's next week after the estate sale. Little Raven will stay around 'cause I need a cook. Jed will stay. Clint I'll keep on until fall or things turn around. The Mexicans will most likely move on after haying as always. The syndicate wants to run this place as a bare bones outfit until they send someone here to work things out the way they think it ought to be run."

"So I reckon you're canning me," I said.

"Yeah, sorry but you know if and when things change you'll be the first I call."

"Should I pack up today?"

"There's no particular hurry. Next day or two. I'll have your pay check in the office when you're ready to collect it," Tom said while looking somewhat blank and his shoulders looking as if he was carrying a heavy load, then he turned and walked off back to the house.

Maybe I'll drop J.W. a line at the Bar X Bar, I thought.

Working a dude ranch can't be all that bad and I'd get to see some new country.

I knew that I'd miss the Milliron slash B but one has to move on and grow, even though Dad would say, "A rolling stone gathers no moss."

*   *   *

I had written to J.W. soon after I had gotten home. It was now close to the middle of August and I hadn't heard back from him and my thought was that maybe he didn't get hired on with the Bar X Bar as he had hoped and that's why I hadn't heard from him by now.

Ma and Dad wanted me to enroll in college but I was too late to enroll for the fall courses. At this time I pretty much just helped out around the house and garden. Kipp was working full time at the Texaco as a mechanic now and his buddies also had jobs.

I'd go to the Hoof and Horn for coffee from time to time and get the local gossip, shoot the breeze with local ranchers as well as see if there were any hopes of someone hiring cowboys. Ben Blastingame was still running the feed lot and Roy, his grandson, was the yard boss. The couple of employees working for Ben were new men.

In talking with Donna at the diner one morning when business was slow she said, "Ben has had such a turnover of employees. They only seem to work a month or a week then quit or Roy fires them."

"Roy has a way of getting under one's skin. He sure has talent that way," I said giving her an exasperated look.

"I think Ben isn't very happy with him running the yard. They don't even sit together when they come in for lunch or just coffee," Donna had noted.

"That's too bad for Ben, he was hoping to have Roy run the whole business for him so he could retire."

"Well between you, me and the lamp post I think Ben is going to sell out one of these days."

Just then Roy entered the diner and without looking around went to his usual seat at a table in the rear of the diner.

"Coffee, Roy?" Donna asked as she picked up the coffee pot and a mug and headed to his table.

"As usual, unless you give haircuts in here now," Roy accused.

"Don't get smart with me, Roy, or I'll have you wearing this whole pot of coffee over your head for free," Donna threatened, "Besides you can read that sign over there that says, 'Reserve the right to refuse service to anyone,' don't you?"

"Yeah," Roy answered as Donna set the mug in front of him and poured coffee.

"Is coffee all you care for this morning or is there anything else you need?"

"Just coffee . . . Thanks," Roy answered, sounding borderline sarcastic.

Donna walked briskly away and came back to me and added more hot coffee to my cup.

I guess it was then that Roy first realized that I was sitting at the counter as I was looking at the jukebox selection on the carousel in front of me. I was checking out B-17 which was, 'Wake Up, Little Susie,' by the Everly Brothers.

"Dakk!" Roy said as he got up from his table with his cup of coffee and came and sat down next to me.

"Roy," I said.

"Ben said the Milliron is being sold."

"Yeah," I answered.

"Are you lookin' for work? I could use you if you are."

Suddenly, for a moment, my ability to speak seemed paralyzed, and then I flat out lied by saying, "No, not really."

"So you still workin' for the Milliron then?" Roy asked.

"No . . . But have plans to start work in Wyoming as soon as they call me," again I lied.

"Well that's too bad, Ben would love having you work for us again."

"Yeah, well thanks, but I need to see some new country." I said, thinking of Roy saying, 'us' in reference to the feed lot work.

I put money in the jukebox and pressed B-17. "Wake Up, Little Susie" began to play and Roy retreated back to his table, spilling coffee on the floor as he walked away. Donna looked at me and winked. I smiled back. The song brought back melancholy memories. I wondered about Sue and what her life was like now that she had married and was a mother.

Roy dropped change on his table and walked out of the diner after drinking his coffee without another word to me or Donna.

"For crimanny sake, someone ought to box that boy's ears real good an' maybe it would knock some good sense in him," Donna said.

"Maybe, but I doubt it," I said as the song, 'Wake Up, Little Susie," ended.

Nepotism can be more of a pain in the ass than it's worth most times, for both employer as well as employees that work with them, I speculated to myself, thinking of Dad and his boss's nephew that he always complained about because he was, as Dad put it when Ma wasn't around, a lazy, good for nothing effin' S.O.B.

I left the Hoof and Horn after talking to a few guys that came in that I knew and also had some lunch before driving out to the Texaco to get gas.

When I pulled in at the pumps a kid came out to give the truck five bucks' worth of gas. I saw Kipp's coupe parked at the side of the station and could see he had had the Ford pin-striped.

"Where's Kipp?" I asked the kid with the grease smudge on his cheek.

"He's inside," said the kid.

I went into the open bay that had a car in it with the hood open. Just then Kipp came out of the crapper wiping his hands and arms up to his elbows.

"Hey, what's up?" he said.

"Noting much, just come by for some gas." I said.

"I'm off as soon as the station's owner gets here and that should be in the next few minutes. You can park your truck next to where mine is and we can get into mine and go cruise the gut and you can see how hot Betsy is runnin'. Here's Joe now," Kipp said.

Kipp introduced me to his boss and after some small talk Kipp and I took off in Betsy to cruise the gut and he peeled a little rubber on our way out and again after shifting into second gear. The tassel from his graduation cap was hanging from the rear view mirror.

"Betsy's got power," I said.

"This is nothin', I'll take you up on the rim and we'll kick ass on that straight away by the airport.

As we got to Grand Avenue Kipp down shifted and the Ford's pipes rumbled. Kipp looked at me and said, "Hot or what?"

"Hot!" I said.

"Wait til we get up on the highway and away from the city cops," he said.

When we got on top of the rim, Kipp put Betsy through the gears and she peeled off at zero to sixty in no time. As we passed the old number 1031 steam switch engine parked on display in the history park by the airport, over the noise of the glass-packed mufflers I asked, "When they bring that old engine up here?"

"Oh, last year. Brought it up on a flat-bed with a semi pullin' it up the grade."

We drove down the Zimmerman Trail back into Billings with the glass-packs clapping all the way down as Kipp used the jake brake by down shifting the gears to slow the Ford. Finally at the bottom we were able to talk again and I asked, "You still seeing that gal you took to the prom?"

"Yeah, you bet. She sure loves doin' it but I still can't get her to let me slip my tongue in her month."

"I hope you're not riding her bare boned," I said.

"No. I'm not into marriage, just getting my rocks off."

"Good, because you know those little pollywogs are good swimmers, use rubbers," I warned.

Then to change the subject I said, "The Crow Pow-wow is next week, you want to go? Jimmy Catchum asked me to come and as he put it, join the festivities."

"Sure, you bet. I've got Wednesday off unless that part for the Packard comes in. But I don't think it will." Then added, "By the way, you still want to drag race me an' Betsy against you an' the old International?"

After Kipp left me off at my truck, I watched him as he took off in a roar with the hot rod burning rubber each time he shifted gears. And I thought back to the early years when we rode our bikes and Kipp always had a card held by a clothespin to make a motoring sound with the spokes as we rode up and down the streets. He always loved the sounds of a motor. Even the time we built a soap box racing car Kipp found a way to make the thing sound as though it had some sort of motor in it. As he raced down the hill in it, it rumbled. His theory was, the more powerful the sound of the engine the better.

*　　*　　*

We drove to the Crow Reservation in my truck. It was a hot day without a cloud in the sky and as we entered the Crow Agency pow-wow grounds, dust rose to a pall in the still air from the cars and trucks moving to parking areas. Grasshoppers of varying sizes and color flew and buzzed off the ground and landed on the parked vehicles only to fly off again in a new direction.

A hundred or more tepees stood all facing east in a gigantic semicircle, the center of which was an enormously wide brush covered arbor. Gone were the buffalo hide tepees, replaced now by canvas coverings most of which were painted in varying designs and colors. Horses of all colors filled a paddock area, most were eating the grasses. People were coming and going as a bustle of excitement. Indian women in buckskin beaded dresses, some with a multitude of elk tusks sewed on them, headed for the arbor, their hair braided on each side of their heads. The men's braids were wrapped in colorful cloth or otter fur. The women also wore long dangling earrings of dentalium shells, and many had around their shoulders fringed satin shawls. Even the children were dressed festively and all ran about in high spirits. The men dancers with their faces painted, their torsos and legs naked and also painted had gathered and walked towards the dance area. All had on two-feathered bustles, a large one at their rump and a smaller one between their shoulders and each dancer wore a roach headdress. All wore bell-leg and arm-bracelets and even belled belts that jingled brightly as they walked around in their beaded moccasins to the dance. Most had on hair-pipe breastplates and carried a rattle in each hand. Cooking fires at the tepees sent a haze that mixed with dust and bright sunlight.

There was an area that sponsored vendors who sold trade items, souvenirs, beaded moccasins and food.

I found a spot to park my truck and Kipp and I followed the masses that were headed for the arbor from which you could hear the booming of kettle drums and the primeval melodic chanting of the participants.

"I didn't expect it to be this crowded with people," I told Kipp over the hubbub.

"Yeah, this place is swinging. Makes me think of the early days and what it was like before white men. You know, mystic," Kipp said.

We wove our way slowly in and through the spectators and waiting participants until we were well into the arbor and just behind the drummers.

The drummers whaled on the drums to a modulating sound as they also chanted, "BOOM! BOOM! BOOM! Hoy ah! Hoy ah! Hoy ah! BOOM! Boom, Boom, Boom, BOOM! BOOM!" along with the sound of bells, rattles and whistles filled the arbor and the surrounding encampment for miles. The atmosphere and aura was a feeling of a primeval time. Puffs of dust rose with the thumping moccasin feet as they hit the ground in cadence with the drum beats. My neck, arms and back felt goose bumps and I found my foot also beating time to the rhythm and looking over to Kipp and saw that his head was also bobbing in cadence.

"I think one of the dancers is Jimmy Catch'um. The one with the blue beaded moccasins on and two eagle feathers in his roach headdress," I said to Kipp, leaning close to him so he could hear me.

"Oh, yeah. Hey, look at the end drummer, ain't that ol' Billy Young Buck?"

"Yeah, it is and he must be sober to be keeping the same beat as the others," I confided close to Kipp's ear. He just nodded and his head went back to following the beat of the drums.

Eventually the women dancers meandered into the dance as the men backed off and the women took over swinging, swaying and gliding around in circle, their shawls spreading in the air. It was as though they were all brightly colored fluttering birds, wailing and chanting to the drumming. "Hay yah! Hay yah! Hay Yah! Yah! Yah! Hay yah! yah!" interrupted with shrills and occasional coyote sounding yelps.

The thirteen drummers sitting on the ground never missed a beat. Billy Young Buck was in his element and as serious looking as the others, chanting and drumming from subdued sound to a peaked crescendo. Blanketed elders sat behind and to the sides of the drummers, some wearing their chiefly feather headdresses and holding eagle wing fans, all chanting along with the drummers.

The ground under our feet felt as though it vibrated and perhaps it did.

"I wonder if this was like the Ghost Dance of 1889 before the government outlawed it," Kipp said to my ear.

I had no answer for him but thought he was most likely right.

After about an hour of watching the dances we made our way to a food stand and bought some brisket sandwiches and drinks. After which he and I went around to the vendors' booths to look at the merchandise that was being offered for sale.

Kipp found a Crow Indian woman selling deer-hide beaded moccasins with rawhide soles. He pulled off his Keds and tried on a pair to make sure they fit.

"How much for these mocs?" he asked as he examined the shoes that were of cow rawhide and still had some of the hair left on the soles. The moccasins had been entirely sewn with sinew thread, including the lazy stitched bead work that covered the tops.

"Fifteen dollar," she said.

He haggled with her some and she let him have them for twelve bucks. "No tax," she said. He gave her two fives and two one dollar bills and wore them while carrying his high tops around. I did find a woven porcupine quill hat band that I bought.

Towards late afternoon and at an interval in the pow-wow, Jimmy Catch'um saw me and came over to talk.

"Look's like you made it here this year," he said, his bells jingling as we walked towards the parking area and his truck.

"Yeah, we made it. This is my brother Kipp," I said as an introduction.

"Hey!" Jimmy said and he and Kipp shook hands.

"You here for the night or are you going back to Billings?"

"I've got to work tomorrow," Kipp piped up.

"That's too bad because there will be a big bareback horse race here tomorrow an' that's a bunch of fun. It's for all ages and they get very competitive about it. Like they use to say in the old days, 'Heap good race'," Jimmy stated, smiling.

"Maybe we'll see it next year," I said.

"Hope you had a good time?" Jimmy said, and then added to me, "I don't figure we'll be workin' the Milliron together now that it's sold."

"I suppose not," I said, "I'm hoping to find work in Wyoming."

"Well good luck."

"Thanks."

"Hey, before you go come on over to my truck. I've got to take this dance stuff off and I want to give your kid brother somethin'," he said as he saw that Kipp was wearing beaded moccasins.

At his truck he took off his dance bustles, bells and roach head dress, then opened his glove compartment and pulled out an eagle feather.

"Here!" he said, handing it to Kipp, "You need one of these if you're playin' Injian. Now all you gotta do is go count coup on an enemy or steal a horse and you can wear it."

"Whoa! Thanks! Much obliged," Kipp said gloating, "Next time you're in Billings look me up at the Texaco an' I'll give you a tune up for free. Thanks again."

Kipp was in 'Seventh Heaven' as we headed back home. All he could talk about is warrior societies and how they worked, the Sun Dance, the Ghost dances and the different Indian battles all of which he had read about. It was almost too much information for me at one time but at least it kept me from thinking about my problems of a job prospect that seemed to always be running through my mind lately.

We got home just after supper time and Ma had kept supper in the warm oven for us. I saw that I had mail postmarked Moose, Wyoming, but was reluctant to rush and open it for fear it wouldn't be what I had hoped for. I went to feed the horses first, and then ate dinner with Kipp while Ma was finishing up the dishes and Dad was watching TV. Kipp had filled the folks in on our pow-wow outing by the time I came back into the house and he was saying, "I can't believe that Jimmy Catch'um gave me this eagle feather. You know that's big medicine to have been given to me."

I hadn't seen Kipp that excited about anything that didn't involve him and the CC's getting into some sort of stupid trouble or his hot rode Betsy.

"Dakk, did you see you got a letter today? It must be from that friend of yours in Wyoming," she said.

"Yeah Ma, I saw it and I'm sure it's from him because the return address is the Bar X Bar Ranch in Moose, Wyoming. I'll read it later," I explained patronizingly.

Up in my room I lay on the bed and opened the letter and read it:

Hey Dakk,

One of the guys is quitting. He gave them a two week notice. He's getting harnessed up . . . (Married) to some gal he got into a family way and is in love with.

I put in a good word for you. Played you up some. Told them you're a top hand and so on.

So if you can come, the sooner the better, then you have a good shot at the job.

Hunting season is just around the corner and they're full up with hunters and they need guides. So if you start work here you should know most of the country before fall. Hope to see you.

Got to run . . . . Let 'em buck! J.W.

P.S. Send them a card saying you're coming for the job.

*　　*　　*

I left for Moose, Wyoming, and the next morning after reading J.W.'s letter I had packed my gear and by five in the morning had loaded my saddle, tack and bedroll into my truck. Kipp would take care of feeding Jeep and Sioux. Ma had insisted I have a breakfast of waffles and sausages before I headed out. I was on the road by seven after Ma had made me a couple of sandwiches and filled my Thermos with coffee. Driving south from Billings down towards the Wyoming border to Elk Basin and on down to Cody, I was hopeful of getting to the Bar X Bar in time to get hired on. I had dropped a card in the mail saying that I was coming the Bar X Bar looking for work though I thought I would get there before it did.

Most of the countryside to the Wyoming border was nothing more than sandy arid ground covered with prickly pear cactus, yucca, sagebrush, few antelope and some cattle on open range. There was a breeze and it caused occasional small dust devils to spin out on the dry ground here and there. The mountains blue gray in the distance raked the sky line while heat waves ahead of me on the road formed mirages of shimmering ponds. The few and distant vehicles coming towards me looked as though they were being driven over water.

I found the town of Cody on the south side of the Shoshone River, surrounded by the Bridger and Absaroka ranges. North of Cody stands Heart Mountain, with Carter Mountains to the south. I would have loved to spend some time in Buffalo Bill's old town but I headed for the East Gate of Yellowstone National Park, driving up the Shoshone River road, edged with large boulders and lodge pole pine forests through the mountain canyon.

Once I was in Yellowstone Park, the first National Park in the Nation, I couldn't help but stop at some of the same places Kipp and the CC's had explored. I had seen many black bears, elk and a few buffalo and wished I hadn't given Dad back his camera. After getting a late meal I wandered into a gift shop. I bought a book called, "A Field Guide to the Mammals" by Burt and Grossenheider. It was the same series as the book I'd discovered by Olaus Murie, "A Field Guide to Animal Tracks." I picked up all sorts of free pamphlets and brochures about the many things to see in Yellowstone. Time had just flown by and I needed to head to Moose and find the Bar X Bar Ranch.

There was more traffic on the two-lane and it was slow going in the park because tourists would stop to photograph elk, bears, moose and any animal close to the road. Of course the bears loved it when the cars stopped because they would come up to the car and beg food. The tourists would hand out food though the slightly rolled down windows, the bears at times standing up on their back legs to take the food away from feeding fingers. Sometimes there was a cub bear or two with the begging mothers. People would jump out of their cars to take photos and allow their children out of the cars, which to me seemed like a very dangerous thing to do. Besides, the park ranger had mentioned to everyone coming through the gate at the park's periphery, including me, that you should not feed the bears while traveling in Yellowstone.

By the time I had passed Jackson Lake and followed the Snake River with Mount Moran and its glacier field to my right and drove into the Grand Teton National Park on the south side of Yellowstone, it was after four-thirty in the afternoon. But it still would be light for sometime. The air was much cooler here than in Billings. I kept driving south, skirting Jackson Lake, then past Leigh Lake and Jenny Lake. The Teton Mountains seemed to have grown out of the lake that reflected their still snow-capped tops. They were a spectacular sight. The mountains were named by Canadian trappers, *"Les Trios Teton,"* The Three Breasts.

At Moose I went into the visitor's center and waited until the tourists had left the information desk and then I asked the lone uniformed ranger with the flat brimmed campaign hat and U.S. gold badge directions to the Bar X Bar Ranch and he gave me guidance.

I followed a narrow winding road at the base of the Tetons through a lodgepole and aspen forest with immense granite boulders scattered throughout and buck and rail fencing followed the road on both sides. In this part of the county you saw very few barbwire fences, only endless miles of rolling six foot high sawbucks supporting panels of horizontal poles, creating a more natural pleasing fence line that allowed game such as deer, elk and moose to jump over without chance of injury by getting tangled in wire. In Jackson Hole there was no shortage of long slim pole timber. Just looking into the woods one saw endless miles of slim lodge pole pines and at their base downed timber in what seemed to be never-ending 'Pick Up Sticks' laying everywhere.

I saw a cow moose with her calf at the edge of a pond as I drove down the gravel road. Finally I came to a side road that had a wood sign that read Bar X Bar 1 mile with an arrow pointing in the only direction you could drive if not just passing by the Bar X Bar.

A half mile up the road a truck was coming my way with two people in it. Both driver and passenger were wearing cowboy hats. As we were about to pass each other the passing truck stopped and so did I. The passenger was J.W. He jumped out of the truck as I got out of mine and we shook hands.

"You Son-a-bitch, you made it! Yahoo!" J.W. exclaimed, "I didn't figure you'd be here for a day or two from now. Glad you made it."

"Yeah, me too. Hope that job is still open," I said.

"This here is Bernie Byatt. Bernie, meet Dakk Lovett!" and we shook hands.

"Glad to meet yuh," Bernie said.

"Bernie here is head wrangler and hunting guide an' he's the one does the hiring," J.W. offered.

"A job is what I'm here looking for," I said.

"We were just headin' for the post office to get the mail an' have a beer at Dornan's. We can talk business there. Turn around up ahead. There's a wide spot an' follow us back to Moose," Bernie said.

At Dornan's store in Moose Bernie picked up the mail and we went across the parking area to Dornan's Restaurant and bar. There were only a few other customers in the barroom and one old rancher cowboy with a very dark sweat-stained straw cowboy hat on and well faded jean-jacket. He sat at the end of the bar smoking his pipe, positioned so he could see everyone that came in. He nodded at us as we entered and we nodded back to him. We sat at a table near the large windows looking up at the three Tetons in the not-too-far distance. Bernie ordered beers all around.

"Tab us, Charlie an' give Jim at the end of the bar a beer on me if he wants another," Bernie told the bartender as he picked up the three open beer bottles and headed back to our table.

Bernie wasn't particularly tall, maybe five-ten or eleven but with three inch high cowboy boots it put him over six feet. He was tanned with a somewhat ruddy face, brown hair and a droopy mustache. Every cowboy including J.W. had on their silk neck rags, doubled around their necks and knotted in the front, as did Jim at the end of the bar.

"J.W., how come you guys still have your spurs on?" I asked, with I'm sure what was a somewhat dumbfounded look.

"Because if there are any out of town ladies out here an' on the loose an' they see us with spurs on, they don't mistake us for those Jackson drugstore cowboys," J.W. gloated with a big smile, "an' we might get lucky."

Bernie was smiling also, "It's all in the look. And that's what they eat up. They go back to wherever home is an' just have tall tales to tell their friends about how good it was in the ol' west doing it with a real cowboy."

"By the way, why do they call this place Jackson Hole?" I asked, "What do they mean by hole?"

Bernie spoke up, "The valley name is after Davy Jackson, a beaver trapper that trapped in this valley and back then any valley surrounded by mountains the trappers called holes. On the other side of the Tetons is Pierre's Hole and there is Brown's Hole in Colorado, an' I suppose there are others around the country also."

We talked more and about horses, dogs, cows and the ladies. After drinking three beers each, we headed for the Bar X Bar. I was hired on.

* * *

The dude ranch, or as they preferred to call it, 'guest ranch,' also outfitted a hunting camp for hunters in the Fall and was owned by James and Judy Lawder. It was situated near a eighty-acre grassy meadow at the base of the south end of the Teton Mountain Range. Aside from the meadow it included a fishing pond with cutthroat trout and an icy mountain stream. The grassy meadow was their hay field and the horses were fenced out of it until after the hay had been cut, baled and stored. The ranch was surrounded by a lodge-pole timber forest and a multitude of aspen groves. The buildings were saddle-notched log structures, chinked inside and out with quarter poles. Old shed bleached elk and deer horns were used to decorate the posts of the porches. The barn, a two story gambrel-roofed building, had stables, tack room, feed room and storage on the main floor while the upstairs was the bunkhouse for the wranglers and guides. Our showers and toilets were downstairs. There were twelve guest cabins strewn apart and situated to face the meadow and the pond. The lodge had a sizeable kitchen with table and benches for the hands to eat at while the guests took their meals in the main dining room. From the dining area was a living room with Molesworth western style furniture, a huge river-stone fireplace, a ping pong table, a billiard table and a console radio and an old cabinet phonograph player with a wind-up crank and filled with vinyl 78 rpm records of big bands. On one wall was a large bookcase filled with books mostly about the west. Next to the bookcase was a locked glass front gun cabinet in which stood with some old vintage Winchester rifles of varying calibers, three double barrel 12 gauge shotguns and a .4-10; the cabinet also held four Savage lever action rifles for the hunting guides that didn't have hunting guns. There was no television, since it was impossible to get reception in the valley in those days.

There was a hay shed for the fall hunting horses but once the Dude string, later turned hunting horses, were no longer needed they all went back to the horse contractor and the lodge closed down for the season with only Dustin Harney staying through the long cold winter to care take the place until spring. The Lawders became what is known as 'Blue Birds" and headed south to a warmer winter climate. Dustin, who we sometimes nicknamed Dusty, had to be sixty plus and was a short straggly bearded old cowboy bachelor. Come spring he left for a couple of months to work for a local rancher doing branding after which he came back to the Bar X Bar to work again.

Dusty bunked with us but didn't take guests or hunters out. He guided for fishermen who wanted to fish the Snake River or Phelps Lake but he was for the most part the fix-it man. He kept the wood pile supplied with up to eight cords of wood when there wasn't something else for him to do. He also made sure the meadow was irrigated during the growing season, as well as put up the hay in the meadow and stored for the next year's feed. In winter his work was the hardest when he had to remove the snow load from the roofs of the buildings. If he had to go to Moose for any reason he would use his long wide cross country skis. Form Moose if he needed a break, he would hitch a ride to Jackson and another back to Moose afterward. There wasn't a lot of traffic on the road there in winter, so it took him awhile to get a ride to town and therefore he would ski towards Jackson until luckily someone happened along. Dustin's time in winter was mostly spent reclusively at the ranch with his fat barn cat he called Cobb.

Dustin had a brother who was also a bachelor and worked for the same ranch as Dustin during branding but for half of the year, he would move his cattle that were mixed in with the ranch's stock to his small outfit on Hog Island south of Jackson. Dustin took his pay from that cow ranch in beef, a live yearling calf, and threw it in with his brother's cows. Over the years they both had built up a sizeable bunch of cows that they bred with one seed bull. The steers they sold off.

J.W. early on told me he was glad that Dustin liked guiding the fly fishermen out to the Snake River fishing because he wasn't about to venture into that river country until after a hard frost in the Fall. The worst part of that job were the thousands of mosquitoes that would bear down on any man or beast and land to the point that you looked like you were wearing a suit of live mosquitoes. They all try to suck some blood out of you at the same time. The cutthroat trout fishing was always good but you had to wear heavy clothing, gloves and mosquito netting over a hat to protect your face.

At four thirty in the morning we'd wake, dress and go saddle the jingle horses kept in the corral. Then J.W. and I would head up into the timber to get the horse string in the dark. We knew the general area that they most likely were. Riding up a trail in pitch darkness, unless there was a moon out you had to rely on your horse's night vision. Unfortunately, your horse didn't account for the fact that you sat three or more feet above its withers and would pass under an overhanging branch that would slap you in the face if not just plain knock you out of the saddle. So you kept an arm up in front of you in hopes of feeling the branch coming at you and ducking in time. The next problem was trying to hear the cow bell hanging on the bell-mare. At times she would know we were coming and not move so we couldn't hear the bell and we'd sit in the saddle with our horse standing still and basically have "a Mexican standoff" until the mare went back to eating. Then we'd hear the jingle and head for the mare. Once we found her the rest was easy and generally by then we had some light. We'd run her with whistling and slapping of our chaps at the thigh, making her hurry down to the ranch, jingling all the way and into the corral. The geldings and other mares would naturally follow after the belled mare.

Once the horses were corralled it was time for us wranglers to eat breakfast and find out how many guests would be riding up into the back country that morning. By seven o'clock the cook's helper would ring the triangle outside to let the guests know breakfast was being served. Then the guests would straggle into the dining room to eat. We would just sit in the kitchen drinking coffee and smoking, waiting for Bernie to find out what the day held for us.

As soon as he knew how many horses had to be saddled for the adults and kids we'd head out and saddle the horses we thought would work the best for our riders that day. Aside from a quick grooming, haltering, saddling, and putting on the animals' headstalls and bits on, we'd check their hooves and make sure they still were shod all around. Then we'd do the morning tick check, pulling off the ticks that had attached themselves to the horse's lower stomach-genital area and kill them. It was not uncommon to find three or more ticks on each animal every day until winter set in. We also had to make sure we had rain gear tied to the back of each cantle because the weather was hard to predict since you couldn't see it coming towards you. The high mountains blocked the northwestern and western view of the oncoming weather.

All we wranglers had our own long yellow slickers rolled up and tied to the back of the saddle's cantle at all times, while the dudes had army surplus ponchos, of 'one size fits all' tied to their saddles. We called our slickers "Fish," so named because the old oilskin pommel slickers were at one time manufactured by the trademark 'Fish' and first became standard cowboy bad weather rain gear around 1880.

The cook always had sourdough pancakes, eggs how we wanted them, bacon, sausage, ham, home-fries, biscuits and gravy, coffee and O.J. ready for us to order and devour. Unfortunately, I found out she would not be our hunting camp cook come fall.

On our table sat a sugar shaker, a salt and pepper shaker that Missis Lawder had picked up in Tombstone, Arizona. Both shakers were shaped like white tombstones, each with their own epitaph; the pepper read:

"Here lies Pepper Tate,
1860-1881
Hanged by mistake
He was right,
We was wrong
but we strung him up
and now he's gone."

And the salt read:

"Here lies Salty O'Day
1861-1881
Hoss Thief,
A rope necktie,
An old oak tree
and salty wasn't
what he used to be."

So if one of us wanted the salt passed their way, he'd say, "Pass O'Day," or the pepper, "Pass Tate."

One morning while waiting on orders the conversation was about what the dangers of the forest were.

"The one thing you've got to be careful about with horses in the timber country is X's," J.W. warned me.

"X's, what are you taking about?" I said.

"You've seen how much dead fall there is in the timber, well one tree falls over another that's on the ground and forms an X. That's what you have to look out for with a horse that's picking its way down off of the mountain. He can easily get a leg caught in the X and break a leg," J.W. cautioned me, "We had a horse bust a leg a month ago and had to shoot it. Some dude let the horse get off the trail into the timber and Bernie riding drag told the old boy to get his horse back on the trail and as the guy turned the horse, a deer bolted up from its hiding place an' spooked the dude's horse an' everything went to Hell in a hand basket. Had to shoot the horse right there. The bears and magpies had a feast off of him for two weeks. So a word of warning, if you find yourself in that down timber predicament, it's best to get off the horse an' walk, letting him pick his own way down."

"Thanks for the good advice," I said.

"As long as we're talkin' lectures about the wilds of Wyoming mountain country," Bernie put in, "here's something else you ought to know. Don't ever get caught between a mama bear an' her cub or cubs, the same goes with a moose cow and her calf. You do an' you're in deep sheep shit. They'll charge you. Also black bears climb trees but grizzlies don't, the thing is grizzlies can haul ass at about thirty to thirty-five miles per hour in a short distance sprint, so try to keep a good quarter mile away from them if possible."

"You ever run into a grizzly?" I asked.

"Only once, up above timber line. A big ol' sow and two cubs. She was teaching them how to get moths from under the rocks on this large scree field. She didn't get wind of me an' I turned my horse around as soon as his ears went flat an' we got the Hell out of there before she caught wind of us. They have piss-poor eyesight but a nose that's as good as any blood hound or horse."

We went out after breakfast and saddled only six of the horses after finding out that only five of the guests' kids wanted to go riding and one adult also. The other horses got the day off. While bridling, I asked Bernie if there still were wolves in Jackson Hole.

"Hell yes. But the rangers an' wildlife people around here say there aren't. But Game an' Fish, as well as I know different. In the four years

I've been in this country I've seen two an' in different areas. I saw one for less than eight seconds, he was black as coal. An' when he saw me or caught wind of me, he hit the timber an' was gonner. Another time was with a hunter I was guiding, we were on the Idaho side of the Tetons. This one was gray an' same thing, as soon as it saw us it was gone like a ghost," Bernie said, "They're as scarce as hen's teeth but they're around, just like cougars. Wolves have been between a rock and a hard spot for fifty years. They didn't all get killed off like the government wants you to think. They survive by being elusive an' keepin' their own numbers down."

Just then the kids came running to the corral for the trail ride that J.W. and I took them on. This time we were lucky and only ran into Steller's jays and gray jays, the almost tame camp robbers, that entertained the kids at lunch time by occasionally flittering from the nearby branches, then gliding down and to take pieces of sandwich bread and lunch meat from the children's hands or out of their held-out cowboy hats. The jays seemed more ravenous than the kids at lunch time.

The following morning Bernie and I had just brought the horses down and had shut the corral gate when we heard a woman scream. Bernie, being still mounted, rode to where he heard the commotion and saw a large black bear lumbering around the cabin with its nose in the air and looking to get into the building. There were no dogs on this ranch and so there wasn't any animal to run the bear off. The bear didn't act as though it was willing to leave so Bernie built a loop and roped the bear by the head and a forepaw as it stood up on its hind legs. He dallied and swung his horse around, spurred the animal to a gallop and towed the bear as it tried to keep from being drug. Bernie then headed for the pond and ran the horse into it, pulling the bear also into the water that was only about three feet deep. After a few lunges he let his rope go and bear and rope took off out of the pond and headed for the woods and high country.

"Looks like you just lost a rope," I said as Bernie came back soaking wet.

"The fun of it was worth it. I always wanted to rope a bear ever since I'd seen a picture of the Charlie Russell painting in which the cowboys are roping a grizzly," Bernie said with a grin on his face.

"Is the bear going to be alright, dragging that rope around?" one of the guests asked.

"Don't worry, he'll just chew it off before he gets a quarter mile away," Bernie said assuring, "but I don't think he'll come back for, how do you say . . . an encore?"

By now every guest was out of their cabin to see what the ruckus was about and had seen the whole show, which would make a great tale once they went home and told the folks and friends about it.

Later Bernie said that Jim Lawder was worried the ranch might get in trouble if the Game and Fish or Park Service got wind of the roped bear scenario and that he hoped the guests wouldn't let the cat out of the bag while in town.

Every day was somewhat different and for the most part we didn't know what the day would bring unless there was a special day activity for the guest. We had a tour bus that took guests to the parks for a couple of days. Or Dusty would take the men that liked to fly-fish on the Snake River or, as J.W. would say, "Feed the mosquitoes," while the women shopped in the town of Jackson with the kids.

That Friday I had gotten a letter from home saying that Readers Digest had accepted my short story called "Cow Camp" and that I had received a check of fifty dollars for the story. So after telling J.W. about it we decided to celebrate. J.W. and I went to Jackson to do a little dancing and drinking. We took the meandering back road to the town of Wilson, and then headed across the Snake River Bridge and on to Jackson and the most popular night spot, the Cowboy Bar.

It was around nine when we entered the bar, which was filled with people, smoke, music, laughter, talk and the clinking of pool balls hitting one another at the pool tables. Cowboys stood at the bar with a foot on the brass foot-rail, elbows on the bar, and drank, smoked and talked to one another. The place was large with a long mirror backed bar and everything had the feel of the west. The most unique thing was all of the knotted burl wood that adorned every post and crowned everything as decoration.

The bar top was covered with hundreds of embedded silver dollars. The Cowboy Bar was really called "The Million Dollar Cowboy Bar." In the old open gambling days, when slot machines, roulette, craps, Black-jack and poker were played it was one very famous watering hole. Now poker gambling still went on but privately and upstairs, on the Q.T., away from the noise of the bar and bands. The Wort Hotel around the corner from the Cowboy Bar also had a bar that was called the "Silver Dollar Bar' because it also had silver dollars implanted in its bar top. Patrons of the night life would take their drinks from bar to bar, when the band stopped playing in one bar, so they could keep on dancing without taking a break.

People crowded the dance floor. We leaned against the wall with a couple of beers and waited for the band to stop playing as they paused after every song and the lead singer made small talk to the audience and dancers.

"Hey, look over there, there's a couple of cute gals sittin' by themselves," J.W. pointed out. And he headed to the table as the band started playing again.

"Howdy, ladies, would you care to dance with us? My friend here an' I are celebratin' his havin' gotten one of his short stories accepted by Readers Digest."

"Sure," said the brunet and she and J.W. went off dancing as soon as he set his beer bottle down on the table.

"So you're a writer, let's dance and you can tell me all about it," said the girl with the raven black hair.

We danced and when the band took their break we ordered more drinks and by now knew the two women's names, Joyce was the brunet and Vicky was the other gal and the one I danced with most of the time.

"Where are you gals from?" J.W. asked.

"We're college students at Berkley in California. We are both working at Jackson Lake Lodge. I'm a waitress and Vicky is a maid but now that things are slowing down since most of the tourists are heading back home, Vicky and I have only two more weeks of work at the lodge and since we both had the weekend off, decided to come to Jackson and have a good time," Joyce chattered.

"Well I'm sure glad we had time off also, otherwise we wouldn't have met," I said.

"You goin' back to the lodge tonight?" J.W. asked.

"No, it's too far for us to drive this late at night. We got a room at the Wort Hotel," Vicky said as she looked at me with that I-want-to-go-to-bed-with-you look. She had been dancing the slow dances real close and tight to me.

"Where do you two work?" Joyce asked.

"We're hands, wranglers at the Bar X Bar Guest Ranch near Moose," J.W. answered as he lit her cigarette.

"We both were working for the Milliron slash B in Montana and that's a cow outfit," I said.

"What made you come here to Jackson Hole to work?" Vicky wanted to know.

"Change of scenery. Plus after the ol' man died, his wife sold the Milliron out to a syndicate cattle outfit," J.W. stated.

Joyce and J.W. were getting very close and very friendly. I saw her kissing him a couple of times and J.W. was teasing her with that I-can-be-had kind of macho cowboy look.

Now and then someone would come up to ask Joyce or Vicky to dance but they would say, "No thank you, we have dates we're with." Only one tall lanky cowboy came and cut in on a dance I was having with Vicky. I let him have the rest of the slow dance and a fast one afterwards. But then Vicky said she had to get back to her date and the cowboy went back to the bar and had the bar maid bring us a round of drinks on him.

"Are you guys heading back to the guest ranch tonight? Or should I say this morning . . . . it's almost closing time," Vicky said.

"Now that the horses are in the hayfield eating the stubble instead of being run up into the mountain timber we don't start work until six-thirty in the morning," I said, starting to feel the effects of the beers.

"Maybe we should leave. Do you guys want to come up to our room at the Wort? We could have a little private party?" Joyce said.

"I don't see why not. The night is still young, what you think, Dakk?" J.W. said, looking at me with a smirk on his face.

"Yeah, you bet, except it's morning now. But I'm game. Got to go with the flow," I said which sounded stupid to me as I had said it.

We left and J. W. and Joyce crossed the street and passed the antler arch to his pickup that was parked in front of Jackson Drug. We waited for them to return before going around the corner to the Wort Hotel. I knew he was going to the truck to get some condoms out of the glove compartment. I had some in my jean jacket pocket. I lit a Lucky as we watched them make out after he retrieved what he wanted out of the truck. Then they cut across the street towards us with J.W. steering Joyce by the hand as a truck made its way through town. The four of us went around the corner of the block and into the Wort and took the stairs to their second floor room.

The room had two single beds separated by an end table and lamp. The open window faced the street from which you could hear people leaving the bars talking and laughing and a few vehicles leaving town. Joyce closed the window and noise out of the room and turned on the radio to soft music. Vicky was quick to begin to unsnap the buttons of my shirt with one hand as she unzipped her skirt and let it drop to the floor and I then helped her undress also. Joyce and J.W. had gone into the bathroom and no sooner than I had my boots and pants pulled off; Vicky was already naked in bed.

"Come on cowboy, let's ride," Vicky said as I climbed into the bed with her and we kissed.

Moments later Joyce and J.W. came out of the bathroom soaking wet after having showered together and jumped onto the next bed. With the bathroom light still on, I could see a pile of their clothes that lay in a jumbled heap on the bathroom floor.

"Oh. Fuck me. Fuck me hard," Joyce was whispering to J.W. as the bed squeaked and the headboard knocked against the wall. Vicky and I were making our own waves.

By five in the morning I woke up to J.W. and Vicky going at it and discovered Joyce was in bed with me and she was working my manhood teasingly. So I was quickly convinced to go for another ride but this time I had Joyce riding me until we both climaxed at the same time.

J.W. drove like he never had before back to the Bar X Bar and we made it in time to see that Bernie had brought only six horses to the corral and we knew it would be an easy day if we went out at all.

"Well, look at what the cat dragged in, a couple of fornicators," Bernie exclaimed with a grin on his face, "You two look like you've got run over by a Mack truck."

"Yeah," we both answered simultaneously without much enthusiasm. "I need some coffee," I said as we headed for the kitchen.

Hot coffee and breakfast woke us from lack of sleep as well as enabled us to face the day with new enthusiasm.

The following weekend Bernie and J.W. had gone to the Stagecoach Bar dancing and drinking. They showed up late the next morning very hung-over. I had the horses saddled and ready to go with the guest family all ready to trail ride.

"You guys go on ahead an' I'll catch up as soon as I have a cup of coffee," J.W. said, "Which trail you takin'?"

"The creek through the flood plain towards the Snake," I said.

"Mosquito Heaven," J.W. said with a grim face.

"Isn't Bernie coming with us today?" the teenage girl asked.

"No, it's his day off. But J.W. will catch up to us," I said.

My crotch was itching and I thought I better take another shower when we get back for lunch. I must have gotten some hay chaff down my shirt and it worked its way to my pubes and now I itched.

We took a trail towards the river going through willow groves and saw a bull moose with sizable antlers eating in a marshy area a good distance away. Each time he raised his head out of the pond from eating at the bottom, water dribbled from his mouth as he turned to watch us. The antlers his crowning glory bear over him royally.

Twenty minutes later J.W. came riding up as we were stopped and watching a couple of beaver swimming in one of the small ponds they had created by damming the creek. As soon as they heard J.W. approach on Llano with his spurs jingling, one beaver slapped its tail on the water and both disappeared into its depth, leaving two rippling circular wakes behind them.

"I made it," J.W. joked, slapping at the mosquitoes that had landed on his face. He didn't look very happy.

"You just missed the beavers," the youngest girl said as she squashed some bugs that had landed on her horse's neck.

"I heard them splash. See that pile of branches an' sticks, well that's their house. An' you see all the aspens they've cut down, that's what they eat. They're vegetarians," J.W. told them in a matter of-fact voice. He wasn't happy in this bug infested area.

"They should be called woodatrians," the boy said.

"Dennis, there's no such thing as woodatrians," the father said and slapped at mosquitoes that had landed on him and instantly killing three that were already in the same vicinity of the wallop.

"Well if all they eat is wood then they should be called woodatrians," the boy argued.

J.W. took the lead and we all rode in file at a trot towards the Snake River's banks with the damn bugs following us as fast as we rode.

To the northwest, the sky had darkened and a few drops of rain hit us, the sound of thunder rumbled over the valley. The wind picked up, causing the mosquitoes to retreat to the willows.

"Let's get our rain gear on, folks. Looks like we're in for a wet one," J.W. warned. Everyone donned their ponchos and we put on our yellow Fish slickers.

"Why don't we have yellow slickers?" asked the boy.

"Because we don't have any to fit you," I put in, smiling, as the rain began to intensify into a downpour with gusty winds that kept up as the weather moved southeasterly. He horses danced and sidled as the ponchos and slickers flapped in the wind.

At one point J.W. dropped back and let everyone go on and he said to me in between rumbling thunder, "Hey, I think I got a case of crabs. I've been itchin' my crotch all day."

"So have I. You think those gals at the Wort gave them to us last week?"

"Yeah, those bitches are probably laughing about it right now," J.W. grumbled.

"How we going to get rid of them?"

"We'll have to get some bottles of Triple X or turpentine an' scrub and comb the little bastards out until we kill them all. Have to wash all our clothes and bedding with hot or boiling water a few times until we get rid of them. Ain't you ever had a case of crabs before?"

"No, lucky I guess,"

By now we had reached the river and J.W. was back in the lead, following the trail that passed a few very nice fishing holes with a pair of river otters frolicking off muddy slides on the river bank.

"What are those?" the boy asked as he pointed to them.

"River otters. And, no, they're not woodatrians, they eat fish and whatever meat they can get," J.W. said, sounding in better humor now that the bugs were in hiding from the rain.

"Look up there," I said to the kids, "there's a porcupine up in that tree. They eat bark so I guess you could call them woodatrians."

When we got back for lunch the rain had moved on and the sun shone again, J.W. went to the bunk house bathroom after borrowing the magnifying glass from the living room book shelf and checked himself out.

"Well, sure as shit I have fuckin' crabs. The little bustards have moved in and started a family. Here, take this magnifier an' go in the crapper an' check yourself out," he urged.

I did and I too had a case of homesteaders.

We told Bernie that night about the parasites and he laughed and mumbled something about shaving our boys down there.

"A little kerosene would eventually get rid of them. I've had them a couple of times myself," Bernie said, "Hell, there's no need to make a mountain out of a mole hill, it ain't syphilis," and then added somewhat dubiously, "I hope you guys had rain-slickers for your juniors when you went in? Otherwise you might find out that those gals had more than lice to hand out."

*   *   *

Once the summer guests had left we worked on the tents, stove, packsaddles, box and canvas panniers getting ready for hunting camp. Dustin and Bernie gave J.W. and me a crash course on packing though I had had some experience in that art from hunting in Montana. We were taught the diamond hitch, double diamond, box hitch with half diamond, the barrel hitch and the basket hitch. We learned about the sawbuck and Decker pack saddles, about how to pack out an elk, slings, a britchin, how to tail a horse and use a brake-always in case of an accident with the animals on the trail. There were a million dos and don'ts. I was one up on J.W. who had never packed before.

"These hunters come in for a five day elk or mule deer hunt. They spend their first night here and the five days with us in camp, then they come out an' spend their last night getting a shower an' a soft bed to sleep in before heading back to their wives, kids an' work. Dustin takes the game meat into Jackson Cold Storage an' they process the elk an' the head goes to the taxidermist to be mounted. Cold Storage sends them the meat and so does Reesor's Taxidermist once he's got the head mounted," Bernie had told us then added, "We then take turns in having' days off during the three days between hunters."

"I got to tell you guys something," he said to J.W. and me, "Neither of you have been Wyoming residents for over a year so when you are guidin' don't have your out-of-state driver's licenses with you, otherwise you could get arrested by the Game and Fish Warden. Guides are supposed to have been in Wyoming for at least a year. So keep your hunters on the level and don't shoot their elk for them even if they ask you," Bernie warned, "So if you have a problem with that an' think you couldn't bullshit your way out of tellin' the Game and Fish you've been around here workin' for over a year, then I'll have to try to hire some local guys, which there ain't any 'cause they're already workin' for someone else. That's been the problem for years now, not enough local guides. I should have told you sooner, it just sort of slipped my mind. I'm sorry. So if you want to quit I won't blame you."

J.W. and I had just found ourselves in a dilemma but decided to take our chances this late in the game. I suddenly felt like my brother Kipp who was always one step away from the law catching up to him for whatever tomfoolery he and the CC's got themselves into.

We kept busy fixing gear and practicing the hitches. This year we had no antelope hunters. Antelope are the earliest big game animals hunted on the Wyoming plains and for the Bar X Bar hunters they are hunted around Pinedale and Daniel, Wyoming.

Nor did we have any hunter that had drawn a moose or Rocky Mountain bighorn sheep permit. You automatically got a black bear license attached to your elk license so you could kill either or both if you got the chance.

"Last year they had some hunter out of Texas that came here to hunt for a grizzly bear and Bernie found him one that almost made the Boone and Crocket record book. You know what that guy paid to hunt a grizzly?" J.W. asked me.

"A couple of hundred bucks maybe," I said.

"Make that five hundred bucks. Bernie said he got fifty dollars as a tip along with a bottle of Jack Daniel's whisky,"

"The guy must have been loaded to put out that kind of money," I said.

"Well he also had to pay the Bar X Bar for the hunt on top of it all," J. W. declared, "He was from Houston, Bernie said, had oil money so he was black gold rich."

"At least he knew how to spread it around," I said.

"Most of these hunters are good tippers, especially if you find them a good bull elk like a six pointer."

One day I happened to notice that Dustin had a horrible scar on his left forearm and my curiosity got the best of me and I asked him about it.

"It happened on one of my bad luck days in January '54," he began, "I'd been out checkin' my trap line, beaver I was trappin' at the time. Had twenty-four drown sets with Victors for about a mile. I remember I'd gotten eight an' it started to snow to beat Hell. I was on skis. Snow was deep. I got to the last of my traps and knew I had another one. But the wire ran down under the ice an' I couldn't see it. An' instead of stickin' my head in the freezin' creek to see what was what, I just reached under the ice and got hold of the taps chain an' jerked it out of the water with my left hand, bein' a southpaw, but the beaver weren't drowned and as I went to use my right hand to toss it on the snow so I could club it, he got me. Sharp ass teeth they have. Took thirty stitches to close me up at Saint John's Hospital. Left a blood trail all the way there. Doc said it was a good thing I used a tourniquet or I'd bled to death before I got to him. Anyway it kinda put the kibosh on trappin' the rest of that year."

"You still trap beaver now though?" I asked.

"Well just 'cause you get bucked off don't mean you don't get back on. I don't run a trap line no more except to get rid of the troublesome ones that are buildin' dams an' messin' with the irrigation ditches where ranchers don't want them. But I'm real cautious nowdays," Dustin said.

The hunting camp for the Bar X Bar elk and fall bear hunters was up the *Gros Ventre* River, which means Big Belly and named by Hudson Bay Canadian fur trappers, then on past Slide Lake which was created during an earthquake in 1925 that dammed the river. On May 18, 1927, the natural dam collapsed and flooded the Snake River Valley which included the towns of Kelley and Wilson, Bernie had told me. We had to ford the river and follow a trail up Redmond Creek on the north side of Sleeping Indian Mountain.

The spike camp was made up of four wall tents and a cook tent that had a cook stove set up in it as well as a long table and folding chairs. J.W. and I had dug a trench latrine that was walled with canvas and had a roof made of spruce boughs, the seats were two horizontal poles twelve inches apart and coffee cans held the TP. Strung between two trees was the food cache that hung on a pulley system so the cook could get to it but not the bears. We also had a pine lodgepole corral, hitching rail and the creek nearby for water. The camp was in a saddle surrounded by forest and grassy meadows at an elevation of about seven thousand feet.

Everything we needed was packed in by the horses which were in pretty good shape since they had been worked most of the summer. From the Bar X Bar to the trail head up Redmond Creek was over twenty horse trail meandering miles with two different river crossings. The Snake River and the Gros Ventre River both were still fast flowing, cold and clear, though not as deep at the crossings as they had been earlier in the year. The crossings in the spring were chest deep to your horse or deeper and extremely dangerous to navigate through because of not only the depth of the water but the strength and speed it moved as well as its temperature being close to freezing.

"See that dead fall over there that has created a catch all for flotsam? Stay away from it with the horses, there's a deep hole just beyond it and the river bends into the shore an' with that cut bank your horse couldn't climb out on that side," Bernie warned. "Stay west of that big boulder. This is the safest crossing in this area at this time of year."

"Ever have trouble crossing the rivers?" I asked.

"No! So far so good. But I know of a local guide that lost his pack mule an' all his gear crossing this river a couple years ago. He almost drowned himself. He dove in an' tried to cut loose the lash ropes from the packs off of his mule an' both got pulled into a hole formed by a log jam. He got out by the luck of God but the mule drowned. The river was too high an' water too fast. Hell, I've seen six elk drown crossing the Snake River once. They just picked a bad spot to try to cross at."

We rode on in file with Bernie at the head and me leading the pack string and J.W. bringing up the drag on Llano. The smell of duff from traveling through the pines and spruce was strong and sparks jumped from the shoes of the horses when we cut over the granite rocks and climbed uphill. Butterflies of varying colors fluttered about and dragonflies darted or held themselves still in the air. The quaking aspens, golden with color, rustled in the breeze, losing a few leaves to the ground. Elk and deer droppings could be seen along the trail as well as bear scat in places where berry bushes flourished. The rose hips had turned red. In the meadows the fireweed turned into fluffy seedy hair, the Indian paintbrush still bore scarlet blooms and the balsamroot, the golden blooms now gone, their leaves turning brown and curling dry, told that winter was around the corner.

There were a lot of outfitters in Jackson Hole and each was assigned a particular area permit to hunt in the National Forest. Hunters had to go out on a hunt only assisted by local guides that knew the hunt areas like the backs of their hands. J.W. and I with the assistance of Bernie had to learn our hunt area and find the elk bed grounds, the bull elk, the high meadows and how to use an elk call to lure the bulls to our hunter. Our hunt area was the Sleeping Indian. Looking northeasterly from the town of Jackson you could see the mountain called the Sleeping Indian. The head of the Indian is to the west and he looks as if he is lying on his back wearing a war bonnet, his nose stands out as well as a saddle under his chin making the neck followed by a large belly, a *Gros Ventre.*

* * *

The first five hunters arrived and I took them and their gear by horseback up Redmond Creek four miles to the spike camp from the Gros Ventre trail head. They had arrived by truck and car from the Bar X Bar driven by Dustin and James Lawder.

Our cook was Charlie Martin a five foot ten, two hundred and forty pounds, with a full white-beard. He was an old cowhand that hailed from Missouri. Fortunately, Charlie was a very good cook and story teller. He could keep everyone entertained with his many tall yarns that he would spin one after another. From which we nicknamed him Tall Tale Charlie. He kept the hunters spellbound and laughing. He loved to play poker and though he was not an alcoholic he kept, as the Lawders expected, plenty of liquor on hand for the evening return of the hunters. On real cold days Charlie would concoct a hot drink for hunters when they returned to camp he called "Bull Shot." It consisted primarily of beef bouillon, Tabasco sauce and vodka. After a few cups of Bull Shot you no longer felt cold but also a bit tipsy which helped you sleep through the cold night. He also kept on hand a large bottle of aspirin for all the aches and pains the out-of-shape hunters had after coming out of the back country on horseback from the day's hunt.

Charlie had a camp jack, a roustabout, a young high school dropout at seventeen because he was one of eight Mormon kids in his family. The seven other siblings were all girls and he wanted to be on his own since he was ten years old. He had blonde hair and icy blue eyes, he was as tall as Charlie and everybody called him by his nickname, Snook. Why he was called that, no one, let alone Snook himself. In grade school he had many fights over other boys calling him Snook but as he aged some, he grew to like the name and quit fighting over someone calling him that. His real name was Clarence Miller. This was his first year of employment with the Bar X Bar and Charlie's roust-a-bout, go-fer. He was a hard working kid who might turn into a real good hand.

Bernie had put up a sign in the cook tent for all to read and pay heed to:

NO SMOKING ON THE HUNTS UNTIL AFTER YOU'VE MADE YOUR KILL. WEAR YOUR RED SO YOU WON"T BECOME DEAD! AND THIS MEANS EVERYBODY ON THE HUNT.

This, he explained to all the hunters, was so the game wouldn't smell the smoke and become wary of human presence in their area, and that wearing red was required by law as most hunters already knew.

Charlie slept in his cowboy tepee range-tent next to his cook wall-tent. Charlie didn't use an alarm clock: he claimed to have one built-in and if he had any disbelief in himself he said the sun or the stars told him the time unless there was weather and he would then rely on his gut feelings. Snook had a cot in the cook tent and it was his job to keep the fire in the stove lit. Charlie kept a clothesline hung over the stove with clothespins so we could hang our wet gloves there to dry. He would send Snook to wake us as soon as he had the coffee and biscuits going in the morning, which was about five a.m. and still pitch dark at that time of year.

In your half-sleep you could hear Charlie moving around lighting the gas lights, checking the fire going in the cook stove, and bagging pots and pans but you stayed in your bedroll until the last minute because most mornings it was below freezing. We had had twelve inches of snow at six thousand feet already six days before the first hunters had arrived in camp. And though the days were warm, the snow stayed for the most part, which was good for the hunt. It made tracking easier, especially if the hunter had made a bad shot and you had to find the animal before the bears and coyotes got to him.

Most hunters came with their own rifles in what favorite calibers they preferred. We, on the other hand, only carried a Savage in our saddle scabbards, and binoculars. We were not supposed to shoot for the hunters and only had the rifles as backup against grizzlies or any possible mishap with a wounded charging wild animal.

We would run the hunts generally twice a day, early morning and late afternoon. But a few hard core hunters wanted to hunt from dawn to dusk. Most of these hunters were nothing like the local townspeople who hunted for their winter's meat to put in the cold storage. The nonresident hunters that came to hunt in Wyoming for big game were head hunters looking for the prize bull elk or deer or what game they came to hunt and paid a high price for that privilege.

In the morning we would split up in groups, each with a guide going in a different direction up the mountain on horseback. We all took along coffee in thermoses and sandwiches. When an elk had been shot Charlie would take the tongue, cook it and make everyone tongue sandwiches which were an epicurean delight for us to eat.

On the second morning I had only one hunter from Texas, a nice guy but I had a hard time understanding him because of his strong Texas accent or rather drawl and pronunciation of the English language.

"Ah sad a prior that this hair is da day I get mah bull," Sam the oil well driller said, "Y'awl find me a beggar elk than George White an' so hep me Ah tip y'awl good. An' mah word is jes' as riot as rain."

"Yes sir," I said, only catching the gist of what he had just said.

"No need y'awl call me sir, son. Y'awl call me Sam. We're all Markins hair, an' your gonna hep me get mah big bull elk."

A couple of miles up the trail we got off our horses and tied them to trees and with our rifles I lead the way to a small open meadow and I could smell the elk. I pulled my glove off, and wetting my little finger, I held it up to make sure I knew the wind direction was in our favor. The light breeze was coming from the front of us.

Sam was no dummy; he kept his mouth shut and watched my hand signals as we advanced quietly through the snow and around the dead fall. When I was close to an opening of the meadow I used the binoculars to glass the elk that were bedded down. Vapor rose from their breaths, their backs frosted over. All were cow and calves except for one young spike elk. Then I saw the bull to our right and counted the points on one side of his horns. Five points. I held up five fingers to the side of my head and then pointed to the direction of the bull. Sam brought up his rifle and looked but from his angle couldn't see the bull, so I slowly moved away from my vantage point at a low crawl, allowing Sam my position to shoot from. He chambered a round slowly into the rifle and looked down the barrel. I knew he saw the elk. He moved forward to rest his rifle on a branch of a deadfall for bracing and aimed again. I looked at the bull through the binoculars; he held his head back and was sniffing the air. Had the breeze changed direction, I thought to myself as I watched the bull. Suddenly a gray jay sang out harshly; the spike stood and the cows also jumped up, followed by the calves and the bull. The cows and calves instantly broke for the timber and the big bull turned and rushed after them with the spike on his heels.

Kaboom! Sam's Remington barked and I heard him eject the cartridge and chamber another round as the bolt slammed forwards.

"Ah mus' be blond to miss that shot, Lard knows what happened," Sam muttered.

"Let's go see if there's blood. Maybe he went down in the timber," I said.

"Ah jes' hate missin'. Ah drawed a good aim on him fur ah fared, that's one thang ah know."

We followed the tracks for some time but we never saw a drop of blood or any hair on the snow. He had missed completely and that was one thing I knew. Back at the horses I made sure he had taken the round out of his rifles chamber and put on the safety before he put the rifle back in the scabbard. I did the same and we rode on up the mountain to the top of the Sleeping Indian's belly and I could see that a lot of elk had been there. We tied the horses again and scouted on foot. Then we hid at the edge of the woods and I bugled a few times but received no answer from any elk, so we rode back to camp. I told Sam that we should come back to the top in the late afternoon and he agreed. On the way down we heard a few distant rifle shots that sounded to be a few miles away.

When we got to camp one of the hunters had shot a four point elk, four on one rack and four and a half one on the other rack and he was happy with what he had shot since it was his first elk hunt and was already celebrating with a few drinks of J.D. whisky. They had brought the head of the elk in and Bernie and Snook had gone back to pack the animal quarters back to camp.

Around four o'clock Sam and I rode back up the mountain to the top and I did my best to keep ourselves downwind at all times. On the way up I pointed to some fresh bear tracks without saying anything. Once on top we tied the horses and traveled on foot keeping low, without making a sound in the soft snow and stopping to glass ahead before moving on. The wind changed and we moved to keep it from picking up our scent and blowing it towards our destination. I thought of bugling but decided against it. We pressed on slowly and found the area we had seen all the elk tracks that morning and decided to wait, hiding in the timber's edge. The sky had become overcast by the time we had reached the top of the Indian and it began to snow.

Sometime later a few prudent cow elk came up into the meadow. They advanced and pawed the snow and began to eat the grasses below. More cows and calves appeared and began pawing and eating as well. They moved forwards, grazing. We waited. What seemed like hours passed, then slowly a big bull elk appeared facing us. He had to be over two hundred yards away from where we hid. Sam took aim kneeling and was using a low tree branch for rest. The bull bent his head and pawed the snow and began to eat. Sam didn't shoot, he waited. Finally the bull turned sideways to us, giving Sam a profile shot at the bull.

Kaboom! Sam's rifle barked.

The elk all sprang into the timber with the crashing of branches and a dusting of snow flew as they ran through the trees. The snow was now coming down hard and at that distance I couldn't tell if Sam's shot had been good.

"Ah got 'em!" Sam exclaimed.

"You sure? I didn't see him go down," I said.

"Hell, jes' as riot as rain ah got 'em. Lard has answer mah prior," Sam babbled.

We walked over to where the bull had been and there he lay. Cautiously I nudged the elk's antler with my foot and he kicked out once and stopped. Sam was aiming at the elk's chest with his rifle but didn't need to fire. This time Sam had proved that he was a good shot. The elk lay dead, its eyes losing their luster as he bled from his neck a puddle of crimson on the new snow. By now the snow had stopped but darkness was closing in. After we had taken care of dressing out the elk, raising its body over fallen timber so it would freeze solid during the night and leaving the gut pile as orts for the coyotes or bears, we then headed back to camp. The night sky had once again opened up to be clear and there was a ceiling of glittering stars without a moon; only my flashlight and the horse's knowledge of the trail got us back to the warmth of the camp, something to eat and the comfort of our cots and bedrolls. Morning would find us on top of the mountain with the pack animals and we would quarter the bull elk and bring the meat and head back down to camp. I asked Sam if he wanted the ivories and he said no, so I dug them out of the elk's jaws and kept them. Charlie got the tongue to cook up after Bernie had caped out the elk head to send to the taxidermist along with the horns.

*   *   *

After the first group of hunters had left the guest ranch I had a couple of days off and went to Jackson on that Friday night. I drove to Moose then south to Jackson; there was a wind out of the west and the road was drifted over with snow in places but was passable. As I drove past the Elk Refuge I saw that some of the elk had already come down out of the mountains to winter there. It was estimated that over seventy thousand elk wintered on the refuge in the winter months.

It had snowed the day we came out of camp and town was covered, the four arches made mostly from shed elk-horn on the corners of the town square were capped with snow. Icicles hung from the porch roofs covering the boardwalks in front of the town buildings. The air was cold and crisp. The snow crunched under foot.

I had a cup of coffee, burger and a piece of pie at the Westerner Restaurant. The waitress had on a name tag that said Linda. Business was slow, only a few early arrival skiers were eating at a table next to the window. She took the time to talk to me as I ate my meal while sitting at the counter.

"Looks like the skiers are here early this year. Snow King Mountain won't open for another month most likely," she told me.

"You get a lot of skiers here?" I asked.

"We get some. A lot more skiers come every year since the ski area was built in 1939. I was just a kid back then and most people that had skis around here used them just for getting around across country, it was faster than using snowshoes."

"So do you ski?" I asked her.

"I do once in a while and I have my kids now that ski going downhill. They love it. It's the speed, they love going like a bat out of hell down the runs. My youngest one Bobby broke his arm skiing a year ago on the last day that Snow King was open for skiing but that doesn't stop him from wanting to ski fast. Do you ski?"

"No, never tried it. I just don't think I could savvy skiing," I said sort of nonchalantly. Working in the cold every winter day was one thing but just playing in it was another. It never appealed to me whatsoever.

She talked to me some more in-between checking on her costumers' needs. She asked if I was staying in the valley through the winter and said that one of the most fun things that went on in Jackson was in February.

"It's the two day cutter races hosted by the Shriners Club. That's one way the Shriners raise money for the kids' hospital down in Salt Lake City. They have the races right out here on Broadway. It's like chariot racing only some run on runners instead of wheels. The chariots are drawn by two horses. They race two abreast. It's like in the movie 'Ben Hur.' They run for a quarter of a mile from start to finish down the street," she went on, "It's a Calcutta auction and there's lots of side betting and once in a while there is a crash or spill because the horses are running on packed snow and ice on the street," she said. "It's a lot of fun and racers come from all over with their teams. It's quite the deal."

"It sure sounds like a lot of fun and I'd love to see them but I don't know if I'll be still here in Jackson then," I told her.

"Well I hope you get a chance to see the races," she urged.

After leaving the restaurant I decided to see a movie since I was in town alone and needed a mental escape from everything. I was in some sort of funk but had no idea why. The job was good and a nice change from working with cows but my mind was out of sorts for some reason. Maybe because I wasn't sure what I was going to do after hunting camp ended and the Bar X Bar shut down for the winter. It may have been the beginning of my getting 'cabin fever.' I walked past the Wort Hotel then around the corner and past the Cowboy Bar as a few folks were entering it and heard the band playing but wasn't in the mood to go in myself.

Teton Theater was playing 'Run Silent, Run Deep' with Clark Gable and Burt Lancaster. This was so far away from my daily life that I thought I could submerge myself in the film and get my mind out of my doldrums. I bought a ticket for fifty cents and went in and sat up in the balcony. Surprisingly, the theater was quite full, then again it was the weekend and outside the bars there wasn't much to do in town at night. They just about rolled up the streets and boardwalks by six o'clock in the afternoon.

The news reel talked about the latest craze, the Hula Hoop and Nikita Khrushchev, the Premier of the Soviet Union. There was a Popeye the Sailor and Bugs Bunny cartoon before the feature movie, 'Run Silent, Run Deep,' a World War Two movie about a United States submarine captain that has an obsession with wanting to kill a Japanese destroyer that sank his previous ship and three others. After getting the Navy Department to give him command of another ship, the USS Nerka, he and his new crew go after the Japanese destroyer nicknamed Borgo Pete, which begets the movie similar in plot to Herman Melville's book, 'Moby Dick' with the submarine captain chasing the Japanese destroyer as Captain Ahab chased after the great white whale for revenge in Melville's book.

After the movie I thought that hunting the enemy with a submarine was not much different than hunting some wild animal except in most cases the animal wasn't hunting you back. Being a sailor on a submarine wasn't for me. It is too confining, too claustrophobic, and the sea, which I had never seen except in movies, news reels and photos, was too unknown and endless to me. The thought of being in a submarine gave me the heebie-jeebies as Ma called it whenever she had a case of goose bumps over something scary. Land had much more to offer, I'd never make a sailor.

I decided to go to the Rancher Bar instead of the Cowboy Bar. It was snowing again lightly. I sat at the bar which only had a few cowboys sitting, drinking and talking while others played cards at the poker tables in back. Each time someone came into the bar warm air and smoke spilled out and a cold blast followed the patron in. The men at the bar automatically looked at who was coming in. I sat at the bar and unbuttoned my coat as the bartender came towards me.

"What's your poison? He asked.

"Jack Daniel's, water back," I answered.

"Howdy," said the cowboy sitting a couple of stools from me. Then added, "Haven't seen you in town before. Who you workin' for or you just passin' through?"

"I'm with the Bar X Bar until after the hunt, then I don't know," I said.

"So, you work for the Lawders. Is Bernie Byatt still with them or has he headed for Nevada again this year?"

"Yeah. He is," I said as the bartender handed me my change from a five dollar bill for my J.D. in silver dollars and change. Most businesses in Jackson gave you change back from a five or ten dollar bill in silver dollars unless you asked for paper and you'd try to only use the silver instead of the paper money you carried, otherwise your pants would fall down to your ankles with all that silver weight in your pockets.

"I've known Bernie since he was a kid," he said, then leaned over and asked in a quiet voice, "I caught wind that Bernie roped himself a big ol' bear and lost his rope in the process. Is that true?"

I just nodded lightly, yes.

"I'll be dog gone, dipped an' damned to hell," he said, "When he was a kid, he roped anythin' and everythin' he saw. Dogs seein' him coming with a rope headed for the hills before he got too close to them."

* * *

I had left the Bar X Bar a short time after our last hunt on the Indian. We had moved the hunting camps tents and equipment back to the ranch in deep snow. The snow was three feet high in the mountains and the elk had all moved down into the valley to winter on the National

Elk Refuge. I remember seeing the *wapiti* as they are sometimes called lined out on a ridge a half-mile long one behind the other; cows and yearling calves, young spike bulls all followed by the mature bulls, some with massive, spectacular horns, all heading into the most beautiful of valleys, Jackson Hole, where thousands of elk winter. It was a magnificent sight.

Breaking camp took three days of packing everything out of Redmond Creek with the horses and it had snowed most of that time. Bernie was going to work feeding cows on some ranch near Bondurant, Wyoming, for the rest of the winter, J.W. headed for California and I went back to Billings to live with my folks and my brother Kipp. Going back to Billings at that time of year turned out to be a longer drive since Yellowstone Park was closed to the public in winter. I ended up driving to Riverton, then north to Worland along the Bighorn River to Billings. I had lucked out with the weather and didn't have to drive in any whiteouts where snow and wind blinded you of what was ahead of you. It was called 'white knuckle driving' due to the fact that you are holding onto the steering wheel so tight for control and fear of colliding into something that your knuckles are white.

Work in Billings was hard to find that winter so I just kept to home banging away at my typewriter and began writing a few short stories and mailing them out to different publications to see if I could sell one or two. 'Field and Stream' bought one and published it, called, 'The Last Hunt' about an elk hunter's last elk hunt since he was getting too old to hunt and was moving to a retirement home for veterans from the First World War. It was good for my ego to have gotten published and I felt that I was headed in the right direction with writing and I enjoyed doing it. I gave my mother the one hundred and fifty dollars I got for the story for my winter's room and board. Come spring I'd sign up for fall classes at Eastern Montana College and put my cowboy career on hold or retirement. Time would tell.

The KCC's were all working and Cooper had bought himself a 1946 Ford coupe and Kipp was trying to talk him into making a hot rod out of it.

"My dad says that if I waste my time and money on hot rodding it up I wouldn't get as much money for it when I wanted to sell it," Cooper said.

Cody's dad had helped him buy a 1948 Crosley sedan which the salesman had said belonged to an old lady. The mileage on the odometer was low but the brake pedal showed a lot of wear. Kipp had to do a lot of work on the car for Cody because the thing had ignition problems as well as steering. He told Cody that he thought the salesman had turned back the odometer on the Crosley. Sometimes Cody's car wouldn't start and he had to turn on the ignition, place the transmission in neutral and open the door, get out and push the door frame until he was trotting at a good pace. Then he'd jump into the car, push in the clutch, put the car into high gear and pop out the clutch and the car would come to life. He always tried to find a downhill grade to park on so he had less trouble getting the Crosley going if the battery or starter wouldn't activate his car.

In April I got a part time job at the Billings Gazette. It didn't pay much but it was a way to get my foot in the door and see how the newspaper business worked. I was pretty much just a gofer and not a writer but it was valuable experience. I even got to work in the darkroom developing photos. I did artwork for some of the ads which included everything from setting my own ad type, paste ups, and writing my ad copy. I saw how the linotype operators and the printers worked. I even had to help hand-collate the papers as the sections came off the big press cut and folded.

They even gave me a chance to go out and take some news photos one day when one of the news photographers was ill. It was a day that was raining as Dad would say, "Like cats and dogs." It was late in the day and everyone was busy trying to put the paper 'to bed,' as they called it.

"Lovett! the assistant editor yelled at me, "You know how to take pictures, don't you?"

"Yes sir, I . . ." and he cut me off before I could tell him I had taken pictures with Dad's Brownie camera.

"Good! Take that camera and head for Livingston and between there and west of Big Timber there's a freight train derailment. A few cars have crashed down some coulee there. Write down the particulars of the accident and bring back some good shots. Keep track of your mileage and the paper will reimburse you for the gas," he said, and then added, "Your photo might make the front page. Get going!" And he left for his office.

I picked up the camera but had no idea how the thing was supposed to work.

The camera was a large Graflex newsman's camera with flash. I had never operated such a camera so I asked one of the news men to show me how to operate it.

"Its tits, here, let me show you," he said and made a quick demonstration of how the Graflex functioned, loaded the film and took a picture of me and I blinked after the flash half blinded me. Then I took one of him. After which he said practice makes perfect with a smile and went back to his job. Then looking over his shoulder as I was heading out the door he warned me, "Don't let the effin' rain hit the lens or your picture will be blurry."

I picked up the camera in its case with extra flash bulbs and film and headed out into the steady rain. I had on my cowboy hat and slicker that almost dragged the ground and made a mad dash for my truck in the Gazette parking lot. I felt as though I didn't look like a reporter dressed the way I was but then this was the west and most people dressed this way and wore cowboy hats and boots even if they never rode a horse anywhere.

The rain for the moment seemed to have eased some and my wipers swished back and forth. The wiper on the passenger side of the International was not doing too good a job of moving the rain water cleanly from that side of the windshield.

I drove through Laurel, Columbus, Reedpoint, Greycliff and Big Timber and just before Springdale I saw flashing lights from sheriffs and other emergency vehicles in the not-too-distant darkness. They had road flares along the highway and one lane closed off on the railroad side of the roadway.

I was stopped by a sheriff's deputy. "Please stay on the other side of the highway," he told me as I came to a stop.

"I'm here from the Billings Gazette. My editor sent me to take some pictures," I said and showed him my press card.

"Okay, cowboy, just park over there and stay out of the people's way that are working here," he informed me.

I parked, snapped the front of my slicker closed and walked down the muddy bank towards the wreck carrying the Graflex. The rain had abated and rivulets of mucky water ran towards the coulee and the small trestle where the train cars lay on their sides at odd angles. The wheel trucks spilled and piled against each other into the coulee. This wasn't just a freight train but a stock train that had been loaded with cattle now bellowing in fear. Men worked trying to get the cattle free of the car. I took pictures of the accident. Most of the cattle cars had made it over the trestle as well as the locomotive before the timbers had broken and the trestle collapsed. Three cars had plunged over into the coulee bank, one being a cattle car which stood precariously at an odd angle still upright. The cows inside had been crowded at the rear end of the wood-sided car and men were hacking at the boards with axes in an attempt to free the panicked animals that mooed almost morosely.

I kept taking pictures. Flood lights had been brought in and stock trucks had already arrived to transport the cows, as well as local ranch cowboys and their horses to help herd the animals. Suddenly the chopped out boards gave way to the pushing of the noisy and frightened animals and with a splitting of wood they spilled out and scattered. Some with broken legs only stood shaking once out of their confinement. Others ran off with bloody wounds. This would be an all-night job for the cowboys trying to gather the now running off cows.

I asked different people in authority questions after identifying myself as press and wrote what they said in my pad.

"Well it looks like one of the trestle uprights was weak and split and the weight of the train caused the others to give way. That's what it looks like to me," said one person I asked.

"How many cows are dead?" I asked a man that had been cutting the cattle free with an axe.

"Just four in the car had been crushed to death. I'm sure we'll have to put down some others that have broken legs or bad wounds. We'll see by morning."

It was a little after nine at night and the rain had started again just before I had reached my truck. I climbed into the cab with my slicker still on and then had to reopen the door because I felt that my left side kept me from reaching to the glove compartment to get some matches to light a Lucky with. The bottom of the raincoat had gotten caught in the closed door when I slammed it shut. After I started back for Billings I noticed that one of the truck head lights had burned out and I drove with my one light on high beam but that was too much reflected light because of the steady rain and I turned it back to low beam. The windshield wiper on the passenger side of my truck was almost useless as it swung in rhythm with the one on the driver's side. I was thankful that at least the one on my side was working well. As the rain increased and battered the truck windshield I turned up the speed of the wipers also. They swung rapidly, wiping water away to little avail. Visibility was poor and the road looked straight.

There was no traffic and I sped up to fifty-five, hoping to get back to the Gazette before it went to print, even though I was pretty sure the presses were most likely running by now. The linotype operators had already been busy writing up columns as I left the Gazette that afternoon.

Suddenly a cow stepped out onto the road and I hit the brakes and tried to swerve to the right to miss her. It was a pure spontaneous reaction but nonetheless I did hit her and she fell. Then she got up and moved back down from where she had come from.

I jumped out of the truck to check on her and in so doing slammed the door behind me and discovered that the hem of my yellow slicker was caught in the door again. As I attempted to open the door to free myself the truck started to roll forwards and before I got the door opened the truck picked up momentum and headed down into a coulee wash, dragging me with it. I had shut off the engine but in haste hadn't set the hand brake or put the International into gear. Now it was going into the coulee, speedily dragging me along on the ground and mud. I saw the cow running away into the rain and darkness limping. Then the slicker ripped and I was free but the rear wheel ran over my right leg just above my ankle.

I must have passed out because when I awoke I was in a hospital bed with my leg elevated and in a cast.

"Where am I?" I asked the nurse, my mind a haze, a blur of a nightmare still spun in my head. They had given me morphine. I had dreamt that Sue was riding off on my horse Jeep. She was saying, "I never really loved you, I love Dick," and she was laughing at me over her shoulder. Dick Long was riding on Sioux next to her with his white chef's coat on. He had his back to me and I could not see his face. "You're stealing my horses!" I yelled at them. And Dad's Luger materialized in my hand. I took aim . . . and awoke in a cold sweat.

"You're in the Livingston Hospital. They brought you in last night. Someone found you off the road unconscious with your leg broken," said the nurse. "We found your press card and called the Billings Gazette to let them know what had happened. They're sending someone out and we have called your parents. They're also on their way here."

The only recollection I had of what had transpired was the cow running off in the rain and the pungent odor of wet sage.

The reporter they sent was the same one that had showed me how to operate the Graflex. He had located my truck that had been towed and was able to get the camera to take back to the paper after visiting me. He told me that my left light was broken and fender dented but to him looked fixable. The cow I hit they hadn't found as yet.

Ma, Dad and Kipp came as the reporter was leaving.

"Oh son! Are you okay?' Ma asked.

"Yeah, I guess, leg hurts some and I'm drowsy," I told her.

"Thank God, you're alive. What happened?" Dad asked.

Kipp was speechless. He just stood with his hands buried in his pockets looking sorry as if it was all his fault that this had happened.

I started to tell them what I remembered when the doctor came into the room to check on me followed by the nurse.

"You're lucky I was able to save your leg. It was beat up, but a clean enough break. I think the muddy ground is what may have mostly saved your leg. If it had been hard ground, your leg bones, the tibia and fibula would most likely have been pulverized and I would have to have amputated it to just below your knee," the doctor said in a serious and subdued tone.

"The bad news is that you're most likely going to possibly walk with a bit of a limp," he added.

A day later I was back home lying in bed reading the Billings Gazette with some of the photos I had taken of the train wreck with the cows spilling out of the cattle car on the front page of the paper and Dakk Lovett photographer was credited to me. Though my leg ached I felt good seeing the photo with my name published under the photo. The article went on telling about the train wreck, the loss of cows and my accident while covering the story.

"This just came in the mail for you," Ma said with a frown.

The letter said it was from the Selective Service Board. It read: You are hereby directed to present yourself for Armed Forces Physical Examination to the local board named above by reporting at: such and such, at 7:58 a.m. on the 27 of July 1958.

* * *

THE END

EPILOGUE

Dakk Lovett was exempted as being unfit for military duty due to his limp from the accident that had broken his leg. He went on to college while working part time for the Billings Gazette. Lovett became a columnist for the Billings paper and as time passed he wrote numerous short stories and six books of fiction on the west and its people. He still rode his horses from time to time. He married after meeting his future wife Diana at the Hitchin' Rail Feed Store where she was employed. He had gone in the store to buy grain for the horses and had become smitten and asked her out on a date, and after dating for a year they were married. They had two boys three years apart.

Kipp Lovett enlisted into the Army in 1963 and became a helicopter mechanic in Vietnam. He was wounded by enemy mortar fire when the Vietcong attacked the American base near Pleiku in the central highlands of South Vietnam. He spent three weeks in a hospital, received a Purple Heart and was honorably discharged in 1966 after completing his tour of duty with the Army. Though he liked working as a helicopter mechanic he was ready to come home to Billings and leave the war. He chose not to re-up for another tour in Vietnam.

Cody Rhodes enlisted in the Army at the same time that Kipp had. He was killed in Vietnam a month after he got there by friendly fire from South Vietnamese troops in a cross-fire fire fight.

Cooper Younger worked his way up the ladder at Casey's Golden Pheasant for some years before deciding to go on to a culinary college to become a Cordon Bleu chef. He then moved to San Diego and worked there as the executive chef in an exclusive restaurant.

Sue Palmer-Long had two more children and moved east to Virginia.

Goo Goo (Rolland) Lewis became an illustrator. He never married but lived with his mother after his father had died. Then he lived on his own after she too later died some eleven years later after his father.

Lee Pekhead drifted to the oil fields and became a driller after having worked his way up in the profession.

J.W. Ramsey suffered from depression and while living in Jordan Valley, Oregon committed suicide by shooting himself, then a month later Llano had colic and died.

Bernie Byatt became an alcoholic who disappeared in the west.

Charlie Martin died of a heart attack while working as a cook in hunting camp. He was telling a tall tale to the hunters but never got to its ending.

But the West lives on . . . Let 'em buck! J.C. Cantle

CPSIA information can be obtained at www.ICGtesting.com
Printed in the USA
LVOW090331151211

259474LV00002B/2/P